SUB-MAJER'S CHALLENGE

Tor Books by L. E. Modesitt, Jr.

The Grand Illusion
Isolate
Councilor
Contrarian
Legalist

The Saga Of Recluce
The Magic of Recluce
The Towers of the Sunset
The Magic Engineer
The Order War
The Death of Chaos
Fall of Angels
The Chaos Balance
The White Order
Colors of Chaos
Magi'i of Cyador
Scion of Cyador
Wellspring of Chaos
Ordermaster
Natural Ordermage
Mage-Guard of Hamor
Arms-Commander
Cyador's Heirs
Heritage of Cyador
Recluce Tales
The Mongrel Mage
Outcasts of Order
The Mage-Fire War
Fairhaven Rising
From the Forest
Overcaptain
Sub-Majer's Challenge
Last of the First

The Corean Chronicles
Legacies
Darknesses
Scepters
Alector's Choice
Cadmian's Choice
Soarer's Choice
The Lord-Protector's Daughter
Lady-Protector

The Imager Portfolio
Imager
Imager's Challenge
Imager's Intrigue
Scholar
Princeps
Imager's Battalion
Antiagon Fire
Rex Regis
Madness in Solidar
Treachery's Tools
Assassin's Price
Endgames

The Spellsong Cycle
The Soprano Sorceress
The Spellsong War
Darksong Rising
The Shadow Sorceress
Shadowsinger

The Ecolitan Matter
Empire & Ecolitan (comprising *The Ecolitan Operation* and *The Ecologic Secession*)
Ecolitan Prime (comprising *The Ecologic Envoy* and *The Ecolitan Enigma*)

The Ghost Books
Of Tangible Ghosts
The Ghost of the Revelator
Ghost of the White Nights

Other Novels
The Forever Hero (comprising *Dawn for a Distant Earth*, *The Silent Warrior*, and *In Endless Twilight*)
Timegods' World (comprising *Timediver's Dawn* and *The Timegod*)
The Hammer of Darkness
The Green Progression
The Parafaith War
Adiamante
Gravity Dreams
The Octagonal Raven
Archform: Beauty
The Ethos Effect
Flash
The Eternity Artifact
The Elysium Commission
Viewpoints Critical
Haze
Empress of Eternity
The One-Eyed Man
Solar Express
Quantum Shadows

L. E. MODESITT, JR.

SUB-MAJER'S CHALLENGE

TOR PUBLISHING GROUP
NEW YORK

This is a work of fiction. All of the names, characters, organizations, places, and events portrayed in this work are either products of the author's imagination or used fictitiously.

SUB-MAJER'S CHALLENGE

A Tor Book
Published by Tom Doherty Associates / Tor Publishing Group
120 Broadway
New York, NY 10271

www.torpublishinggroup.com

Tor® is a registered trademark of Macmillan Publishing Group, LLC.

EU Representative: Macmillan Publishers Ireland Ltd., 1st Floor, The Liffey Trust Centre, 117–126 Sheriff Street Upper, Dublin 1, D01 YC43

The Library of Congress has cataloged the hardcover edition as follows:

Names: Modesitt, L. E., Jr., 1943– author.
Title: Sub-majer's challenge / L.E. Modesitt, Jr.
Description: First edition. | New York : Tor, 2025. | Series: Saga of recluse ; 25 | "A Tom Doherty associates book"
Identifiers: LCCN 2025015741 | ISBN 9781250326829 (hardcover) | ISBN 9781250326836 (ebook)
Subjects: LCGFT: Fantasy fiction. | Novels.
Classification: LCC PS3563.O264 S83 2025 | DDC 813/.54—dc23/eng/20250424
LC record available at https://lccn.loc.gov/2025015741

ISBN 978-1-250-32684-3 (trade paperback)

First Tor Trade Paperback Edition: 2026

Printed in the United States of America

10 9 8 7 6 5 4 3 2 1

For Dr. Michael G. Stults
With gratitude and great appreciation

ALYIAKAL'ALT,

SUB-MAJER

Lhaarat Post

Summer, 103 A.F.

I

Sub-Majer Alyiakal walks to the window, noting that the light of the Summer afternoon is fading into twilight. *Fourth Company shouldn't be this late, not on a routine patrol.* Except no four-day patrol to Kraaslaen, the small town just south of the border with Cerlyn, could be called routine, not less than a year after Alyiakal had removed all Cerlynese armsmen from the high road in Cyadoran territory, effectively destroying more than three Cerlynese companies and gutting the fort that had been their base.

That battle, and the skirmishes that led up to it, had occurred in Harvest, too late for Cerlyn to mount a counterattack, given the usual severe Autumn and Winter weather, but Alyiakal has continually worried that Duke Taartyn might well launch such an attack in early Summer, once the Spring planting is finished. *Just about now.*

As he turns from the window, Crendaak, the ranker manning the desk outside Alyiakal's study, says loudly, "The lookouts just sighted Fourth Company leaving Gairtyn and heading for the bridge, ser."

"Thank you." Alyiakal still wonders what caused Fourth Company's delay, since the green-blue sky has been cloudless, even over the tallest peaks of the Westhorns to the east and northeast of Lhaarat Post.

While Alyiakal would like to be at the stables to find out what happened, he's always disliked superior officers who pressed for instant answers and has vowed not to be one. *At least not unless it's truly urgent.*

So he waits, almost a glass, before Captain Paersol hurries into his study, closing the door.

Alyiakal motions for Paersol to take one of the chairs in front of the desk. "You're a bit late in returning. That's not like you." *Not this late, anyway.*

"Ser . . . we stayed longer in Kraaslaen because the headman wanted to talk about all the Cerlynese armsmen they've seen on the road to the north. Scores of them, according to the locals."

"Did you see any?"

"No, ser. I did lead third squad over the bridge and up the road a ways, close to the border between Cyador and Cerlyn. We stopped a hundred yards short of there, just to be careful. There were more than a few hoofprints, but we couldn't see anyone."

"It sounds like they were avoiding you."

"That's why we stayed a little longer—around two glasses yesterday. I wanted to see if we could spot any armsmen. I sent scouts along the circular road to the west, the one that splits off where the high road crosses the bridge, but there weren't any hoofprints there, not for more than a kay, anyway."

"What did Headman Nauraal have to say?"

"He's very worried. He promised to send a messenger if the Cerlynese move into Kraaslaen or make attacks on the town."

"How long do you think it will be before they attack?" asks Alyiakal.

"I'd guess it'll be in the next few days. They've likely been watching our patrols. You've varied the frequency so there's not a regular schedule, but there's always at least an eightday between patrols to Kraaslaen, and sometimes two."

"I'd have to agree, but they might wait until after the next patrol, or keep popping up for the rest of the Summer until we believe they won't attack—which is when they will. Or they'll wait until mid-Autumn when we can't get there." Alyiakal stands. "Thank you. I look forward to reading your report, and I'll see you at the mess."

"Yes, ser."

After Paersol leaves the study, Alyiakal walks to the small window, but his eyes are focused elsewhere.

Lhaarat Post doesn't have the resources, either of golds or provisions, to maintain a company either in Kraaslaen or at the unnamed hamlet with the bare-bones barracks located a day's ride south of Kraaslaen. Doing so would also be expressly against his orders from Mirror Lancer headquarters. Besides, a company wouldn't be sufficient to stop a large-scale assault. *Unless you're leading it.* To have the post commander that far from Lhaarat for any lengthy period isn't feasible, either.

Alyiakal shakes his head. He can only hope that Headman Nauraal will send a messenger when the Cerlynese assault begins. One way or another, he has no doubt that Duke Taartyn will attack Kraaslaen, and likely with a far larger force than the one the Mirror Lancers had destroyed the previous Harvest.

But you've known all along that dealing with the Cerlynese would be a challenge—especially given the limitations imposed by Mirror Lancer headquarters.

Alyiakal smiles sardonically.

II

On fiveday morning Alyiakal leads the chestnut gelding out into the post's courtyard, mounts, and rides to where Undercaptain Maarkyn is mustering Third Company. Alyiakal reins up beside the undercaptain and waits.

In less than a third of a quint, Maarkyn turns and says, "Third Company, ready to ride, ser."

Alyiakal nods and says, "At your command, Undercaptain."

"Third Company! Forward!" Then Maarkyn follows the lead of the two scouts to the post gates, with Alyiakal riding beside him, and the three squads of the company behind them.

Once the company leaves the post and rides west on the east road, through the town proper of Lhaarat, Alyiakal creates his usual unseen order funnel to collect the tiny chaos bits that flow from the white sun that is just clearing the peaks of the Westhorns. While he doesn't expect to see raiders on the patrol along the high road, not after all his efforts as deputy post commander and then post commander, there's always that possibility. In some situations, that extra chaos can make a difference, even if Maarkyn and the Mirror Lancers he leads never notice that Alyiakal's firelance sometimes discharges more firebolts than it can actually hold.

A third of a quint later, the company turns north onto the road leading to the stone and timber bridge over the River Lhaar and then to Gairtyn, the small town that had barely been more than a hamlet when Alyiakal had been posted to Lhaarat nearly two years earlier.

Few townspeople look up as the company rides by, past log-walled dwellings, and then past the gristmill and the sawmill before turning north onto the road just below the eastern end of the valley, a road being built slowly over the past year by local laborers and a few lancers on disciplinary duties.

Some three kays north of Gairtyn, the company turns north on what had once been a logging trail, but is now a passable road through the evergreens, angling to the northeast along a hillside before reaching a flat that had been logged a generation earlier. At the north end of the flat, Alyiakal looks closely at the handful of local workers with picks and shovels widening the trail ahead into a road passable to wagons. He just hopes they can finish the basic road by the end of Harvest.

Once past the workers, the company rides single file along the trail for another two kays until the lancers reach the high road, a trading road through the hills below the western slopes of the Westhorns from Jakaafra, just north of the Great Forest, all the way to Cerlyn.

At the junction with the high road, Maarkyn calls for a break to allow the remainder of the company to join first squad and to rest the horses and give the lancers a chance to stretch their legs.

After the break, Maarkyn looks to Alyiakal. "North on the high road, ser?"

Alyiakal nods, then says, "To the old way station. Then we'll see." Alyiakal can't help thinking about how he discovered the high road—simply because he followed tracks in an old logging trail, tracks that belonged to a Cerlynese scout, which in turn led to patrols on a road that no lancers then knew about. All that led to barbarians forced into attacking his company by the Cerlynese, and eventually in Mirror Lancer headquarters ordering Lhaarat Post to remove Cerlynese armsmen from the high road where it crossed Cyadoran lands, resulting in skirmishes and the battle in Kraaslaen.

Once the company is again moving north on the high road, Alyiakal uses his order/chaos senses to discern what living things might be in the evergreens extending in both directions from the road. He finds no traces of men or horses, but order/chaos patterns of red deer, a single mountain cat, and more than a handful of the mountain foxes whose coats turn white in Winter.

Before long, the scouts report a trader with two mounted guards, and Alyiakal and two lancers ride forward.

The dark-haired teamster is the trader, and, after he halts the wagon, he looks at Alyiakal, then says, "You're the majer from Lhaarat, aren't you."

"I am. And you are?"

"Ghamyt, from Ilypsya, ser."

"How far north did you go?" asks Alyiakal. "As far as Kraaslaen, or farther?"

Ghamyt shakes his head. "We don't go into the rocky lands. We turn back where the trees get thin."

"What's in the wagon?"

"Brown wool, not that it's worth that much. Evergreen nuts in one barrel, sage in another, tragon in another . . ."

Alyiakal listens and senses but discerns no untruths. After a moment, he asks, "You didn't happen to see any armed riders, did you?"

"None except you. Should we?"

"Not if you're headed south or back to Ilypsya. Thank you."

Three quints after seeing the trader, Alyiakal sights the crude way station, but there's no one there, scarcely surprising in late morning.

In early afternoon, the company turns off the high road and rides down the side road to the still-unnamed hamlet that holds the barracks built by the Cerlynese roughly two years earlier and used by the Mirror Lancers on extended patrols to Kraaslaen. Not that Third Company will be headed that far on the current patrol. None of those working the fields and plots give more than a passing glance to the lancers.

While the company dismounts at the barracks and the lancers water their mounts, Alyiakal does the same for his chestnut, then tethers him, and walks to the nearest field and the wiry, dark-haired man laboring there.

The grower looks up. "Good day, Majer."

"The same to you, Taemlin. How are your crops?"

Taemlin shakes his head. "They've been better."

"But you get to keep everything now," Alyiakal points out.

"That is true, but we have more mouths to feed."

"Before long, they'll be old enough to help."

"When they get older enough to really help, they'll soon have families, and they won't be able to help then, either."

"I'm afraid we can't help with that," replies Alyiakal with a smile. "You're getting more traders now, aren't you?"

"They want more than we can give."

Alyiakal offers a sympathetic smile, knowing that, while the grower likes to bemoan matters, there are more than a few predatory traders, and not just those based in Cyad, Fyrad, or Summerdock. "Have you heard anything interesting from them?"

"Nothing I haven't heard before. A lot of 'em still won't take the high road beyond Kraaslaen. Afraid the Duke's men'll charge them with trading with the Grass Hills barbarians."

Alyiakal can understand the traders' reluctance. The Cerlynese have tortured and killed traders who traded with the barbarians, although the majority of the impoverished small growers in the Grass Hills northeast of Cyador aren't really barbarians, even if most everyone calls them that.

"That should work to your advantage, for goods they don't want to carry back."

"Not often enough."

"You haven't seen any raiders or armsmen, have you?"

"Only your Mirror Lancers." Taemlin frowns. "You always ask, and we never see any."

"That's what I'd hope, but you're here all the time, and we're not."

Alyiakal spends another fraction of a quint with the grower before walking back to the chestnut, untying him, and nodding to Undercaptain Maarkyn.

A few moments pass before the undercaptain orders, "Mount up!"

The ride back is quiet, and Alyiakal worries that there are so few traders at a time when there should be more.

Third Company finally rides back through the gates at Lhaarat Post in late afternoon. After grooming and settling the chestnut, Alyiakal heads back to his study in the headquarters building.

"Did we get any dispatch riders today, Crendaak?"

"No, ser," replies the duty ranker at the desk outside Alyiakal's study. "Are you expecting anything special?"

"I'm always hopeful," *unless it's from headquarters.* Alyiakal smiles, knowing he can't expect a letter from Saelora any time soon, because he'd sent off his last letter to her on oneday, although he had hoped for one from Hyrsaal. He walks into his study, still wondering when and how the Cerlynese will attack.

III

When he wakes on oneday morning, Alyiakal can't shake his concerns about the Cerlynese or that he's heard nothing from Kraaslaen.

Maybe the Cerlynese were just scouting for what they plan to do later.

That might be, but Alyiakal knows he can't keep a company in Kraaslaen all the time, or even half the time, not and keep it adequately supplied. That means that he'll have to react when and if he gets word about Cerlynese actions. *But you can make sure that you'll have three companies ready on less than a day's notice.*

Those thoughts are still in the back of his mind when he sits down at the head of the table at the morning mess.

Once everyone is served, Staalt, the undercaptain about to be promoted to captain, asks, "Are you still planning to come with Second Company this morning, ser?"

"More than ever. I'll borrow a few lancers and make a side trip to Lestroi to see if Headwoman Kiefala has heard anything from traders or travelers. Sometimes, they'll tell her more than they'll tell us."

Staalt nods. "Thank you, ser."

Dhraak, the senior captain, asks, "Do you think we'll get any instructions from headquarters about Kraaslaen?"

"We already have," replies Alyiakal dryly. "Don't create a post there, and don't spend much time there, but keep the Cerlynese out of Cyadoran lands. All we can do is be ready to set out on less than a day's notice with three companies."

"That's not exactly realistic," Paersol says.

"Because we've managed to do that for a year," replies Alyiakal, "they obviously think it's no problem." He pauses, then adds, "Or rather, it's a lesser problem than others that the Mirror Lancers face."

"The other borders are quiet right now, ser," states Paersol. "What other problems are more important?"

"From the directives all the posts have been receiving, the Imperial Treasury isn't exactly overflowing. I suspect the Majer-Commander is under pressure not to build new posts or increase the number of Mirror Lancer companies."

"The new Emperor of Light doesn't seem much better than the last one," says Staalt dryly.

That's likely because he's indebted to the Merchanters and doesn't want to rein them in . . . or feels he can't. But that's a feeling Alyiakal can't prove and definitely can't voice. So he says, "I imagine that Emperor Kaartyn feels that he's doing the best he can. He's been emperor only a year."

"Must be nice to have that excuse," says Dhraak. "I don't think saying that would work well for most Mirror Lancer post commanders."

"Unless they're senior enough and have ties to those high in the Triad," replies Staalt, clearly avoiding looking in Paersol's direction.

"It depends on what kind of ties," says Alyiakal evenly. "Some ties mean that even more is expected from the post commander. By the time an officer gets command, those ties seldom protect an officer from the consequences of serious misjudgments or mistakes."

"You say 'seldom,'" replies Dhraak.

"I don't know, personally, of any senior officer who made such a mistake and retained command. I have heard of one instance where that appeared to be the case, but I don't know all the facts."

Dhraak nods slowly.

"I'm reluctant to comment more," adds Alyiakal, "because I've been in a position where the facts seemed unfavorable when taken out of context. I was fortunate enough to have a superior officer who wanted to know all the facts and the context. I try hard to be as honest and fair as he was. Good examples are one of the things that hold the Mirror Lancers together." Alyiakal laughs. "Now that you've heard my pontification, we need to finish breakfast and get on with the day."

After breakfast, Alyiakal makes his way to the stable, where he saddles the chestnut, leads the gelding out into the stable courtyard, then mounts and rides to meet Staalt as the undercaptain musters Second Company.

After the company is mustered and leaves the post, Alyiakal spreads his order funnel and rides beside the undercaptain as the two follow the scouts and lead the company up the east road and into the hills overlooking the post and the town.

Alyiakal notes the traces of logging wagons as well as some wagon and cart tracks, but the company encounters no one on the ride to the Lhaar River overlook. At the overlook, Staalt calls a break that lasts slightly more than a quint before the lancers remount and continue on the east road, passing the turnoff onto the road that eventually leads to Jakaafra.

When Second Company nears the rock wall and the narrow timber gate marking the entrance to Lestroi, Alyiakal smiles as he recalls the hidden entrance that had been concealed by a dead evergreen until the previous Autumn. He turns to Staalt. "If you'd detail four lancers to accompany me."

"Yes, ser."

"Keep on heading east for another half glass, then take a break and come back. If we're not here, we will be shortly."

Staalt nods.

Then Alyiakal rides over to the high gate, senses the order/chaos pattern behind it, and calls out, "Majer Alyiakal to see Headwoman Kiefala." He waits for the watcher to open the peephole.

After several moments, the gate swings inward.

While Alyiakal doubts there will be trouble, he says, "Kaastyrn, lead the way," and extends his shields to cover the lancer.

Alyiakal follows, glances to the older woman who has opened the gate, and nods politely. "Just the five of us, today."

"Thank you, Majer." The woman immediately closes the gate behind the last lancer and drops both bars back into place.

Behind the gate is a narrow stone-walled passage barely wide enough for two mounts abreast. It extends some ten yards and seems to end, but doesn't, because there is another gate on the left, a gate now open, Alyiakal can sense, but one that can be quickly closed. When Kaastyrn reaches the second gateway, he guides his mount through and turns onto the ancient road cut into the stone, rides forward several yards before reining up to wait for Alyiakal and the other three lancers.

Once all five are on the stone road, Alyiakal leads the way down toward the gorge that holds the hamlet of Lestroi—a hamlet cut into the walls of the gorge by the dissidents before they were removed by the First.

Kiefala—the silver-haired headwoman—stands waiting outside the door of the first dwelling.

Alyiakal reins up and inclines his head politely.

"Do you bring more difficult news, Firstborn?" An amused smile belies her serious tone.

"Difficult for us. Not so much for you."

Kiefala raises her eyebrows.

"The Cerlynese are gathering armsmen just north of Kraaslaen."

"Did you expect otherwise?"

Alyiakal barks a short laugh. "Hardly. Have you heard anything?"

"We only know by what we have not seen or heard."

"Then there haven't been any traders or peddlers or travelers from the north?"

"Not a one in the last four eightdays."

Indicative, but hardly conclusive. "What did those who came earlier have to say?"

"They didn't say much, but they didn't even have any knives to sell. Will you destroy them again?"

"We'll do what we can . . . as necessary."

"And next year . . . when they try again?"

"I'm hoping we can be persuasive enough this time that there won't be a next time."

"You cannot persuade the dead," replies Kiefala.

"But often the dead can persuade the survivors," says Alyiakal dryly. "What do you know about towns or hamlets north of Kraaslaen?"

"There are hamlets, but the only town anyone mentions is Kula. It is at the east end of the Grass Hills on the road to Clynya. How far beyond Kraaslaen . . . that would be a guess."

Alyiakal nods. "How is Taaryan faring?"

Kiefala smiles warmly. "Well. He works hard, and he is cheerful. He would not make a good lancer." She pauses. "Rather . . . being a good lancer would be hard on his spirit. You knew that, though."

Alyiakal shakes his head. "I felt it. I didn't know it."

"Trust your feelings, Firstborn, but I shouldn't have to remind you of that."

"We all need reminders, now and then." Alyiakal then asks, "How is Lestroi doing this year?"

"We seem to fare well, but what we lay in for the Winter will tell."

"Have any other young people asked to join you?"

"Two girls, and an older woman fleeing an abusive consort."

"Will that cause trouble?"

"It's unlikely. The consort attacked the headwoman of Laankor. She slit his throat."

Laankor? For a moment, Alyiakal has to think before he remembers that is the name of the community with the log fort at the junction of the east road and the high road. "Have you ever met her?"

"Not yet. It's likely we will now that you have your lancers patrolling the high road."

She pauses, then adds, "It would be good to work together while you remain."

"I should be here for at least another year, but that's up to Mirror Lancer headquarters."

"You will only be here until you stop the Cerlynese, and they need you more elsewhere."

"That won't happen this year," replies Alyiakal.

Kiefala raises her eyebrows. "It might be best for everyone if it did."

"Your thoughts or your feelings?" asks Alyiakal.

"Both."

Alyiakal smiles. "I'll keep that in mind. I won't take any more of your time now. Give my best to Taaryan."

"I will."

Alyiakal turns the chestnut, and the four lancers follow him.

Once they're away from the gorge, Kaastyrn eases his mount forward and asks, "Begging your pardon, ser, but why does the headwoman call you Firstborn?"

"She means it as a term of power and respect." *More of the kind of power harking back to the magus who subdued the Great Forest and broke the dissidents.*

"I've never heard that before," says Kaastyrn.

"Until she called me that, neither had I," replies Alyiakal. "But she seems to insist on it."

As he rides up the old stone road to rejoin Second Company on the way back to the post, his thoughts circle back to Kiefala's last observation. *It's a risk, but she just might be right. Then again, not acting decisively might be an even greater risk, given Duke Taartyn's approach to ruling.*

IV

One of the more cryptic utterances of the Second Emperor of Light, made near the end of his reign, was that no man—or woman—can tame or temper the extremes of passion in others until he has tamed those extremes within himself. He went on to say that great men too often fail because there is no one strong enough to require that they tame themselves and that those passions inevitably destroy them and, unfortunately at times, what they have built.

Yet what he constructed in building the Empire of Light, physically and socially, still endures, and we know of no force strong enough to stand up to him. Even the great forest was not his match, yet he spoke as though he had faced such power . . .

Fragment, Mirror Lancer Archives
Zaenth'alt, Captain-Commander
Cyad, 45 A.F.

V

Immediately after breakfast on fourday, Crendaak appears in the doorway to Alyiakal's study. "Ser, there's a young fellow at the duty desk. He says he rode almost straight through from Kraaslaen, and he needs to see you."

From Kraaslaen? That can only mean one thing. "I'll see him immediately. Oh . . . and send word that Third Company's patrol is immediately canceled. You'll have to hurry on that."

"Yes, ser."

In less than half a quint, Crendaak escorts the youth, barely more than a boy, into the study. His worn brown clothes and face are dusty, and his toes extend over the front of his sandals. His eyes are bloodshot, with dark circles beneath them.

"He says his name is Nathaam," Crendaak offers.

"Ser . . ." The boy shudders. "It was awful . . . the green demons . . ."

"The Cerlynese?" asks Alyiakal. "They attacked Kraaslaen?"

The boy nods. "They were killing everyone. My father, he would have sent me, but they killed him. I was in the fields, and Porthan came . . . he told me. I could only save my sister . . . Mother told her to run to her hiding place . . ."

"Is Nauraal your father?" Alyiakal is guessing that the headman of Kraaslaen would be the one sending the message.

Nathaam nods.

"You rode all the way here?"

"Yes, ser . . . well, Premyah rode with me to the hamlet on the other side of stony hills. I had to stop. The growers there, they were nice. They said I should stay . . . but who would tell you? I had to leave Premyah there . . . She couldn't ride anymore."

"He was riding a horse with Cerlynese tack," says Crendaak.

"How did you get the horse?"

"Porthan and his sister helped. We had to wait. She asked the armsman . . . well . . . she did something, and Porthan hit him with a bladed spade. He had to hit him a lot. The armsman stabbed Porthan, but Porthan killed him. He said he'd be all right . . . but that I had to go."

Alyiakal has no trouble sensing the absolute truth of what Nathaam has said . . . and what he has not. After quietly asking more questions, Alyiakal turns and says, "Crendaak . . . if you'd see that Nathaam gets something to eat and a place to rest."

"Ser . . . I have to go with you . . . to the hamlet. Premyah . . . there's no one else."

"The Cerlynese killed your mother, too?"

"And Dylina and maybe Askar. They were killing everyone."

Alyiakal pauses. "You can go with us as far as the hamlet where your sister is. We can't leave until tomorrow morning."

Nathaam swallows. "Not until then?"

"It takes time, Nathaam. Most posts would take days to do it." Alyiakal looks to Crendaak. "Have all the officers report here immediately. Then you can help Nathaam." He turns to the youth. "You can wait here until Crendaak returns."

Half a quint passes before Crendaak appears and leads Nathaam away. Then Dhraak, Paersol, Staalt, and Maarkyn enter the study.

"Does this have to do with canceling today's patrol, ser?" asks Maarkyn.

"It does," replies Alyiakal. "But you'll have your hands full for the next eightday or so because you'll be doing all the patrols here—just in the valley, though. The Cerlynese have attacked Kraaslaen and massacred a number of people . . ." Alyiakal goes on to explain. When he finishes, he adds, "We'll set out with three companies and three wagons at first light tomorrow. Any questions?"

"Could the Cerlynese set this up as a trap?" asks Paersol.

"The boy was telling the truth. He saw his friend kill a Cerlynese armsman with a shovel. The Cerlynese are brutal, but I don't see them letting a local grower murder one of their armsmen as a setup." *For one thing, that's too indirect for them.* "They'll have figured that we'd get word before long. So they may set up some sort of ambush or attack. We'll just have to outmaneuver them when we get there." *Even if you have no idea how many armsmen and what else you'll be facing.*

"Is there any point in waiting?" asks Dhraak in a tone that suggests he knows the answer.

"I don't see any. That just gives them more time to torture the locals and to prepare for our attack." Alyiakal smiles wryly and says, "You all know what to do. I'll be checking with each of you."

After the four leave, Alyiakal walks to the window, although there's no breeze and the early-Summer air is already damp and heavy, which won't be the case on the high road, but it will be damper and hotter in Kraaslaen.

Amid all the preparations for an early departure the next morning, dispatch riders appear in late afternoon with directives and an announcement from Mirror Lancer headquarters, as well as letters from Hyrsaal and Saelora.

The key section of the first directive reads:

> *. . . belt knives worn by Mirror Lancers shall be forged of cupridium or bronze; the blade length shall not exceed six digits. No Mirror Lancer officer or ranker shall wear and/or have on his person more than one belt knife at any one time . . .*

So what is that all about? Off-duty rankers carrying shortswords in place of belt knives? Or is it about knives not being of iron?

The remaining directive deals with proper documentation of tack and wagon gear replacements.

The announcement surprises Alyiakal slightly.

> *With the recent death of the honorable Hystaan'mer, the Merchanter Advisor to the Emperor of Light, Emperor Kaartyn'elth has chosen Traasjan'mer, of the Yuryan Clan, as the next Merchanter Advisor, in line with the custom of choosing an advisor from a different clan or house than his predecessor. The principal clans and houses are the Dyljani Clan, the Yuryan Clan, the Hyshrah Clan, and Bluyet House. While lesser clans or houses may be considered, to date no emperor has chosen outside the four largest.*

Alyiakal initially questions why the announcement was sent to him and other post commanders, but then understands. Not only could post commanders potentially get involved with powerful traders, but potential future commanders will need to know which trading concerns are powers.

After taking the directives and the announcement to Crendaak, Alyiakal opens the letter from Hyrsaal first.

> *Alyiakal—*
>
> *There's not much new here, just one small barbarian raid after another. Once in a while, we sight a squad of Jeranyi troopers, but they always give us a wide berth. These days, some of their armsmen carry those polished bronze shields you mentioned.*
>
> *Inividra is hundreds of kays north and west of Lhaarat. You'd think that it would be cooler here than Lhaarat, and it was. For about the first two eightdays of Spring. It's already getting hot and dry. Just like you said Pemedra was. I can hardly wait for full Summer. At least I won't drown in sweat. Maybe shrivel up like a dried pearapple, though.*
>
> *Catriana complains—not really—but she wrote that Haarlt already is taking after me. She says that his hair is thick and just as red and that he charms everyone who sees him. That last part isn't mine. I think it's more her, but she doesn't agree. Sometimes, it seems so strange that I have a son*

that I've never seen and won't see for another year. I still think it was the right thing for us to get consorted . . .

Alyiakal can't help smiling at Hyrsaal's happiness. He also wonders if he and Saelora are being foolish in waiting. *But that's her decision as much as yours.*

After putting away Hyrsaal's letter, he turns to Saelora's letter, saving the best for last and smiling warmly at the first words.

I miss you, sometimes a little, and sometimes a whole lot, but you know that.

Some days, it's hard to believe it's been almost two years since you were here. Other days, it seems so much longer.

That's true of other things as well. It only seems like a few seasons ago that Laetilla and I built the distillery, but we're now working on adding to it. The main difficulty will be getting copper in any form, especially without Vassyl, but both Dyrkan and Faadyr think they can help, and Catriana has some ideas. She always has ideas, and most of them are good.

Part of trying to expand is based on hope, and part is because we've got more land filled with greenberries and because there are some possibilities to use maize and distill a clear liquor. Something that strong doesn't sell all that well here or anywhere in Cyador, but, as Mother has said more than once, outland traders are interested in anything strong. For us dealing with outland traders is easier and more profitable than dealing with the trading clans out of Cyad . . .

Alyiakal can certainly see that, just given his brief time acting as an Imperial tariff enumerator.

When he finishes her letter, he tucks it away with the others, then leaves the study to check on how the wagon loading is going . . . and to look in on Nathaam.

VI

By sunrise on fiveday, Alyiakal rides beside Paersol at the head of Fourth Company just beyond the end of the new roadbuilding beyond the logging road. From there, the company travels the trail toward the high road. Dhraak and First Company follow, while Second Company and the supply wagons are taking the longer east road to the high road. Not for the first time, Alyiakal wishes he could squeeze more silvers out of the post's budget to complete the shorter road to the high road, but Mirror Lancer headquarters hasn't seen fit to provide much in the way of support, and on a few occasions Alyiakal has personally added silvers to advance the roadbuilding.

Once the sun clears the trees, Alyiakal creates his usual unseen order funnel to collect the chaos bits that flow from the white sun. While he doesn't expect to see raiders on the high road, he knows once he and the three companies near Kraaslaen, any additional chaos he holds could make a difference, even if the Mirror Lancers he leads never notice his firelance sometimes discharges more firebolts than it can actually hold.

Another glass later, at the junction with the high road, Alyiakal orders a break to rest the horses and to give Fourth Company the chance to catch up and re-form before the two companies resume their ride toward Kraaslaen. Then he glances back to where a worried-looking Nathaam rides beside Senior Squad Leader Baarth at the head of first squad.

Alyiakal wonders how many times Baarth has kept Paersol from making some mistake. *But as long as Baarth keeps him from making those mistakes, you don't have any grounds for removing Paersol.*

After both companies are rested, Alyiakal orders them north on the high road, knowing that Second Company won't rejoin them until well after First and Fourth Companies reach the unnamed hamlet with the former Cerlynese barracks, where all three will spend the night.

A glass later, Alyiakal sights the weathered and crude way station ahead on the left. As he rides closer, he senses no one near, and it appears unused. That's not surprising, since the scouts haven't seen much in the way of tracks on the road, and the companies haven't encountered any travelers or traders.

And we likely won't see anyone but locals from here on, not with the Cerlynese holding Kraaslaen.

Several kays past the way station, the lancers reach the section of the road that curves around hills for more than five kays but remains comparatively level. Through that stretch, Alyiakal checks the paths leading from the road into the hills. While most show hoofprints and cart wheels, few are recent.

Once the lancers pass the curve of the high road, more than a glass elapses before the scouts ride back and report. The side road ahead, leading to the valley to the northwest, holds few tracks but none that appear to belong to Cerlynese mounts.

A quint later, the scouts lead the way down the side road between a rocky hillside and a straggly evergreen forest. It ends at a slope covered with irregular sharp-edged chunks of rough black rock extending to the valley. Below the boulder field is a hamlet, of sorts, with a few more dwellings than the previous Summer.

Alyiakal sees a few figures working in the scattered fields, and even a few children, most unlikely if the Cerlynese were present. Even so, he remains wary until Fourth Company nears the hamlet, when he can definitely sense that the stark barracks building is empty.

Alyiakal doesn't have to seek out the grower who is the de facto headman, because Taemlin hurries from his field as soon as Alyiakal reins up.

"Is the youth with you, Majer?"

"Over there." Alyiakal gestures. "Is his sister well?"

"She's worried . . . and scared."

"Can he stay here with her? At least until we return?"

"We can do that. Can he work the fields?"

"I imagine so. That's what he was doing when the Cerlynese attacked Kraaslaen." Alyiakal pauses. "Have you heard anything from the north?"

"No one has come that way since the youth. There are never that many, but there have always been a few."

That doesn't surprise Alyiakal. The Cerlynese would want as much time as possible before word reaches Lhaarat Post. "It may take us a while to deal with the greencoats."

"We will be here." Taemlin hesitates, then adds, "Somewhere."

"You have hidden places if raiders or greencoats should come?"

"We cannot be too careful."

"I can't blame you, but we'll do our best to see that you don't need to use them." He glances over to see a gangly figure guiding his mount toward the grower. "Here comes Nathaam. I'll leave him in your hands, at least until we return." Then Alyiakal turns to the youth. "Taemlin says your sister is well. You're to stay here until we return. Then we'll talk about your future."

"I would go with you."

"If anything happens to you, your sister will have no one. You can't do that to her. She's lost too much already."

Nathaam looks indecisive, but Alyiakal senses both fear and worry.

"You will be safer here," adds Taemlin. "She needs you."

Alyiakal eases the chestnut away and back toward Paersol. There will be plenty of time to ready the barracks and post sentries on the high road, since Second Company and the wagons won't arrive for several glasses. *And for you to consider alternatives in dealing with the Cerlynese.*

VII

Slightly after sunrise, under a cloudless but hazy green-blue sky promising a hot, windless day, Alyiakal leads all three companies and the supply wagons from the unnamed hamlet. The high road shows no recent tracks, except for the hoofprints of Mirror Lancer road guards.

After adjusting his visor cap, Alyiakal creates his order funnel to gather more chaos bits to add to those he'd gathered on fiveday. He continues to study the road and the terrain on each side for the next several glasses. Then he calls a break at a small stream just short of the handful of hillside dwellings on the road's west side, knowing that there is no water for more than ten kays.

After the break, the companies ride less than a kay before reaching the more rugged, rockier, and drier terrain flanking the road. The few trees are stunted and twisted, and the white sunlight seems even hotter, although the amount of sun-chaos bits Alyiakal collects doesn't change in the slightest. He finds himself continually blotting away the sweat oozing from under his visor cap and taking frequent swallows of the order-infused water in one of his water bottles.

In time, the road turns slightly northwest and winds through lower hills forested with evergreens. Alyiakal halts the companies at the next stream to water the horses and give the lancers a midday break.

Three quints later, Alyiakal reaches the top of the rise overlooking the wide, grassy valley containing the hamlet of Lastop and, at the far side, the town of Kraaslaen. This early in Summer, the valley looks more like it belongs in the Grass Hills, rather than in the hills below the Westhorns, but then, as Alyiakal well knows, the southeast part of the Grass Hills lies just beyond the hills that form the north side of the valley.

More than a glass later, Fourth Company reaches the valley floor, and tallgrass flanks the road angling toward Lastop . . . and Kraaslaen beyond. Alyiakal hasn't ridden a kay before an antelope bolts across the road and into the taller grass on the west side of the road.

As the afternoon drags out, Alyiakal finds himself sweating more, most likely because the air is more humid than in the hills. Finally, the tallgrass thins enough to reveal fields and plots on the south side of Lastop, as well as the hamlet's crude mudbrick dwellings and their woven grass-thatch roofs.

Neither the scouts nor Alyiakal see any sign of Cerlynese armsmen, which surprises him. Even as Fourth Company enters the outskirts of the hamlet, he senses nothing that suggests armsmen or scouts.

When Fourth Company nears the hamlet's center, a square of packed dirt with little more than a small chandlery besides the scattered dwellings, Alyiakal turns to Paersol.

"Set up camp in that area we've used before, just north of the stream and east of the road to Kraaslaen. Detail two lancers to accompany me. I'm going to talk to the chandler."

"Yes, ser."

Alyiakal and the two lancers ride to the chandlery, where all three dismount, tie their mounts to the railing, and enter the small, low-ceilinged building.

The blond-haired chandler, likely only a few years older than Alyiakal, stands alone, although Alyiakal can sense two people in the back room, one likely the chandler's consort and the other, his son.

"I told you that the Cerlynese would be back," declares the chandler.

"You did. I'd hoped they wouldn't be that foolish." Alyiakal smiles blandly. "It appears that they aren't patrolling this far from Kraaslaen. Have they sent any riders here?"

The chandler pauses, as if debating how to answer. "There was a patrol three days ago and one this morning."

Alyiakal senses the reluctant truth. "A squad or so?"

"A score of riders."

"Did you or your family encourage their return?"

"I'm scarcely one to be consulted on such matters."

"I don't believe you answered my question."

"Why should I?"

"Because it's in your best interest to do so."

"Overcaptain—"

"Majer," corrects Alyiakal.

"My apologies, Majer, but the senior members of the family are the ones who determine what is in the family's best interests."

From what Alyiakal has seen, both now and earlier, the chandler and his extended family aren't all that different from the worst of the Cyadoran traders. *But Vassyl, Saelora, and Catriana were never that cruelly indifferent to the fate of those who aren't traders or Merchanters.* Not about to voice his thoughts, he replies, "In turn, chandler, my apologies for your unfortunate position."

"That sounds like a veiled threat."

"Mirror Lancer commanders don't make threats. It's most unwise. Like your family's leaders, we do what we think best."

"Then it might be best for you to leave matters as they are."

"I can see why you believe that. While it might be best for Cerlyn, and your family, there's considerable doubt as to whether that would be beneficial for Cyador, or for that matter, for most of the people of Kraaslaen and other towns and hamlets on the high road."

"You would decide that?" asks the chandler with a hint of the sardonic.

"Cyador doesn't torture outland traders for trading with people it doesn't favor," replies Alyiakal coolly. "Good day, chandler."

Alyiakal leaves the chandlery and remounts, thinking how grateful he is that Saelora isn't like so many traders and Merchanters. Then he and the two lancers ride to rejoin Second Company and the wagons.

When Alyiakal and the two lancers reach the camp, the companies are just beginning the process of setting up, getting sentries posted, mounts watered and picketed, lancers detailed for various duties, and meals prepared.

Still accompanied by the two lancers, Alyiakal rides farther south and up on a low rise beside the road, where he studies the terrain, extending his senses as far as he can. He discerns no trace of riders, although he does sense an antelope with a single offspring. For a time, he just thinks, then turns the chestnut back toward the campsite.

Once he's taken care of the chestnut, Alyiakal summons Dhraak, Paersol, and Staalt to join him beside one of the supply wagons.

"There aren't any Cerlynese here," Alyiakal begins. "According to the chandler, they patrol this far every other day or so, and the last patrol was this morning. What do you think that means?" Alyiakal gestures to Dhraak.

"They don't want to spread their forces. Not before they're ready, anyway." Dhraak offers a crooked smile. "Or maybe they don't want to lose any more men than they have to."

Alyiakal nods to Paersol.

"They don't intend to fight here, but they want to remind the locals that they're back."

"Staalt?"

"Lastop doesn't matter to them," replies the undercaptain. "They want to engage us where they think they have the greatest advantage."

"You're all correct," says Alyiakal. "And we need to engage them either where they don't expect us or where they do, but where they don't have the advantage that they think they do."

"How do we find that out?"

Alyiakal smiles wryly. "We'll have to go to Kraaslaen, but not all the way on the main road. That's one reason we've scouted and mapped the back lanes over the past year."

"You always thought this would happen, didn't you?" asks Paersol.

"Without a post here," *or without going into Cerlyn,* "it was bound to happen sooner or later. Most people, especially rulers, only respect some form of force. We're the unfortunate ones who have to apply that force." He stretches. "That's all I have for now."

VIII

Alyiakal sets scouts well away from the camp—in addition to the usual sentries—suspecting that the chandler, or someone else, might attempt to sneak around the Mirror Lancers and inform the Cerlynese. Although he suspects that the Cerlynese will not attempt a night or predawn attack, his sleep is still light at best, because he could easily be wrong. He wakes early on sevenday and finds the sentries have seen and encountered no one. By dawn, the three companies and wagons are moving north on the high road toward Kraaslaen, roughly nine kays away. The grass isn't quite as tall as it was the last time they fought the Cerlynese, but that's understandable since it's earlier in Summer.

Alyiakal still leads with Fourth Company, followed by Dhraak and First Company and then Second and the supply wagons. He calls a halt a hundred yards short of the low rise he'd used as a partial concealment in ambushing the Cerlynese last Summer and rides to the top of the rise where the scouts wait.

"Have you seen any sign of armsmen?"

"No, ser. Not even any dust, and it's dry enough that there should be some," replies Raayls.

That means they want us to come to them, either to be ambushed or against a fortified position where they can use archers.

Alyiakal studies the area between the rise and the town. Looking to the far side of the town, he notes that the mudbrick fort on the low hill beside the stream appears unchanged, although he sees trails of smoke from there and elsewhere around the town.

"We'll take the west lane that circles the town. It's about a kay ahead on the left. It's wide enough for the wagons, if barely. Once I let the other officers know, I'll signal you."

"Yes, ser," replies Raayls.

Alyiakal rides back and rejoins Paersol at the head of Fourth Company before passing the word to the other two companies.

It's close to a half quint later before the Mirror Lancers resume riding, and another quint passes before Alyiakal sees and senses a squad of armsmen to the northeast, clearly heading toward the rear of the Mirror Lancer column and the supply wagons.

He concentrates on discerning riders ahead, but can't sense any, *not yet, anyway,* and turns to Paersol. "We're about to be harassed from the rear. Draw in the scouts to fifty yards but keep moving. Order ready arms. I'm heading back to Second Company. I won't be long."

Paersol nods and begins to relay the orders as Alyiakal turns the chestnut to the rear at a fast trot.

As Alyiakal nears Second Company—which is split, with two squads leading the wagons and a squad as rear guard—he confirms that the pursuers comprise but a squad and suspects that their purpose is to slow them and disable the wagons, if possible.

Slowing the chestnut as he nears Second Company, Alyiakal sees that the senior squad leader is in charge.

"The undercaptain's in the rear, ser!"

"Excellent! Keep moving!"

By the time Alyiakal reaches the last rank, where Staalt rides, he sees that the Cerlynese pursuers are a little more than two hundred yards behind and the leading riders bear polished bronze shields. *Shields, not bucklers, and that means archers behind them.*

Alyiakal leans toward the undercaptain. "The Cerlynese have archers behind the first riders, who have polished shields to deflect firebolts. Detail four lancers to accompany me. The Cerlynese shields won't cover their mounts' legs. I'll take care of that, but the lancers need to target the archers in the rear."

"Last two ranks, form on the majer! Under his orders!"

As the four form behind Alyiakal, he tells them what he told Staalt, then adds, "Keep tight and close behind me until I order you to spread and open fire. Save your firelances until then. Fast trot toward the greencoats. Now!"

In less than a tenth of a quint, Alyiakal senses archers loosing shafts, and broadens his shields enough to cover the rankers, waiting until he's close enough to use a firelance without straining himself. Only a few shafts strike his shields, and without enough force to be more than merely uncomfortable.

Then, with two quick bursts, he brings down the leading horses, then those behind. As he shouts "Spread and open fire!" he continues to target the remaining mounts and riders, using order to guide the quick bursts.

In another fraction of a quint, the remaining three greencoats turn and flee, moving quickly out of firelance range.

"Back to the company!" orders Alyiakal, slowing and turning the chestnut. "Fast trot!" He doesn't see or discern other greencoats nearby, but he can't sense that far in front of Fourth Company, and that bothers him.

". . . shafts dropping all around us . . ."

". . . why he wanted us tight . . ."

Alyiakal doesn't comment until the five reach the rear of Second Company. "Good work! You're returned to Undercaptain Staalt's command." He turns to Staalt. "Leave the bodies and arms and keep a close watch. They might try again."

"Yes, ser."

Alyiakal quickly rides forward past First Company to rejoin Paersol, who immediately asks, "What happened, ser? We couldn't see much except a few firebolts."

"The greencoats sent a squad after the supply wagons. The leading riders tried to shield their archers with big polished shields. Doesn't do much good if you can't shield your mount. Once the leading riders went down, our lancers could take out the mounted archers. Just keep that in mind."

"Yes, ser."

"Have the scouts sighted any more greencoats?"

"Not yet, ser."

"In another kay, we'll be coming to another lane on the right. It leads directly to the town square." As he speaks, Alyiakal force-funnels enough of the chaos he has gathered into his firelance to replenish what he has used.

A half quint later, Raayls signals, gesturing to the northeast, then turns and rides back to Alyiakal, reining up and reporting. "Five companies, maybe six, riding toward us on that side lane. The ones leading and some of the others have those bronze shields."

Alyiakal turns slightly, studying the grass to the east-northeast, then remembers that much of the ground farther north and to the east has been planted in potatoes. That means that the Cerlynese can cross it more easily, then halt at the edge of the fields and loose shafts over the tall grass, which would require the Mirror Lancers to charge through the grass. *But that can work both ways.*

Abruptly, Alyiakal turns to Paersol. "Send a messenger to Dhraak and Staalt. They're to halt and hold their position and face the lancers to the east, in case the Cerlynese attack through the grass. Tell them that there are five companies of greencoats moving toward us, and that Fourth Company will make a diversionary attack. The greencoat shafts can't reach them until they're in the grass."

"Yes, ser."

Once the ranker messenger has ridden off to convey the orders, Alyiakal says to Paersol, "We need to get to the lane before they get too close. You're going to hold at the crossroad with second squad. I'll take first squad to attack their lead company while it's in the potato fields. If we can turn them, I'll signal for you to join us. If not, we'll withdraw and join you."

"Ser . . . one squad?"

"We don't have to win it all at once. We took out one squad attacking the wagons. If we take out another squad or a company and withdraw, we'll have removed most of their numerical advantage. Now . . . Fourth Company! Forward!"

Fourth Company shifts into fast trot.

When the company reaches the lane leading to the center of Kraaslaen, Paersol orders, "Company! Halt! First squad! Direct command to the majer."

"First squad!" orders Alyiakal. "On me. Fast trot. Ready arms!"

As he rides, he concentrates on creating an illusion of an empty road, projecting it in front of the squad. While some Cerlynese armsmen may detect an illusion, they won't be able to see what's behind it.

He senses that the first two companies of the Cerlynese have ridden off the lane and are moving to the western end of the fields. While the shield-bearing armsmen in front are over a hundred yards away, the archers in the rear are much closer. *Which means we need to deal with the archers first.*

"First squad! Halt. Face left! Staggered formation!"

Once the squad has turned and faces the flank of the Cerlynese force moving toward First and Second Companies, Alyiakal orders, "Target the archers in the rear! Open fire!"

With the first firebolts, Alyiakal has to drop the illusion and concentrate on directing his own firebolts at the rear of the lead Cerlynese company. Unfortunately, that also means that first squad will soon be under attack from archers in the Cerlynese forces still on the lane east of first squad.

Alyiakal quickly drops as many archers as he can; so many black death mists leaves him feeling chilled within. Abruptly sensing shafts flying toward the squad, he extends his shields, and orders, "First squad, cease fire! To the rear, ride!"

Baarth, the senior squad leader, relays the order, then rides up beside Alyiakal.

The sudden and rapid movement of first squad results in only a few shafts striking Alyiakal's shields before the squad is beyond the immediate range of the archers.

Even before first squad reaches Paersol and the rest of Fourth Company, Alyiakal is doing his best to discern where the various Cerlynese companies and forces are. He quickly discovers that, despite the loss of most of their archers, roughly two companies are advancing slowly through the grass toward First Company. Another company is moving to follow those companies, while the remainder of the Cerlynese force, possibly two companies, remains on the side lane, unmoving.

When first squad is within yards of second squad, Alyiakal turns to Baarth, and orders, "Re-form the squad so that the company is ready to advance."

Then he turns the chestnut and reins up beside Paersol. "We may be attacking shortly."

"You just withdrew."

"There wasn't much point in staying at that moment and losing lancers to the archers. If I'm not mistaken, their rear companies will mistake our withdrawal for a retreat and move to support the attack on First and Second

Companies. That's when we'll attack their flank, sweeping in and firing from the side, the same way first squad did."

"The flank firing maneuver?" Paersol's tone is even, but Alyiakal can sense his doubt.

"Exactly. Pass the word. We might only have to wait a bit or a half a quint."

"They're attacking First and Second Companies."

"I know. Pass the word to stand ready for a flank fire attack."

"Yes, ser."

Alyiakal already senses death mists from both the Cerlynese and First Company, but less than a third of a quint passes before the remaining Cerlynese companies surge forward into the fields, following those greencoats riding through the grass toward the Mirror Lancers.

"First Company! Forward! Fast trot!" Alyiakal orders.

Once again, Alyiakal interposes the illusion of an empty road between Fourth Company and the Cerlynese, lifting it only when first squad is parallel to the trailing Cerlynese riders. "Company! Halt! Staggered formation! Full flank fire!"

Firebolts rake the trailing company, taking out most of the rearguard archers even before they realize they're under attack.

"Full flank attack!" Alyiakal orders. "On me!" He turns from the lane into the potato field while quick-targeting every greencoat he sees.

In a fraction of a quint, Fourth Company has taken out the majority of the trailing two companies and nears the end of the field.

"Fourth Company! Hold! Hold and re-form! Line-abreast! Line-abreast. Fire only as necessary!"

It's not that Alyiakal doesn't see greencoats ahead; it's that advancing farther will take the company into range of First Company's firelances.

For two quints, Fourth Company holds, the lancers picking off any greencoats trying to escape the firelances of First Company.

Then, there is largely silence, and the sickening odor of ashes and burned flesh. While Alyiakal surveys the area of death and burned vegetation, all he sees are Mirror Lancers, although he has the sense that possibly a score of greencoats may have escaped. But there certainly aren't any nearby.

"Fourth Company, re-form!" orders Alyiakal. Then he force-funnels some of the remaining sun-chaos bits into his firelance, vaguely surprised that he hasn't used it all, and rides over to the head of the company and Paersol, who looks slightly dazed.

Abruptly, Alyiakal realizes that Paersol really hasn't ever been in a battle like this, only skirmishes, and the aftermath of the burning of the fort in Kraaslaen the previous Summer.

"Ser?" asks Paersol.

"Casualties, Captain?" Alyiakal asks tiredly.

"Two dead, three wounded." Paersol pauses. "So far. Baarth is checking with the other squad leaders."

"How badly wounded?"

"One of them . . . it looks serious."

"Let me take a quick look."

Alyiakal dresses the wounds of two lancers, who should recover, if he can watch them. The third is dead before Alyiakal can get to him.

After dealing with the wounded, Alyiakal turns to Paersol. "Take your time but deal with weapons and stray mounts. Then form up the company ready to head into the town. I'll need two lancers to accompany me to check with Dhraak and Staalt."

"Yes, ser." Paersol's voice is subdued.

A third of a quint later, Alyiakal reins up beside Dhraak. "How are you doing? I'm afraid you took the brunt of the attack."

"Not too bad." The captain frowns. "I couldn't tell with all the grass and firebolts, but it seemed like there were a lot of greencoats."

"Five companies, possibly six," replies Alyiakal.

"There's almost no one left. How'd you manage that, ser?"

"You managed most of it. I led a squad and attacked their flank. We took out maybe half a company and withdrew when they started loosing shafts. They decided they'd routed Fourth Company and went to support the companies moving on you. We had to wait just a bit. Then we made a flank fire pass, followed by an attack on their rear. That took out a lot of their archers and likely pushed more of them toward you."

"At first, there were a lot of shafts flying, then only a few . . . and after that we could really attack them." Dhraak pauses. "You left me a really solid company, ser."

"Thank you, but you were in command, and without a good commander, they wouldn't have done as well. What about casualties . . . and captives?"

"We lost eight, and another eight wounded. Most I've ever had." Dhraak shakes his head. "But I have to say I've never fought a pitched battle before, either."

"Just your fortune. Captives?"

"Oh . . . two of them. Both unhorsed in the grass."

"I'll need to talk to them, but the wounded come first."

Another glass passes before Alyiakal finishes dealing with the First Company wounded, two of them with small but sucking chest wounds that he seals with order-infused dressings, hoping he can keep the wounds sealed long enough to give the two a chance of surviving.

Then he checks with Staalt, but Second Company has no casualties, most likely because the archers couldn't reach them before being eliminated. But the lancers did catch five greencoats trying to escape the carnage inflicted by First Company.

Alyiakal decides to interrogate the captives while the companies reorganize, gathering weapons and any loose mounts, and preparing to resume the advance on the town, although Alyiakal doubts there's any real resistance left.

He begins with one of the captives held by Second Company, asking quietly, "What's your name, armsman?"

The man looks at Alyiakal, swallows, then says, "Baathun . . . ser."

"Are you from the grasslands, or Clynya, or Kula, or one of the other towns."

"Caarn . . . north of Kula."

"Were you posted to the fort at Kula?"

Baathun hesitates, then finally says, "Yes, ser."

"Did two or three of your companies come from Kula?"

"Two, ser."

"One from the grasslands, and three from Clynya?"

"I wouldn't know, ser."

"Who was in command?"

"Overcaptain Mherak."

"What do you know about the overcaptain?" asks Alyiakal pleasantly.

"I couldn't say, ser. He was the overcaptain."

"Was the overcaptain close to Duke Taartyn?"

"Not likely, ser. The overcaptain never met the Duke. That's what the captain said."

Alyiakal can sense, without even straining, that Baathun has a considerably less than favorable opinion about Overcaptain Mherak . . . or the Duke.

After interrogating, if briefly, all seven captives, about all that Alyiakal learns is that there were seven companies posted to Kraaslaen, that none of them were told much about why they were there, and none of them liked the overcaptain. Alyiakal suspects the captains likely didn't either, but that's more his intuition than anything even semi-factually based.

Another glass passes before three companies reach the main square, with the simple fountain in its center. All the doors and shutters of the small shops on the west side of the square are closed, as are those of the inn. There's no one in sight, although Alyiakal can sense that more than a few are watching.

When the companies reach the area below the mudbrick fort, Alyiakal sees that the gate is ajar. That's no surprise, because he can't sense anyone in the fort or in any of the mudbrick dwellings nearby.

He does see dust in the distance on the road that leads to Kula . . . and to Cerlyn, a road he'd very much like to take, but will not. Starting wars with other lands is not something decided by sub-majers, even if it means that some other sub-majer, or majer, will have to deal with Duke Taartyn in the future. But that's not his decision.

Alyiakal thinks—and hopes—the near-total destruction of ten companies of armsmen over two years will persuade the Duke not to risk any more armsmen for at least another year or so. Beyond that is problematic.

He also knows that he'll have more nightmares in the nights to come.

ALYIAKAL'ALT,

Sub-Majer

Lhaarat Post
Harvest, 104 A.F.

IX

In the late afternoon of the second threeday of Harvest, Alyiakal rides beside Maarkyn as they turn off the high road and lead Third Company onto the narrow, but passable, road leading two kays downhill to the logged-over area.

"Not a single trace of a raider or brigand," says the undercaptain. "Not on the whole patrol. Do you think headquarters will cut back on the number of companies here at Lhaarat?"

"If they do, it will likely encourage Duke Taartyn, but who knows? They're cutting back on the size of port companies, and I practically had to beg for the few golds to finish this road." Alyiakal gestures vaguely at the road. The part they're riding was only completed in mid-Summer, after two years of work by a combination of local laborers and a few lancers on disciplinary duties.

"It's made patrolling easier, and more traders are using it," says Maarkyn.

"We know that, but I'm not sure that headquarters is overly impressed by a few kays of road along a long border."

Maarkyn laughs, if softly.

"They're more worried about what's happening with posts like Pemedra, Isahl, and Inividra." *And with reason, based on what Hyrsaal's written you.*

"Do you think we'll always be fighting on the borders, ser?"

"Mostly likely, unless matters change." Alyiakal doesn't see that happening any time soon.

He frowns momentarily as he senses an order/chaos pattern to the north, before he recognizes it as a red deer.

After traversing the part of the road through the logged-over area, Third Company reaches the repaired and improved old logging road which extends to the valley floor and then runs south along the valley's east end. When they reach Gairtyn, the townspeople barely glance up as the company rides by, past the sawmill and gristmill and toward the stone and timber bridge over the River Lhaar.

"They don't even look at us anymore," Maarkyn says. "You got the road built, and they have more traders."

"People are like that," Alyiakal says dryly. "As far as they're concerned, it just happened."

"Just like there are almost no raids anymore," adds Maarkyn.

"A lot of that was because Headwoman Kiefala got together with the headwoman of Laankor and with the local council of the walled valley."

"The fact that most raiders don't live very long might have helped," suggests Maarkyn.

"Most good things come from more than one source," suggests Alyiakal. *And people forget that one bad actor can upset everything if people aren't careful . . . and vigilant.*

Less than a glass later, the company enters Lhaarat Post, and Alyiakal rides straight to the stable, leaving Maarkyn to deal with releasing the company to duties.

After grooming and settling the chestnut, Alyiakal crosses the courtyard to the headquarters building and makes his way to his study.

"Ser," says Crendaak, standing, "we had dispatch riders from Terimot. There are several large envelopes from Mirror Lancer headquarters, and several directives."

Dispatch riders from Terimot means priority, Alyiakal knows. Otherwise, the directives would just wait at Terimot until Alyiakal sends outgoing dispatch riders from Lhaarat Post.

"Likely orders for Captain Paersol," replies Alyiakal. "Or orders extending my time as post commander here."

"Wouldn't you be posted elsewhere, ser?"

"I'm afraid I'm rather junior for any larger post, and too senior for any smaller post." *At least, if you're extended another year, you're due home leave before the extension.* Alyiakal steps past Crendaak, closing the door behind himself as he enters his study.

He settles himself behind the desk and looks at the envelope that reads "Post Directives," which can wait, and turns his attention to the two envelopes addressed identically to him. Both are large and thick, as if each contains other envelopes. Alyiakal picks up one in each hand, then decides to open the slightly lighter envelope.

Inside is a single sheet noting that orders for Paersol are enclosed, and that the captain will be detached no later than the fourth eightday of Harvest for reposting to Chaelt as senior captain and port commander.

Alyiakal nods slowly and sets aside the single sheet and the sealed envelope addressed to Paersol. Then he opens the heavier package, which contains two envelopes addressed to him. He opens the thicker of the two, holding a smaller envelope and an official letter from the Majer-Commander.

His eyes widen slightly as he reads the second paragraph.

> *. . . for effective accomplishment as post commander, Lhaarat Post, as ratified and confirmed by the Majer-Commander on Twoday, Seventh Eightday of Spring, 104 A.F., you, Alyiakal'alt, are hereby promoted to Majer, effective Oneday, First Eightday, Summer, 104 A.F. . . .*

Majer? At least a year earlier than usual, if not longer? He has a feeling that what's contained in the other envelopes will explain the promotion.

With a wry smile, he opens the second envelope, which holds the insignia of a Mirror Lancer majer. Since it's well past the effective date of the promotion, he takes the time to replace his sub-majer's insignia with those of a majer.

Then he opens the last envelope, which contains two sheets, also from the Majer-Commander. Alyiakal focuses on the key sections of the first.

> *Alyiakal'alt, Majer*
> *Commander*
> *Lhaarat Post*
>
> *You are hereby ordered to Pemedra Post, for duty as post commander, for two years, with the possible command extension for an additional year.*
>
> *You are detached from Lhaarat Post effective the third eightday of Harvest 104 A.F. Up to five eightdays of home leave are authorized. You are to report to Pemedra no later than the end of the last eightday of Harvest.*
>
> *As commander of Pemedra Post, as has been past practice, you will report directly to Mirror Lancer headquarters, but you are encouraged to inform the Commander of Syadtar Post of any evolutions that might traverse areas close to Syadtar . . .*

The remainder of his orders contains travel and leave authorizations and other information.

The second sheet is brief, noting that his successor is Majer Vordahl, who has previously been the deputy commander at Assyadt. Vordahl will arrive sometime during the fourth eightday of Harvest, as will a junior captain Laaryst to replace Paersol.

Pemedra? As post commander?

Alyiakal has a definite feeling that headquarters remains concerned about Cerlyn and Duke Taartyn, and that his posting to Pemedra is anything but coincidental, since it's the only other Mirror Lancer post that borders Cerlyn. But he also recalls what Subcommander Ciasyrt told him years before, when he'd received his orders to Pemedra as an undercaptain—that the commanding officer at Pemedra was usually in his last assignment and more interested in holding the barbarians at bay than in attempting to obtain a prestigious staff position in Cyad.

Alyiakal can only hope that he's being posted to Pemedra because of his success with barbarians and the Cerlynese. He also wonders about the timing of his departure and Vordahl's arrival.

Almost as if headquarters doesn't want us to meet. But are you reading too much into the timing? It just might be that's the only timing that works out for headquarters. But he still wonders. He's just relieved that his replacement isn't Baertal, who's gone out of his way to try to poison other officers against him from their first day at Kynstaar.

He stands, shaking his head. *At least you'll get home leave . . . and to see Saelora.*

Then he walks to the study door, opens it, and says, "If you'd find Captain Paersol . . . I need to see him."

"Yes, ser." Crendaak stands and heads out.

Alyiakal returns to his desk, first opening the directives and glancing through them, before thinking over the promotion and his orders. He doubts that he'll know any of the officers and suspects he'll know only a few rankers at Pemedra, given that he left there six years ago. *But you never can tell.* His thoughts also drift to Hyrsaal, since he knows that Inividra has to deal with continual Jeranyi and barbarian raids.

A little less than half a quint later Paersol appears in Alyiakal's doorway. "You wanted to see me, ser?"

Alyiakal senses some concern from Paersol, possibly because the captain hasn't done anything wrong and can't imagine why Alyiakal wants to see him. Then Paersol frowns. "Ser . . . are congratulations in order?"

"Oh . . . I just found out I was promoted, effective the first of Summer, but that's not why I sent for you." Alyiakal gestures. "Close the door and have a seat." Once Paersol is seated, Alyiakal hands him the sealed envelope. "I understand this holds your orders to Chaelt as senior captain and port commander." Alyiakal pauses. "Go ahead and open them. Then we'll need to talk."

"Ah . . . yes, ser." Paersol opens the large envelope and begins to read. After a time, he stops and looks up. "The orders are just as you said."

"I had no doubt they would be, but there are a few things you need to know that are not in those orders or in what you may be told." Alyiakal clears his throat. "First, the post commander there three years ago was killed by cammabark explosives, apparently set by smugglers. He was replaced by a very able senior captain, a Captain Aaltyn. I don't know if you'll be succeeding Aaltyn or his successor, but if you're succeeding Aaltyn you should find very accurate records."

"How do you know this, ser?"

"Aaltyn was a company commander at Luuval when I closed the post there. We both did temporary duty at Fyrad after that, and he received his orders just before I left. Now . . . I'll offer an observation that I believe to be true but cannot personally verify. Several officers who have had port and smuggling duty, both at Chaelt and elsewhere, have suggested to me that dealing with outland smugglers is far less hazardous than dealing with Cyadoran smugglers and even some Cyadoran traders."

Paersol frowns once more. "Why would that be?"

"I can think of a number of reasons, but since I've never had that duty, my thoughts would be speculative. I would caution you that port and smuggling duty is anything but risk-free. The risks are lower than at border posts, but they still exist." Alyiakal stands. "That's all I have for you."

"Thank you, ser." Paersol gets to his feet quickly.

Once Paersol leaves the study, Alyiakal begins a letter to Saelora to let her know roughly when to expect him because the dispatch riders from Terimot will leave at dawn. It might be an eightday before there's another dispatch run, and he won't order one for his personal convenience.

He has written close to a page before he has to set it aside and slip it into a drawer so that he won't be late for the evening mess.

When Alyiakal enters the mess all four company officers are waiting and looking at him expectantly. He grins. "Yes, I did get promoted, and I'll fill you in on everything after we're served."

In moments, the officers seat themselves, and the mess orderly fills the wineglasses, after which Alyiakal lifts his glass and says simply, "The best to us all."

"The best to us all."

After a sip of the modest red wine, Alyiakal says, "First, as Paersol may have told you, he's being posted as port commander to Chaelt and will be leaving during the fourth eightday of Harvest. I've been a majer since the first day of Summer, but just found out. I'm being posted to Pemedra as the commanding officer. I have a very fixed detachment date, and that's the third eightday of Harvest. My replacement will be Majer Vordahl, currently the deputy post commander at Assyadt. He'll arrive within a few days of my departure. Captain Paersol will be departing about the same time as Majer Vordahl arrives. Paersol's replacement will be Captain Laaryst, but headquarters hasn't yet indicated when he'll arrive." Alyiakal looks to Dhraak. "You'll be acting post commander for a few days."

"As few as possible, thank you, ser," replies Dhraak dryly. "And I hope Duke Taartyn doesn't get word of your departure."

"I doubt he even knows who I am, except possibly as the difficult commander of Lhaarat Post." *If that.* "From what I've gathered from the few prisoners I've interrogated, he scarcely knows the names of his own senior officers, let alone the names of anyone in the Mirror Lancers."

"I still don't see why his armsmen fight for him," offers Paersol. "They keep getting slaughtered."

"Because they don't have much choice and because they hate us," replies Dhraak. "Our rankers live better than their officers . . . and they live longer, too."

"I've heard that Merchanters buy copper from Cerlyn," says Maarkyn quietly. "That doesn't make sense. We're killing their armsmen with cupridium firelances and sabres made from their copper, and they still sell it to us?"

"It's a bit more complex than that," says Alyiakal. "The Duke—or his traders—needs the golds. Copper fetches golds. So they sell it to the Suthyans, and our Merchanters buy from them. No one else pays more."

"But . . . that means we're paying even more that way."

"Trade doesn't always make sense," says Dhraak. "It always makes golds, but often not sense."

And the passion for golds wins out over common sense and Mirror Lancer lives . . . and even Cerlynese lives. Alyiakal merely nods, his thoughts on the letter he needs to finish and on what awaits him at Pemedra, but he smiles as he thinks about his home leave—and Saelora.

X

On fourday morning, Alyiakal watches the dispatch riders leave with his letter to Saelora, and a shorter letter to Hyrsaal, as well as a recommendation to Mirror Lancer headquarters to consider promoting Senior Squad Leader Baarth to undercaptain. He likely should have made the recommendation earlier, but he'd needed Baarth to keep Paersol from making too many mistakes. *And now that Paersol is leaving . . .*

He shakes his head and walks back toward the mess, thinking.

While Hyrsaal should be ending his posting at Inividra in late Harvest, it looks unlikely that the two of them will cross paths on home leave, since Alyiakal's detachment from Lhaarat is earlier than expected. In his last letter to Alyiakal, Hyrsaal wrote that he hoped to get a posting in Geliendra or at one of the Great Forest posts, but that he hadn't yet heard, and that he wouldn't be detached until his replacement arrived, because the barbarian and Jeranyi raids will likely continue into Autumn.

More raids everywhere—possibly why you're headed to Pemedra? Or just to keep Duke Taartyn in line so headquarters can concentrate on supporting the northern border posts?

Regardless of what Alyiakal thinks, it will be some time before he finds out, if ever, since the Majer-Commander seldom explains any more than is absolutely necessary. In the meantime, he needs to make sure all the post records—and the maps for each company—are up to date.

When he steps into the mess, Dhraak is the only other officer there.

"Good morning, Majer."

"The same to you. What are you planning for your patrol today?"

"With your approval, I'd like to bypass that short stretch leading to the walled valley and head farther on the south road."

"Something there that I should know?" asks Alyiakal.

"No, ser. Just that it's been a while since we've gone very far south, and the locals ought to see us a bit more."

"We're getting more traders from Cyad that way, and that's fine with me . . . provided you don't see lots of hoofprints coming out of the walled valley." Alyiakal offers an amused smile, because no one has seen such tracks over the past few years. The people in the valley only enter and leave through the western end of the valley using the road that winds its way to Westyll.

Dhraak chuckles, then asks, "Do you know anything about Captain Laaryst?"

"Not a thing. Headquarters didn't tell me anything. But when I was first posted here as deputy post commander, Majer Byelt didn't even know he was getting a deputy."

"The post didn't have a deputy commander before?"

"No, and given how few officers we seem to have, I'm not sure that it will again." Alyiakal isn't about to offer his speculation that he ended up in Lhaarat because headquarters had no idea where to put him.

"Why are we short of officers, do you think?"

"My best guess is that because the Emperor doesn't have the golds to pay for more."

Dhraak glances toward the door, then says, "Maybe he shouldn't spend so many golds on refurbishing the Palace of Light."

"I hadn't heard that," replies Alyiakal.

"Why would you, ser? You've spent almost all your career fighting on the borders." Dhraak looks toward the mess door again.

"Do you know who Paersol's contacts in Cyad are?" That's a guess on Alyiakal's part, but not much of one.

Dhraak shakes his head. "It's just that he's let a few things slip."

"I've always thought he comes from an elthage background, but he's always avoided it around me."

"The same around the rest of us as well, but he says he came from Sollend. No one comes from Sollend. It's where the consorts or unconsorted daughters of wealthy Magi'i spend the summers. He also only did a year at Kynstaar."

"And just two years at Westend before he was posted here." Alyiakal might have said more, but Paersol steps into the mess, followed moments later by Staalt and Maarkyn. Instead, Alyiakal walks to the head of the table and seats himself.

When everyone is seated and finished serving themselves, Maarkyn asks, "Ser, with everything that arrived yesterday, was there any news from Cyad or headquarters?"

"Strangely enough, there wasn't, well . . . except for more directives, including another ordering all posts to minimize the unnecessary use of firelances." Alyiakal takes a bite of the ham strips and then of the fried apples.

"As if we rode around throwing chaos at trees," says Dhraak sardonically.

"Do any of them in headquarters remember when they were actual Mirror Lancers?" asks Staalt sarcastically.

"Most likely do," replies Alyiakal, "but they send the directives to placate the Magi'i and the Emperor."

"Do you think the Magi'i are that dense, ser?" asks Paersol, his tone verging on the snide, as it often has.

"Most of them are very bright," answers Alyiakal, "but they don't understand what we do and what it requires because they've never faced what you do, and they usually look down on anyone in their family who becomes a Mirror Lancer officer."

"Have you ever met with real Magi'i, ser?" asks Paersol.

While Alyiakal can't believe that Paersol has asked the question, especially since he *knows* Paersol knows he has, he replies evenly, "I have, on a number of occasions. I even met with the Third Magus personally once. You might recall that Senior Magus Thiaphyl was here two years ago, and I escorted him to Lestroi. That was the second time I worked with him."

"Do you recall the name of the Third Magus?"

"The Third Magus I met with was called Verinaar. That was six years ago. Someone else might be Third Magus now, for all I know."

Alyiakal can sense his reply disconcerts Paersol, and he says, "They have their priorities, and we have ours, and that's the way it is. On a more personal note, where do you plan to take your home leave?" He eats several more bites of the eggs, ham strips, and fried apples.

Paersol hesitates, then says, "With family, at least for most of it."

"No young lady in your future?" asks Dhraak amiably.

"Not yet." Paersol turns back to Alyiakal. "What about you, ser?"

"I'll spend most of it with friends in Vaeyal and possibly Fyrad. I spent more time in that area growing up. Both my parents are dead, and themselves were only children."

"I'd think that there might be more than a few women who'd be more than pleased to consort you," suggests Paersol, "especially now."

"You must know how it is," replies Alyiakal. "I'm not terribly interested in women who'd consort for the rank and the survivor stipend . . . and who have no understanding of what Mirror Lancer officers do." He laughs. "It doesn't mean I won't consort, just that no woman whom I could love has agreed." All of which is true, but not in the way that Paersol will take it.

"That's why so many senior officers don't consort until they're close to getting their stipend or even until they do," Dhraak points out.

"That's one way of looking at it," says Paersol. "But don't you risk missing much of life?"

"Every officer has to choose what's right for him," says Dhraak. "My choices might not be right for you. Yours might be a disaster for me."

"And we could all be wrong and end up miserable," says Alyiakal dryly, adding to Paersol, "I hope you enjoy your home leave, and that I enjoy mine." He takes a small swallow of ale, before finishing his breakfast, then waits until he sees the others are finished before standing and saying to Dhraak, "Have a good patrol. I look forward to hearing if you find anything interesting beyond the walled valley. If you do, I hope it's not too interesting."

Dhraak chuckles. "So do I, ser."

Alyiakal offers a parting smile, then leaves the mess, heading for his study and the records he needs to review and update before he leaves Lhaarat.

XI

For the next few days, Alyiakal goes through all the personal records of every ranker and officer at Lhaarat. He also makes sure that the maps are up to date, and that the supply records are current. While he finds a few missing or incorrect items, which he corrects, he doesn't discover any real problems.

On oneday afternoon, he requests Dhraak join him in his study.

The senior captain arrives promptly. "Ser . . . you wanted to see me?"

Alyiakal gestures for Dhraak to close the door and seat himself. "I did. You know that I'm ordered to depart before Majer Vordahl is scheduled to arrive. You're the most senior captain. I'll leave a letter naming you acting post commander until a new commander arrives. I'll also post the patrol schedule for the two eightdays after I leave, but you may have to change it if there's severe weather or if Captain Laaryst is delayed. The head cook may also request silvers to pay for local produce and meat. Those funds are in the strongbox in the locked room off the armory . . ."

For the next quint, Alyiakal details what Dhraak needs to know, then asks, "Do you have any questions?"

The captain grins. "What if I forget?"

"Ask Crendaak how I did it. He won't tell you what to do, but he will tell you what I've done. Anything else?"

"If I might ask . . ."

"Yes?"

"You're not that keen on the Magi'i . . ."

"I worry that the most senior Magi'i concentrate their efforts too much on what happens in Cyad and not enough on what happens elsewhere in Cyador. They also keep women who have the talents to do magery limited to healing. That limits the number of mages at a time when I suspect we could use more."

"Because the outlanders are getting stronger?" asks Dhraak.

"Also, because I get the feeling that there are fewer strong mages than there were in the time of the First. All you have to do is look at what they built and how much more time it takes for us to do far less." Alyiakal shrugs. "Then it may be that some skills and knowledge have been lost as well."

"Do you think that's necessarily bad?"

"When we fought the Kyphrans, they had a mage. Just one mage. If they'd had two, it could have been very different. We lost more than two companies. I don't know of any other encounter where we lost that many officers and men."

"Hmmm . . . I see what you mean, ser." After a moment of silence, Dhraak continues. "Is that the only reason you worry about the Magi'i?"

"That and the fact that they don't seem to see the possible threat from outland mages, and that they seem to think that the chaos towers will last forever and that the Great Forest will always remain contained."

Dhraak nods.

"Anything else?" asks Alyiakal.

"One other thing . . . You're more than a field healer, not that any lancer who knows that will ever say more, except maybe Paersol. What does headquarters know?"

"I can do a little bit of healing," lies Alyiakal, "and at least some Magi'i know it. Some of my superiors have suspected it, but they've said nothing, most likely because they're thinking it can't do any harm and it benefits the Mirror Lancers. I wouldn't dare to try surgery or anything like that." He smiles wryly. "I think we've gone over everything I can think of that you'll need to know." *And a bit more.* "You'll do just fine." Then Alyiakal stands.

So does Dhraak. "It won't be the same without you, ser."

"Every commander likes to think that. Sometimes, they're right. Mostly, they're not, but we all like to hope," he concludes dryly.

After Dhraak leaves, Alyiakal walks to the window, not really looking out, before returning to his desk.

Two quints later, Crendaak peers in. "The dispatch riders brought more directives, it looks like." He holds up a single large envelope. "Mostly letters, though. Nothing personal for you, Majer."

"Thank you. It's a little early for letters." Alyiakal stands and takes the envelope, then returns to his desk, where he slits open the envelope, which contains three sheets.

The first sheet is an announcement whose first lines capture Alyiakal's attention immediately.

> *Captain-Commander Mheryt has been selected as the Majer-Commander of the Mirror Lancers of Cyador, following the sudden death of Majer-Commander Waarkyt. Waarkyt'alt died on the second twoday of Summer, as the result of a red flux so violent that even the best healers in Cyad could not save him.*
>
> *Senior Commander Laartol will succeed Mheryt'alt as Captain-Commander, effective immediately . . .*

The remainder of the announcement details Mheryt's past postings, including time as post commander at Inividra, Geliendra, and Syadtar, and those of Laartol, who had commanded at Isahl, Assyadt, and Guarstyad.

Alyiakal lowers the sheet. Especially with the announcement, he has no doubt that Laartol had something, if not everything, to do with his assignment to Pemedra. And since Laartol does nothing without forethought and purpose, exactly what does he expect of Alyiakal? Or did he arrange for Alyiakal to take command there to preclude anyone else from getting the command billet there? But why?

Because he wants someone he can trust to deal with Duke Taartyn and the Jeranyi . . . or because you've been able to defeat larger forces when outnumbered . . . and the Mirror Lancers are spread too thin?

All of those surmises make sense, but Alyiakal knows that Laartol has always thought far ahead . . . and that concerns him.

After several long moments, he glances at the other two sheets from the envelope. The first is a directive to reduce the cost of local food procurement wherever possible and by using a list of possible methods.

Alyiakal sets that one aside and looks at the second directive, which encourages post commanders to recommend "highly qualified" and "experienced" senior squad leaders for consideration as potential undercaptains.

At least you've already complied with that directive.

But his thoughts go back to Laartol and his own promotion.

XII

By the third sixday of Harvest, Alyiakal has all the records updated, and has his and Paersol's detachment and travel documentation completed. There have been no raids or brigandage over the last eightday and no reports of Cerlynese armsmen. Alyiakal just hopes that there won't be any trouble or difficulties until after he leaves on eightday, and hopefully, not until after Vordahl arrives to take command.

Late that afternoon two dispatch riders arrive, with only a few directives and a number of personal letters, two of which are for Alyiakal, one from Saelora and the other from Hyrsaal.

After reading the directives, which only make slight changes to existing Mirror Lancer policies, Alyiakal makes the changes in the directives book and then opens the letter from Hyrsaal, noting the traces of chaos around the seal before he begins to read.

> *Congratulations on your promotion. I've always said that you would do great things, and you have. I'm glad Headquarters recognizes that. They can use you at Pemedra, but so could we here at Inividra. They'll probably send you here sometime. We don't lose that many lancers at any one time, but*

losing a man every third or fourth patrol from late Spring to early Autumn adds up over the year. Having a good field healer would also help . . .

That doesn't surprise Alyiakal. From what Healer Vayidra had told him and what he's seen and heard, between a third and half the fatalities in most companies are from wound chaos if there's no healer available.

At least you've been able to do something about that.

It's looking like I'll be detached sometime in the last eightday of Harvest, and I won't get to Vaeyal for another eightday. But the good news is that I'll be promoted to overcaptain, effective the first oneday of Autumn, and posted to Northpoint as officer-in-charge for two years. I understand that they're reducing the complement there, and possibly even doing away with the command billet in the future . . .

Alyiakal nods. His father had been a full majer when he commanded at Northpoint, but it's still a good duty for Hyrsaal . . . and far closer to Fyrad and Vaeyal. And while duty patrolling the Great Forest isn't risk-free, it's nowhere near as dangerous as Inividra.

. . . Catriana says that Haarlt is not only walking but running and climbing everything. She says it must come from my family, like the red hair. I'm so looking forward to seeing them both. It's hard to believe I've never even seen my son.

It's good that she and Elina are both in Fyrad where they can help each other and that Dyrkan's family has been so supporting . . .

Catriana also wrote that Loraan House occupies half the space at Haansfel, and she's now a full Merchanter. She and Saelora are the only women Merchanters anywhere along the Great Canal.

Half the space at Haansfel? Are they planning to take it over? Or do they have the space because Haansfel is slowly failing?

I don't know if you heard, but you might recall Naeyal from Kynstaar. I wrote him after he was posted to Syadtar, but I never heard back. I didn't hear anything about him after that, but he went from there to Ilypsya for a short posting and then to Eastpoint and then to Isahl . . .

Alyiakal just remembers that Naeyal had ignored him and Fuhlart in the brief time that the three were all at Syadtar.

. . . but I just heard that Jeranyi raiders attacked his company in a rainstorm, and they ended up hand-to-hand. With all the rain, his firelance malfunctioned and incinerated him. At least, that's the story . . .

Alyiakal winces. *More like a ranker took him out, and no one will say anything because he'd pissed off too many of his men.*

It doesn't look like we'll see each other on this home leave. I wish we could, but I'm most certain Saelora will give you a warm welcome, and that's an understatement.

Alyiakal grins.

Alyiakal sets Hyrsaal's letter aside and studies the seal on Saelora's letter with his senses. As is usual, there are traces of chaos there as well. He supposes there always will be, at least as long as he's a Mirror Lancer officer. Then he opens it.

Alyiakal—

I'm so looking forward to seeing you. I can hardly wait. It's been so long, and you know how I feel.

I'm so proud of you. I couldn't resist telling Mother that you'd been promoted to full majer. She didn't say much, except that at least I had the sense to love a capable man, even if he wouldn't consort me. I hope you don't think I'm horrible because I didn't tell her that it was my choice.

I don't know if I wrote you before that Charissa is also helping as she can at Loraan House, because Mother does like to spend some time with Gaartyn and Rendara. Gaaran likes driving the wagon, and he's using it to carry and sell goods to some of the nearby towns and hamlets . . .

Laetilla is also training the twins—Charissa's cousins—to help with the distillery now that we've got things worked out with the clear maize liquor. We decided to call it Crystalflame. Most of that goes straight down the Great Canal to Fyrad and various outland traders. I don't know that we could have worked that out so well if Dyrkan hadn't come up here and helped last year. He came up with the idea of a special short "aging." The twins are also a great help around the factorage . . .

Elinjya still comes by at least every eightday, sometimes more often, often with the children. They're well behaved, and they call me Auntie Saelora . . .

When he finishes reading Saelora's letter, he sets it aside for the moment, although he'll read it again later, and turns to writing a response to Hyrsaal. While it won't be dispatched until eightday, when Alyiakal departs Lhaarat and he and a few lancers accompany the dispatch riders back to Terimot, he knows that sevenday will be filled with last-moment chores. Hopefully, he won't have forgotten anything that will require any great amount of time to rectify.

He takes a sheet of paper and picks up his pen.

XIII

Alyiakal rises early on eightday morning, first dressing and readying his duffels, then making his way to the mess. All four officers are there, waiting for him.

"We all thought we should join you for an early breakfast," declares Dhraak, smiling broadly.

"You didn't have to," says Alyiakal, "but I appreciate it." He gestures toward the table, then takes his place at the head, where he discovers platters of ham strips, cheesed eggs, and fried apples, not exactly the simple fare he had expected for an early breakfast. "This is much better than I expected."

"It was Drassyl's idea," says Staalt. "He said you'd never asked for anything special for yourself, only for the lancers."

But that's the way it should be. Alyiakal manages a ragged grin. "I'm not about to argue with the head cook, and I certainly won't turn down such a good hot breakfast. Neither should any of you." He immediately serves himself and passes the platters, waiting for the other officers to serve themselves before he takes a mouthful of the fried apples.

"You were posted to Pemedra some time ago," says Paersol after several moments. "Isn't it unusual to be reposted to a previous post?"

"I'm sure it's happened before. When I was there, the deputy post commander had been posted there earlier in his service. My father commanded a post where he'd served before as well."

"Do you know anything about the new commander, ser?" asks Maarkyn.

"Some," admits Alyiakal. "We were at Kynstaar at the same time, and his father was, and still might be, a senior commander at Mirror Lancer headquarters."

Dhraak tries to conceal a wince, but Alyiakal doesn't think the other three notice.

"That could be . . ." Paersol doesn't finish the sentence.

"Very good, very bad, or not make any difference at all," says Alyiakal, "depending on the individuals and the circumstances. For what it's worth, Majer Vordahl did very well at Kynstaar. He was very professional the entire time he was there."

"Was he as good with blades as you?" asks Staalt.

"We never sparred, so I can't say."

Dhraak clears his throat, then asks, "Was that because you only sparred with the best of the officers?"

"I had the advantage of being trained by my father from the time I was twelve."

Paersol looks confused, although he should know.

Except he might not because he was only at Kynstaar for the last year. Alyiakal doesn't want to explain and looks to Dhraak.

"Sometimes," Dhraak says, "when an officer candidate is very good with blades, they don't often spar with other candidates because it doesn't teach those candidates anything, and they don't learn anything new, either."

Staalt nods. "That makes sense."

"Do you think we'll have any more trouble with the Cerlynese?" asks Maarkyn.

"Yes. At least so long as Taartyn is duke. It's only a guess, but he might wait until next year, or even longer, before he tries anything with Kraaslaen. Then, he might attack sooner. He likely won't attack in Harvest because that might limit the number of armsmen he could use, unless he's building up a force like the Mirror Lancers. That gets costly, though. Cerlyn's not that wealthy, and it may have taken him some time to replace all the armsmen he's lost."

Before Alyiakal realizes it, he's finished his breakfast, and he realizes that he needs to get on the road, because, even riding with the dispatch riders, it will be three long days before he reaches Terimot.

"Unfortunately," he says as he stands, "I need to get moving. Thank you all . . . and I need to thank Drassyl as well."

Alyiakal walks to the half-open kitchen door, but before he can even enter, Drassyl steps out.

"Majer."

"I just wanted to thank you for the breakfast . . . and for all you've done while I've been here . . . and before."

"It was my pleasure, ser." Drassyl smiles and hands Alyiakal an apple. "I thought you might like this for your horse. You usually ask for carrots, but . . ."

"Apples are more special. Thank you."

From the kitchen, Alyiakal goes to his quarters to retrieve his duffels, which he carries to the stable. There he spends some time talking to the chestnut gelding. He's chosen not to ride the chestnut to Terimot because he doubts the ostlers there will appreciate him, while those at Lhaarat Post are more able to match him to someone who can appreciate him, although the chestnut will likely be a spare mount for a while.

"That's the best I can do for you, fellow." Before Alyiakal leaves the stall, he offers the apple to the chestnut, and waits for him to finish it. Then he pats him and leaves the stall. He swallows several times.

He quickly saddles one of the spare mounts, fastens his gear behind the saddle, takes a firelance from the officers' rack, checks it, and places it in its holder. Then he leads the roan mare out into the courtyard, where he mounts and rides to join the small group headed for Terimot.

Except that he finds all four companies mustered on foot in the main courtyard, and he looks to Dhraak, standing with the other officers in the front.

The senior captain grins. "Wasn't my idea, ser. The senior squad leaders asked permission. One thing I've learned is that when they all agree, it's a good idea." Dhraak's grin broadens. "As I recall hearing you tell some under-captains, listen to your senior squad leaders. So we took your advice."

Alyiakal swallows again. He hasn't expected anything like this. After a moment, he manages to say, "I can't argue with that." Then, with a ruefully amused smile, he looks to Chaaltyn, at the head of First Company. "You wouldn't have had anything to do with this, would you?"

"Only a little, ser. Me and Baarth. Lots of the lancers agreed it was the only way we could show our appreciation."

Alyiakal turns his mount so all the rankers can see him and begins to speak, using a touch of order so that they all can hear. "I'm going to miss all of you. Every lancer here had a part in accomplishing what we did. I asked a great deal of each of you. Every time we faced the Cerlynese, we were outnumbered, and there was no one near to reinforce you. But every one of you did what was necessary, without question or hesitation, and you did it well." Alyiakal pauses, not knowing what else he can or should say. "For now, all I can do is to thank each of you and wish you well."

Then he inclines his head in respect, before turning the roan toward the dispatch riders and the four lancers who will accompany him.

XIV

Alyiakal arrives in Terimot after three long days of riding, and two nights with little sleep, only to find that a firewagon is waiting for him, ready to depart the moment he dismounts and unstraps his duffels from behind the roan's saddle. He spends a few moments on necessaries, and then heads for the firewagon, but each of the lancers carries a duffel for him.

The driver's assistant stands beside the open door to the front compartment. "Majer Alyiakal, ser?"

Alyiakal nods and offers his seal ring and orders.

"No need of that, ser. There's no other majer around here. We'll be off as soon as you're settled."

"Thank you." Alyiakal looks into the front compartment, which is empty, then takes the duffels one at a time and puts them behind the rear seats. He turns to the two lancers. "Thank you both. Be careful on your ride back."

"Thank you, ser. Good fortune in Pemedra."

The two step away, and Alyiakal steps up into the compartment and seats himself in one of the forward-facing seats. Immediately the driver's assistant closes the door.

Alyiakal remains seated only until the firewagon is up to speed, headed west through the growing twilight toward Ilypsya. Then he stretches out and closes his eyes.

Tired as he is, his sleep seems fitful at first, but he wakes sometime in the dark when the firewagon makes a brief stop and then again sometime right after dawn.

In late afternoon of fourday, the firewagon reaches Ilypsya, where Alyiakal discovers that the next firewagon to Fyrad won't leave until fiveday morning. So he avails himself of the quarters for senior officers passing through and cleans up thoroughly before making his way to the small mess, where he ends up at the senior officers' table with another majer and an overcaptain.

Alyiakal doesn't recognize the considerably older majer, and deferring to him as the three are being served, he says, "Majer, I'm Alyiakal, going on home leave before heading to Pemedra."

"Trastyr, headed home from Chulbyn to enjoy some quiet years in Doorm."

"I can't say I've heard of Doorm," Alyiakal admits.

"Most haven't. Just off the Great Canal about twenty kays north of Fyrad."

Alyiakal looks to the overcaptain. "I didn't catch your name."

"Haarnt, ser. Headed for duty at Fyrad."

Trastyr tilts his head. "Pemedra, you say. Your first full command?"

"Actually, it will be my fourth."

"Oh?" The older majer looks surprised, a surprise that Alyiakal can also sense.

"Oldroad Post, reporting to Guarstyad; command to shut down Luuval Post; and two years as post commander at Lhaarat."

Trastyr laughs. "Just shows how old I'm getting. I have to say you look young for a majer."

"I am, and I was just promoted to full majer."

"I'd guess you come from a lancer family then."

"It's a good guess. My father and grandfather were both lancer officers. You might have run across my father—Majer Kyal."

Trastyr frowns, then nods. "Kyal . . . never met him personally, heard good things about him. You mentioned Guarstyad. Was that dustup there with the Kyphrans really as bad as some say?"

"They had firelances, a battle mage, and over fifteen hundred troopers. We had four companies. In the end they had maybe twoscore survivors, and we lost two companies and their officers."

"You obviously survived. Given your subsequent postings, you must have been effective."

"I was promoted to overcaptain and given command at the new Oldroad Post on the east side of the Westhorns. Small post, just two companies."

Trastyr nods again. "You fight from the front, don't you?"

"I've done what I thought necessary."

"That's quite a scar on your forehead. You don't usually get those laying back."

Alyiakal laugh ruefully. "I guess I haven't mastered effective command from the rear."

"Lhaarat . . ." ventures the overcaptain. "Were you there last year when the lancers wiped out an entire Cerlynese garrison at some town?"

"Kraaslaen. It's just across the border from Cerlyn. We destroyed their fort and four companies two years ago. Last year they sacked the town with seven companies. Less than a score survived after we got there. It's a long two-day ride from Lhaarat."

"That's why Lhaarat sounded familiar," says the older majer.

"Then you're the one," says the overcaptain, shaking his head.

"The one what?" asks Trastyr.

"Another officer, his last post was Lhaarat, and he said there was an overcaptain . . ."

"Was that officer Captain Dhaerl . . . or maybe Overcaptain Dhaerl?" asks Alyiakal.

"Yes, ser. I mean he was Captain Dhaerl, but now he's Overcaptain Dhaerl."

"Good. He deserves the promotion," says Alyiakal.

"You didn't recommend him?" asks Trastyr.

"I couldn't. When he was reposted, I was the deputy post commander. I didn't take command until a season later."

Trastyr shakes his head. "You've had an eventful career. Headquarters is posting you from one troubled border post to another. You're headed to Pemedra. In ten years, you'll either be a commander at headquarters . . . or you'll be dead." The older majer looks at Alyiakal sadly. "Guess I was fortunate not to face what you have. A few raiders here and there at Isahl, smugglers at Summerdock."

"Some of it's chance," says Alyiakal.

"Chance, and what you make of it," replies Trastyr.

"What was the strangest or most difficult situation you ever encountered?" asks Alyiakal, not wanting to talk more about himself.

"That's all in the past," demurs Trastyr.

"The past is a very good instruction for facing the future," insists Alyiakal. "I really would like to hear what you have to say."

"The strangest situation? Hmmm . . ." The older majer pauses, thinking, then says, "I suppose one of the oddest things I came across was east of Jakaafra. I was just an undercaptain, and I had a company patrolling the Great Forest. We were heading back to the barracks at Northpoint. Just ahead in the twilight, I saw a woman and a girl. They were walking toward the wall. Then, all of a sudden, they were gone, and there was one of the giant black cats, with a cub following her . . . and then they both disappeared."

"Disappeared?" asks Haarnt.

"Disappeared. My senior squad leader saw them, too. We never reported it. Who would have believed it?"

"Strange things happen around the Great Forest," says Alyiakal. "A Mirror Engineer told me that one day all the wards on one section lost power, right after a huge cat appeared on the wall." Not all of that is true, but Alyiakal doesn't want to be entirely truthful. "But I was thinking more about something more difficult not involving magery."

Trastyr chuckles. "Lots of difficult times, but there's nothing strange about them. I got sent on a patrol to track some raiders north of Isahl in mid-Autumn. Sunny morning when we left the post, chilly but clear and windy. Should have guessed that a wind that strong wasn't good, but I was young. Anyway, dark clouds started moving in just as we sighted the raider band, maybe three, four kays away. They saw us, but they didn't hurry any. We got within a kay when the rain came down, more like a waterfall. Well, there wasn't much point in pursuing. We couldn't see that far, and in that much rain, firelances aren't much good. So we turned back. Good thing, not that we had much choice. There's no cover in the grasslands. We rode another three kays, and the air got even colder, and the rain changed to sleet, and the water froze on and in our uniforms, and before long the sleet changed to snow. Took us four glasses to cover the last three kays back to the post."

Alyiakal smiles, recalling his encounter with thundersnow.

"You look like you've been through something like that," says Trastyr.

"Similar circumstances, except it was thundersnow, when I was a fresh undercaptain at Pemedra. Dropped enough snow to be knee-high in about two glasses, but it was cold enough that we didn't have to worry about rain freezing on us."

"I wager you always look for the wind and the clouds now," declares Trastyr.

"Always." Alyiakal turns to the overcaptain. "What about you, Haarnt?"

"Not rain or snow, like you two. But there's an inland valley south of Chaelt that's a real desert, with strange orange sands, and we were following smugglers . . ."

Alyiakal listens, glad to have someone else doing the talking. He's also looking forward to a decent night's sleep.

ALYIAKAL'ALT,

MAJER

Vaeyal

Harvest, 104 A.F.

XV

The firewagon to Fyrad leaves Ilypsya at first light on fiveday, and Alyiakal shares the front compartment with three other officers—an older undercaptain, likely promoted from senior squad leader, and two captains. All three are headed to Fyrad. Because the two captains appear to be friends, they sit in the rear-facing seats, while Alyiakal and Undercaptain Wuultz sit in the forward-facing seats.

Alyiakal wonders why Majer Trastyr isn't on the same firewagon, but it could just be that there are two headed south along the Great Canal . . . or Trastyr left earlier . . . or would depart later. *Or that officers still on full duty take priority.*

Alyiakal pushes those thoughts aside and dozes for a time, and when he wakes, he finds the view out the side windows hasn't changed much, just the same whitestone road going south through fields and hamlets whose names remain largely unknown except to those who live there.

When the undercaptain wakes, Alyiakal asks, "Where are you coming from?"

"Kynstaar, ser."

"Recruit or officer candidate training?"

"Recruit training."

"If I might ask, what part of training?"

"Blades and firelances. Mostly blades. Especially after headquarters ordered us to cut back on the amount of chaos we used." Wuultz pauses, then asks, "Do you know anything about that, ser?"

"Only that they sent a directive requesting that all post commanders take steps to reduce unnecessary use of firelances. The directive didn't give a reason."

"Seems like headquarters doesn't like to explain."

"Except when they spend pages explaining," replies Alyiakal dryly. *Usually, those directives are about matters that don't need explanation.*

Wuultz chuckles. "There is that, ser."

"How were you doing on getting recruits?"

"Plenty of recruits. Enough that we didn't have to keep those who might not make the best lancers. Hasn't always been like that."

"More from grower families . . . or from Cyad and the bigger towns?" asks Alyiakal.

"More this past year from the larger towns, I'd say." Wuultz shrugs. "That's just my feeling."

"Do you know what you'll be doing at Fyrad?"

Wuultz offers a crooked smile. "Same thing as at Kynstaar, except I'll be working with naval marine recruits, and it'll be mostly blades and truncheons."

Alyiakal can see that. Using firelances on ships could create considerable problems. "Where are you from originally?"

"Cyad."

Alyiakal smiles. "What's it like? I've never been there, but I've heard tales that the city's a marvel and filled with danger."

Wuultz snorts. "Like everything, it depends on where you go and how prepared you are. The streets around the Palace of Light are the safest place in the whole world. Same's true of the Magi'i quarter, but I wouldn't go near the warehouses and inns used by the outland traders at night without half a squad behind me."

"What about the warehouses used by the Cyadoran clans and traders?"

"In the light, they're safe enough. At night they're not much better than the outlanders' places."

"So the Imperial Tariff Enumerators don't have any role in keeping traders in line?"

"Never heard of anything like that. The city patrollers keep the peace, mostly, and the places where folks live are pretty safe. Doesn't mean you shouldn't be careful, but away from the worst of the trading quarter, Cyad's safer than most places."

"Why'd you join the Mirror Lancers?"

"My father was a tinsmith. My older brother liked that sort of work." Wuultz shakes his head. "I just couldn't see it. Still can't. What about you, ser?"

"Third-generation Mirror Lancer." Alyiakal manages a rueful grin. "I never thought about anything else. So far, I haven't regretted it."

After some more casual conversation, Alyiakal leans back and closes his eyes.

For the rest of the day, there's some brief conversation, usually at rest stops.

It's late afternoon when the firewagon stops at Vaeyal and the driver's assistant opens the door to the front compartment. "Vaeyal, Majer."

Alyiakal steps out into the damp warmth, glancing up at the dark gray clouds to the northeast that appear to be moving toward Vaeyal, then retrieves both duffels and sets them beside the waystop, little more than a three-sided hut with roof and a backless bench. He watches the firewagon depart, then looks around. He can't see Loraan House from the waystop, and, as late in the afternoon as it is, the factorage isn't usually open. He did write Saelora that he'd be arriving late on either fiveday or sixday afternoon, and she should have received that letter before now. *But that doesn't mean she did.*

He'd rather not carry the two duffels farther south to the bridge, then across the canal and back up to the factorage. *But if that's what it takes.* He decides to wait, at least a little while, just in case Saelora or Gaaran might be coming, although he doesn't want to wait too long and have to lug the duffels in the rain.

Then he hears the sound of wheels on stone and sees the Loraan House wagon crossing the bridge and turning north on the whitestone road beside the canal towpath. He can both see and sense that Saelora's driving.

He can't help smiling at the sight of her in the stylish Merchanter blues that so compliment her mahogany hair and piercing brown eyes, and the moment she brings the wagon to a halt, his smile broadens. "I hoped it would be you and not Gaaran."

"Do you really think I'd wait to see you?" The warmth of her voice and the emotions behind her words sweep over him.

"I'm so glad you didn't."

"Because of me or because you don't want to get soaked?"

Alyiakal grins. "You. But I'd rather not get soaked." He lifts one of the duffels and turns.

"The rear doors are unbarred."

"Excellent!" In moments, he has both duffels in the rear of the wagon, with the doors secure, and climbs up beside her, putting an arm around her tightly. "If this weren't so public . . ."

She turns her head and kisses him, firmly but swiftly. "You're fortunate it is."

"Is that a promise?"

"Absolutely." She returns her attention to the horse. "You likely need to wash up, and I did think we'd have dinner after that . . . but it will still be early."

"That will make it the best evening in three years."

"I'd hope so."

Alyiakal watches her as she carefully turns the wagon back toward the bridge. He notices she wears the electrum and blue zargun bracelet he had given her. "You've gotten defter in handling the wagon."

"After three years, I should have." She glances at him for an instant. "A full majer. Hyrsaal wrote that you have to be one of the youngest ever. He also said that you deserved it for all you've done."

"I've had some advantages he hasn't had, but I'm so happy he'll be an overcaptain."

"So is Catriana." Saelora pauses. "With all you know . . . about the Great Forest . . . is there any way . . . ?"

"I can write him about how to approach situations along the wall . . . and some other suggestions. I can write those down while I'm here. If he stops here, then I won't have to post them. I can write more that way."

"I can help."

That surprises Alyiakal.

"If you write it out, and then I copy what you write, I can destroy your words, and there's no physical link to you."

"If you would . . . that would be the best."

"I'd be happy to do that, and Hyrsaal will definitely appreciate it." Saelora's tone alone tells Alyiakal that she *will* make it clear that her brother should appreciate the advice. She guides the wagon across the bridge over the Great Canal and then north on Canal Street.

When they near the factorage, Alyiakal studies the front of the building, but he can't see much in the way of change, except that it looks newer somehow. "Did you refinish or . . ."

"Early in Summer, I had the trim repainted, and Gaaran made some repairs to the front."

"It looks good. Are things working out well with Charissa and Gaaran helping with Loraan House?"

"Very well. I also have them both to dinner once every eightday or so, sometimes with the children, sometimes not."

The green and white awning of the coffeehouse up Canal Street from

Loraan House is folded up, indicating that it's closed for the day, but Alyiakal smiles, recalling the first time he and Saelora had been together.

Before long, they reach the older graystone road leading to the distillery, Saelora's house, and the swamp. Knowing they still have another two kays to go, Alyiakal asks, "Now that you've improved the end of the road, has anyone followed your example?"

"Things haven't changed much." She offers an amused smile. "Some people now call it the road to the distillery rather than the old road."

"Not the road to the Lady Merchanter's house?"

"That would be expecting too much."

As the wagon nears the house, Alyiakal immediately sees that the distillery is twice as large as it had been three years ago. "You mentioned that you'd added on, but I didn't realize just how much."

"The guest quarters are the same, but . . ."

Alyiakal understands what she doesn't want to say and immediately asks, "You won't mind having me around all the time?"

"I haven't waited three years to miss having you any more than absolutely necessary. I did make some changes to the house."

"I'm sure I'll like them. You have excellent taste, and I've liked everything you've done."

"I still worry."

He reaches out and squeezes her shoulder gently. "Don't."

After Saelora brings the wagon to a halt just outside the stable, Alyiakal climbs down and studies the approaching dark clouds, sensing the swirl of order and chaos within, then asks, "Do you want to put the wagon in the stable? It's definitely going to rain, most likely hard."

"If you wouldn't mind . . ."

"Mind? I insist."

Even with two of them, it takes almost two quints to get the wagon into its place in the stable and to settle the horse. Then Alyiakal carries the two duffels into the kitchen through the door from the stable.

Laetilla turns from the prep table and smiles pleasantly. "It's good to see you, Majer. I'm so glad to see you're here safely."

"Alyiakal, please. It's good to see you as well. Saelora's written me about what you've done, especially with the distillery, and I suspect you've done a great deal more."

"She certainly has," Saelora replies.

"There's warm water in the tub," Laetilla says directly to Alyiakal, "and a hot kettle here on the stove. It will be about a glass before dinner is ready." Then she smiles. "Take whatever time you need."

"I'll come for the kettle shortly," says Saelora.

"It has been a long trip," adds Alyiakal, "and it's so good to be here."

"Come along, dear," says Saelora, leading him out of the kitchen, into the front parlor and past the small dining room. Everything looks as it always was to Alyiakal, who has to be careful with the duffels in the narrow hall leading past the closed door to the study, and to Saelora's bedroom and bath chamber in the rear.

After entering the bedchamber, Alyiakal looks around, not seeing anything he readily recalls as different. Then he notices a second armoire against the wall to the right of the door leading to the bathing chamber. "The armoire?"

Saelora smiles shyly. "If we're to be together, I thought you might like some place for your clothes and uniforms."

Alyiakal studies the armoire, goldenwood like hers, but of a different style. "I've never had anything that elegant . . ."

"I found it last year and had it rebuilt and refinished. Go ahead. Open it."

Alyiakal does. On one side is an actual hanging bar, with hangers, and space at the bottom for boots, while the other side holds drawers, with a flat open shelf at the top. The only item in the armoire is the lancer-green robe Saelora had given him on his last leave with her.

He shakes his head. "You shouldn't have."

"I want you to feel at home."

Alyiakal looks straight into her eyes. "Here . . . with you . . . is home, the only real home I've had since . . ."

"Since your mother died?"

Alyiakal nods. "My great-aunt's house and officers' quarters were never home."

"Do you want to unpack or bathe first?"

"If it's all right with you, I'll just unpack a clean uniform for dinner and then bathe."

"While you get out that uniform, I'll fetch the kettle and heat up the water in the tub." There's a twinkle in her eyes as she adds, "You'll bathe without me present. That would be too tempting for me. I'll be with Laetilla, and you can join us when you're ready."

Definitely tempting for me as well. At the same time, Alyiakal knows he's sweaty and grimy and sore in places from the long glasses spent in the fire-wagons.

All in all, he spends a little less than two quints shaving, bathing, and getting into a clean uniform, but he does drain the spent water from the tub. He also hangs up his remaining clean uniform. Then he makes his way from the bedchamber.

Saelora meets him at the archway to the parlor. "You look like you feel better."

"I do. Very much. Thank you for the hot bath. I haven't had a hot bath . . . well . . . since I left here. Even moderately senior Mirror Lancers bathe or shower with cool or cold water."

"Just sit down here, and I'll get us some wine."

"You're sure?"

"I haven't spent six days traveling."

Alyiakal takes the blue upholstered armchair from which he can most easily watch Saelora as she heads into the kitchen. He hears the heavy rain pounding on the roof, and he's glad they put the wagon in the stable.

Saelora quickly returns and hands him a Merchanter-blue, crystal wine-glass, obviously part of the stemware Vassyl gifted her once she became a Merchanter.

"Take a sip."

Alyiakal takes a small careful sip. "This is excellent." He frowns. "It's not Alafraan, is it? If it is, it's better than any Alafraan I've ever had."

"It's not Alafraan." Her lips curl into an amused smile before she says, "It's Fhynyco."

"I've heard it was good, but obviously, I didn't know how good. I haven't been here for two glasses, and you've already surprised and spoiled me."

"I do hope so." She takes the other armchair.

"And I don't have any gifts for you. I haven't been anywhere—"

"I know that. Your being here is a gift."

"I'm glad you feel that way . . . because you've been the best thing that's ever happened to me." He chuckles. "In that way, the second-best thing was meeting and becoming friends with Hyrsaal. If you tell him that, you'd better tell him that he should understand."

"He's already told me that you're the only lancer officer he'd ever allow near me." She takes a modest swallow of the Fhynyco. "Did you meet anyone interesting on your way here?"

"An older majer who had just left his last duty and was returning to Doorm and an undercaptain headed to Fyrad to train naval marine recruits in hand combat . . ." Alyiakal relates what he'd learned and is finishing with Wuultz's comments about recent recruits when Laetilla appears and announces, "Dinner is ready."

Alyiakal stands and then offers a hand to Saelora. While she takes his hand, she rises gracefully without actually placing any weight on him. Each carrying a wineglass, they walk to the small dining room.

There, Alyiakal is greeted by the same table, with the same blue crystal, silver utensils, and Merchanter-blue tablecloth. The light from the three candles of the single candelabrum warms the cream walls and replaces the fading light of early evening. Alyiakal lets Saelora seat herself because that is her preference.

Laetilla serves, first a plate before Saelora and then one before Alyiakal, before refilling their wineglasses and slipping from the dining room.

"You're getting a variation on something you had before," says Saelora.

Alyiakal looks at his plate, a casserole of sorts, accompanied by thin slices of apple and thin wafery flatbread. "It looks like the lamb emburhka, but it's not. Fowl emburhka?" He grins. "But the way Laetilla fixes it?"

Saelora laughs softly. "Exactly."

Alyiakal waits for her to take the first bite, then quickly samples the savory casserole of rice, cheese, and tender fowl strips with the spices he still does not recognize but definitely appreciates. "In some ways, I like this even better than the lamb. It's a bit more . . . subtle."

"Not as hot-spicy, you mean?"

"That's true, but I did mean subtle, even if I'm often not."

"I like you the way you are."

"I'm glad you do. I'm not sure I could be otherwise." Feeling slightly embarrassed, Alyiakal asks, "What do you have in mind for tomorrow?"

"Breakfast, of course. By ourselves. Laetilla has made almond rolls, and there's fruit. Afterwards, that depends mostly on what you need to do."

"Me? The only thing I really need to do is ride to Geliendra and order some new uniforms."

"Would you mind if I came with you?"

"I'd like it if you would, but riding both ways will take a good part of the day. Can you spend that much time away from the factorage?"

"I can now. Gaaran knows all the stock and most of the customers in Vaeyal. The twins are working out well so that there are always two people there." She pauses. "I told them all I wouldn't be there as much for the next four eightdays, possibly not at all some days. Gaaran told me that if I came in at all tomorrow, he'd be most disappointed in me."

"I definitely wouldn't want you to disappoint your brother."

"I could always blame you," replies Saelora.

Alyiakal doesn't conceal his wince.

"It serves you right."

Since she's right, Alyiakal takes several more bites of the emburhka and then another swallow of wine. "I do like this."

"You said that before, but I'll tell Laetilla that you praised it twice. She knows you well enough to know that you're not excessive with praise—except when you're praising me."

"I'd like to rebut that, but—"

"Enough, dear," Saelora says gently.

Alyiakal shuts his mouth and decides to finish his emburhka. He enjoys every single bite, and every swallow of wine.

Shortly, Laetilla appears and removes both plates, then returns and places a smaller plate before each of them before departing.

"Greenberry-pearapple tarts. Excellent," declares Alyiakal.

"You'd say that about anything we'd serve you."

"Of course, but that's because you've never served me with anything less." He pauses. "Go ahead. Tell me it's not true."

Saelora flushes, then shakes her head.

The two take their time over the tarts, remaining at the table even after Laetilla clears away the plates and then leaves for her quarters in the distillery. As the light from outside fades and the candles provide a gentler light, Alyiakal can't help but think how striking Saelora is in candlelight and almost starts to say that, then laughs, more to himself.

"Laughing, yet?"

"At myself. I looked at you in the candlelight, and how beautiful you are, and I was about to say that, but then, I said that before, and I didn't want to repeat myself, but now I've ended up doing the same thing."

Saelora tries not to laugh, but fails, then shakes her head. "Only you."

"Except, after all that, it sounds so calculated, and that wasn't what I meant at all. I mean, being calculating."

"Dear, there are times when you don't need any more words." Saelora stands, takes the snuffer, and damps out the candles.

XVI

As the morning light creeps into the bedchamber, Alyiakal wakes and glances at Saelora, who lies next to him in the wide bed, still sleeping. Even as he looks at her, she turns toward him.

"That's the nicest way to wake . . . knowing you're looking at me like that."

"So is waking to find you next to me." Alyiakal smiles and draws her to him.

In time, they rise, and Alyiakal pulls on his robe, and Saelora hers, and they make their way to the kitchen, where Saelora cuts summer apples into thin slices arranged neatly on two plates, along with an almond roll for each, and Alyiakal pours two mugs of ale.

She carries the plates to the dining room, and he follows with the ales, smiling as he sees the two empty wineglasses remaining from the evening before.

Once they're seated, he lifts his mug and says quietly, "To you, and the best morning in three years." He grins and adds, "So far." Then he takes a swallow of ale.

Saelora barely sips her ale before setting it down and picking up a slice of apple, and then taking a bite of her almond roll.

"You were hungry," says Alyiakal.

"And you weren't?" With a perfectly straight face, she adds, "In more than one way?"

He smiles again. "You're right. I can't deny it."

"So was I." Saelora takes another bite of her almond roll.

Neither speaks for a brief time.

Then Saelora looks from her empty plate to Alyiakal's and says, "I'll get us each another almond roll."

"There's more?"

"I know what you like for breakfast . . . and before." Saelora stands and carries her plate to the kitchen, returning with two more almond rolls, one of which she slips from her plate onto his.

"Thank you."

She doesn't answer but reaches out with her free hand and squeezes his shoulder gently.

After they each finish their second roll, Saelora rises from her chair and says, "We probably should get ready for the day."

Alyiakal stands as well. "Is it still all right if we go to Geliendra today? I really do need new uniforms."

"As long as we're together."

"If you have any more broken jewelry, we could stop by the goldsmith's shop."

"I have some. We'd have to stop by the factorage."

"We can do that." Alyiakal hesitates. "I have a favor to ask."

"You only have to ask."

Alyiakal hesitates again but doesn't sense any reservations. "I don't spend very much, and even for me it's dangerous to carry the golds that I've saved. At the post, I can stash them in the strongroom, but even that worries me. If you'd keep them for me . . ."

Saelora wrinkles her brow. "How many golds?"

"About two hundred thirty. I made two and a half golds an eightday as a sub-majer. It's three as a majer."

Saelora just looks at him, stunned.

"I know it's a lot to ask, but you could use them to help build up Loraan House, couldn't you? Wouldn't that help?"

After another long moment, she says, "You're willing to give me total control of everything you've saved?"

"Well, that doesn't include the thirty golds or so I'd keep for new uniforms and just in case. I love you. You're the most important person in my life, and you're also an excellent Merchanter. I certainly trust you with my life; so how could I not trust you with my golds?"

Saelora shakes her head.

"It might be better if you didn't tell your mother, though," Alyiakal says wryly.

She steps closer to him. "So far as I'm concerned, we're consorted. Even if the formalities have to wait."

"Are you sure? We could get consorted quietly."

"No formal consorting stays quiet, dear, and consorting now wouldn't be for the best for either of us."

"I know why it could be a problem for me, but why would it be a problem for you?"

"You might recall that the head of the Imperial Tariff Enumerators went out of his way to send an enumerator to Oldroad Post, and that both an enumerator and his assistant vanished at Luuval, and that someone sent a senior magus to investigate you at Fyrad."

"And if we consort, that will make matters harder for Loraan House?"

"Especially because that didn't stay quiet. There have been rumors. There are always rumors. But a recorded consorting is more than a rumor, and we'll both be targets from both sides."

"I should have thought—"

"No. Even I didn't realize it until lately. Catriana was the one who's been hearing the rumors. Someone wanted to know if her consort was friendly with a certain sub-majer who's not that highly regarded by some Merchanters in Cyad and high tariff enumerators."

"And if we consort, both of you will face more problems."

"There are always problems. Other Merchanters want to know why Loraan House deals with so many outland traders. I tell them it's because the outlanders want what we can make or procure, and they're willing to pay more. That's true, mostly, but the more I find out about the trading clans in Cyador, the less I have any desire to get any more involved with them." She turns and looks directly at him. "I could use those golds, and if it works out well, we'd both be better off. Possibly a great deal better off. But trading can be risky."

"I know that, but there's risk for both of us, and there's no one else I trust more. I'd trust you even if I didn't love you." He leans forward and brushes her cheek with his lips. "And I do love you."

After they wash up and dress, as well as straighten up the bedchamber, and Alyiakal sets aside all his dirty uniforms for the wash girl Laetilla has found, the two leave the bedchamber, Alyiakal in uniform, and with his sabre, and Saelora in full Merchanter blues.

Saelora stops by the closed study door and says, "I never had the chance last night to show you the changes I made to the study."

"That's all right," says Alyiakal sheepishly. "I missed you too much to even think about the changes you've made, except the ones you pointed out."

"You were a little intent on a few other things . . ."

"I don't think I was the only one."

Saelora laughs softly, then walks to the closed study door and opens it.

Alyiakal manages not to gape. Instead of an old and wide desk, a bookcase, and a narrow bed, there are two narrower desks against the side walls, staggered slightly, each with a chair, and the bookcase is now set under the small window.

"This way," Saelora says, "you can work here if you need to. You can also use one of the desks at the factorage if you want when I have to be there."

"You are amazing."

"You're kind, but we need to be heading to the factorage if we want to go to Geliendra and get back before it's too late."

"You're right." He holds up a small leather case. "The golds are here. In a leather pouch inside."

"Keep them until we get to the factorage."

When the two step outside, the white sun has already burned off any lingering haze, leaving the green-blue sky clear, and the air warm and moist. Although the ground is damp, the stone paving from the stable to the old road is dry.

A quint or so later, Alyiakal and Saelora have both horses saddled and ride west on the old stone road.

"Should we tie the horses out front or in the rear lane?" he asks.

"Out front. We won't be that long, and Gaaran's mount will be in one of the rear stalls. So will Charissa's if she's here."

"Are the twins Rhobett's children?"

"No . . . they're from Charissa's mother's brother and his first consort. Their mother died a year after they were born. Charissa said that she was never the same after she had them. There never have been any real healers here in Vaeyal . . . until now."

"I haven't had any experience with something like that." *You certainly weren't able to keep Vassyl alive.* "But then, that's how you learn." *And sometimes fail.*

Once they've tied their mounts in front of the factorage, Alyiakal follows Saelora inside, where Gaaran hurries through the door to the rear and halts behind the counter.

"I thought you weren't coming in today." Gaaran turns to Alyiakal. "It's good to see you, and congratulations. Full majer, no less."

"Thank you."

"We won't be long," replies Saelora. "We're heading to Geliendra. I needed to pick up something and drop something off. Where are the twins?"

"They're cleaning the stalls," replies Gaaran. "If they've finished there, they'll be stocking those kegs of lavendula oil you picked up late yesterday."

Saelora shakes her head. "They should have been here last eightday. Cheslya will likely be here in a while. She asked about them the other day."

"She may wait for you," replies Gaaran.

For a moment, Alyiakal wonders who Cheslya is and why she'd wait for Saelora, then recalls that Saelora had once mentioned her as running the only reputable brothel in Vaeyal.

"If she does come in, tell her to wait a moment, and then have Kaasya talk to her. If she's reluctant, have Kaasya tell her that she'll have a hard time catching me for the next few eightdays. I'll mention it to Kaasya so that she's not surprised."

Once Alyiakal and Saelora leave Gaaran and walk through the door to the part of the factorage that holds two desks, as well as a circular conference table, Alyiakal takes out the leather pouch filled with golds and hands it to Saelora. She moves to a locked door in the left wall and unlocks it, as well as the lock on the next door, and then descends a narrow staircase.

In less than half a quint, she returns, relocking the doors. She carries a small leather case.

"Various bits of jewelry?" asks Alyiakal.

She nods, then turns and calls, "Kaasya, Kaastyl!"

After several moments, two lean figures emerge from the rows of heavy shelving at the back of the factorage. Both are roughly a few digits shorter than Saelora, with sandy brown hair, although the slightly taller one is clearly male. Alyiakal finds himself briefly surprised because, for some reason, he has thought that the twins were both women, rather than brother and sister.

Saelora gestures. "I thought you'd both like to meet Alyiakal, the majer you've heard so much about but never met."

"Ser," they both say simultaneously, with voices not that different in pitch or timbre.

"I'm pleased to meet you both. Saelora has written how helpful you've been."

"She's been good to us," says Kaasya. "Jobs are hard to find here in Vaeyal."

"Very hard," adds Kaastyl.

Saelora turns to Kaasya. "As I told you, I won't be here much. You've met Cheslya, as I recall."

Kaasya nods.

"She's been waiting for the lavendula oil, but she'd rather not deal with men. So I told Gaaran to have you help her if she comes in. She gets it one part in twenty less than what's on the list, and make sure you tell her that."

"Yes, ser."

"That's all. We're headed to Geliendra. Alyiakal has something to take care of there, and I can do some business as well."

Alyiakal smiles pleasantly and says, "It's good to see you both."

Once Saelora and Alyiakal have left the factorage and are riding on the main road east toward Geliendra, Alyiakal asks, "Have they had a hard time growing up?"

"It wasn't always the easiest, Charissa told me. Their father was very much in love with their mother, and they got the feeling he'd rather have her than them."

"That could hurt. My father grieved a long time after Mother died, but he still loved me in his own way. He just had a hard time showing it."

"Kaalyt may have felt the same way, but if he did, and I'm not sure of that, the twins didn't sense it. You did."

"Not at first, but the older I got, the more I understood," Alyiakal admits.

"That's true of all of us."

As the two ride past the last of the dwellings set close together, they approach a man leading a horse pulling a cart filled with something but covered by canvas.

The man glances toward them, sees Alyiakal's uniform, and says, "Good morning, Majer."

"Good morning to you," replies Alyiakal.

After they've ridden a bit farther, Alyiakal asks, "Do you know him?"

"If I have, I don't remember him."

"You remember everyone you've met, I suspect."

"Not everyone. The one who's really good at that is Catriana."

"You two work well together, don't you?"

"We do. We couldn't have done half what we have without her." Saelora pauses. "It's too bad we can't get together more often, but it's just not practical. I'd love to see more of Haarlt, too. He reminds me of Hyrsaal when he was a boy."

"Hyrsaal's still got that boyish streak. I'm not sure I ever did."

"I love my brother, but at times the boyishness wears. I much prefer the way you are."

"That's good, because I doubt I'm going to change in that way."

More than a glass later, as they're nearing Geliendra, Alyiakal asks, "You don't mind if we go to the tailor's in Southpoint Post first?"

"Southpoint? I thought we were going to Geliendra."

"Everyone calls it Geliendra, but the post is officially Southpoint, just like most people say Jakaafra when they really mean Northpoint." He smiles. "Even Mirror Lancers."

By the time they're riding along the avenue that the road has become once it enters Geliendra, more than a few people look at them in more than a passing fashion. Alyiakal can sense surprise all too often. *Is a Mirror Lancer majer riding with a Lady Merchanter that strange—or do people expect that we should be in a carriage or coach?*

Alyiakal is still concerned about that when the two ride past the market square and continue by the striped awning of the coffeehouse toward the post's main gates.

"I've never been near the post," Saelora confesses.

"It's one of the larger posts. Partly because it has housing for rankers and officers." Alyiakal gestures toward the tall shimmering sunstone gateposts ahead, set far enough apart to allow two carriages abreast. "The north gates are equally impressive. Those are the ones the Great Forest patrols use."

As they near the gates, one of the lancers on guard duty steps forward and looks from Alyiakal to Saelora, then back to Alyiakal, clearly recognizing the insignia of a majer.

Alyiakal halts his mount and extends order and a sense of command. "I'm on home leave, lancer, but after three years at Lhaarat, I find I need to replace some uniforms. I do know where the tailor's shop is . . . assuming it's where it was three years ago."

"Oh, no, ser. It's still there."

"Excellent . . . and thank you." Alyiakal urges the mount forward.

Saelora keeps pace. After they've ridden through the gates and circled the entry square with the statue of the second Emperor of Light and headed down the side lane toward the tailor's shop, she asks, "Shouldn't I be with you?"

"Officially, I can only bring family on post, and that's if there are family quarters. But Geliendra has family quarters. You're all the family I have, and I'm not about to leave you alone outside the walls." He smiles. "Besides, we won't be that long, and most rankers aren't about to question a majer accompanied by a Lady Merchanter."

Since it turns out that the tailor has all of Alyiakal's measurements from his last visit, and he hasn't changed much, he spends less than a quint in the shop. Even so, it's close to midday when they mount up once more.

Once they're riding back toward the gates, Alyiakal says, "Since my uniforms won't be ready until after the next sixday, if there's a day when you have to meet with outlanders or catch up, I can come and get them then."

Saelora frowns momentarily, then smiles ruefully. "I'm sure I'll have to spend some time in the factorage, but I'll have to see."

"The goldsmith's next?"

"Do you have something else in mind?"

"I do, but after the goldsmith."

Alyiakal recalls that the goldsmith's shop is roughly five blocks west of the Southpoint Post gates and three blocks south.

When they rein up in front of the shop, Saelora says, "I'm impressed. You've only been here twice, years ago."

He grins. "Three times, years ago. The first time I had to come back because the shop was closed."

"You also persevere," she says lightly before dismounting.

Alyiakal dismounts and ties both mounts to the railing, then adds a bit of order to keep anyone from cutting or untying them, not that he won't be watching with eyes and senses, and walks beside Saelora.

A younger man stands behind the counter as Alyiakal and Saelora enter the shop, but he looks at them and says something quietly. Even before Saelora reaches the counter, the muscular man that Alyiakal recognizes from before appears beside the younger man. Alyiakal can't help noticing that the older goldsmith now has lines in his face and strands of gray in his hair.

"The Lady Merchanter from Vaeyal, I recall." The goldsmith looks to Alyiakal. "You're a majer, now. Should I know why?"

Alyiakal smiles. "There's certainly no reason you shouldn't. Time passes. I did my duty well enough that headquarters decided I should be promoted."

Saelora's eyes go to the younger man. "Your son?"

"Indeed. He'll be the fourth generation of goldsmiths. You still wear that bracelet, I see."

"It was well-crafted and given with care."

The goldsmith looks to Alyiakal, then back to Saelora. "Obviously. How might I help you?"

Saelora lifts the leather case and sets it on the counter. "The last time I was here, you suggested I come back in a few years if I had any more pieces that you could melt down or rework. I also brought a few complete pieces, in case you might be interested . . ."

Alyiakal steps back, keeping his senses and eyes more on the horses than the transactions in progress. Unlike his previous visit to the goldsmith with Saelora, he neither sees nor senses passersby of concern.

After Saelora and the goldsmith finish, Alyiakal leaves the shop with her. He doesn't say anything until they're both mounted. "Did you get a fair price?"

"I think so. Not as much as when you were here last, but more than twenty-five golds. He took all the broken jewelry, and two other pieces. He wanted those for his son to learn from. That's what he said, anyway."

"Or he thinks he can sell them for more than he paid you."

"That's possible, but the golds are more useful to me than the jewelry." She hesitates, then asks, "Where are we heading now?"

"You said you'd never seen the Great Forest. I thought I'd show you . . . from a respectable distance."

"That's for my benefit, isn't it? You could enter it safely, couldn't you?"

"With me, you likely could as well. The greatest danger for either of us would be if someone observed a Mirror Lancer majer or a Lady Merchanter entering the Forest."

Saelora nods.

The two turn their mounts and ride north until they near the west wall of the post, then turn west for several long blocks before again heading north toward the Great Forest.

"The dwellings here aren't kept as well," says Saelora quietly.

"Most people with golds are uneasy living close to the Great Forest, although very few of the creatures that leave attack people. They prefer livestock. But losing livestock is a greater burden on those who are poor."

"Isn't everything?" asks Saelora rhetorically.

"Always."

After riding two kays, they leave the scattered ragtag dwellings behind and enter an area of small plots and fields, divided by a mixture of fences and hedgerows. Farther to the northwest stand woodlots and larger fields. The ground between the sunstone road and the wall that it parallels is bare earth.

Alyiakal and Saelora rein up in a narrow lane less than two hundred yards from the whitestone walls shimmering in the afternoon sun.

For several moments, Saelora says nothing.

Alyiakal waits.

"I hadn't realized just how tall the trees are. They make the wall look small, as if it didn't matter."

"The wall is to keep people out. The wards maintained by the Mirror Engineers are what keep the creatures of the Great Forest inside the wall. The Mirror Lancers do a little of both."

"How big is it?"

"Not quite a hundred kays on a side. There's a chaos tower powering the wards every thirty-three kays."

"Chaos towers have a lot of power . . . and that's all they do?"

"So far as I know. I can sense the flows, and they don't go anywhere else." Alyiakal lets his senses take in the Great Forest but doesn't intrude. As with each time he's encountered the Forest, he finds it hard to believe the amount of order and chaos within the walls . . . and that the Great Forest agreed to be contained by the First.

It must know that confinement will end.

Even as he thinks that, an image surrounds him—one that he's experienced before, except this one lasts longer.

For an instant, the white walls remain, but the power of the wards is fading and intermittent, and indistinct figures weave a mesh of sorts over the wall, and a feeling of restless sleep ensues . . . until there is a flash of brilliant chaos so bright that, while it is but an image, Alyiakal's eyes burn, and he can see nothing.

When he can see once more, only isolated parts of the white walls remain, with stones strewn across the sunstone wall road, and vines entwined around the sections of the wall that still stand and the same tall trees that dominated the Great Forest before now also tower over lower undergrowth everywhere.

Alyiakal can't help shuddering.

"Alyiakal . . . what was that?" asks Saelora, an anxiousness in her voice that he's never heard.

"Did you see anything?"

She shakes her head. "I just . . . felt . . . surrounded by some sort of overwhelming force, and I felt . . . or maybe I saw . . . a searing white flash."

"That was the Great Forest . . . reminding me that, in time, the walls will shatter and that it will again be free."

"Soon?"

Alyiakal shakes his head. "Long after us. Even Cyador cannot last forever." *But the Great Forest just might.*

"You . . . talked . . . with it."

"More like . . ." He pauses to think. ". . . it gifted me with three visions."

"Why you . . . and not the Magi'i?"

"I think . . . and this is only a guess . . . that it's because they see the Forest as an enemy, and I just see it as it is." *Thanks to Adayal.*

"Because you tried to talk to it?"

"More to listen . . . and to let it know that I wasn't an enemy."

"It's helped you . . . to be a better mage, hasn't it?"

Alyiakal considers, momentarily. "It's certainly given me a greater understanding of many things . . . and that understanding has made me more able."

She smiles wryly. "You could have just said 'yes.'"

"Yes."

"Is there anything else?"

"No. I didn't plan on what just happened. I just thought you should see the Forest."

"I have a question for you," says Saelora. "When you see the Great Forest, do you think about her?"

"Adayal? I can't help but think about her occasionally, but it's more the wondering kind of thought, like what ever happened to her. She was right about us living different lives. Every time I see the Great Forest, I can see that."

"Do you miss her?"

"No. It's more that . . . there have been so few people in my life who made a difference and having both her and Triamon vanish . . . without them I wouldn't have been able to do what I learned from the Great Forest. I'd at least like to have thanked them both."

"You still might," says Saelora.

"Not Triamon. I had the feeling he was dead, the moment I got that letter from my father. With Adayal, it's unlikely. She'd have to write me somehow."

"With your talents, you could find her." Saelora's voice is even.

"What for? Besides, it could take eightdays, and I'd be taking time from being with you, and that's far more precious to me."

"You don't feel like you owe her that?"

"I owe her that," admits Alyiakal, "but I love you, and I also owe you far more. You've been with me and in my thoughts for ten years. I saw Adayal a few times for less than a season, and that was before you ever wrote me. If the opportunity comes, I will thank her, but not by slighting you in any way."

Saelora offers a smile that's both warm and somehow amused, then says, "We can head back to Vaeyal now."

Alyiakal isn't about to protest, although he senses that more time had passed while he'd seen the images than he'd immediately realized.

Once they're through the west side of Geliendra and on the road to Vaeyal, another thought strikes Alyiakal. He's always wondered about the "dream" he'd had of the first great magus destroying another mage who opposed building the wall around the Great Forest. Had the Great Forest planted that dream in his thoughts? Could it be that the dissidents were followers of that mage? And that the First magus destroyed the other mage and his followers to save Cyador from the Great Forest?

Alyiakal doubts he'll ever know. *Not for certain.*

XVII

On eightday morning, Alyiakal is organizing his now-clean uniforms and taking the last items from his duffel when he pulls out a small wooden box and smiles.

"What is it?" asks Saelora.

"I'll show you." Alyiakal opens the box, extracting an object wrapped in felt. When he removes the felt, he reveals a small silver bird perched on a silver limb. "I don't think you've ever seen this."

Saelora smiles, clearly realizing that the bird is a miniature traitor bird, so well-wrought that even the bird's posture captures its mischief and calculation of whether to call out to reveal a hidden person or possible prey.

"It's a traitor bird, isn't it. It's marvelous . . . but why do you have it?"

"Because I bought it right after I bought you the bracelet. I thought I might have a use for it at some future time, but I figured that it might be best to have purchased at a time when no one could trace it . . ."

Saelora laughs, then says, "Who would ever believe you're that devious?"

"No one, I hope." Alyiakal rewraps the bird and returns it to the box. "Except perhaps your mother. I'm just glad we don't have to have dinner there until next eightday." He pauses. "Why did she ask us at all?"

"She didn't. Charissa did, even if it was likely at Mother's suggestion." Saelora offers an amused smile, then adds, "Now that you're a full majer and visiting Vaeyal, you're important enough as a Mirror Lancer post commander for her to be able to drop your name. Also, she doesn't want to be in the position of having to admit that she hasn't entertained you . . . and Vaeyal is small enough that she can't afford to lie about it. Exaggerate, yes. But not lie."

Alyiakal shakes his head. "She doesn't even like me."

"No, but she respects you. And when you become more important, she'll be able to talk about Hyrsaal and you being friends and about how she knew you when you were a mere captain."

"But not about her successful Mirror Lancer son and her Merchanter daughter?"

"That will come when we're consorted," says Saelora. "Then she can brag about her successful children and their consorts. Right now, as far as she's concerned, I'm at best a kept woman." Before Alyiakal can say anything, she adds, "That's my choice, and we aren't going to discuss it. After all, Hyrsaal and Catriana were sleeping together long before they consorted. While Mother didn't care for Catriana, she certainly wasn't objecting to Hyrsaal sleeping with her."

Alyiakal sees no point in revisiting the issue and says, "What would you like to do today?"

"I'd just like to stay here and talk to you . . . and then have dinner."

"And play some Fyrr so you can display your superiority there?"

"Only if you try a little harder."

Alyiakal chuckles. "I can manage that."

"Then I'll get the pastecards and the board while you finish up here."

"I won't be long."

"You never are . . . except when you want to be." She grins. "Or to please me."

Alyiakal flushes.

XVIII

Over the next few days, Alyiakal and Saelora spend most of the time together, although she stops by the factorage briefly almost daily, and on fiveday they take a ride south along the road bordering the Great Canal to visit a grower who turns out to have some maize about to be harvested that he'd like to sell—and which Saelora agrees to purchase.

After they return to the factorage, while she works out the transportation details, Alyiakal writes out his observations and comments about the Great Forest for Hyrsaal. He's careful to couch his recommendations as advisory since he's never ridden an actual patrol along the Forest walls.

On sevenday, Saelora decides against accompanying Alyiakal to Geliendra because she can use the time at the factorage.

Alyiakal borrows one of Saelora's canvas carrying bags and straps it behind the saddle and then rides beside her to the factorage before he continues eastward. He reaches the Southpoint Post gates around midmorning.

The two Mirror Lancer guards nod respectfully as he rides past and makes his way to the tailor's shop, but he can sense that they exchange a few words and one of them leaves the gate and heads for the headquarters building.

Someone must have passed the word about the strange majer.

Alyiakal rides on to the tailor's shop, where he inspects his new uniforms and tries them on. After that, he pays the tailor and has him pack them in the canvas bag, which he carries out to where he's tied the gelding. As he's fastening the bag behind the saddle, he sees an officer approaching, but finishes securing the uniforms in place.

The approaching officer is an older overcaptain, likely close to being stipended and who says politely, "Are you new here, Majer?"

"I'm afraid not, Overcaptain. I'm Majer Alyiakal, and I'm taking home leave in Vaeyal before my next posting."

"I just wondered. It's rare to see a majer here who's not part of the complement. It's good to meet you. I'm Laartas, the supply officer." The overcaptain gestures toward the tailor shop. "Uniforms?"

"I'm afraid so. My last posting was Lhaarat. Duty there is hard on uniforms, and there's no place anywhere close to near there." *Not that there is with any border post.*

Laartas frowns. "I'm likely out of date, but wasn't a Majer Byelt the post commander there?"

"He was. I was posted there for a year as deputy post commander, and a little less than a year later, he was promoted to subcommander and posted to overall command in Biehl. I was promoted to post commander. My posting after home leave is as post commander at Pemedra."

"Pemedra?" The overcaptain's eyes widen just slightly. "It's not often we see another post commander here. I'm sure that Subcommander Hurtaal would appreciate it if you could spare a moment."

"I can certainly spare a few moments." Alyiakal unties the gelding and starts to lead the gelding toward the headquarters building, since riding while Laartas walks would be discourteous, to say the least.

Laartas immediately matches steps with Alyiakal. "You seem quite familiar with Southpoint."

Alyiakal chuckles. "Somewhat, anyway. I first came here as an officer candidate on my way to Kynstaar. Then after my first duty at Pemedra, I stayed here on home leave before I was posted to Guarstyad. I usually pick up new uniforms here." Alyiakal can sense the overcaptain's growing disconcert and finds it both amusing and unwelcome. "I didn't want to intrude. I just needed to get new uniforms without much fuss."

"I'm afraid, ser, that unknown majers are far more likely to be noticed than unknown captains."

"A very good point, Overcaptain, and one I should have considered."

When they reach the headquarters building, Alyiakal quietly uses order to lock the uniform bag to the saddle. Then he ties the gelding to the hitching rail near the entrance and follows Laartas to the subcommander's study, which appears not to have changed much in the six years since he last stood there.

"If you'll excuse me, ser, I'll tell the subcommander you're here."

Alyiakal nods and waits.

When Laartas leaves the subcommander's study, he's noticeably subdued. "Ser . . . I had no idea." He gestures toward the open door.

Alyiakal smiles warmly. "That's my fault. I should have notified Subcommander Hurtaal I was here. I didn't realize that trying to replace uniforms quietly would cause a problem." Then he enters the study, closing the door behind himself.

Subcommander Hurtaal is already standing beside his desk.

"Alyiakal, Subcommander," says Alyiakal warmly. "A pleasure to meet you." *If a dubious one, under the circumstances.*

The slightly graying and thin-faced Hurtaal studies Alyiakal, then offers an amused smile. "It's my pleasure to meet you. You really should have known that you'd be more than welcome. Headquarters has apprised all post commanders of your success in dealing with the Cerlynese."

"As I told Overcaptain Laartas, I was just trying to get some uniforms replaced without disturbing anyone, and I apparently ended up creating more of a disturbance."

"A welcome one. I have to say that I wondered how so junior a senior officer managed so effectively, but when Laartas mentioned where you'd been posted . . . everything made more sense. I have the feeling you didn't tell him everything."

"Not quite. After serving as the officer in charge at Oldroad Post, reporting to Guarstyad, I was reposted slightly early and sent on temporary duty to close Luuval."

Alyiakal senses mild surprise but waits.

"So Pemedra will be your fourth command?"

"Yes, ser."

"I understand there was some difficulty involved in closing Luuval."

"There was. The Imperial tariff enumerator there didn't want the post closed, and the two commanders prior to me both died unexpectedly."

"You phrased that as if there happened to be some connection."

"I suspected it. There was no proof."

"Didn't the post collapse into the water immediately after it was closed?"

"It did. The morass encroached on the post more quickly than anyone anticipated, and I closed it roughly an eightday before the planned date. The Imperial tariff enumerator was not pleased. I don't think he believed me. Unfortunately, I was right. He and his staff died when everything collapsed."

"You seem to have good timing."

"No, ser. I just measured the speed of the morass's encroachment and noted it was increasing. Since my orders only stipulated that Luuval be closed by a certain date, there was no reason not to close it earlier and every reason not to hazard the lives of the lancers unnecessarily."

Hurtaal nods. "There is one other thing. There was a report that you were accompanied by a woman in blue the other day when you came."

"Oh, I was. That was Overcaptain Hyrsaal's younger sister. She's a full Merchanter with her own factorage. She had some business dealings in Geliendra, and it made sense for her to come from Vaeyal with me. I've been staying with the family, since Hyrsaal is my best friend. Unfortunately, my parents are both dead, and I have neither siblings nor cousins. Since lancer families are permitted at posts with family quarters, that didn't seem to be against regulations."

"Now that you explain it, I can see that. You likely know the post commander regulations fairly well, don't you?"

"Since the time I made overcaptain, I've always been close to the youngest and most junior senior officer I knew. I thought that I should be very certain of what the regulations demanded, prohibited, and expected."

"Would that more young officers understood that." Hurtaal smiles pleasantly, not effusively, but not at variance with his feelings. "It's good to meet you, and I wish you a restful home leave and a successful posting at Pemedra."

"Thank you, ser." Alyiakal inclines his head and departs, leaving the study door open.

Since Laartas is standing there, likely waiting to talk to the subcommander,

Alyiakal says, "It was good to meet you, and I appreciate your courtesy. I also apologize for inadvertently putting you in a difficult position."

"Ser, it was good to meet you. Best of fortune in Pemedra."

Alyiakal senses that the overcaptain means every word. "Thank you."

As he walks back to where he tied the gelding, he wants to shake his head, knowing he should have paid a courtesy call on Hurtaal first. *But you were thinking like a junior officer . . . and majers definitely aren't, especially majers being sent to a major command.*

He doesn't think it turned out too badly, all things considered. *But you can't afford to make another mistake like that.*

XIX

On eightday, Alyiakal and Saelora leave the house slightly after second glass of the afternoon, although dinner is set for third glass. Once they saddle the horses and lead them out, Saelora eases two carefully wrapped crystal decanters into one of her saddlebags.

"Where did you get the crystal for the lavendula oil?" asks Alyiakal, after Saelora mounts, and the two ride down the stone drive to the old road.

"When I knew I'd get the oil, I had Catriana get me some perfume decanters. She offered a cup of oil free to anyone who'd give her perfume bottles or decanters. Then she sent a few of them with the oil. Mother was complaining about how everything bothers her skin. I thought this might be worth a try, and I know Charissa would like it. She asked when the oil arrived."

"That's very thoughtful of you."

"I do try."

More than Marenda deserves. "I know. You've always been that way with everyone."

"Most everyone," replies Saelora wryly.

"I take it that Karola and Faadyr will be there," says Alyiakal as they ride west past the distillery toward Canal Street.

"They were invited, and Karola won't refuse because she can use the dinner as a time to see Mother when others are around."

"So everyone comes so that your mother can't focus on any one person's shortcomings?"

"She'll mention or allude to all of our shortcomings. It's harder for her dwell on any in depth, and she likes an audience."

"You're all better than she deserves."

"She was much kinder when she was younger, especially before Father died."

"I can see how that might have affected her. My father was much more withdrawn after my mother died."

"Did he talk about it . . . or her?"

Alyiakal shakes his head. "My great-aunt told me that when she died most of the light in his life vanished, and that I was all he had left."

"You never mentioned that."

"I thought I had."

"Sometimes, dear, you think I can read your thoughts."

Alyiakal chuckles. "Sometimes, you can."

More than a quint passes before they reach the house where Gaaran and Charissa live, if still owned by Marenda. Alyiakal takes a quick glance at Marenda's cottage to the rear on the east side, as neat and well-kept as when it was built four years earlier.

Gaaran waves from the side porch, then calls, "Take the first two empty stalls. Karola and Faadyr will bring the chaise."

Since there's no point in unsaddling the two geldings, Saelora and Alyiakal quickly stall both horses and walk quickly to the side porch.

"No children?" asks Alyiakal.

"Charissa persuaded Kaasya to take care of Gaartyn and Rendara for the afternoon. She has a good chance of eating uninterrupted." Gaaran looks to the perfume decanters Saelora carries. "Gifts, yet."

"More practical than they look," replies Saelora.

"You mentioned that." Gaaran grins. "You saw that look on Charissa's face the other day, didn't you?"

"I knew she wouldn't ask. This way she doesn't have to."

Gaaran gestures to the door. "I know what you both drink, and I'll get it while you're exchanging greetings and offering gifts."

Alyiakal opens the door and holds it for Saelora. Gaaran follows, limping, a reminder that he'd lost the lower part of his leg on duty at Isahl. Then Alyiakal steps into the parlor and closes the door.

Saelora swiftly walks toward her mother, seated in the dark green upholstered armchair she occupies as if it were a throne, with a beaker on the table beside her. Alyiakal watches, noticing that Marenda's hair is now mostly gray with only a few strands of flame red remaining.

Saelora stops short of her mother, but then nods to Charissa. "I brought you both a little something. It's a fragrant oil that's good for your skin."

"That's very kind of you, and in a crystal decanter too," says Marenda pleasantly. "But you do know that some oils don't suit me."

"It's also good for skin rashes and for keeping insects away," replies Saelora. "I thought it might prove useful . . . and if it doesn't, you can use the decanter for something else." She hands one decanter to Marenda and then walks to the settee and hands the other to Charissa.

"Oh . . . when I saw the two decanters," Charissa immediately exclaims, "I knew. You're so thoughtful. Thank you."

"Well . . . if it doesn't suit me," says Marenda dryly, "I know who will enjoy it." She turns to Saelora. "You are very practical, I must say."

"Practical *and* thoughtful," interjects Alyiakal. "It's good to see you, Marenda. You're looking well."

"I'm looking older, and we both know it. You, at least, have something to show for it."

"So do you," replies Alyiakal cheerfully. "You have three successful and happy children, and grandchildren who dote on you."

"Those that I see, anyway."

Before Alyiakal says more, Gaaran returns with two wineglasses. "It's a very good white Alafraan." He hands one to Saelora and the second to Alyiakal. "I'll be back in a moment." Then he looks out the window. "A bit more than a moment. Here come Karola and Faadyr."

"Early, yet," says Marenda as she sets the decanter on the side table beside her apparently untouched beaker. "Quite a wonder." She looks to Charissa. "Did you tell her we were starting at two quints past two?"

"No. I just told her that the fowl would be overcooked if anyone was terribly late." Charissa takes a swallow of her ale, then sets the beaker down on the side table, not too close to her decanter.

"Better that way," replies Marenda.

Alyiakal moves to stand beside the other settee, where Saelora has taken a seat, both waiting for Karola and Faadyr to join the group, but it's close to half a quint before Karola enters, followed by Faadyr and Gaaran.

"It's so refreshing to see you so early," declares Marenda.

"I thought it would be good for a change," replies Karola cheerfully before turning to Charissa. "Faadyr brought a keg of ale for you and Charissa." Then she turns back to Gaaran. "And for your occasional beaker."

"That is very thoughtful." Marenda turns to Faadyr. "Very thoughtful, indeed."

For the first time since he arrived, Alyiakal detects no snide undertones, and in moments, everyone is seated in the parlor, with beverages in hand or nearby.

"You're headed for command at Pemedra, I hear," Gaaran says to Alyiakal. "How did that happen?"

"I made the mistake of making defeating the Cerlynese look easy. Comparatively easy, anyway. So headquarters is sending me to the other post where the Cerlynese might be a problem."

"This is your fourth combat command," Gaaran says. "I've never heard of an officer getting four in a row."

"That's because he's too good," says Marenda, a remark that stuns Alyiakal. "Your father always said that headquarters tried to kill off officers who were too effective. That was why he took his stipend as early as he could. They were going to send him back to Inividra right after he'd commanded at Isahl." She turns to Alyiakal. "They have you in a difficult position. You're a new majer, a good three postings or more from being able to take a stipend. You're also even more stubborn than my youngest daughter, and that's saying something. You might make commander, but it's more likely you'll get killed. At least you haven't consorted and left Saelora with a child."

"Alyiakal won't do that," says Saelora quietly, "and now that we've discussed that," she turns to Karola, "how are the children doing?"

"Karmara has the same temperament as Hyrsaal, but she can already give anyone a cutting look, and she's not afraid to disagree. So far, she's polite," says Karola. "Daarfyn is more of a cross, quiet like Faadyr, with a touch of you. It will be interesting in a few years when Karmara and Gaartyn get together."

"When parents say something is interesting about their children, it often suggests problems to come." Marenda looks to Saelora. "Your father said you were interesting, but he never thought you'd be a Merchanter living beside a swamp and running a distillery catering to outland traders."

"They pay well, and they're not as condescending as traders from Cyad."

"Most everyone I've met from Cyad is condescending," says Faadyr. "Not that I've met many." He looks to Alyiakal. "What about officers from Cyad?"

"I couldn't say. I haven't run across that many actually from Cyad." Alyiakal offers an amused smile and adds, "But every single Imperial tariff enumerator I've met has been from Cyad, and all of them were condescending."

"Almost all Imperial tariff enumerators come from Merchanter families in Cyad," says Saelora.

"As a woman . . . in trade . . . dear," replies Marenda, "you should expect such behavior."

"I never thought otherwise," Saelora responds sweetly. "It is interesting, though, that Merchanter heirs who aren't good enough to be Merchanters are the most condescending, just like the most arrogant Mirror Lancer officers are often the least effective."

Marenda looks to Alyiakal. "Do you find that to be true, Majer?"

"Not in all cases, but often."

"Then why are so many promoted?" asks Faadyr.

"I'll answer that another way," replies Alyiakal. "So far, I've seen several arrogant majers. Very few of them made subcommander." *But then very few majers make subcommander regardless.*

"Hyrsaal says it's unlikely he'll even be a majer," says Karola. "Why are you a majer when he's only an overcaptain?"

"Hyrsaal's been promoted on the usual schedule." *More or less.* "I got promoted to overcaptain early because there was no one else available and qualified to be officer in charge at Oldroad Post, not within hundreds of kays. Something similar happened at Lhaarat, because the majer in command wasn't as prepared as he should have been, and I managed to salvage the situation. Headquarters didn't want to admit that. So they promoted me early to sub-majer and sent him to Biehl on a pre-stipend posting."

Charissa glances at Gaaran, then rises and slips out of the parlor, likely checking on the progress of dinner.

"That doesn't explain your promotion to majer," Marenda points out.

Alyiakal smiles ruefully. "I'm seen as too good a combat commander to waste, but no post commander would want me as a deputy, nor would the subcommanders at Assyadt or Syadtar want me commanding posts reporting to them. As a sub-majer I'd be too junior to command at the only other combat post, which is Pemedra. So they promoted me and are posting me there because they expect more problems with Duke Taartyn of Cerlyn or possibly with the Jeranyi."

"And hope that you don't survive the next three years," says Marenda tartly.

Saelora starts to open her mouth, but stops as Charissa reappears, inclining her head to Marenda. "If you would, dinner is ready."

Marenda stands, taking her beaker of ale, and leading the way to the dining room, where she takes her place at the head of the table, with

Charissa to her right and Gaaran to her left, followed by Karola next to Gaaran, and Faadyr beside Charissa, with Alyiakal beside Karola, and Saelora beside Faadyr. The seating arrangement doesn't surprise Alyiakal in the slightest.

A serving girl appears, but Alyiakal doesn't think she's the same one who'd been there the last time he'd eaten at the house, three years earlier. Each diner receives a plate with two slices of roast chicken with a white gravy, mashed potatoes, and fried quilla strips.

Alyiakal looks at the quilla and then to Saelora. They both stifle smiles.

"To family," says Marenda, lifting her wineglass, "for all our differences."

"To family."

Everyone at least sips their wine or ale, and then, after Marenda lifts her utensils, they all begin to eat. Alyiakal devoutly hopes that the comparison between his career and Hyrsaal's is over.

When no one says anything more, after several mouthfuls of the moist and flavorful chicken, he asks Charissa, "Do you ever use tri-spice in cooking?"

"I've heard about it, but never have used it. Isn't it rather . . . costly?"

"I've been told so," replies Alyiakal, "but some of the growers near Lhaarat have found a way to raise it there. I thought the valley was too cold, but traders are seeking it out there."

"If it's costly," says Marenda, "someone will find a way to grow it or steal it."

"The other rare trade good the hill people have is mountain musk oxen wool," says Alyiakal. "We ran across a trader who traveled hundreds of kays from Jakaafra along the back road to Laankor just to obtain some. It's the only other place besides the foot of the mountains northeast of Guarstyad that I've seen mountain musk oxen."

"Laankor?" asks Karola.

"A small land in the Westhorns east of Lhaarat. It's just north of Lestroi." Alyiakal looks to Saelora.

After a brief amused smile, Saelora says, "Lestroi? Isn't that where you discovered that hidden community built by the dissidents who opposed the First?"

"Dissidents who opposed the First?" asks Faadyr.

Alyiakal then explains and describes the hidden community, and the questions and comments last through dinner and dessert, a better and moister version of the lemon cake Charissa baked for the last dinner he'd had at the house.

After the final crumbs of the cake have vanished, Karola rises and looks to Marenda. "This has been lovely, Charissa, Mother. Thank you so much. It is a long drive back."

"I'm so glad you both could come," replies Marenda, "and thank you for the ale, Faadyr. We will enjoy it."

Alyiakal and Saelora stand as well, followed by Gaaran and Charissa, as Karola and Faadyr leave the dining room.

Marenda rises from her chair slowly. "I do hope the oil agrees with me, Saelora, but even if it doesn't, I appreciate the thought."

"If it doesn't," interjects Charissa, "I'll have more to appreciate. Thank you."

"I do appreciate your including me." Alyiakal nods to Charissa and then to Marenda. "You're the only family I have." *For better or worse.*

For a fraction of a moment, Marenda appears stunned. Then she smiles. "Alyiakal, I'd tell you that you've proved enough. Most officers haven't done half what you have, and none as young as you are. But you've got more to prove than Kayral did, and that was a lot. So . . . for Saelora's sake, just don't get yourself killed."

Alyiakal doesn't know quite what to say to Marenda's unexpected words. Then he manages to say, "We share the same view on not getting killed."

"Then don't."

"I won't."

Alyiakal and Saelora are barely outside and walking toward the stable when she asks, "What made you say that about family?"

"Because I realized it was true. I've chosen you, but family comes with you, and all families have thorns around the roses, so to speak."

Saelora reaches out and squeezes his hand. "Thank you."

Neither says much until they're riding south on Canal Street toward the old stone road that leads to Saelora's house.

"Your mother was a bit less acerbic this afternoon," Alyiakal observes. "She also let on that she cares for you."

"Even what little she said was hard for her."

"But she said it."

"I wonder if she decided against consorting Father unless he left the Mirror Lancers," muses Saelora.

"Because of what she said this afternoon? I thought they weren't consorted until after he was stipended."

"That part is true. But they never talked about their courtship or what came before." Saelora pauses. "I don't want us to be like that."

"Neither do I." He laughs softly. "That turned out to be quite an afternoon." *In more ways than one.* "Do you think, in time, she might come to your house for dinner?"

"She just might, but I can't say when."

Most likely not until we're consorted. "Then we won't hold our breath." *And we still have the evening to ourselves.*

XX

Alyiakal wakes in the dark and glances around, but Saelora isn't in the bed. He immediately gets out of bed, hurrying toward the faint light in the hallway leading to the dining room and front parlor. As he nears the archway into the parlor, he hears voices, and someone sobbing.

Then he sees Saelora in one of the armchairs, and Marenda in the other. Saelora's eyes are red, and she holds a letter. Somehow, Alyiakal recognizes the letterhead, and knows what it signifies . . .

He tries to explain, that it was a mistake, that he's still alive, but neither Saelora nor Marenda even knows that he's there.

"No . . . it's just a dream. I'm here. I'm really here . . ."

Grayness swirls around him, and he's riding toward a burning house, where a woman steps around the corner, bow in hand, ready to shoot.

His firelance flashes, turning her into ashes, and the house explodes, enveloping him in flame . . .

. . . except the gelding carries him through the wall of flame toward scores of armsmen in green and brown, their faces burned away, all running toward him with blades of flame. His firelance sweeps over them . . . and nothing happens, except the blackened Cerlynese armsmen draw closer and closer . . .

Then something enfolds him in the darkness, and he struggles to escape, fearing he'll be trapped and the flaming blades will turn him to ashes . . .

"Alyiakal . . . it's just a dream, just a dream. You don't have to fight me," murmurs Saelora, her cool face against his hot sweaty one.

Alyiakal shudders, swallows, and finally says, "I'm really here. I am."

"Of course you are. And I'm here, too."

"Thank . . . the Rational Stars . . ." He puts an arm around her, holding her tightly for several moments before relaxing his grip. "I'm sorry. It seemed so real." He laughs briefly, a hoarse and hollow sound. "It always does, but this was worse . . . than most." He sits up and uses a corner of the sheet to blot away the sweat on his face.

"Do you want to talk about it?" Saelora asks.

"Not the details." He shudders again, trying not to see Saelora holding the letter and sobbing. "Not the details."

"I'm right here, dear."

Neither speaks for several moments.

Then Saelora asks, "Would you like something to drink?"

"I don't think so." After a time, Alyiakal continues, "It was such a mix of terrible things . . . the girl archer I had to kill years ago . . . then all the Cerlynese armsmen blackened and burned attacking from all sides . . . and worse." Alyiakal isn't about to tell her what upset him the most. It's bad enough that he's had that vision, and he knows that Saelora must have at least thought about the possibility of his death.

But none of your future dream visions have come to pass.

Not yet.

XXI

Saelora looks across the table at Alyiakal and asks, "You really don't mind coming with me today?"

"Hardly. I'll still be with you, and it won't hurt if the twins get to see I'm a real person." Alyiakal laughs softly. "At least, I hope it won't hurt. Do you think I'll see Elinjya?"

"It's unlikely, but possible. She stops when she can. Why do you want to see her?"

Alyiakal chuckles. "You've been writing and telling me about her for years. I just wondered what she looks like."

"You'd like her."

"Good. Do you know when this outland trader is supposed to show up?"

"Sometime after midmorning. He didn't say, but I suspect he'll ask to see the distillery."

"Because he's suspicious and wants to know that you're not buying the Crystalflame from someone else?"

"He didn't say, according to Catriana, but he won't commit to buying more without seeing where it's produced."

"He's willing to spend four or five days traveling to find that out?"

"He supposedly procures goods for the largest trading house in Austra."

"Out of Valmurl, then?"

Saelora nods. "You can see why that connection might be useful, both ways."

"I can." Alyiakal can also see several other reasons why she wants him there. He takes the last bite of his second almond roll, and then finishes off his mug of ale.

After washing their dishes and leaving them in the drying rack, the two ready themselves for the day.

"Are you going to take the wagon or ride?" asks Alyiakal.

"Ride. If Trader Elbarak needs a mount, he can borrow Gaaran's. If he wants to see the wagon, it will be here when he comes to see the distillery." She looks to him. "You're not wearing a new uniform?"

"That wouldn't help you any. A somewhat worn uniform will likely be more useful, as will my very worn sabre."

"That makes sense, but I wouldn't have thought of it."

In another two quints, the two ride down the old road toward Canal Street.

"Does this trader have any goods you'd find useful?" asks Alyiakal.

"He hasn't mentioned any. He's more interested in buying the greenberry liqueur and Crystalflame. He's willing to buy a considerable amount, if I'll guarantee not to sell it to another trader from either Austra or Nordla."

"Is that sensible?"

"Yes. I can still sell to traders out of Hydlen or Lydiar and anyone from Hamor. Besides, we're not producing enough to sell in all those places, let alone places like Suthya or Spidlar."

"Are you thinking of expanding the distillery?"

Saelora laughs. "Not soon. It took more than a year to get all the copper we needed for the last expansion."

Copper again. Alyiakal can't help but wonder why the Emperor isn't interested in the difficulty in obtaining copper, particularly since the Empire of Light needs copper to make cupridium.

"That's one reason why I'm inclined to work something out with Elbarak. We both can profit more, and it's less complicated than negotiating over the price of smaller lots with traders in Cyador."

"You can't just set the price?"

"They'll still insist on haggling and complain to other traders that I'm unreasonable. If I sell a large share of the year's production of Crystalflame to Elbarak's house, Catriana can handle the rest out of Fyrad . . . and because it's scarce, she can ask higher prices."

Alyiakal's very glad that Saelora's comfortable with all that, especially after his comparatively brief experiences with traders and Imperial tariff enumerators.

Saelora and Alyiakal have only just arrived at the factorage and are settling the two geldings into the two empty stalls behind the factorage when Gaaran appears.

"No one's come yet."

"He won't be here before late midmorning at the earliest," replies Saelora.

"I'm glad you're here," Gaaran says to Alyiakal. "Rank has certain advantages."

"Disadvantages as well," returns Alyiakal, adjusting his visor cap and closing the stall doors, one after the other. "Let's hope the advantages prevail."

The three walk through rows of shelves and into the open area set with desks, the conference table, and chairs.

"Kaasya's out front," Gaaran says. "Kaastyl's out with the pony cart collecting greenberries."

Alyiakal looks at Saelora questioningly.

"We had to get the cart and pony because Gaaran needed the wagon to sell and deliver things to other towns."

"Sometimes the twins do that, too," adds Gaaran.

"Does Charissa like the lavendula oil?" asks Saelora.

"She really does. She also used it on a rash Rendara had. Even Mother admitted that it was soothing."

After a moment, Alyiakal says, "Why don't you two do what you need to do? I'll just look around here and nearby, and if I see anyone looking like a trader, I'll be back."

"I had some questions . . ." ventures Gaaran.

Alyiakal smiles at Saelora, then heads toward the door to the front counter.

As he steps through the door, Kaasya starts, then says, "I'm sorry. You surprised me, Majer."

"I wish my appearance had that impact on the Cerlynese and a few others." He pauses. "How do you like working here?" With those words he extends a bit of order embodying the need for truth.

Kaasya glances toward the door behind the counter, then lowers her voice. "At first, I didn't like it at all. Then it was all right. Now . . . there's no place I could find in Vaeyal or nearby that would be any better. You won't tell her that I didn't like it at first, will you?"

"I suspect she already knew that and hoped you'd come to like it."

Kaasya looks toward the door again, then asks, "Is it true that you wrote letters to each other for years before you met?"

"Almost six years."

"That sounds like one of those old tavern songs Grandmother used to talk about."

"I've never heard one like that," replies Alyiakal, "and I'd appreciate it if you don't make up one about us." He smiles cheerfully.

"Oh, no, ser. I wouldn't do that."

"At least not until we're both old and gray." He half turns. "I'll be back in a bit."

Alyiakal takes his time walking north on Canal Street, past the side street leading to the alley behind the factorage and to the coffee shop where, years ago, he and Saelora had sat and talked for the first time. Keeping his eye on the factorage, he turns south, taking the time to study the canal and the passing firetows and the barges they pull.

He finally returns to the factorage to find Gaaran behind the counter.

"She's going over the ledgers. She said she won't be long. Kaasya's in back filling some jugs with lavendula oil."

"For Cheslya . . . or someone else?"

Gaaran grins. "For one of the other brothels. I stay away from them."

"Can't imagine why," returns Alyiakal.

"Imagine what, dear?" asks Saelora as she comes through the door.

"Gaaran deciding that he's better not dealing with certain customers."

"I think Charissa might be the one who decided that," replies Saelora.

"She never said a word," protests Gaaran.

"Did she have to?" asks Saelora, smiling.

Gaaran shakes his head.

Less than two quints later, after Gaaran has gone back to the rear of the factorage to go over duties with Kaasya, three men rein up outside. Alyiakal sees that two of the three are canal guards. One dismounts with the trader. The other ties the horses to the hitching rail but remains there.

The trader leads the way to the door, followed by the guard, and steps inside. He is of modest height with a trimmed reddish-brown beard.

Saelora steps forward. "Trader Elbarak?"

"The same. You are Merchanter Saelora?"

"I am," she replies, "and this is Majer Alyiakal."

For a moment, Elbarak's eyes narrow.

Alyiakal smiles. "I'm a friend of the family, and happened to be on home leave. One of my postings gave me modest insight into trading. So I asked Saelora if I could meet you."

"I would not have thought that a military officer, especially in Cyad, would be interested in trade."

"Some years ago, I was the commander of a small post on the border between Kyphros and Cyad. I acted as an Imperial trade enumerator for over a year." Alyiakal senses Elbarak's well-concealed surprise, but merely smiles politely.

"That is rather unusual, I take it?"

Alyiakal chuckles. "So far as I know, I'm the only officer with that experience. The situation was unique, but I did encounter some traders from both Austra and Nordla."

"I hope they were reputable."

"They were extremely well-prepared and very polite."

Elbarak laughs. "Excellent."

Alyiakal steps back. "I won't keep you from your business." He turns to Saelora. "I'll stay here until Gaaran returns."

"Thank you," she replies. "I'd like you to accompany us to the distillery."

"I'll be here. Just let me know."

Less than a third of a quint after Saelora and Elbarak leave the front area of the factorage, and the guard rejoins the other guard outside, Gaaran joins Alyiakal.

"What do you think of the trader?" Gaaran asks.

"He seems pleasant enough. I'm going with them to the distillery. That might tell me more. What do you think?"

"He's calculating."

"I suspect all traders are. Saelora is. She's usually pleasant and polite about it. I'd guess she's just polite when she's angry or irritated."

"Is that really a guess?" asks Gaaran.

"Mostly. I've tried not to do something to upset her, but I've seen her with your mother."

"I've never really understood why Mother gets so upset with Saelora."

Alyiakal has a few ideas, but only says, "I've heard that ties between mothers and daughters are either close and warm or strained and turbulent, with little in between."

"It happens, but I can't say I understand."

"Let's just hope the meeting and negotiations with Elbarak go well," declares Alyiakal, not wanting to comment on Marenda.

"They will. Saelora's very good at it."

"She seems good at all aspects of merchanting."

"She definitely is," agrees Gaaran.

More than a glass passes before Saelora and Elbarak step into the front of the factorage.

She says to Alyiakal, "We're ready to ride to the distillery now." Then she says to Gaaran, "I don't know how long we'll be, but I'll be back after Trader Elbarak leaves."

Gaaran nods.

Elbarak adds, "We'll wait for you out in front."

"We'll be there shortly," replies Saelora.

After Elbarak leaves the factorage, Alyiakal and Saelora walk to the stable. There they unstall their horses, lead them into the alley, and mount, after which Kaasya closes the doors behind them.

As Alyiakal and Saelora ride up the narrow alley, Alyiakal asks, "What do you think?"

She shrugs. "There are possibilities, but he's not making any commitments yet. He definitely wants to see the distillery. I think that will determine how interested his house will be."

"If his decision rests on the distillery, he'll buy everything he can."

"And if he doesn't?" she asks.

"It's for reasons you can't control, possibly ones he can't control, either, and in time he'll regret it."

"We'll see how he likes the distillery."

Once Alyiakal and Saelora join the others, she and Elbarak lead the way north on Canal Street, followed by Alyiakal and the two guards.

Elbarak asks questions, many of which Alyiakal cannot hear, despite his order/chaos sensing, but most of what he can hear appears to be about Vaeyal and where she obtains greenberries and maize. From what Alyiakal can determine, Saelora avoids being too specific.

When the group nears the distillery, Alyiakal senses a feeling of definite surprise when Elbarak realizes that the neat but significantly sized structure is indeed the distillery, though the trader says nothing to that effect.

After the three dismount, Alyiakal ties the horses and merely watches and listens as Saelora leads Elbarak through the distillery, explaining in general terms, again without specifics.

When the three walk out of the distillery two quints later, Saelora says, "That's all there is."

Elbarak nods. "I have to say I'm surprised. Your factorage here is far more . . . capacious than I expected after first seeing the town. The distillery is large and very well kept."

"What else would you like to know?" asks Saelora.

Elbarak gestures to the house, with its expanded stable. "Your distillery master lives there?"

"No, the distillery mistress has quarters at the west end of the distillery. The house is mine."

"It is modest."

"I rebuilt the interior. It's very comfortable and has everything I need," replies Saelora. "Large and elaborate dwellings do not make golds. Lands, distilleries, and factorages do."

Elbarak laughs, for a moment. "You own all of Loraan House?"

"Not all. The vast majority. Catriana—the house Merchanter in Fyrad—has an interest."

"But you do not require the approval of anyone else?"

"No. I do, however, seek the advice of others, such as Majer Alyiakal here, and a few trustworthy and knowledgeable holders and traders."

The Austran trader looks to Alyiakal. "You are young to be a majer, are you not?"

"I'm likely one of the youngest majers."

"You mentioned you commanded a small post . . ."

"That was my first. After home leave, I'll be headed for my fourth. Aside from one temporary posting, all my command posts have been combat posts."

"You are not from Cyad, then?"

"No. I'm a third-generation Mirror Lancer officer."

"But . . . with such posts . . . you've never been posted to Cyad?"

Alyiakal shakes his head. "I had the good fortune to serve under the current Captain-Commander when he was post commander at Guarstyad. That's about as close to headquarters as I've gotten. He's a very solid and remarkable officer."

"Do you have any . . . acquaintances among the Magi'i?"

"I've worked with one of the senior Magi'i twice, and I met the Third Magus once. Other than that, not really."

"You have an interesting background, Majer. I can see why Merchanter Saelora values your advice. Do you have any you'd care to share with me?"

"Only that you'd be better off not trading with Cerlyn, and definitely not going there."

Elbarak frowns. "Why?"

"They've been known to kill and torture outland traders who deal with any who displease the Duke, even when those traders did not know of that displeasure."

"Hmmm . . . that's interesting. From whom did you learn that?"

"From the Grass Hills barbarians who tried to get various goods from the dead traders. Also from some Cerlynese factors in towns just outside Cerlyn."

"I was under the impression those barbarians only talked with blades and arrows, that is, with Mirror Lancers."

"They'll talk if you've removed their weapons and their mounts."

Alyiakal waits.

But Elbarak turns to Saelora. "I'd like to ride back to the factorage where we can discuss matters. It shouldn't take long."

The ride to the factorage is similar to the previous ride, with Saelora and Elbarak side by side and Alyiakal and the two guards trailing. This time, neither Elbarak nor Saelora says much.

Back at the factorage, Alyiakal stalls both mounts, and heads to join Gaaran at the front counter, while Saelora and Elbarak take seats on opposite sides of the conference table. While Alyiakal senses no hostility, he does glean a hint of puzzlement on the part of the Austran trader.

As soon as Alyiakal steps through the door to the factorage's front counter, closing it after himself, Gaaran asks, "How did it go?"

Alyiakal shrugs. "He doesn't reveal much. From what I can tell, he's surprised at what Saelora's built, and he's puzzled. He doesn't dislike me, but likely thinks I'm an impediment of some sort . . . one he can't completely ignore." He smiles. "I did my best to hint I'm not just any junior majer."

"You did more than hint."

"You're right. I'm not that subtle. We'll have to see." *One of your least favorite, but overused and accurate, phrases.*

Close to another glass passes before the door behind the counter opens. Saelora and Elbarak emerge and walk to the front door, where they both halt.

"A pleasure to meet you, Merchanter Saelora. We look forward to working with Loraan House."

"As we do with Valtrad House," she replies. "Be careful on your way back to Fyrad."

"That we will."

Once Elbarak leaves the factorage, Saelora, Alyiakal, and Gaaran watch until he and his guards are out of sight.

Then she takes a deep breath.

"Can we ask how it went?" Alyiakal inquires.

"He placed and paid for a modest order of both liqueur and Crystalflame, to be delivered to the Valtrad warehouse in Fyrad before the end of the third eightday of Autumn. If it sells well, there will be more orders to come."

"That won't be until next year, most likely," says Alyiakal. "Not for something shipped to Valmurl."

"We couldn't supply more than what we just sold until then."

"Modest order?" questions Alyiakal.

"It's a modest order for them," replies Saelora with a smile. "Sometimes, they'll buy enough of something to take the cargo space of an entire ship."

"That sounds like it merits congratulations," declares Alyiakal.

"Hearty congratulations," adds Gaaran.

"Will you have to add to the distillery?" asks Alyiakal.

"Not yet." She pauses. "But it might be a good idea to keep an eye out for more copper, especially tubing." Then she looks to Gaaran. "Can you and Kaasya handle things for the rest of the afternoon?"

"We can. Kaastyl should be unloading the greenberries at the distillery before long, if he hasn't already."

"Then we'll leave," says Saelora. "We'll be by sometime tomorrow. You know where to find me if there's anything urgent."

"I do," agrees Gaaran. "I doubt there will be."

More than a quint passes before Alyiakal and Saelora ride north on Canal Street, where very few people are out in the hot late afternoon.

"I hope I didn't upset things," says Alyiakal. "I sensed that I puzzled Elbarak and made him a little uncomfortable."

"That was for the best. He wanted to know who you really were and why you were here." She smiles. "I told him that you and my older brother, a Mirror Lancer overcaptain, were friends, and that Hyrsaal asked you to make sure that his little sister was safe when dealing with outlanders."

"I'm sure Hyrsaal feels that way," says Alyiakal, "even if he didn't know about this meeting."

"Elbarak asked me if you exaggerated anything. I said you'd done far more than you'd mentioned, which was why Mirror Lancer headquarters regarded you so favorably. He could see I told the truth. That bothered and intrigued him."

"Did he say why he found my descriptions of Cerlyn interesting?"

"I noticed that, and I asked. He didn't say much, but he said his house didn't like trading in 'unsettled areas.'"

Alyiakal frowns. "They clearly don't trade with Cerlyn, but Suthya and Jerans border Cerlyn. I wonder if Cerlyn is encroaching on Suthya. The Suthyans are known far more for trading than fighting, unlike the Jeranyi." He pauses. "I'd appreciate it if you'd keep an ear out for anything that might bear on the subject."

Saelora smiles. "I can do that."

"Anything else?"

She shakes her head. "I'm ready to have a leisurely afternoon, or what's left of it, and dinner with you."

"Excellent." Alyiakal smiles fondly at her.

XXII

Early in the morning on the ninth twoday of Harvest, Alyiakal stands by the waystop on the west side of the Great Canal, his two duffels beside him. Somehow, his home leave is over. It seems like it's only been a few days since he'd gotten off the firewagon and Saelora had driven up with a love and warmth he'd immediately sensed.

Now, she stands beside him, holding his hand, while Gaaran sits on the teamster's bench of the Loraan House wagon, drawn up on the far side of the waystop.

"You know," Alyiakal begins, "the past five eightdays have been the best of my life."

Saelora smiles and squeezes his hand. "You said that last night. More than once."

"When things are true, I repeat myself." *Especially when I want you to know how I feel.*

"I know you have to go," she says, "but I'll always be with you."

"You have been for years, when no one else was." That, too, is true.

There's so much to say, Alyiakal feels, and yet he's already said it, as Saelora has pointed out, far more than once. So he stands there, holding her hand, both waiting for the inevitable arrival of the firewagon.

Less than half a quint later, Alyiakal catches sight of the curved glass canopy shielding the firewagon's driver and his assistant, then squeezes Saelora's hand, before she steps back, and the firewagon comes to a halt opposite Alyiakal's duffels.

The driver's assistant steps out. "Majer Alyiakal? Going to Ilypsya?"

"To begin with."

"That'll do, ser."

Alyiakal puts one duffel behind the forward-facing seats and the other beneath his seat, then takes the remaining forward-facing seat, likely reserved for him by the assistant, since the other three officers are all captains.

In moments, the firewagon is heading north.

The captains introduce themselves—Thurylt, Sartaan, and Naasm—and Alyiakal gives his name, then asks, "Where are you headed?"

Naasm answers immediately, "Home leave in Ikaryn, northwest of Ilypsya. After that, duty in Guarstyad."

"Duty at Dellash," replies Thurylt.

"Inividra," declares Sartaan, the captain sitting beside Alyiakal. "What about you, ser?"

"Pemedra."

"Is that as far out as I've heard?" asks Thurylt.

"It's more than two days' ride from Syadtar for a courier, three days with a squad and wagons."

"Then you've been there before?"

"My first posting out of Kynstaar. Have any of you been posted there?"

All three shake their heads.

"It's an interesting post," says Alyiakal. "The fourth Emperor of Light built it to be the first of several posts farther east and north. After his sudden death, none of the others were built, and Pemedra was never constructed to the size the emperor envisioned—except for the post walls, which are about the same size as those at Geliendra." Alyiakal stretches slightly and leans back in his seat, pulling his visor cap down, as if he intends to nap, which he might. He just wants a little time to himself, especially since he can sense that none of the captains really want to talk, or at least not to him.

None of the three know the post commander at Pemedra is always a majer, confirming his suspicion that none have ever been sent to northern border posts before.

The rest of the journey to Ilypsya is quiet and polite. Alyiakal has used his senses to eavesdrop on the whispers between Thurylt and Naasm, which consist of a few inaccurate speculations about him and far more conversation about their various women-friends. Alyiakal ignores this after the first few words.

When the firewagon arrives in Ilypsya, well after dark, Alyiakal exits first. The driver's assistant beckons, and a lancer ranker with a handcart materializes and places Alyiakal's duffels on the cart, then says, "The next firewagon to Syadtar doesn't leave until at dawn on fourday. The senior officers' quarters, ser?"

"Please." The delay doesn't exactly please Alyiakal, but delays happen, there are only so many firewagons, and complaining isn't going to change matters. He does appreciate the ranker's help.

As he heads for the senior officers' quarters, the ranker following, he wonders if the two delays he's experienced at Ilypsya, both involving Pemedra, might have any significance. Then he shakes his head. Attributing personal meaning to random and not-uncommon occurrences is foolish. *On the other hand, if the number of random delays increases over time, that would have a cause.*

Once he deposits his duffels in the quarters, he heads for the officers' mess, knowing that, while it's well past the evening meal, the mess has ale and a few items for transient officers at all times.

The mess orderly immediately rises from his seat in the corner as Alyiakal enters.

"What do you have?" asks Alyiakal.

"Just ale to drink, ser, but there are small loaves of bread and some cheese, and travel biscuits . . . oh, and some fresh apples."

"Thank you."

Once Alyiakal pours himself a mug of ale, slices some cheese onto a plate, and adds bread and an apple, he turns toward the senior officers' table, belatedly seeing a much older overcaptain who has said nothing.

When he nears the table, he says, "I'm sorry. I didn't see you when I walked in. It's been a long day."

The overcaptain smiles knowingly. "If you're here now, it had to be. I'm Lydaal, headed for Geliendra."

"Alyiakal, to Pemedra. Good to meet you." Alyiakal seats himself across from Lydaal, who has barely begun to eat, it appears.

Alyiakal takes a swallow of ale and is about to speak when two captains enter. Alyiakal recognizes them as Thurylt and Naasm, two of his firewagon companions.

Both captains stiffen at the sight of the two senior officers.

"As you were." Alyiakal gestures to the serving table. "There's plenty."

Both captains resume walking toward the table.

"You know them?" asks Lydaal.

"We were on the same firewagon to Ilypsya. I introduced myself, and they did the same. It was clear they didn't want to talk. So I didn't press them."

Lydaal shakes his head, murmuring, "Young idiots. When else would they have a chance to talk to a combat-tested post commander? Except they don't know enough to know." Lydaal grins and raises his voice as he continues. "No one commands at Pemedra without successful combat experience. I take it you're no exception."

"Pemedra, Guarstyad, and Lhaarat," Alyiakal replies conversationally.

Lydaal lowers his voice slightly. "And since you're young for a majer, I'd guess not much else."

"Temporary duty closing Luuval post."

Lydaal chuckles. "Heard that more than a few overcaptains turned that down."

"As a less senior overcaptain, I found that refusing would not have been in my best interest."

"Wise of you. Have you been to Geliendra recently?"

"My home leave was nearby. I was at the post twice, to get new uniforms, and I did pay an inadvertent courtesy call on the subcommander."

"Inadvertent?" Lydaal raises his eyebrows.

"I just wanted to get new uniforms, but Overcaptain Laartas happened upon me and insisted that I pay a visit to Subcommander Hurtaal. We had a short and pleasant visit, during which he politely reminded me that even junior majers were always noticed."

"He was right, Majer."

"Obviously, and I did apologize to Overcaptain Laartas and thanked him for his courteous handling of the situation."

"Good for you. Laartas will remember your courtesy . . . or he should."

"I'd guess you're likely his replacement, since Geliendra usually only has one overcaptain in complement."

"Most likely, but I haven't been told."

"Are we ever?" asks Alyiakal dryly.

"Not usually. I've known once in twenty years. What can you tell me about Geliendra?"

"I can't say much about officers there now, but I do know that Mirror Engineers often visit to check the chaos towers and wall wards. Once, the Third Magus showed up. A firewagon shuttles from here directly there, in case you didn't already know. There's a decent coffee shop not too far from the main gates."

For about a quint, between eating and sips of ale, Alyiakal tells Lydaal what he can about Geliendra and Southpoint Post.

When Alyiakal finishes, Lydaal nods. "Thank you. How do you know so much about a post where you've never been posted?"

"Because my father was a Mirror Lancer majer." Alyiakal shares details of being there as an officer candidate and spending home leaves there or nearby.

"Thank you. I appreciate it." Lydaal glances toward the junior officers' table, where both captains are clearly avoiding looking anywhere near the senior officers. "I wish you well at Pemedra. You'll need it."

"Thank you. Unless there's something I don't know, you should have a good posting at Geliendra. I wish you well."

The two stand simultaneously, and Alyiakal gestures for Lydaal to precede him, then follows. He can't help thinking how unlikely it is that either captain will get much higher in the Mirror Lancers.

But then, most officers would find your making majer unlikely.

ALYIAKAL'ALT,

Majer

Pemedra

Harvest, 104 A.F.

XXIII

On threeday morning, Alyiakal wakes early, washes, shaves, and dresses, and heads for the headquarters building, hoping to find the post commander before encountering him at the morning mess, assuming the post commander goes to the morning mess, since some subcommanders don't always do so.

"Ser?" asks the ranker in the anteroom.

"I just wanted to pay a courtesy call on the post commander, since I'll be here for another day."

"I'll tell Subcommander Bekkan that you're here, Majer . . ."

"Alyiakal."

While the ranker's tone is deferential, there's a hint of unvoiced annoyance, even as the ranker stands, knocks on the closed door, and then enters.

Bekkan? The same Bekkan who was the deputy post commander at Guarstyad when you were detached from Oldroad Post? Wasn't he in charge of firewagon security here before being posted to Guarstyad? But then, he was detail-oriented, and firewagon post definitely needs attention to detail. At least the post commander isn't Jaavor.

The ranker returns immediately and says, "You can go in, ser." The underlying annoyance has vanished.

Alyiakal enters and closes the door behind himself.

"Well . . . if this isn't a pleasant surprise," declares Bekkan, smiling and standing.

The surprise to Alyiakal is that Bekkan genuinely means it, from his thinning red hair down to his immaculately polished boots. "A surprise to me as well, Subcommander. I had no idea you were the post commander here. I just thought I should pay my respects because I'll be here for another day. The last time I was here was less than a glass."

"Why don't we walk to the mess together?" suggests Bekkan. "I was about to head there."

"I'd appreciate that."

"Good." Bekkan gestures toward the door.

Alyiakal takes the hint, turns, and opens the door.

Bekkan doesn't say anything until they're in the hallway leading to the front entrance. "Where are you headed?"

"Pemedra."

The subcommander nods. "That makes sense. I heard that when you were in command at Lhaarat, you wiped out a Cerlynese post they'd set up on our lands."

"Twice actually," replies Alyiakal. "The first time they had about four companies, the second time, a year later, they had about six."

"How many companies did you have? I assume you led them."

"I did. Three companies each time. I had to leave one near the post to deal with other duties."

"Mirror Lancer casualties?"

"About half a squad the first time, a squad the second time."

"You do have an ability to prevail with extremely low casualty figures. Commander Laartol—well, Captain-Commander Laartol now—said you lost very few wounded who survived combat."

"It helps to be a field healer, but it helps less the more lancers I command."

Bekkan gives a short harsh bark of a laugh. "That gets more so in everything the higher in rank you get. The less you can do personally, and the more you have to rely on others. If you're very good at what you do, it's hard to find subordinates who can do what you did. You have to teach them, and even then, it can be frustrating."

Thinking of Captain Paersol, especially, Alyiakal has to smile wryly.

"From your expression, I can see you've already seen that. I hate to tell you, but it gets worse." Bekkan pauses. "I'll have to introduce you at the mess. How much do you want me to say?"

"Just that I progressed from a small command on the Kyphran border to a larger command at Lhaarat, and I'm on my way to take command at Pemedra . . . if you think that's appropriate."

"I like it. It's short and not boastful or excessively modest."

When they reach the officers' mess, Bekkan calls out "As you were" the moment he steps through the door, then walks with Alyiakal toward the senior officers' table.

The number of senior officers already standing around the senior officers' table surprises Alyiakal—four overcaptains, including Lydaal, two sub-majers, and one majer, not to mention the six captains and ten undercaptains at the junior officers' table. He would have wagered that as many as a third of the junior officers were in transit, two of whom he recognizes—Captains Sartaan and Thurylt. Belatedly, he realizes that among the Mirror Lancer officers are a scattering of Mirror Engineer officers, including one overcaptain.

Bekkan motions to the majer already at the table, listens for a moment, and says a few words, then gestures for Alyiakal to sit to his left, before saying, "Please be seated." He remains standing, waiting until the officers seat themselves.

"Some of you may have noticed new faces at the senior officers' table. This morning, we're pleased to have senior overcaptain Lydaal, who's headed to a posting at Geliendra, and Majer Alyiakal, who's progressed from a small command on the Kyphran border to a larger command at Lhaarat and is now on his way to command at Pemedra." Bekkan smiles and adds, "That's all I have. Enjoy your breakfast." He then seats himself and says, "Alyiakal, I'd like you to meet Majer Accarrl, deputy post commander."

"Pleased to meet you, ser," says Alyiakal.

"Ser?" asks Accarrl, with a twinkle in his eye.

"You have to be senior to me," replies Alyiakal cheerfully.

Both Bekkan and Accarrl laugh.

"Somewhere I heard," says Bekkan, "that your father was also a Mirror Lancer majer."

"He was. Majer Kyal. He commanded at Northpoint, Isahl, and Inividra."

Accarrl nods. "I never met him, but I heard about him."

"After a while," says Bekkan, "in a group of officers, someone will know or have heard of every good majer in the Mirror Lancers. Not always, but usually."

"Your posting to Pemedra suggests there may be trouble with Cerlyn," suggests Accarrl. "What do you think?"

"As long as Duke Taartyn rules Cerlyn, there's a likelihood of trouble. He may lay back for another year, but sooner or later, he'll stir things up . . ." Alyiakal mentions a few of the signs he's observed as he eats ham strips and a helping of indifferent egg casserole, which some warm dark bread makes slightly tastier.

"You don't have a high opinion of the Duke," replies Accarrl.

Alyiakal laughs softly. "I don't have a high opinion of anyone who makes trouble, whether they're from Kyphros, Gallos, Cerlyn, or Jerans."

"Every border commander would agree with that," says Bekkan, hesitating momentarily before asking, "Have you ever seen the entire post here?"

"The only buildings I've seen, except in passing, are the firewagon terminal and the temporary quarters for officers," Alyiakal admits.

"We should remedy that." Bekkan looks toward an older, but prematurely gray, overcaptain, whose insignia indicate he is a Mirror Engineer. "Faaklyn . . . could you spare a glass or so this morning to show Majer Alyiakal the post—the transport support areas in particular?"

"Yes, ser. Be happy to do so."

Bekkan turns back to Alyiakal. "You obviously understand logistics on the post level, but you should find it interesting on a larger scale."

Alyiakal doesn't miss Bekkan's choice of words. *"Should," as in must, not "might."* "I'm certain I will, and I appreciate the opportunity."

In less than half a quint, Bekkan finishes eating, but before he rises to leave, he says, "I'm sure I'll see you tonight at mess, but not tomorrow morning, since the firewagon north leaves at first light."

"I'll be here this evening."

As the senior officers begin to leave the mess, Overcaptain Faaklyn says to Alyiakal, "Would starting the tour now be convenient, Majer?"

Alyiakal understands that the question is rhetorical. "Very convenient. I appreciate your time. I suspect you have a lot on your platter." *The last thing you want to do is escort a visiting majer.*

"The past few days have posed a bit of a challenge, but I can fill you in as we go."

"I'm in your hands, Overcaptain." Alyiakal walks beside Faaklyn as they leave the mess and head for the doors to the post courtyard. These are separated by a good hundred yards from the larger courtyard dominated by the firewagon terminal.

The older man strides across the court and through an archway between two buildings, one of which is clearly a rankers' barracks, and into another courtyard. He stops and gestures to his left at the small oblong building. A drive leads right up to a door big enough to allow a carriage to pass through. "That's the repowering building. The door on the other end of the building is where the firewagons enter and are inspected. The walls are a double course of graystone."

"To prevent an unexpected release of chaos?"

"Exactly."

"I take it you don't have a chaos tower here. Do you get cupridium reservoirs filled with concentrated chaos from Fyrad or Cyad?" As Alyiakal finishes his question, he senses a certain surprise from the overcaptain, but just waits.

"We do, but how did you know?"

"I wouldn't know, except when I was at Guarstyad we had to recover some territory occupied by the Kyphrans that contained a ruined building dating from the first years of Cyad. The old basement walls concealed chambers with weapons and equipment from that time. There was also a wheeled cart that held what looked like a cupridium reservoir."

Faaklyn frowns. "I never heard about that."

"Headquarters wasn't happy with what we found. Neither was the First Magus, I understand." While his last phrase is a surmise, Alyiakal doubts that the First Magus would disagree. He goes on to explain about the dissidents, adding, "That was what got me thinking about how you replenish the chaos for the firewagons."

"It comes in heavy cupridium cylinders," admits Faaklyn. "Each one is stored in a separate stone compartment."

"Do you have to replace or rebuild the machinery driving the wheels often?"

"Not the engines, or not often. The wheels have to be replaced regularly."

"What's the bigger problem—chaos supply or maintenance?"

"Maintenance right now. Parts, specifically. We're on the edge with spare parts. We get the parts from Fyrad. When the subcommander's asked for more, he's been told that the Mirror Engineers are short on mages, and they're doing the best they can." Faaklyn lowers his voice. "Rumor is that a lot of the mages are tied up in Cyad, but no one seems to know why or with what. Even the subcommander can't find out." The overcaptain shrugs. "We do the best we can. The driver and his assistant inspect the firewagon at each major stop."

Alyiakal wonders if the mages are involved in refurbishing the Palace of Light, as Dhraak suggested, but decides not to raise the issue, not on a single rumor. Instead he says, "I know it must vary by how much distance the firewagons cover, but how often does the chaos have to be replenished, and how do you tell?"

"There's a geared device linked to one of the axles that tells how many kays the firewagon has traveled. When it reaches four-fifths of the usual number of kays the chaos will last, it displays a small red indicator, and the driver knows that the firewagon needs replenishment. Firewagons leaving Fyrad, Chulbyn, or here on long routes are replenished before they leave regardless of the kays traveled since the last replenishment."

"I take it that the system works well enough that no one gets stranded."

"We've only had two firewagons deplete their chaos in the last two years. In one case, the indicating device had a gear malfunction that didn't reveal itself. In the other instance, we had no idea. So we replaced everything in the device."

"It's too bad you can't measure how much chaos remains stored in the firewagon reservoirs," observes Alyiakal.

Faaklyn frowns again, then concentrates on Alyiakal, who can sense the engineer's chaos probe.

"The Third Magus confirmed I'm not a mage," says Alyiakal cheerfully, "but I have order levels high enough that I'm a decent field healer, and I noticed that the Magi'i who investigated the dissident equipment couldn't tell whether it still held chaos. So I asked." All except being a field healer is technically a lie, but the Mirror Engineers and Magi'i hadn't been able to determine chaos levels.

Faaklyn looks at Alyiakal curiously. "So this isn't just a courtesy tour?"

"More an educational tour so that I know enough not to make stupid or impossible logistical requests."

Faaklyn shakes his head. "That's so like the subcommander." He resumes walking toward the structure adjacent to the repowering building, which has several doors large enough to accommodate a firewagon. One is open and several engineer rankers are working on a firewagon. "That's the main repair and maintenance building."

Standing outside another door is a firewagon of a kind Alyiakal has never seen before but whose purpose he can easily discern. "Supply and freight hauler?"

"Just for the Mirror Lancers and Engineers. If we had to, one of those could carry two squads of lancers—without mounts, of course, for a few glasses. Be very uncomfortable, though, and the maintenance is brutal. There are only two, and the Magi'i have insisted they won't help build another."

Because of maintenance or for some other reason? That's another question Alyiakal won't ask because it's clear Faaklyn believes what he's been told.

The rest of the tour is far more mundane, dealing with the supply warehouses, the scheduling center, which contains a miniature model of Cyador and all the whitestone roads used by the firewagons, and the armory, which holds discharged firelances awaiting recharging, or, if damaged, transport to Fyrad for repair or scrapping.

"I thought most firelances were recharged in Fyrad," Alyiakal says.

"All those used south of here go there. We replenish as many as we can here without jeopardizing our supply. It just depends."

"On how many need repowering and how much chaos you have?"

"Exactly."

The tour ends near the senior officers' quarters, where Alyiakal inclines his head to the overcaptain. "Thank you very much. You were very informative."

Faaklyn smiles amusedly. "So were you. In case we don't talk again, best of fortune in Pemedra."

"I'll doubtless need it."

As Alyiakal watches the overcaptain walk in the general direction of the maintenance building, he can't help but wonder why Bekkan had arranged the tour, since Bekkan has never engaged in anything without a purpose and has, in the past, been rather short on requests for information he thought was unnecessary or irrelevant.

Captain-Commander Laartol's hand again?

Except Laartol would have had to have briefed Bekkan well in advance, not that Laartol didn't plan everything in advance. But that didn't explain Bekkan's genuine pleasure at seeing Alyiakal.

This time, Alyiakal is the one to shake his head.

XXIV

Some among the Triad, other than the Mirror Lancers, have questioned the need for firelances, when cupridium blades, lances, and shafts can be created far more cheaply than firelances and are far superior to the weapons now possessed by the barbarians on the borders of Cyador, and when the chaos towers required to power the firelances could be used for other purposes, such as powering more fireships to protect Merchanter cargoes, or building greater numbers of splendid edifices or wondrous devices to ease the labors of many, as proposed by the vanquished dissidents . . .

Firelances are more than mere weapons. They are a continual and ever-present tool and symbol of the power and might of Cyador. No matter how greatly the barbarians improve their weapons, or even their tactics, or how many more armsmen they bring against the Mirror

Lancers, every firebolt that turns a barbarian to ashes creates a respect and fear beyond all other weapons and beyond the fear of mere death, for both body and essence are destroyed by that firebolt. That respect allows Cyador to hold and protect its lands with far fewer armsmen, and at a lesser cost than in other lands . . .

There is also the undeniable truth that chaos used to create excessive luxuries weakens any land, as does chaos used to multiply the profits of the traders of those luxuries . . .

Fragment, Mirror Lancer Archives
Zaenth'alt, Captain-Commander
Cyad, 45 A.F.

XXV

On fourday morning, Alyiakal eats at the early-morning mess and settles himself in the forward compartment of the firewagon heading for Syadtar at first light, along with two undercaptains and a captain, none of whom he recognizes.

All four officers doze, or at least try, for a glass or so, but Alyiakal finally sits up and looks out the side windows, not that there's anything remarkable to see beyond stretches of grass, trees, scattered holdings, and occasional hamlets.

Finally, Captain Waerdyn, sitting next to Alyiakal, clears his throat. "Majer . . . ?"

"Yes?" replies Alyiakal politely.

"With your rank . . . going to Syadtar . . ."

"I could be going to Isahl, Pemedra, or Syadtar," replies Alyiakal, "and you'd like to know which. We have a little time. You tell me where you think I'm headed, and why. If you're wrong, I certainly won't be offended."

"I'm only guessing, ser, but I'd say you're headed for Isahl."

"Why do you think that?"

"You're young for a majer, and I've heard that only very . . . experienced majers go to Pemedra or are picked to be deputy post commanders, like at Syadtar."

Alyiakal nods. "Your reasoning and logic are correct, but . . . it happens that I'm headed to Pemedra as the post commander." Before Waerdyn can say more, Alyiakal offers a sympathetic smile and adds, "When I got my orders, I had similar thoughts, especially since my first posting, years ago, was to Pemedra. In turn, I'd say that you're headed to Isahl, but I could be wrong."

"Your guess is better than mine," admits Waerdyn. "Isahl."

"Why do you think I asked for your reasons?" asks Alyiakal.

"I don't know that I could say, ser."

"Fair enough. Too often, we all make mistakes of judgment, not because our reasoning is flawed, but because our assumptions are incorrect or incomplete. Pemedra has a reputation for requiring older and experienced majers. The unstated assumption there is that all majers experienced in combat are older. Many older majers are, but not all. Likewise, most junior majers have less experience handling combat and directing multiple companies, but not all."

Waerdyn remains silent for a time, then asks, "Might I ask where else you've been posted, ser."

"Guarstyad, Oldroad Post on the Kyphran border, briefly at Luuval and Fyrad, and last at Lhaarat."

"All of those, except the brief postings, are combat posts, aren't they?"

Alyiakal nods.

"If I might ask . . . how much combat?"

Alyiakal laughs softly. "More than you'd ever wish, Captain." Alyiakal reinforces the words with a sense of cold truth.

Waerdyn shivers. "Are you expecting the same at Pemedra?"

"It's likely. You also might see some at Isahl from the Jeranyi. I don't know if they're still using them, but at one time the Jeranyi supplied the barbarians with spear-throwers that had about the same range as a firelance and large, polished bronze shields that could deflect firelance bolts."

"What's the best way to deal with them?"

"It depends. If they're mounted, they can't shield their mounts. Take out the mounts. If they're on foot and in a tight formation, without shields beyond the front ranks, you can arc in firelance bolts over the front ranks, but you'll need to do it in a passing attack in a semi-spread formation, and you'll still risk some casualties from the spears. If they're on foot with enough shields to form a turtle, with spear-throwers in the middle, any frontal attack will cost you men, but if they march forward, either their lower legs or their heads are vulnerable." Alyiakal pauses, then adds, "And those are just general approaches. They might not work in all cases. The best attack is always what they don't expect, and the captains who are most successful are those who can work out ways to surprise their opponents, preferably before they even know you're there."

"What about splitting your company?"

"It's usually not wise, except when it's necessary." At Waerdyn's frown, he adds, "All the standard maxims about tactics have a basic element of truth. Almost all of the time, they're right. In a very, very small set of circumstances, they're not."

"How do you know that?"

"Usually, when everything you've tried doesn't work," replies Alyiakal dryly, then shakes his head. "I've said too much. Some of that just has to come with experience."

For the rest of the journey to Syadtar, Waerdyn and Alyiakal talk more about places, and Alyiakal prefers to listen, although he doubts that he'll ever visit Gedaan, a small town west of Cyad, where Waerdyn grew up.

In time, late in the afternoon, the firewagon passes through the open, white-oak gates in the white sunstone walls of the city, continuing on to the central square before turning north. Alyiakal nods as the firewagon passes the green and white awning of a coffee shop, and then another square containing the statue of the second Emperor of Light, and shortly comes to a small circle where it slows to a halt before the open gates.

Moments later, the driver's assistant opens the door. "Syadtar Post, Majer, sers."

Alyiakal pulls out his two duffels and heads for the gates, showing his seal ring as he nears the guards, who incline their heads politely. Since the headquarters building is directly behind the gates, Alyiakal decides to go there first, realizing, belatedly, that he never actually entered the headquarters building before, but only the building dealing with personnel and supplies for Isahl and Pemedra.

Once inside the building, he sets down the duffels and walks to the duty ranker.

"Ser . . ."

"I'm Majer Alyiakal, heading for Pemedra, but also calling on the post commander."

"Yes, ser. Subcommander Zekkaat said you'd be here. If you'd follow me . . ."

Alyiakal follows the ranker down a hallway into an anteroom, where another ranker sits at a desk set midway between two open doorways.

"Majer Alyiakal to see the subcommander."

The second ranker rises and escorts Alyiakal into the study on the right. "Majer Alyiakal, ser."

Zekkaat is a black-haired, burly officer, not quite going to fat, and moderately tall, if a digit or two shorter than Alyiakal. He stands as Alyiakal enters, motioning for the ranker to close the door. "Welcome to Syadtar, Majer."

While Zekkaat's tone is warm and friendly, his eyes smiling as well as his mouth, Alyiakal senses no warmth behind the words and expression. "Thank you, ser."

Zekkaat gestures to the chairs before the wide desk, largely covered with stacks of paper, then seats himself.

Alyiakal seats himself as well, and since Zekkaat says nothing, he says, "Since part of my duties are to keep you informed of any actions or events that might affect either Syadtar or Isahl, I came to meet you as soon as I arrived."

"I appreciate that courtesy, Majer, and your recognition of the relationship between Pemedra and Syadtar. But then, since you were once posted to Pemedra, your immediate arrival here makes sense." Zekkaat leans back slightly in his chair and frowns briefly. "I understand that you were post commander at Lhaarat for the past two years, and that your . . . activities . . . may have provoked Duke Taartyn."

"That well may be the way the Duke views matters, but that is at variance with the facts. He continually sent armsmen across the border into Cyador, and he built a fort in the small town of Kraaslaen and garrisoned it with between five and seven companies of armsmen. Those armsmen attempted attacks on our patrols of the high road—"

"The high road?"

"The road that runs along the lower heights of the western side of the Westhorns from north of Jakaafra all the way to Clynya. I was explicitly ordered by the Majer-Commander to remove all Cerlynese armsmen from Cyadoran territory. We did so—twice—and destroyed the fort in Kraaslaen. At no time did we cross the border into Cerlyn."

"You used the term 'remove,' advisedly, I also understand. The Duke has suggested you slaughtered his armsmen to the last man."

"We were outnumbered two to one the first year and were two days' ride from Lhaarat Post. They attacked us. We fought two short battles. In the first, we took out almost an entire company. When the Cerlynese refused to leave Kraaslaen, we took the fight to them. Roughly a squad survived."

"Was that brutality necessary?"

"Ser, I'm not fond of giving someone who wants to kill my lancers a second chance, especially when we're fighting on our territory."

"You did the same thing a year later, or so I heard."

"Not exactly. Last year, the Duke sent roughly seven companies into Kraaslaen, killed all the men that they could find, and assaulted the women and girls. Less than half a Cerlynese company survived. Again, we did not cross into Cerlyn."

"How were the Cerlynese armed?"

"Polished bronze shields, blades, lances, or horn bows."

"How did you manage that with only your complement?"

"In both instances we only used three companies."

"Just three companies?"

"One needed to remain to deal with any other matters during the eightday absence of the other companies."

"Did headquarters verify the number of Cerlynese dead?"

"The current Captain-Commander visited Lhaarat after the first instance and verified the deaths and the number of blades and shields recovered. The spoils compensation to the rankers was considerable in both instances." Alyiakal senses that his mention of Laartol definitely disconcerts the subcommander, although his face shows nothing beyond a pleasant expression.

"You seem to have covered everything, Majer. You understand that I prefer to verify matters when I'll be receiving reports from another officer."

"I understand." *That someone has been sowing doubt.* "I learned a long time ago, by careful observation, not to report as factual anything that I could not support."

"You phrased that carefully."

"If I hear reports from others I cannot verify, I'll report that is what I was told."

"A very good policy, Majer. I won't keep you longer." Zekkaat stands. "My deputy, Majer Baertal, will arrange the logistics for your travel to Pemedra."

Baertal! Everything makes sense. While Alyiakal knew from the questions that someone had fed Zekkaat a great deal of slanted information, he should have realized that the amount of venom behind Zekkaat's questions could only have come from Baertal. *And it's perfectly logical that Baertal's here, given that Vordahl was deputy post commander at Assyadt.*

The subcommander walks to the door, opens it, steps into the anteroom, opens the half-ajar door to the adjoining office, and gestures for Alyiakal to enter, saying, "Majer Alyiakal, Majer Baertal, I believe you two know each other."

Alyiakal smiles broadly. "Majer Baertal and I go a long way back." He turns to the other majer. "Congratulations. Deputy post commander of the largest border post."

"You've also done well, Alyiakal. I always knew your talent with weapons would be deadly."

"I'll leave you two to work out the logistical details of getting the supplies and replacements to Pemedra." Zekkaat offers another warm smile over an internal coldness and a certain amusement, then turns and leaves the study.

That veiled amusement suggests strongly to Alyiakal that the subcommander is likely playing them both. *And Baertal has absolutely no idea that's what's happening.* Alyiakal knows, from past experience, that it would do no good even to hint at it, and he says cheerfully, "Shall we get to it?"

"Of course."

As Baertal seats himself, Alyiakal does the same and studies the other quickly. Baertal is one of the few Mirror Lancer officers taller than Alyiakal, but only by a digit now, if that. He's also black-haired and burlier, with the slightest hint of thickness around his waist, and his blue eyes suggest guilelessness.

"You've got a squad's worth of replacements," begins Baertal, "and there's a junior squad leader from Pemedra here to accompany you and three wagons of supplies. They've been waiting for you."

"There was a firewagon problem in Ilypsya, and I was delayed two days there." *At least if I'd been able to take a firewagon immediately when I arrived there.* "Have you noticed whether there have been more incidents like that recently?"

"There are always some," replies Baertal diffidently.

"Are there any other personnel from Pemedra?"

"Just the squad leader."

"Do you have his name?"

Baertal glances at a sheet in front of him. "Faaln." He hands Alyiakal a large envelope. "The supply manifests, the wagon custody forms, and the replacement rosters are all there."

"What about firelance replacements?" asks Alyiakal.

"A hundred fully powered firelances. They're listed on one of the supply manifests."

The last time Alyiakal had traveled to Pemedra, the supply wagons had carried five hundred firelances. "That's quite a cutback."

"We got a dispatch from headquarters on oneday cutting back our resupplies as well. With it was a directive curtailing all unnecessary use of firelances." Baertal smiles sardonically. "As if any officer or post commander goes around wasting chaos." He pauses. "You wouldn't know anything about that, would you?"

"We got a directive to minimize the use of firelances before I left Lhaarat. That's as much as I've heard from headquarters. A maintenance overcaptain at Ilypsya told me that they were having delays in getting spare parts, and that he'd heard more mages were involved in something in Cyad."

Alyiakal senses momentary surprise before Baertal says, "Good to know. Thank you."

"What's the current situation with regard to barbarians and brigands to the northeast?"

"There haven't been any reports of either in the last two eightdays. As you know, that can change."

"Quickly," agrees Alyiakal. "Any heavy rains recently?"

"It's been drier than usual."

Alyiakal discerns no traces of untruth or evasion, and that bothers him slightly, given his history with Baertal. "Is there anything else I should know or that might be useful?"

Baertal frowns, as if considering the matter, then says, "Not that I can recall."

"Are you up for reposting soon?"

"Not until a year from now. That could change, though."

Alyiakal stands. "I appreciate the information, and I'll see you at mess."

Baertal does not stand but smiles pleasantly. "You're welcome."

Alyiakal departs, leaving the door open. While he'd like to use a concealment and remain to hear what Baertal and Zekkaat might say, the duty ranker's eyes are fixed on him as he leaves the anteroom. Once he is in the hall, he senses Baertal entering Zekkaat's study and closing the door.

He shakes his head and walks to the front to reclaim his duffels before heading to the visiting officers' quarters. He barely gets his gear into his temporary quarters before he goes hunting for Squad Leader Faaln. Fortunately, just outside the study for senior squad leaders, a squad leader hurries up to Alyiakal as he approaches.

"Are you Majer Alyiakal, ser?"

"I am, and I presume you're Squad Leader Faaln?"

"Yes, ser."

"Excellent. I understand it's you, me, a squad of replacements, and three wagons. Have I missed anything?"

"No, ser."

From Faaln's tone, and his disturbed order/chaos balance, Alyiakal notes the squad leader is worried. "Let's go out into the courtyard and talk." After those words, Alyiakal can sense a lessening of apprehension.

"Yes, ser."

Alyiakal leads the way to a shaded and slightly cooler corner of the courtyard and asks, "What's the problem?"

"It's the replacements, ser."

"Most of them are little more than recruits, and the few that aren't may have other problems, is that it?"

"Pretty much right on, ser. There were two squads of replacements, but the deputy post commander took most of the experienced ones for the complement here."

The experienced ones he didn't take are likely troublemakers. Alyiakal nods. "That's nothing new. We'll have to conduct some intensive training on the way to Pemedra. This sort of thing happens occasionally. We'll have to deal with it." *Complaining to the subcommander about Baertal's actions won't change anything and will make matters worse.*

"Still doesn't seem right, ser."

"It happens." Alyiakal then asks, "Faaln . . . did anyone tell you anything about me?"

"No, ser. Overcaptain Baassyn just gave me your name."

Alyiakal manages not to sigh. "The previous post commander has already left?"

"Yes, ser. Majer Moryah got a dispatch and left with Captain Faeth and the dispatch riders two eightdays ago. He appointed the overcaptain acting commander. Captain Faeth didn't come back, but we got Undercaptain Suraat."

"Did you see any signs of raiders, brigands, or barbarians on your ride from Pemedra?"

"No, ser, but I rode with the dispatch riders."

"Just you?"

"Yes, ser."

Frig! "Very interesting." Alyiakal pauses. "It's time for the evening mess. Meet me here after the meal. We have a lot to organize before we leave tomorrow."

Faaln's eyes widen.

"There's no point in staying at Syadtar any longer than necessary. We'll talk about it after dinner. I'll see you then."

"Yes, ser."

As Alyiakal turns and walks away, it's clear that Faaln is the most junior squad leader at Pemedra, and, if he's reading Faaln correctly, the situation at Pemedra is anything but good. *But don't jump to conclusions. It might not be that bad.*

Alyiakal manages not to get lost in making his way to the officers' mess, although years have passed since he last was at Syadtar. When he enters, he's struck by the difference in his own perceptions over time. On his first posting to Pemedra, he had been surprised by how few officers there were. Now, he's vaguely surprised at how many there are, especially after his own years in the Mirror Lancers.

For a brief moment, he's the most senior, but then Baertal and a much older sub-majer appear, followed by Zekkaat. Alyiakal sits at the subcommander's left, across from Baertal. Beside Baertal is the older sub-majer. The other two at the senior officers' table are both overcaptains, one of whom looks old enough to be close to getting his stipend.

After Zekkaat's perfunctory introduction of Alyiakal and quick toast, the sub-majer beside Baertal says, "I'm Smaalt, handling supply here."

"I'm pleased to meet you. Do you foresee any problems with our leaving tomorrow morning?"

"There shouldn't be. The wagons are mostly loaded already, except for the firelances, but they won't take long."

"That's good to hear," replies Alyiakal. "I understand that firelance replenishment is getting to be a problem."

"It wouldn't be," says Zekkaat, "if some of the border posts didn't go through firelances so fast."

"I suppose you could look at it that way, ser," replies Alyiakal, "but one could also say that they wouldn't go through so many if the Cerlynese, Jeranyi, and others didn't send so many armsmen and raiders into Cyador. Of course, they might be doing that to test how much chaos we can replenish. The Cerlynese, in particular, don't seem to mind losing large numbers of armsmen and their mounts, or weapons."

"That's because they're little more than barbarians," declares Baertal, "and there are always more of them."

Alyiakal nods. "Someone once told me that they breed like coneys, and no matter how many you kill, there are always more."

For an instant, Baertal is stunned, most likely at Alyiakal's quoting Baertal's own words from the past back at him, before he replies, "And they don't respect rank in the slightest."

"Which is one reason why," replies Alyiakal, "it's best not to allow them to fight again."

"You don't believe in quarter, Majer?" asks Zekkaat mildly, amused behind the pleasant façade.

"Not when those you're fighting have the disturbing tendency to massacre the men in any town they take and despoil the women who survive."

"Are the Cerlynese really that bad?" asks the younger overcaptain.

"Yes," replies Alyiakal, before taking a sip of the indifferent red wine and following it with a mouthful of sticky noodles covered in thick brown gravy. Then he cuts a small slice of the pounded beef and eats that.

After several moments of silence, Sub-Majer Smaalt speaks. "You may be the only Mirror Lancer officer who has seen both sets of ruins built by the so-called dissidents. Why is that, and what can you tell us?"

Alyiakal wonders how the sub-majer knows that particular piece of information because it's clear from the reactions of both Zekkaat and Baertal that neither of them does.

"I think it's fair to say that very few, if any, officers have ever heard of the dissidents. I certainly hadn't, even after I investigated an apparent dead-end road and discovered the old road cut into the cliffs. Only when we removed the Kyphrans from the ruins on Cyadoran lands east of the Westhorns and learned those ruins had been built by someone with the skills of the First, did headquarters tell the post commander about the dissidents." Alyiakal gave a quick and factual description of both dissident sites.

Smaalt nods, then asks, "Do you have any thoughts on why the Oldroad Post was thoroughly reduced while Lestroi was essentially looted and the inhabitants removed?"

"I'm only guessing, but even today getting to Lestroi is difficult. Back then it would have been far harder. Also, it appears that Lestroi was attacked somewhat later, and the First may have not seen the necessity to expend massive amounts of chaos to destroy an isolated refuge. Possibly, they also didn't want to call attention to the dissidents. I was told that there are only a handful of mentions of the dissidents in any Mirror Lancer records."

"You use the word 'refuge,' Majer," says Zekkaat. "Why?"

"The location was well-hidden, and was designed and cut out of the gorge walls in a way not to be revealing. That suggests those who built it didn't want to attract the attention of the First in any way."

"Yet you discovered it," declares Smaalt evenly.

"A hundred years later with the help of a very good scout," replies Alyiakal cheerfully. "We weren't looking for it but tracking some raiders. We did find them as well."

"Thank you," says Smaalt.

"You're welcome." Alyiakal senses that the interchange amused Zekkaat and irritated Baertal and confirms his feeling that the subcommander likes to play subordinates against each other. *But with Baertal, that could come back to bite him.*

He wonders, though, how Smaalt knows about the dissidents.

The remainder of conversation at dinner is far more conventional.

After Alyiakal leaves the mess, he heads off to meet with Squad Leader Faaln, who is waiting as instructed.

"Good evening, ser."

"The same to you, Faaln. The sub-majer in charge of supply said the wagons are mostly loaded. Let's go look at them now, before it gets any darker."

"Yes, ser." Faaln leads the way to the wagon house.

All three wagons resemble those Alyiakal shepherded over the Westhorns at Guarstyad, those at Lhaarat, and those used to close Luuval Post, and look sturdy enough. While Alyiakal doubts anyone would deliberately weaken a wagon, there's always a possibility where Baertal's involved, or there might simply be an undetected weakness. Alyiakal studies each wagon carefully, with both eyes and senses. The only thing he discovers is a crack, or fracture, in the cupridium tire of one of the spare wheels, as well as cracks in several spokes. A thin layer of dried mud covers all the cracks.

After he points that out to Faaln, he says, "Make sure that's replaced first thing tomorrow."

"Yes, ser. How did you know?"

"I didn't know. I just know that people often don't check the spare wheels, and it's a long way to Pemedra or back to Syadtar."

"Yes, ser."

"Now, let's go back to the rankers' mess and take a table. We have quite a few things to go over, including the training we'll conduct on the ride to Pemedra."

"You've done this before, ser?"

"Training while traveling? More than a few times. Now . . . I have some questions. Have there been many patrols to the east that have gone more than ten or fifteen kays?"

"I've been here just over a year, ser. I don't know of any."

"What about to the north, into the barbarian lands bordering Jerans?"

"No, ser."

"What about raiders entering the valley?"

"Three or four this Summer. Each time, they were gone before the duty company got there."

Alyiakal nods. While he'd like to say more, now is not the time. *Just like Lhaarat before you got there. What the frig is going on? Pressure not to use firelances or lose Mirror Lancers? Is lack of initiative and training another reason why you've been posted to Pemedra? Or something you haven't even thought about?*

He pushes those thoughts aside for the moment and motions toward the wagon-house door. "We have a lot to plan, so let's get started."

XXVI

Alyiakal is up very early on fiveday, hurrying to the officers' stable well before morning mess because he didn't have a chance to pick a mount the night before. After studying and sensing the available horses, he settles on a gray gelding, and spends a little time with him before meeting with Faaln briefly. Afterward, he makes his way to the officers' mess, where Sub-Majer Smaalt stands to one side of the senior officers' table, with the overcaptains and Baertal on the other side.

"I understand you're heading out this morning," ventures Smaalt.

"There's not much point in delaying," replies Alyiakal, "especially since my predecessor has apparently already departed. Do you know whether he was going to another post or stipended?"

"Stipended, I understand." Smaalt glances past Alyiakal momentarily before he adds, "Earlier than he planned, I believe, but that's just my impression." He smiles. "Here comes the subcommander."

Alyiakal and the other senior officers seat themselves, and Zekkaat sips his ale. Initially, there's little conversation, but Zekkaat turns to Alyiakal and says, "Once you're settled in, I'd appreciate anything you can pass on about barbarian activities."

"Of course," replies Alyiakal.

"Your predecessor always seemed to be reacting," Zekkaat adds.

"I'll keep that in mind. Is there anything else that's changed recently?"

"Barbarians are barbarians. They always want what we have. The only thing that changes is how often they raid and where. As I'm certain you know."

"Alyiakal knows quite well," adds Baertal. "He understands the way they think, most likely why headquarters posted him there."

"Headquarters always has its reasons," replies Alyiakal, "but I've seen officers who thought they understood those reasons be mistaken more than once. As for Pemedra, we'll just have to see."

"So we will," agrees Zekkaat cheerily.

For the rest of breakfast Alyiakal is pleasantly polite, and when he leaves the mess, Zekkaat offers a parting, and perfunctory, "Best of fortune, Majer."

"The same to you, Subcommander."

Alyiakal collects his duffels and hauls them to the stable, where he quickly readies the gray gelding and fastens the duffels behind the saddle. He fastens his healer's satchel on top of it all. Then he leads the gray into the courtyard and rides to where Faaln musters the squad of recruits, picking up a firelance along the way. Skeptical as he is, he compresses a bit of free chaos and forces it into the firelance reservoir, judging from the resistance that the weapon is fully replenished, or close to it.

He reins up beside Faaln. "Who did you choose for a scout?"

"Dagaard, to start. I thought he and Flednaar could alternate."

Alyiakal nods.

Once the squad and wagons form up, Alyiakal nods to the squad leader, and they turn their mounts and move to the head of the short column, directly behind the scout.

"Squad! Forward!" Alyiakal orders.

While the replenishment group leaves Syadtar relatively early, Alyiakal hasn't seen any company from Syadtar forming up for a patrol. In less than half a quint, the last wagon and the two rearguard rankers pass through the north gates, and the de facto squad takes the sunstone pavement that ends less than a kay farther at a split in the road. The squad turns onto the right fork, which leads to Pemedra.

As usual when riding, Alyiakal spreads his unseen order funnel to gather chaos bits, hoping he won't need the additional chaos, but with almost no experienced rankers and three supply wagons, once the group is farther northeast and well away from Syadtar, there's always the possibility that barbarians might risk attacking an apparently small group of lancers.

As the group continues through the rolling grasslands, Alyiakal doesn't yet see any traces of winter graying on the scattered trees or the intermittent clumps of bushes. Nor does he sense any antelopes nearby or grass cats lurking in the autumn-browned, high grass stretching away from the road.

After another two quints, Alyiakal says to Faaln, "Start ordering changes in formation spacing."

"Squad! Single file! Arms ready!"

Alyiakal senses the sluggish response, hardly unexpected, then waits until the rankers are reestablished.

"Squad! Two abreast! Double-spaced! Stow arms!"

After riding another two glasses, ordering intermittent formation changes and arms drills, Alyiakal calls a halt to give a rest to men and mounts.

That remains the pattern for the rest of the day, until Alyiakal calls a halt on a rise near a small stream, an area often used by supply wagons in the past. While he'd like to go through blade drills, he doesn't have any wooden wands, and he's not about to use actual blades with replacement lancers who are largely recent recruits.

Sixday continues the same pattern as on fiveday, until around midday, when the replenishment group nears a section of road along the crest of a long rise that Alyiakal remembers well, since he experienced his first skirmish with barbarian raiders here.

"Faaln," says Alyiakal quietly, "there's a lower rise beyond the downslope ahead. In the past, barbarians have made at least one attack there. Have there been any lately, that you know about?"

"Not in the year I've been here, ser."

"Just to be cautious, have the scouts check out the area even more carefully."

"Yes, ser."

Alyiakal doesn't sense any order/chaos patterns ahead or to either side and sees no sign of riders or their dust, even once his group starts down from the rise. He does note a trail worn in the side of the low rise, but no barbarians. For the rest of the day, the only other people he sees are those working around the scattered hamlets they pass. He also makes certain to work in drills with five-man fronts, and staggered spacing, carefully explaining the need for it, should the squad of replacements run into raiders.

Alyiakal halts the group for the night just past the last hamlet, before the road climbs through the steeper hills separating the lower valley from the long higher valley ahead. The winding road through the hills is the last place where barbarians can approach without being seen until they're almost upon any riders.

On sevenday, Alyiakal has the replenishment squad riding out at dawn, but the slope into the hills is farther than he recalls, and it's a good two glasses and one break before they reach the beginning of the steeper climb into the hills.

Knowing that barbarians could attack without warning, Alyiakal is glad he's gathered two days' worth of compressed sun-chaos, an amount that he's slightly uncomfortable having linked to him, but with so many barely trained replacements, he'd feel even more uncomfortable without it.

While Alyiakal discerns one grass cat and several antelopes over the next glass or so, he senses no other riders besides those with him, but he's getting an uneasy feeling as he looks ahead.

The road curves to the right for half a kay as it angles up the slope before curving back to the left then straightening between two hills. While Alyiakal cannot see farther than the crest of the road, where it straightens, he has a vague sense of order/chaos patterns farther ahead, most likely somewhere amid the scattered trees on the left hillside, because the hillside on the right shows only brown grass.

"Scouts! Look ahead to the left!" orders Alyiakal, boosting his voice with a touch of order.

Flednaar keeps looking, then signals that he sees nothing.

Dagaard, a good hundred yards behind Flednaar, offers no signals.

"Squad! Fast trot! On me!" orders Alyiakal, knowing full well the wagons won't be able to keep up, but he wants the bulk of the squad on the flat at the crest of the road before the possible raiders can reach them.

Even before Alyiakal reaches the crest, he definitely senses riders ahead of the scouts on the left. Moments later, he can see the scattered trees and sense order/chaos patterns amid them.

"Scouts! Back to the squad!"

Both Dagaard and Flednaar look surprised but turn their mounts. Then Dagaard looks back and sees riders emerging from the trees onto the road, spurring their mounts toward the scouts and the squad.

Alyiakal estimates that there must be close to thirty raiders. He's never seen a road-raiding group that large. "Squad! Halt! Five-man front! Staggered spacing! Ready! Arms! This is not a drill! Ready arms!"

As he gives the orders, Alyiakal moves to the road's right shoulder, just ahead of the first rank, where even wildly errant firelance bolts are unlikely to strike, although he does check his shields.

As the scouts near, Alyiakal gestures for them to rein up beside him and orders, "Ready arms!" Then he turns his attention to the approaching raiders. The riders in the rear carry horn bows and will loose shafts once they're in range of the squad. Knowing he can extend his shields enough to protect a group as small as a squad, Alyiakal doesn't call attention to the archers.

When the oncoming raiders are less than two hundred yards from the squad, shafts begin to fly, and Alyiakal extends and hardens his outer shield, angling it so that the shafts strike and slide to the other side of the road.

"When they're less than a hundred yards from us," Alyiakal tells Faaln, "you and I will open fire. If they get to fifty yards, I'll order the squad to open fire."

"Yes, ser."

Although Alyiakal senses puzzlement from Faaln, he doesn't have time to explain.

The moment the lead riders, now moving at a full gallop, near a hundred yards, Alyiakal lifts his firelance and looses quick bolt after quick bolt, guiding each into a raider. Faaln adds his firebolts. In a fraction of a quint, the leading riders are down, as are some mounts, and the charge has turned into confused riders and disorganized riderless mounts.

Alyiakal continues to take down riders, and where necessary, mounts.

From his best count, Alyiakal guesses that possibly eight or nine raiders survive and gallop down the road before turning off into the grass roughly half a kay away.

"Squad! Order arms!" Alyiakal lowers his firelance and turns to Faaln. "Detail two men for spoils, and four to capture any mounts and collect arms and gear."

"Yes, ser!"

Alyiakal catches a few words that Dagaard murmurs to Flednaar.

". . . majer took out most of 'em in moments . . ."

"Scouts! Forward two hundred yards. Keep an eye out for raiders."

"Yes, ser!"

Dealing with the dead raiders—their tack, weapons, and the surviving five mounts that can be caught—takes a glass before the squad can resume riding. The spoils turned over to Faaln are minimal—four thin gold rings, five bronze wrist-guards, and seventeen coppers.

Once the squad and wagons move well away from the ambush site, Alyiakal takes a few moments to compress some of the sun-chaos he has gathered into his firelance.

The squad covers another two kays before Faaln, who keeps glancing at Alyiakal, finally speaks. "Ser . . . how did you know the raiders were waiting there for us?"

"I didn't *know,* Faaln. I've been here before, and there are only a few places where raiders can get close enough for an effective surprise attack without being seen. I caught a hint of movement where there shouldn't have been any." Which is true, if not in the way that the squad leader will take it.

"They had more riders than I've ever seen at one time here."

"They did," agrees Alyiakal, who suspects the number of raiders and the comparatively small squad escorting the supply wagons might not be purely coincidental, nor just the result of raider scouting. *But if that's so, there's no way to prove it and likely never will be.*

"I've never seen an officer as fast and as sure with a firelance, either."

"We may have to do some training on that," replies Alyiakal, knowing that his non sequitur will preclude further comments about his skill. He's also glad that no one noticed, or at least did not speak about, all the raider arrows along just one side of the road. That wouldn't have passed unnoticed with a squad of experienced lancers.

Another glass passes before the squad and the wagons emerge from the hills into the high valley. Before long, they ride past the southernmost hamlet, set to the west of the road between two low ridges covered with grass and sparse clumps of bushes. A mudbrick wall surrounds the houses and low barns, while a line of scrub trees marks a stream. Ahead in the distance is Pemedra, if not yet visible above the dried tan grass that covers the mostly flat lands of the long valley.

Over the next four glasses, the squad passes several more hamlets, all surrounded by mudbrick walls, and none of which appear markedly different from what Alyiakal recalls.

When the squad nears the post, Alyiakal sees that it is also unchanged. Smooth-finished graystone walls, close to ten cubits high, form a hexagon, each side half a kay long. Short stone watchtowers, never manned in Alyiakal's experience, sit atop each wall corner, while the last half kay of the road leading to the white oak gates is stone-paved.

Alyiakal shakes his head, thinking of what could have been, had Emperor Kieffal lived.

As he also recalls, two Mirror Lancers on foot guard the gates, each with a short firelance.

Alyiakal slows his mount and announces, "Majer Alyiakal, arriving to take command, with a squad of replacement lancers, and three supply wagons." He pauses. "Is there any company out on patrol?"

"No, ser. Second Company returned about a glass ago."

"Thank you."

Once inside the gates, Alyiakal can sense the surprise of the replacement lancers. Although the avenue from the gate leads to a circular plaza, the pedestal in the center is vacant. Behind the circle, graystone-walled buildings line each side of the avenue, including obvious barracks.

Alyiakal leads the squad and wagons to the massive and long graystone stables, a good third of a kay north of the other buildings. Beyond the stables, the avenue stretches to the north gates through ground that is empty except for the walls and a series of corrals.

After dismounting and leading his mount into the stable, Alyiakal takes one of the empty stalls away from the door, on the side reserved for officers, then unloads his duffels, setting them outside the stall, before unsaddling and grooming the gray.

As he finishes, a ranker hurries up. "Majer, can I help with your gear?"

"I'd appreciate that," says Alyiakal, "if you'd just leave it in my quarters. I need to find Overcaptain Baassyn."

"He's in his study, ser."

"Thank you." Alyiakal extracts his orders and the related directives from the one duffel, then turns and leaves the stable, walking quickly up the avenue to the headquarters building on the east side of the avenue facing the square. Even now, the stone masonry looks crisper than any building in Syadtar.

The duty squad leader sitting at the worn oak table desk at the back of the entry area watches as Alyiakal approaches, then stands quickly as he sees the insignia on Alyiakal's collar.

"Ser, no one expected you until after oneday."

"I understand." *But I hope it's not a harbinger of the situation here.* "I know where to find the overcaptain."

Alyiakal offers a polite smile as he strides past the squad leader and makes his way down the hallway. When he enters the anteroom to the studies of both the post commander and deputy commander, the ranker at the desk looks up and immediately stands. "Majer Alyiakal?"

"The same. As you were." Alyiakal senses which of the two studies holds someone, presumably Overcaptain Baassyn, and enters the smaller chamber.

The overcaptain rises from behind the desk. "Welcome to Pemedra, ser. We didn't expect you until later." Baassyn's baritone voice is smooth and unhurried, and his green-trimmed cream uniform appears unwrinkled.

"So, I heard. I apparently have this tendency to catch people unaware."

"Surprises are often less than pleasant, I fear, ser."

"But are usually more revealing," replies Alyiakal with a cheerfulness he doesn't feel. He studies the well-tailored, midsized officer whose apparent blandness immediately suggests protective coloration rather than lack of ability. "In any case, Squad Leader Faaln and I escorted a squad of replacement lancers and three supply wagons from Syadtar. Along the way, near the end of the hills at the south end of the valley, close to two squads of barbarian raiders attacked us. We suffered no casualties. We did gain five additional mounts and the tack, weapons, and gear of twenty-two dead barbarians. I'd appreciate it if you'd make sure the captured horses and equipment are handled and recorded properly."

"Yes, ser. You said *two* squads?"

"That was a rough count. They attacked in force. I counted seven or eight fleeing. With only a squad, most of whom are barely out of training, and the need to protect the supply wagons, it would have been foolish to pursue."

"I can see that, ser."

"Excellent. I won't keep you for the moment. I assume the evening mess will be at the usual time since no one is out on patrol. That will be a good time to meet all the officers. After dinner, you and I can repair here and go over transferring command, and you can brief me on recent events."

"This evening?"

Alyiakal smiles. "The sooner, the better, don't you think?"

"Yes, ser."

"Then I'll see you at the evening mess."

Alyiakal senses that Baassyn is both disconcerted and upset and wonders why. It's not as though he's done anything that should have given Baassyn any real concern.

Alyiakal still ponders the overcaptain's reaction as he makes his way to the post commander's quarters, effectively a three-room suite, where he quickly unpacks, then takes a shower and shaves, before donning a clean uniform. He leaves his quarters under a concealment and makes his way to the mess, where he slips inside and waits for the officers to arrive.

The first two are likely the most junior, although under a concealment Alyiakal cannot tell, but junior officers are prone to be early, rather than late.

Both glance around before one says, "The new majer just arrived. He had only a squad leader, and a squad of green replacements. Twoscore raiders attacked them in the hills at the south end of the valley."

"That doesn't sound good."

"Not for the raiders. Maybe a half score escaped. The majer killed most of them. That's what I heard. He never even had the replacements use their firelances. There weren't any lancer casualties."

"None? Usually, their archers at least wound someone. Did they have archers?"

"The spoils he brought back had bows and quivers . . ." The officer breaks off as two other officers arrive.

"Did you hear the first thing he asked the gate guards?" says one of the newcomers. "He wanted to know who was on patrol."

Alyiakal quietly slips out of the mess and far enough away to drop the concealment without notice. Then he waits for Baassyn to arrive.

"I thought you might be early," says the overcaptain jovially as he moves toward the mess door.

"Not too early for the mess. That's hard on junior officers." Alyiakal gestures, and the two enter the mess together.

The four other officers stiffen.

"As you were," declares Alyiakal, moving to take the seat at the head of the table. After he sits, he's relieved that the mess orderly is pouring wine, because he doubts that the grass ale tastes any better than it had on his previous posting at Pemedra.

He lifts the wineglass. "To a good year for all of us."

"To a good year . . ."

"Now, while I've met Overcaptain Baassyn, I haven't met any of you before, and most of you likely don't know much about me. My first posting out of Kynstaar was here at Pemedra, my second at Guarstyad, where I commanded a company against the Kyphrans. After that, I was promoted to overcaptain and given command of Oldroad Post on the Kyphran border. I was detached a season early to close the post at Luuval, then posted to Lharaat as deputy post commander. A year later, I was promoted and made post commander. At the end of that posting I was promoted again and posted here. I'm also a qualified field healer." Alyiakal pauses. "Now . . . a few words from each of you as you introduce yourselves." Alyiakal looks to the older captain seated across from Baassyn.

"Chaem, ser. Almost twenty years in the Mirror Lancers. Came from Pyraan, small town not far from the Accursed Forest."

"Not far from Westend," says Alyiakal. "My great-aunt lived there. You might have known her. Zhalena."

"Zhalena . . . the old healer . . . she was your great-aunt?"

Alyiakal nods. "She was." *She was a healer?* His father had never mentioned that, and Alyiakal wonders how he couldn't have known and why he'd never mentioned it to Alyiakal.

"Everyone respected her," adds Chaem.

Alyiakal chuckles and adds, "I certainly did." Then he turns to the other, considerably younger captain.

"Kessmyr, ser. I'm from Rewaal, east of Cyad. First Mirror Lancer in my family."

"That can be quite an accomplishment," returns Alyiakal.

"Yes, ser," Kessmyr returns wryly.

Alyiakal's eyes go to the senior undercaptain.

"Nolaan, ser. From Chulbyn."

"Lancer family?"

"Yes, ser." Nolaan grins. "But I'm the first officer."

"Good for you."

The junior undercaptain then says, "Suraat, ser. From Cyad."

Alyiakal suspects that Suraat comes from either a Merchanter or Magi'i family, simply because he doesn't say more, but he doesn't press the junior undercaptain.

There's a momentary silence, and the order/chaos swirling around the other five officers, including Baassyn, suggests that none of them quite knows what to say.

Chaem clears his throat. "I might be mistaken, ser, but you said you commanded one of the companies that fought the Kyphrans? Possibly the one that inflicted the most casualties on them."

"We all did our part."

"Were you behind the destruction of the Cerlynese invaders last year?"

"Not behind. I led the three companies personally."

Nolaan and Kessmyr exchange glances, while Suraat frowns.

"Thank you, ser," says Chaem. "I thought that might be so, but I've learned that assuming things is unwise."

"It can be," agrees Alyiakal, picking up his fork, and looking at the spring beans on his plate, fare that he'd hoped never to see again, then turns his attention to the breaded and fried fowl strips covered in a white sauce.

After taking several mouthfuls, Alyiakal says, "Chaem, you grew up near the Great Forest, but did you ever serve at any of the posts there?"

"I can't say that I did, ser." The older captain chuckles. "Near on every other kind of post, Esalia, Fyrad, Chulbyn, Isahl, Luuval before it fell into the water, even Terimot and Sycaast."

"Sycaast? That's somewhere I've never heard of," admits Alyiakal.

"It was on the north coast, about a hundred kays west of Biehl. Used to be a port there, not much of one, but it silted up. Only spent a year there before they closed it. I couldn't see why they even had a port. The land there was rocky, not even much good for sheep. I couldn't say I was unhappy to leave."

"With that description, I can see why," replies Alyiakal, before turning to Kessmyr. "Rewaal's another place I'm not familiar with. Could you tell me a bit more about it?"

"There's not a lot to say, ser. That's one place where whitestone comes from. Not as many work in the quarry these days, and some of the folks who live there have jobs in other towns but live in Rewaal because the houses are cheaper. A couple of Magi'i live there. They make sure the stonecutters work right. Most people only stay a year or two. Those who know say the Magi'i working at the quarry are being disciplined, but the Magi'i never talk about it."

"I never heard about anything like that," says Baassyn.

"Neither have I," adds Alyiakal, "but it wouldn't surprise me." *Not after having met the Third Magus and a few other Magi'i.* "That's definitely interesting." He turns to Nolaan. "Did seeing all the Mirror Lancers coming and going through Chulbyn make you want to be a Mirror Lancer?"

"No, ser." Nolaan grins again. "It made me want to be an officer. I never wanted to be crammed into the rear of a firewagon."

The other officers at the table smile, even Baassyn.

"Suraat, since I've never been to Cyad," begins Alyiakal, "I'd be interested to know what part of the city you think is the most interesting and why you think so?"

Suraat doesn't answer immediately, most likely because he expected a more personal question, which is why Alyiakal didn't ask one.

Finally, the undercaptain says, "The Magi'i quarter, I suppose. The dwellings are large, but not garish. They convey power, but the kind of power that doesn't need to be flaunted . . ."

As Suraat speaks, Alyiakal studies him with eyes and senses, finding that the junior undercaptain has slightly higher innate levels of both order and chaos, but no trace of shields. The undercaptain's order/chaos levels, combined with his precise speech, strongly suggest a Magi'i background.

". . . dwellings in the Merchanter quarter range from modest houses to sprawling small palaces, but even the modest houses have a trace of the overdone or garish."

"That's very interesting," says Alyiakal, meaning every word. "How would you describe the Palace of Light?"

"Imposing, but even shining in full sunlight, there's a feeling of shadowed depth."

"As I said, I've never been there," replies Alyiakal, "but I imagine that's often the case where great power is involved."

"Some senior officers are like that," adds Chaem. "You get the feeling that there's something else there."

"The current Captain-Commander's like that," Alyiakal says.

"You know him, ser?" asks Kessmyr.

"Years ago, he was the post commander at Guarstyad when I was there. Then, several years ago, he visited Lhaarat after we discovered the second dissident hamlet."

"Dissident hamlet?" asks Baassyn.

Alyiakal explains the dissidents, and by the time the discussion is over, so is dinner.

Alyiakal and Baassyn are the first to leave, walking from the officers' mess across the avenue to the headquarters building and into the post commander's study. There, Alyiakal lifts a striker to the wick of the wall lamp but uses chaos to light the lamp. Then he sets the striker down on the corner of the desk and seats himself behind it, gesturing for Baassyn to take a seat. "Before we get to talking about the post and transferring command, I'd like to know your thoughts about the raider attack."

"The number of raiders seems quite unusual, but the report from Squad Leader Faaln and the spoils certainly support that. I'd guess their harvests were poor, and they know we get more supplies in late Harvest and early fall. When their scouts saw how few lancers escorted those supplies . . . they couldn't resist."

"That makes sense," agrees Alyiakal, "except for one detail—the number of raiders. According to Squad Leader Faaln, the recent raids around Pemedra have involved far fewer. In the past, there haven't been any raider hamlets in the valleys south of Pemedra. Even if the raiders saw us on the second day, there wasn't enough time for them to send for more men and reach us by midday today."

"That's a disturbing observation, ser."

"There are several possibilities, of course," replies Alyiakal. "They could have had scouts watching the roads closer to Syadtar, but I was told that no one at Syadtar had seen any raiders within a day's ride of the post. Or they could have sent a larger band on the hope that Pemedra would get more supplies with fewer lancers guarding those supplies, but that has certain . . . improbabilities."

"Ah . . . yes, ser. I can see why you're concerned."

"Do you have any further thoughts on the matter?"

"Not at present, ser."

Alyiakal senses that he's disconcerted the overcaptain, again, but only says, "Now about the post . . . how would you describe its current situation and state of readiness?"

"With the replacements you escorted here, all the companies are at full complement. The hundred firelances that came with the supplies will allow one spare firelance for each ranker and officer. That obviously limits any firelance training with actual firebolts."

"Go on," Alyiakal prompts.

"My best estimate is that two-thirds of the rankers currently have little or no experience in dealing with anything except occasional raids."

Given what Faaln said, that means most don't even have experience with large numbers of barbarians or raiders. "What about mounts?"

"There are currently twenty-one spare mounts. That includes the five you captured."

Alyiakal goes through his mental list of questions, including the state of stores, supplies, and fodder, and listens as Baassyn replies. At the end, he nods and says, "That will do for now. There's also one other matter that I want you to know about first."

"Ser?"

"Starting on oneday, there will be daily patrols, and I'll accompany each officer on a patrol."

"There's already a schedule posted . . ."

Alyiakal holds up a placating hand. "I'm sure the officers will understand. I'd like to see the revised schedule before you post it tomorrow. I'd also like to see the current directives book this evening, since it's been a season since I saw any directives. I need to catch up on the latest from headquarters, as well as read any instructions directed specifically at Pemedra."

"Yes, ser."

"Where are the master account ledgers?"

"Those are normally kept by the deputy post commander." Baassyn's voice doesn't convey the defensiveness he feels.

"I understand, but as post commander, I'm responsible for what's in them. So why don't you get them and the directives? I'll wait."

Alyiakal senses Baassyn's resignation even before the overcaptain says, "I'll be back shortly, ser."

Only a fraction of a quint passes before the overcaptain returns with the two ledgers and the clipbook of directives.

"Thank you, Baassyn." Alyiakal successfully stifles the strong desire to yawn. "I need to do some reading here, and I won't keep you any longer tonight. I'll see you in the morning, and we can go over and sign the change of command papers then."

"Yes, ser."

Once Baassyn has left, Alyiakal begins to read the directives beginning with the most recent, dated the fifth sevenday of Harvest, updating the requirements for training lancer recruits by those posts authorized to conduct such training. Then he reads through the others until he reaches the directives he'd received at Lhaarat. After that he skims through the directives beneath, looking for any that are specific to Pemedra. He stops after going through the directives for the past year, only finding one addressed to Pemedra. That one, sent the previous Autumn, instructs Majer Moryah to provide a full squad to escort all large shipments of matériel and provisions to Pemedra, if requested by the commanding officer of Syadtar Post.

Three wagons apparently don't amount to a large shipment for Subcommander Zekkaat, or perhaps Baertal.

Then he returns to another directive he'd marked and rereads it carefully, noting one particular phrase:

> *. . . post commanders should take care not to create situations requiring excessive force to resolve, particularly excessive use of firelances, when other measures could prove equally effective in obtaining satisfactory resolution of a given situation . . .*

Alyiakal frowns. He doesn't recall that directive. He checks the date, which turns out to be fourth fiveday of Harvest, just after he'd left Lhaarat, but certainly before the directive would have reached the post.

Alyiakal sets the directives clipbook aside and picks up the first of the account ledgers. After looking at the entries on the latest ten pages, he gets the feeling that something is not quite right, but even after half a glass, he cannot discover what bothers him. *But that might be because you're tired and your eyes are burning.*

He closes the ledger he's been perusing and stands, then stretches, before putting out the wall lamp.

After he leaves the study that is now his and walks back to his quarters, Alyiakal considers what he's seen, beginning with an attack by one of the largest raider groups he's ever encountered, and ending in his meetings with the post officers. Chaem seems solid, but Alyiakal feels he'll likely be too cautious on his own, especially after what Alyiakal has seen just so far about the immediate past post leadership. Kessmyr looks to have the right outlook, but painfully little real experience, and both undercaptains are greener than spring grass. Then there's Baassyn, but Alyiakal needs to know more about the overcaptain and the post before making any decisions or judgments he could come to regret.

And you've got raider problems and likely are going to face difficulties with the barbarians to the north or the Cerlynese, if not both.

XXVII

Alyiakal, predictably, does not sleep well, and wakes with images of raiders being turned into ashes going through his head, no matter how much he tries to tell himself that they were the ones who attacked and that he couldn't have trusted most of the replacements to do anything but waste chaos.

Much as he wants to go back through the ledger accounts for the post, doing that can wait. What's more important is finding out just how prepared and capable his officers and rankers are.

He arrives at the officers' mess moments after Baassyn, offers a cheerful "Good morning," and then motions all the officers to the table, where he joins them and immediately sits. He serves himself from the platters on the table and follows with a sip from his mug to allow the others to eat. He tries not to wince as he tastes the grass ale, even more bitter and "off" than he recalls.

"How are your quarters?" asks Baassyn.

"I was so tired that I really didn't notice much last night," replies Alyiakal. "But this morning I found they're more than sufficient . . . and quite clean." He takes a bite of the egg scramble, then asks, since no one else is talking, "Have you had any grass fires in the last few years?"

"I heard that there was one two years back," says Chaem. "Started just north of the post. Couldn't tell it now."

"It's been hot enough this year," adds Baassyn, "so dry that we haven't even had the dry thunderstorms that usually spark that kind of fire."

"Dry Winters as well?" asks Alyiakal.

"No," answers Baassyn. "Maybe not quite as much snow as usual, but not dry."

That doesn't surprise Alyiakal, since the previous Winter at Lhaarat had been much the same.

After more casual conversation, Alyiakal finishes his breakfast and, reluctantly, the mug of grass ale, then says, "For Pemedra to continue as an effective Mirror Lancer post, I need to understand your capabilities. For that reason, I'm having the patrol schedule changed, and I will accompany each of you on patrol for the near future, starting tomorrow. Areas being patrolled may be changed, and you'll be patrolling farther from the post than in the recent past. My experience yesterday suggests that raiders and barbarians may attack with more riders. The Cerlynese may well encourage new groups of raiders to attack in the areas for which Pemedra is responsible, and, in the future, we could see armsmen from Cerlyn, as Lhaarat Post has over the past several years."

The last phrase gets the full attention of all the officers, even Baassyn.

After a moment, the overcaptain asks, "Why do you think the Cerlynese would attack Pemedra?"

"I don't know whether the Duke will or not, but I can't believe that he's pleased about losing close to ten companies of armsmen to the Mirror Lancers. He could attack either Lhaarat or Pemedra. While Pemedra is closer, he likely attacked Kraaslaen because it's the closest actual town in Cyador, and there's a decent road from Cerlyn to Kraaslaen that follows the front of the Westhorns all the way to Jakaafra."

From his previous posting at Pemedra, Alyiakal well knows that there are only trails from the hills north of Pemedra all the way through the valley beyond until they reach the stream that marks the border of Cerlyn.

"It sounds to me that he's more likely to attack Kraaslaen again," says Baassyn.

"You may be right," agrees Alyiakal, "but if he raises a large force, we're the closest other Mirror Lancer post. We'll need to be prepared for that eventuality."

"Do you think anything will happen this Autumn?"

"That's up to the Duke. We'll just have to see, but I wanted you all to understand that we might be involved."

"We don't even patrol that far," says Baassyn.

"Not recently, I understand," replies Alyiakal.

"There's little beyond the hills, just barbarians."

"Four hamlets of peaceful barbarians, as I recall," says Alyiakal, "and one of hotheaded and arrogant raiders."

Chaem and Kessmyr exchange quick glances.

"You've been there, ser?" asks Baassyn cautiously.

"Years ago. I was sent by headquarters to do an in-depth reconnaissance of the grass valley beyond the north hills." Alyiakal briefly describes what his company discovered, then adds, "We'll need to discover how much that's changed."

Baassyn looks like he might say something, but then just nods.

Alyiakal looks at his empty plate and makes sure that all the officers are finished eating before he stands, then turns to Baassyn and asks quietly, "When will you have the papers ready?"

"In a quint or so."

"I'll see you then."

After leaving the mess, Alyiakal goes to the officers' study down the corridor, alone, since no other officers follow him, not that they have to, given that it's eightday, and no patrols are scheduled. He surveys the table desks, one for each company, each with a file chest, before turning his attention to a map of the area north of Pemedra laid out on the Third Company desk. From what he sees and can recall, there are no changes to the map since he left, and, in fact, some changes he made are missing. He finds it unlikely that there have been no changes in six years, and wonders if that's because the Third Company post commanders haven't bothered with the map . . . and if none of the company officers have dared to.

Another thing to look into.

Alyiakal leaves the officers' study and makes his way across the avenue to the headquarters building.

Arriving at his study, Baassyn joins him immediately. "I have the transfer-of-command papers here, ser."

"Good." Alyiakal takes the proffered sheets and reads through them, then sits behind the desk, and looks for a pen and an inkwell, finding them in the single desk drawer. He signs both copies and returns one to Baassyn.

"I'll have a new patrol schedule for you to look at shortly, ser."

"I'd like to start with the most junior undercaptain on the first patrol. That's Suraat, isn't it?"

"He is, by a year. Nolaan should be up for captain next Summer. If that's all, ser?"

"For now. I'm sure I'll have a few more questions."

When Baassyn leaves, Alyiakal returns his attention, briefly, to the account ledgers, but closes them when he realizes that it will take more time than he wants to devote at the moment to ferreting out possible errors or other discrepancies.

Next, he opens the file chest on the side table, hoping to find recent patrol reports. After ascertaining that they're current, he returns to his desk to begin writing his own report on the resupply and replacement patrol, which will include the outsized raider attack. He'll also have to make a copy for Subcommander Zekkaat, with a brief cover note, even if he won't be sending either until the next dispatch run.

More than a glass later, having finished with the report and the copy, he starts reading the file on each of the company officers, and on Baassyn. Among the interesting facts he gains from them are that Chaem is indeed a former senior squad leader who has been rated as a solid company commander at previous postings, none of which were border postings, and who won't earn a stipend for another two years, when his current posting at Pemedra will end. Kessmyr is from Rewaal, has just made captain, and ranked tenth in his group leaving Kynstaar. Nolaan was in the middle of his Kynstaar group, but ranked first in blades and weapons, while Suraat's best area was riding and horsemanship. Baassyn is older than he looks and spent almost ten years as a captain, with middling ratings, before being promoted to overcaptain.

Not exactly the most prepossessing group of officers . . . and you have more actual patrol and combat experience than all of them put together.

He sets aside the officer files and begins to read through the patrol reports, starting with the most recent.

A Second Company report from the previous fiveday states that raiders were sighted northwest of Pemedra approaching a hamlet five kays north of the post but disappeared before the company could reach them. There were no signs of hoofprints or other tracks farther south or on the trails to the north. The company could not discover where the raiders entered the hills.

Alyiakal shakes his head, then continues reading.

After a glass of reading, it's clear to Alyiakal that the scope of the company patrols and the distance they ride from the post are far less than when he was at Pemedra, but so far he's found nothing to indicate why, except possibly the instructions from Mirror Lancer headquarters to be sparing in firelance use, but there's no reference to that anywhere.

When Alyiakal senses Baassyn entering his study, he stands and walks to join the overcaptain.

Baassyn looks up from his desk. "Yes, ser?"

Alyiakal takes one of the chairs in front of the desk. "I've been reading the patrol reports. There's something that most have in common."

"Raiders, I'm sure," replies Baassyn.

"That's only part of it. I'd be interested to know Majer Moryah's standing orders about dealing with raiders. I haven't been able to find anything in writing."

"I don't believe he ever put anything in writing, ser."

"So what were the company officers supposed to do?"

"Capture or kill any raiders they encountered."

"How successful would you judge they have been recently?" Alyiakal asks conversationally.

"By what standard, ser?"

"By the standard you just mentioned."

Baassyn stiffens slightly. "The raiders don't stick around once they see a patrol, so they've never captured any."

"So far as I can tell from the patrol reports, no one seems to know exactly where the raiders come from, except from the north or northwest."

"The majer felt that protecting the valley was the mandate of the post."

"I didn't see any reference to that."

"Majer Moryah received a number of dispatches from Subcommander Zekkaat. I'm most certain that he wouldn't have done anything that the subcommander felt was unwise."

"I'm sure he wouldn't," replies Alyiakal, keeping the sarcasm he feels out of his voice. Then he stands. "Thank you, Baassyn. You've made a number of things clearer."

"Yes, ser."

While Baassyn's voice is pleasant, Alyiakal senses that the overcaptain is definitely concerned. *As he should be.*

XXVIII

On oneday morning, Alyiakal carries his healer's satchel and two bottles of grass ale cut with order-infused water to the officers' side of the stable, where he saddles the gray gelding, leads him out and mounts, then obtains a firelance from the armorer's cart, and rides to join Undercaptain Suraat as Third Company forms up.

"Good morning, ser."

"Good morning, Undercaptain," replies Alyiakal.

"Might I ask about the patrol route, ser? The schedule only stated that it was to be along the northwest perimeter."

"We're going to be looking for possible routes that raiders are using to enter the valley, since it appears that such knowledge is currently lacking."

"Ser . . . but if they're already here . . . ?"

"Exactly, Undercaptain. If you know all the possible routes into the valley, you also know all the possible ways out of the valley. That should make finding or following them easier, and will make it easier to reduce the number of raiders and their enthusiasm for raiding." Alyiakal pauses, then adds, "You'll still give the commands. I'll give you the directions. After the company is formed up, have them head north out of Pemedra."

"Yes, ser."

In less than half a quint, Third Company rides north on the wide sunstone avenue toward the northern gates as the white sun clears the hills to the east.

After half a glass, Third Company passes two hamlets, one to the right of the road and one to the left, each set a kay or so from the main road. More than a glass later, the company nears the split in the road.

"Call a break when we reach the split. What else should you do?"

"Have the scouts check and report on any tracks."

After the company halts and Suraat orders the scouts out to report, Alyiakal asks the undercaptain, "How many patrols have you taken since you got here?"

"Three, ser. This will be the fourth."

"Did Overcaptain Baassyn ever accompany you on patrols?"

"He did on my first patrol."

"Have you taken the company into the hills?"

"Not yet, ser."

Half a quint later, the scouts return.

"No tracks to the northeast, sers."

"No tracks to the north, sers, but a horse and a cart to northwest, sers."

As soon as the scouts move away, Alyiakal says, "We'll see where the carter is going, since we're headed in that direction anyway."

Another half quint later, the company remounts and takes the northwest trail, which turns south at the edge of the base of the hills after several kays. Before long they reach a trail angling northwest into the hills. The carter's tracks also turn onto the trail.

"What do you know about that trail?" Alyiakal asks.

"It heads into Jeranyi lands. That's about all," replies Suraat.

"Have you gone that way?"

"Only for a few kays. I wasn't to leave the valley yet."

"It leads to the West Branch valley. It's easier to get there from Isahl, but the advantage of going this way is that the route is more open, and it's harder for the Jeranyi to mount a surprise attack."

"You've been that way, ser?"

"On my first posting." *When I was as green as you.* "Just keep that knowledge in mind. You might find it useful."

The company continues south along the trail at the base of the hills. After a time, Alyiakal looks north, sees the gap between the two ridges, but decides not to mention it to Suraat.

As Third Company nears the point where Alyiakal recalls the path leading into the hills, at first, he doesn't discern any traces in the high, golden, autumn grass that lies between the trail and the rocky ground at the base of the hills. Then, just ahead to his left, he sees a line of barely disturbed grass that angles toward the hills and a defile he can barely make out beyond an area of sparse grass, and a few bushes and scrawny evergreens. He also sees hoofprints coming from the south that turn in to the grass on the north side of the trail, hoofprints the scouts either didn't see or ignored.

"Halt the company, and call in the scouts," Alyiakal says quietly.

Once Suraat issues the order, Alyiakal rides forward to where the hoofprints enter the grass, keeping to the center of the road, while pointing and saying to Suraat, "Stay to the left, away from the hoofprints."

When Alyiakal halts, he asks, "What are the scouts' names?"

"Ahuur and Laakyn. The taller, thinner one is Ahuur."

Alyiakal waits until the two scouts rein up short of the two officers.

"Sers?"

"Scout Ahuur," asks Alyiakal, pointing to the sandy earth at the edge of the trail, "how old do you think those hoofprints are?"

"Several days, ser, but less than an eightday."

"How many mounts, do you think?"

"Five or six, I'd say."

"What do they tell you?"

Ahuur swallows. "They head into the grass, ser."

"And why would anyone head into the grass?"

"To go somewhere that the trail doesn't, ser?"

"Let's see where they go." Alyiakal turns to Suraat. "Detail five lancers to accompany us." At Suraat's questioning look, he adds, "You're coming, too, Undercaptain."

Alyiakal leads the way, following the traces of bent grass for more than a hundred yards to the point where the grass dwindles to sparse clumps, and he sees a continuation of thc hoofprints. Hc reins up and points.

"What do you see here, Scout Laakyn?"

"Hoofprints, ser."

"Where are they headed?"

"Toward the hills, ser."

"Since it looks like they're following a path," says Alyiakal, "so will we." He guides the gray along the path as it winds through the low bushes and scattered reddish rocks set in sandy red soil too poor for anything except occasional scrub evergreens. He reins up when he reaches the loose sand over the hard and rocky ground at the base of the hills.

He can see occasional hoofprints leading to the defile between two large boulders, although the winds have wiped away some of the prints and filled others with loose sand. He motions to the nearest scout. "Laakyn, follow this path between the boulders there. Ahuur, you follow him. Then come back here and report."

"Yes, ser."

Once the scouts are a few yards away, Alyiakal turns in the saddle and looks to Suraat. "Do you think these hoofprints might be from the raiders no one could find on fiveday?"

"They might be, ser."

"Let's see what the scouts have to say."

Little more than a half quint later, Ahuur and Laakyn return.

Alyiakal senses their worry, but he simply asks, "What did you discover?"

The two scouts exchange glances. Then Laakyn replies, "There's a narrow trail that goes up the hillside and then winds between two hills and heads east. There are hoofprints as far as we could see."

"Is it wide enough for a cart or wagon?" asks Alyiakal.

"No, ser," replies Ahuur.

"That's enough for now," says Alyiakal. "Those riders are long gone. We'll head back to the company."

Two quints pass before Third Company re-forms and proceeds south.

Shortly afterward, Alyiakal asks, "Is there any indication of that trail on your map, Undercaptain?"

"No, ser."

"Don't you think it might be wise to add it when you get back to the post?"

"Yes, ser." Suraat's voice is definitely subdued.

Alyiakal has Suraat take the patrol south far enough to reach one of the narrow roads east and has the company follow it back to Pemedra. He says little more to the undercaptain, except to issue quiet orders.

Once they return to the post, and after Suraat dismisses the company, Alyiakal looks to the undercaptain. "My study in two quints."

"Yes, ser."

As Alyiakal rides to the stable, he can't help wondering what happened to Pemedra. He can't blame Suraat, but he definitely has to question Majer Moryah's leadership. He unsaddles and grooms the gray, then heads to his study. Once there, he leaves the door ajar and walks to the slightly open window. Standing there, he takes a slow deep breath and thinks about how to handle Suraat. Finally, he sits behind the desk.

Half a quint passes before the undercaptain arrives.

"Ser?" ventures Suraat cautiously.

"Close the door, Undercaptain, and take a seat."

Suraat sits on the edge of the chair.

"What do you think our purpose is here at Pemedra?"

"To stop raiders and possible armsmen from Jerans or Cerlyn from entering Cyador and raiding."

Alyiakal smiles pleasantly. "How can we stop them from entering if we don't encounter them until they're in the valley?"

Suraat frowns, then says, "By making them pay for attacking the hamlets?"

"I've read through all the patrol reports for the past year. If I recall correctly, only three raiders were killed, and none were captured. None of the reports mentioned any loss to the hamlets. Are you aware of any goods or women being taken?" Alyiakal projects a sense of need for truth.

"Ah . . . some goods . . . two women that I know of, but all that happened before I got here."

"Is it likely that those were the only losses?"

"No, ser."

"I'll leave you to think about how effective driving off raiders appears to be, especially *after* they've already obtained goods and women." Alyiakal pauses momentarily. "Should I have been able to notice those hoofprints before your company scouts did?"

"No, ser."

"Did you see that many hoofprints on the northwest trail, either before or after the road to the West Branch Valley?"

"No, ser."

"Then what tentative conclusions should you draw?"

"That the trail you found leads in some way to the northwest road to the Jeranyi lands."

"What else?"

Suraat frowns.

"Where did the raiders come from?" presses Alyiakal. "How did they get to that trail if we didn't see any tracks elsewhere on the patrol?"

"The raiders had to come from the northwest, possibly Jerans, or there has to be a way from the north through the hills to get to the trail you discovered."

"Since the raiders went that way, at least one of your suggestions has to be accurate. Both could be, but we won't know until someone follows that narrow path through the hills. What concerns me is that neither you nor your scouts noticed the tracks at the side of the trail."

"Yes, ser," says Suraat.

"You have a few things to consider, Undercaptain. That's all for now."

"By your leave, ser?"

Alyiakal nods, sensing that Suraat is both cowed and angry, even though Alyiakal never raised his voice or spoke sarcastically.

How did it come to this? It's as though the officers have been given the message not to patrol very far. That makes sense for Suraat for a while, but what Baassyn has said suggests that it applies to the other company officers as well, with the implication that they're not to use firelances except as a last resort. While Alyiakal has noted the recent directive to cut back on the firelance use, the officers at Pemedra were doing that well before that directive was issued, at least from what Baassyn and Suraat both indicated.

How far back had the change occurred?

Draakyr was deputy post commander for the two years after Alyiakal had left, and he certainly wouldn't have put up with such sloppy patrolling.

Alyiakal takes a deep breath, stands, and walks to the file chests, where he looks for—and finds—the command-succession folder. He quickly reads through the entries and discovers that Overcaptain Draakyr was briefly acting commander of Pemedra in Harvest of 100 A.F., prior to his taking his stipend. *Draakyr wouldn't likely put up with laxness . . . but could that be why he took his stipend? Or did the laxness come later?*

Alyiakal keeps reading, finding that Majer Taayt commanded after Majer Klaavyl, but just for two years, when he was succeeded by Majer Whyllt, who held the position for only a year, until replaced by Majer Moryah in Autumn of 101 A.F., but the record doesn't show why Whyllt only commanded for a year. *So what happened to Whyllt? Death, ill health, removal by headquarters?*

The history of the company officers shows that Overcaptain Quaelt succeeded Draakyr, then Baassyn. *So Baassyn never served under Whyllt.*

Does anyone at the post know what happened? Then, Alyiakal nods, stands, and leaves his study and the headquarters building.

He strides down the avenue to the building holding both officers' and rankers' mess, as well as the officers' study and the study for senior squad leaders, and heads to the kitchen. As he walks through the rankers' mess hall toward the kitchen doorway, one of the cooks steps out of the kitchen. "Majer."

The cook looks familiar, and then Alyiakal smiles. "Famuur!"

"It's really you, ser? I heard the new commander was a Majer Alyiakal, but I couldn't . . ." The cook breaks off his words and smiles. "You looking for a carrot for your mount?"

"Not at the moment. I was just coming to see if there was anyone left here from when I was a company officer."

"There's me . . . and Laandar . . ."

"You're the head cook now?"

"No, ser. Laandar is." Famuur grins. "But I'm deputy head cook."

"Good for you!" Alyiakal pauses. "Doesn't that mean you deal with the hamlets in procuring provisions?"

"Yes, ser."

"How is that going?"

"Not as well as it might, ser."

"Poor harvests?"

"From what the headmen tell me, the harvests are about the same. It's the raiders. They're picking off lambs and calves and sometimes even girls." The cook glances around. "The headmen think that Majer Moryah didn't care that much unless folks or lancers were killed."

Frig! Not that Alyiakal hasn't expected something, but it's still a shock to hear Famuur say it. "They said that?"

"Yes, ser. More than one of them."

Alyiakal looks around the mess hall and sees the mess boys scurrying to set up the serving line. He hadn't realized it's that late, and he says, "We need to talk, but that can wait for a bit. I don't need to get in the way of the men getting fed." He smiles. "Until later."

"Yes, ser."

Alyiakal walks from the rankers' mess hall and stops. *You're almost at the officers' mess. You might as well take advantage of the situation.* He heads toward the officers' study, then steps into a vacant side hall, where he raises a concealment before carefully making his way to the officers' mess. While the mess orderly is already there, none of the officers are, and Alyiakal waits half a quint before two officers enter.

"Did you talk to Suraat?" asks the taller officer, Kessmyr from his height and voice. "What did he have to say about his patrol?"

"Not much . . . except that things would be very different," replies the other, who has to be Nolaan. "He wouldn't say how, just that we'd find out. Did you find out anything from Chaem?"

"He said that the majer looks to be the kind of officer you don't see much anymore, the kind that knows a lot more than you think and can do everything better than his junior officers."

"The kind you don't argue with, it sounds like."

"I said that, and he shook his head. Said that that kind usually listens. Won't always agree."

"So why didn't Suraat say more?" asks Nolaan.

"I still say he comes from the Magi'i. They don't take well to someone who knows more."

"So why's he here?"

"What else can a Magi'i son do if he can't handle chaos? He also might come from the wrong side of the bed."

Kessmyr's observation impresses Alyiakal, but then he senses other officers entering the building. He slips out of the mess and down the hall to the officers' study, now vacant, where he drops the concealment, then waits until the hallway is clear before making his way back to the officers' mess.

He says, "As you were," as soon as he steps into the mess, and then takes his place at the head of the table.

He lifts his wineglass, then takes a sip of the barely passable red wine that he finds far better than the grass ale. The platters before him hold sliced beef slathered in something too thick to be juice and too thin to be gravy, near-potatoes in a cheese and cream casserole, and the inevitable spring beans. He takes modest portions of the beef and near-potatoes, and even less of the beans, then cuts a portion of the beef and eats it.

The other officers begin to eat.

After a short time, Baassyn asks, "On your patrol, ser, did you find any great differences since the last time you were here?"

"The grass looks very much the same," replies Alyiakal with a pleasant smile. "So do the hills. We'll have to see about the rest. In reading over some of the recent patrol reports, I did notice that there isn't any mention of the arms used by the raiders."

"Well, ser," declares Chaem, with a twinkle in his eye, "when I came here two years ago, they were using big blades and horn bows. They used the blades badly, and the bows decently, and I don't see that's changed."

"If that's the case," replies Alyiakal, "we should be grateful that the Jeranyi and the Cerlynese haven't gotten around to providing the barbarians with bronze shields and spear-throwers again."

"Again?" asks Baassyn.

Alyiakal explains briefly about the weapons and shields the Jeranyi provided to the West Branch barbarians and the shields the Cerlynese used, then takes a small swallow of wine and some more beef and near-potatoes.

"Ser," asks Nolaan, "did you know a Captain Torkaal?"

"I did. I take it that he instructed you in blades at Kynstaar?"

"Yes, ser."

Alyiakal smiles. "I gather he was rather demanding."

Nolaan laughs ruefully. "You could say that, ser."

"One of the best officers I've worked with," adds Alyiakal. "Do you know if he's still at Kynstaar?"

"I believe he should be, ser. He was promoted to captain just before I left Kynstaar. I heard they extended his posting there for a year, possibly two."

"Because he was that good?" asks Kessmyr.

"That's what we thought, but no one said so," replies Nolaan. "None of the other officers were anywhere as good."

"I'm not surprised," says Alyiakal. "He was an excellent patrol officer, too." He takes another small swallow of wine, not wanting to pursue the matter, because it would only be seen as self-serving.

Kessmyr looks at Nolaan, but says nothing, although Alyiakal has no doubt that Kessmyr will want to know more later.

After dinner, Alyiakal makes his way back to his study, thinking that he needs to begin a letter to Saelora because the post is likely to receive dispatch couriers sometime in the next eightday, and he doesn't want the letter to be rushed.

When Alyiakal approaches his study door, however, Baassyn rises from behind his desk and walks out to meet him. "How was your patrol with Undercaptain Suraat?"

"It was instructive for both of us," replies Alyiakal, heading into his study and motioning for Baassyn to follow. "We'll have to see if the patrols with other officers follow the same pattern."

"Instructive?"

Alyiakal gestures for the overcaptain to take a chair, then settles behind the desk. "That's as good a term as any. I learned some more about Suraat, and he learned a few things as well." Alyiakal pauses only briefly. "Where were you posted before Pemedra?"

"Ruumyl."

For a moment, Alyiakal couldn't recall the name. "The waypost north of the Great Canal on the whitestone road to Ilypsya?"

Baassyn nods. "I was officer in charge of the supply post there."

"From there to here seems a bit odd." More like bizarre, but Alyiakal isn't about to say that.

"As I heard it, ser, Majer Whyllt became . . . eccentric. While Majer Taayt could handle operational duties, Overcaptain Quaelt did not have the skills to deal with the logistics of a post such as Pemedra but covered those shortcomings. After Majer Moryah arrived and discovered various discrepancies, the majer requested a replacement as deputy post commander with a stronger background in supply and logistics."

Some of what Baassyn said doesn't make total sense, because Quaelt remained as deputy for two years before Baassyn became the deputy post commander. *There's not much you can do about the past except be very careful . . . and quietly skeptical . . . as if you don't already have enough problems.*

Abruptly, he realizes something that he should have caught. Baassyn has only been at Pemedra for a year and had nothing to do with his predecessor's shortcomings. There's also nothing in the logs and files even hinting at the situation except Majer Whyllt's short time as post commander, but Alyiakal realizes no officer would want to suggest that both the post commander and his deputy were incompetent. "I see. That was an unfortunate coincidence, apparently."

"Unhappily," agrees Baassyn.

"Is that why there are so many updates and corrections in the account ledgers? And some entries that are . . . unbalanced, for lack of a better word."

"There are still some discrepancies that remain unresolved."

"Unresolved?"

"Payments made for supplies that apparently were never received. I have an accounting of those."

"You didn't send them to headquarters?" asks Alyiakal.

"Majer Whyllt is, or was, the son of the previous Majer-Commander. He was allowed to take a stipend earlier than usual. He died in Cyad shortly thereafter."

Alyiakal doesn't even try to hide his wince. "And Majer Moryah was ordered not to do anything that would call attention to Pemedra Post?"

"That was my assumption. The majer never said anything to that effect."

"What about Overcaptain Quaelt?"

"I have no knowledge about the overcaptain, other than his ineptly creative accounts. He departed Pemedra a considerable time before I arrived."

What a frigging mess! After a long moment, Alyiakal asks, "Is there any reason why you cannot now note those accounting discrepancies and bring them to my attention so that I can forward them to the Captain-Commander . . . as a matter of information only? You could note that the discrepancies all occurred before your arrival and were so numerous that it took almost a year to discover what you did, and that it's unlikely the remainder can be resolved."

"The Captain-Commander, ser?"

"I was under the impression that he is responsible for less urgent matters. These discrepancies began, from what you tell me, four years ago and ceased about a year ago. They're not your fault, and certainly not mine, but I'd rather not have either of us accused of hiding improper and possibly unlawful accounting practices."

Baassyn nods slowly. "I have a draft . . ."

Alyiakal can feel a sense of relief, and he has a strong suspicion that Majer Moryah had procrastinated in informing headquarters, at least officially, or possibly refused to do so. "If you'd provide that, I can go over it, and we'll proceed from there."

"Yes, ser. Now?"

"Now or first thing in the morning."

After Baassyn leaves, Alyiakal just sits there for several long moments before taking out paper and pen.

XXIX

Alyiakal rises early on twoday, since he wants to see if Baassyn's draft report dealing with Pemedra's previous accounting discrepancies is ready so that he can read it before going on patrol with Kessmyr and First Company. When Alyiakal reaches his study, the report is waiting in his box. He reads it through, sees that it is well-written and that the numbers make sense, then writes out a few suggested changes in the margins and hands it to Baassyn before the two head for the mess.

"Your report is well-written," says Alyiakal. "My suggestions are more political, as you'll see."

"You're showing a certain urgency, ser."

"Necessary urgency," replies Alyiakal. "The rapid timing should make the situation clear."

"It may not reflect well on Majer Moryah."

Alyiakal knows full well that the rapid transmittal of a detailed report by the deputy post commander immediately after Alyiakal's arrival, especially one addressed directly to the Captain-Commander, will suggest to Laartol that Moryah was in no hurry to report the matter. "Do we have any choice, if it's not to reflect badly on both of us?"

"Put that way, ser, I can't argue."

"Do you know if Majer Moryah had any ties to headquarters?"

"I do not. He just wanted me to return logistics and accounts to working order. He never talked about headquarters, but there were dispatches and letters to and from headquarters addressed to him. He didn't share all of them with me, and he deflected any questions he didn't wish to answer in any detail with generalities."

"Interesting . . ." *And worrisome.*

"Yes, ser."

Since Baassyn believes he's telling the truth, and most likely is, if a slightly biased truth, it's almost certain that Moryah was keeping aspects of the matter hidden, but Alyiakal suspects some of those aspects may surface later.

All four company officers are in the mess when Alyiakal and Baassyn enter. Alyiakal simply gestures to the table, then seats himself. He takes a sip of ale, then serves himself some of the cheesed eggs and ham strips, waiting until all the officers have done the same before beginning to eat.

After several moments, Nolaan clears his throat, then asks, "Ser, will you be conducting blade drills here?"

Alyiakal senses Kessmyr's amusement, but smiles pleasantly. "Only if necessary, as Captain Torkaal may have mentioned. There will be formation drills, of course, once I've observed all companies on patrol."

"What kind of formation drills, ser?" asks Suraat.

"The kind necessary to deal with other armed and disciplined forces." Alyiakal senses the three younger company officers hide varying degrees of indifference, if not annoyance in the case of Suraat, but that Chaem not only approves but offers a slight nod.

"Do you think you'll really encounter armsmen, and not just raiders, this fall?" asks Baassyn.

"It's more likely late next Spring or next Summer, but that's up to the Jeranyi or the Cerlynese."

"Why do you think that?" asks Suraat.

"Because the weather in Autumn makes an attack riskier, and, at least at Lhaarat, we didn't see any signs of scouts once we were well into Harvest . . . and none of you have reported seeing scouts." Alyiakal doesn't sense any untoward personal chaos or unrest, which suggests no one saw and failed to report scouts, although it could also mean that they didn't see scouts or their tracks, which is definitely a possibility, especially where Suraat is concerned.

The remainder of breakfast conversation deals with speculation about the weather and when the first snow will arrive.

After breakfast, Alyiakal gets his riding gloves, jacket, and healing satchel from his quarters, then stops by the kitchen, where Famuur hurries up.

"This time, I would like a carrot. I have to do a patrol, but I'll be back to talk to you later."

The cook holds up a carrot. "I thought as much. I heard that you would be riding patrols."

"I can't seem to give that up." Alyiakal grins and accepts the carrot. "Until after the patrol."

He makes his way to the stable, and after dealing with the gray and giving him the carrot, leads him out, mounts, and rides to where First Company is forming up. After he rides up to Kessmyr, he gives the young captain the same instructions as he had Suraat, since First Company will begin by heading north out of the post. He watches closely as the rankers and squad leaders move into formation.

Less than a quint later, First Company rides through the north gates under a cloudless but hazy green-blue sky with a cool wind blowing out of the northeast.

A quint passes before Alyiakal asks, "Just how far is Rewaal from Cyad?"

"About fifteen kays, ser."

"What kind of town is it?"

"It's a small town in the center of the oilseed fields. Everyone there either grows oilseeds, presses them, or uses the oil for other purposes. There's a factorage that makes all the paint used in Cyador."

"I have to admit I didn't know that. How did you get to the Mirror Lancers from there?"

Kessmyr offers a chuckle and a wry smile. "My father owns one of the presses and the mill that makes feed from the seeds. I'm the fourth son. The dust or something in the mill made me cough all the time and gave me red blotches. So my father sent me to Kynstaar. Even with the tutoring and blade training he arranged for over the year before I left, he doubted I'd last the three years."

A year's worth of tutoring suggests to Alyiakal that Kessmyr's family is at least moderately well-off. "Then he must be pleased."

"More like relieved, ser."

"What about you?" asks Alyiakal with a touch of humor in his voice.

"I'm glad to be even here. I'm breathing air, not dust, and how successful I am depends on me, not on the price of oil."

"It also depends on your lancers."

"Yes, ser. I didn't mean to say—"

"I understand, Captain, but they depend on your leadership, and you have to depend on their skill and willingness to follow you." *Especially their willingness to follow you and your orders.*

Before long, the company passes the hamlet closest to Pemedra. The faintest trace of gray smoke rises into the hazy green-blue sky, and several people are working in gardens just outside the mudbrick walls, some turning the soil and others picking late vegetables, Alyiakal surmises.

A glass later, First Company reaches the split in the road, and Alyiakal has Kessmyr order a brief rest stop and have the scouts check the three trails for tracks. Then he asks, "How often do you take the northeast trail into the hills?"

"Whenever we've been ordered to, ser. Not as often as the north trail. The north way is much shorter."

"To and from Pemedra," Alyiakal agrees. "We'll take the northeast trail today."

After the rest stop, and after the scouts report on tracks, which appear limited to carts and footprints, the scouts lead the way northeast. A little more than three kays later, Alyiakal points to a much narrower trail heading off to the south-southwest. "Where does that lead?"

"Toward the post."

"Have you ridden it?"

"No, ser."

"It leads directly to the hamlet closest to the post, but not to the post itself."

The company continues on the northeast trail for another two kays until it reaches a point where the wider trail turns close to due north and a narrower trail runs south along the base of the hills bordering the eastern side of the valley.

"Call a halt," orders Alyiakal, "and have the scouts check both trails for tracks."

"Yes, ser."

When the two scouts return, the shorter lancer reports. "There's a horse-drawn cart heading south, with someone walking alongside the horse, and a pair of riders heading north. Older tracks of horses heading south. Those could be from two-three days ago."

"Good," says Alyiakal.

The company continues south for the next two glasses. Along the way, neither Alyiakal nor the scouts see any hoofprints leaving the trail, and Alyiakal suspects the carter is headed for the midvalley hamlet, with which Alyiakal had become all too familiar in his first posting. He doesn't see other riders, and the only significant order/chaos patterns are those of a grass cat tracking an antelope and her calf, but the antelope keeps the calf well away from the predator.

Shortly after that, Alyiakal orders another break.

During the break, Kessmyr asks, "Has the valley changed much since your posting here?"

"There's less trace of the burned-out stead north-northwest of the post, and it appears that raiders or smugglers have rediscovered a back road into the valley from the west. So far, here, I don't see much change. Sometimes, though, the changes you don't see are the ones to worry about."

Kessmyr frowns, then nods. "Because you don't think things have changed and you can be caught unprepared?"

Alyiakal just nods.

The company resumes riding south and after another glass reaches the junction with the narrow road leading to the midvalley hamlet. As Alyiakal has suspected, the cart tracks turn toward the hamlet.

"Have there been any recent raids on the hamlet?" asks Alyiakal.

"Not this year, ser. Early last Harvest there was one. I don't know the details. Third Company was the one that responded."

"Under Captain . . ." Alyiakal can't remember the name of the captain who had departed Pemedra earlier in Harvest.

"Faeth," supplies Kessmyr. "He was posted to Eastpoint."

"Have you ever met the headman?"

"No, ser." After a pause, Kessmyr asks, "Did you, ser?"

"Several times." Alyiakal doesn't volunteer more, and Kessmyr doesn't ask.

Alyiakal smiles when First Company passes the side road to the hamlet because he sees the cart tracks heading to the wooden gate in the middle of the mudbrick wall.

More than three glasses later, First Company rides through the southern gates, having encountered only a few local carts on the ride north to the post.

Once Kessmyr dismisses the company to duties, Alyiakal turns to Kessmyr. "I don't have much to say to you right now, Captain. I will be accompanying you again, selectively. There is one area where you need some improvement. In this valley, you should know where every path or road that a horse can take leads and its condition."

"Yes, ser."

"I'll see you at the evening mess." Alyiakal rides the gray to the stable, deals with him, then carries his healing satchel back to his quarters on his way to his study.

Once there, Alyiakal reads the clean and corrected version of Baassyn's report, then drafts a cover letter to Captain-Commander Laartol. The letter simply states that, as the incoming post commander, he feels that Mirror Lancer headquarters should be aware of past discrepancies in the post accounts, and that it has taken Overcaptain Baassyn, in addition to his other duties as well as acting as post commander, almost a year to trace accurately the expenditures and outlays over the three years prior to his arrival.

After completing it, he asks Baassyn to join him and read the transmittal letter. When Baassyn finishes, Alyiakal asks, "Is there anything I misrepresented or misstated?"

"No, ser."

"Then, let's sign and seal them. We need to send them off not later than fiveday, earlier if we get dispatch riders from Syadtar."

"We likely won't, ser."

"I suspect you're right, but I don't want to be seen as excessively hasty."

"Yes, ser."

Since the report is not an operational matter, Alyiakal only asks for a copy for the post files. He does not ask for a copy for Subcommander Zekkaat, especially given that Baertal is the deputy post commander at Syadtar.

After that, he leaves the study and makes his way to the kitchen, where he asks Famuur to step out into a corner of the rankers' mess hall.

Once there, Alyiakal says, "Before I forget, Famuur, my gray appreciated the carrot."

"I'm glad, ser."

"The other thing I wanted to ask you was how the post has changed, especially after Overcaptain Draakyr departed."

"The patrols were shorter, and less frequent. I could tell because the lancers returned to the post earlier in the afternoon, and the officers never asked for trail rations. That helped, especially the year Majer Whyllt was in charge, because we didn't have as many silvers for provisions. We got a few more silvers once Majer Moryah took over, but less than before. Last year was a little better."

"It helps to know that," says Alyiakal. "What can you tell me about Overcaptain Quaelt? In terms of supplies and provisions, that is."

"Beggin' your pardon, ser, but he didn't know sowshit about either. Cut back on what we could spend with the locals, as if there's any other way to get provisions. He couldn't understand that most of the grains for regular ale won't grow here, and that it's a bitch to get ale as good as we do. He didn't like us buying grass antelope, either." Famuur winks. "We just wrote it in the logs as beef calves, not that the locals ever sell calves. But he didn't understand that, either . . ."

Alyiakal just listens for half a quint, hoping he can remember everything—or most of it, anyway. When Famuur pauses, Alyiakal asks, "What about Overcaptain Baassyn?"

"Not all that friendly. Cold, sort of, but he knows his stuff. Watches close, but doesn't get in the way, unless he sees something out of line. All that's fine with us."

After what he said about Quaelt, that's almost a recommendation. "I appreciate that, Famuur. If there's anything you think I should know, just tell me." Alyiakal smiles and adds, "Over carrots and the like."

"Yes, ser. Best that way."

From the kitchen he returns to his study, where he starts a letter to Saelora, beginning with his safe arrival.

> *. . . travel to Pemedra took longer than I expected because of delays at Ilypsya, but I did get to meet the subcommander in charge as a result. I spent the night at Syadtar, where I met Subcommander Zekkaat. I was surprised to find his Deputy Commander was Majer Baertal, one of the officers I went through Kynstaar with years ago. Baertal hasn't changed a bit . . .*

That should be enough. Especially since he has mentioned Baertal's maneuverings when he's been in Vaeyal.

> *Then we had the long ride to Pemedra with supply wagons . . . a bit longer since we were attacked by a large band of raiders. That didn't go well for them, and we ended up with extra mounts, which are always useful. We suffered no casualties . . .*

Alyiakal stops writing after describing Pemedra briefly and saying the post itself had changed little, nor had the endless grass. He can add to it over the next day or so, ensuring she knows how much he appreciates and loves her, but he wants that to be at the end.

He tucks the letter into a drawer, stands, and heads to the evening mess.

XXX

On threeday, Alyiakal accompanies Chaem and Second Company on a patrol out the north road a little more than fifteen kays, five more than the older captain has patrolled before. Although they see scattered hoofprints and a few local wagons, they find no traces of large groups of riders, which, as Alyiakal well knows, doesn't preclude raider scouts.

Fourday morning finds Alyiakal joining Nolaan as Fourth Company forms up.

"Where to, exactly, ser?" asks the undercaptain.

"North out of the post. We'll decide when we see what the roads tell us when we reach the split."

When they reach the fork, roughly two glasses later, while the main body of the company takes a break, Alyiakal and Nolaan ride up the northeast road.

"What do you see?" asks Alyiakal.

"Not much, ser. Some wagon-wheel traces that have to be several days old, heading south. Grass-cat prints cutting across the road, and a single rider heading north. I can't tell where he came from."

"If he's heading north, where do you think he came from?"

"We didn't see those hoofprints coming north. He's most likely coming from the northwest or from the west side of the valley."

"Most likely, but let's check the north road first."

Alyiakal and Nolaan ride back and start up the north road, which shows cart tracks and little else.

When they check the northwest road, they find the same hoofprints, and Alyiakal says, "We might as well have the company go this way." He gestures. "You need to get the company moving."

Less than a quint later, Fourth Company rides along the northwest trail. Three kays farther along, the trail curves south to parallel the base of the hills. In time, they approach the trail leading into Jeranyi territory.

"Now where do you think the tracks are coming from?" asks Alyiakal.

"I'd guess from the northwest," replies Nolaan, "but I don't have anything to support that. What do you think?"

"I'd agree with you because I've never seen a single rider from one of the valley hamlets traveling out of the valley alone. But I'm guessing, too."

When they reach the trail angling into the hills and heading northwest, Nolaan says, "Guesses or not, ser, they came from the northwest."

Alyiakal studies the tracks, then realizes that the trail doesn't look as little used as it had when he'd ridden it years before. In fact, it's more like a narrow road. *Traders . . . raiders . . . both?* "We'll follow them for a while," he declares.

After Nolaan issues the orders and the company heads into the hills, Alyiakal asks, "How far out this way have you gone?"

"Less than five kays. Majer Moryah didn't want us going that far outside the valley."

Alyiakal senses that Nolaan is shading his response, and his wording suggests he went at least five kays, but he only asks, "Did he ever say why?"

"He just said there wasn't any point in it. That our job was to protect the valley and not waste chaos on raiders if they weren't trespassing."

"The problem with that," says Alyiakal, "is that you have no idea if trouble's coming until it hits you. This road sees a lot more riders and wagons than it used to, and that means more trading, either between Jerans and Cerlyn, or Jerans and the raiders living in the grassland north of the valley."

"We did see some wagons a few times this Summer."

"And tracks of more that you didn't see?"

"Yes, ser."

As he rides, Alyiakal looks not only for other riders, but also for possible trails branching off to the southwest. On the long slow climb into the hills, he sees neither riders nor side trails and only senses small birds and possibly a vulcrow. After that the road starts to descend into a dusty vale.

"Have you gone this far?" Alyiakal asks.

"The farthest I've gone was the crest of the road we just passed," admits Nolaan.

Alyiakal refrains from smiling, because they're certainly more than five kays beyond the valley floor. Half a kay farther along, ahead on the left, Alyiakal spies a path between two scrub evergreens. "You see those evergreens ahead? Have the company halt when we get there."

"Yes, ser."

Once the company halts, Alyiakal rides slowly toward the path, with Nolaan following. He sees no hoofprints, but he notices faint wavy lines in the sandy dirt.

"See those faint lines?" says Alyiakal. "Someone probably used an evergreen branch to brush away tracks. Lots of tracks, I'd guess. Raiders or smugglers. Send one of the scouts down the path to see if there are hoofprints farther from the road." Alyiakal senses no one within several hundred yards. *But majers don't go scouting when there are scouts available.*

"Yes, ser."

The scout returns in under a quint, reining up in front of the two officers.

"Did you find any hoofprints?" asks Alyiakal.

"Yes, ser." The scout grins. "Horse droppings, too. Tracks and droppings are several days old, maybe older. Hard to say how many mounts, maybe a half score or a little more. The clear prints look alike."

"Shoed by the same farrier?" asks Alyiakal.

"I'd say so, ser."

"How far does the trail go?"

"Looks to follow the low spots as far as I could see."

"That's very helpful," returns Alyiakal.

After Nolaan orders the scout back into position, Alyiakal gazes to the southwest. At a glance, the lower section of the hills parallels those closest to the valley and likely runs to where he'd rediscovered the path possibly used by raiders. Not absolute proof, but he'd wager on it. He turns to Nolaan. "It's likely we've found one of the ways raiders enter the valley without using obvious routes. Now, let's see if we can find another trail, one heading northeast."

Once Fourth Company resumes riding northwest, Alyiakal says quietly to Nolaan, "You might want to put a mark or note on your map. It'll remind you, and your eventual replacement will appreciate it."

Alyiakal senses something in Nolaan and guesses. "If you've made a personal map, that's fine, but adding the trail on the company map would also be good."

Nolaan nods, then asks, "Why would the raiders or smugglers even use that trail? The regular trails are faster."

"This isn't a smugglers' trail. It's for raiders."

Nolaan looks puzzled.

"Would you like to lead a patrol single file down that trail chasing raiders? Especially when they could post archers in the rocks looking down on you?"

"No, ser."

"Neither would I. Now, keep your eyes open, especially on the right."

Alyiakal studies the road, trying to see if he can discern more hoofprints heading northwest. He thinks there might have been some, but enough travelers have been through over the eightday that he can't be sure.

Although Fourth Company rides another five kays, they find no sign of another side trail that could accommodate a full-grown red deer, let alone a mounted raider. Nor does Alyiakal sense anyone near the road.

The company doesn't return to Pemedra until late afternoon, and after debriefing Nolaan and dealing with the gray, Alyiakal returns to the headquarters building.

Before entering his study, he asks the duty ranker outside his door, "Any dispatch riders today?"

"No, ser."

"Thank you." Then he turns and stops in Baassyn's doorway. "If you haven't done it already, please arrange for dispatch riders to leave tomorrow morning."

"I put them on notice that it was likely."

"Good. I appreciate that."

"How was your patrol?"

"We likely located the other end of that trail that raiders have been using in the hills to the west. It comes out on the northwest road to Jerans about ten kays from the valley floor. It's definitely been used recently."

"You think by the raiders sighted last fiveday?"

"According to the patrol report, they disappeared before Second Company could reach them. That would fit. On twoday we found hoofprints on the valley end of the trail. Today we found hoofprints where the trail meets the northwest road . . . and the side of the road and the entry to the trail had been swept with an evergreen branch. We rode another five kays but couldn't find another trail they might have taken."

"So they could have come from either the north or from Jerans?" asks Baassyn.

"Either's possible, with what we've found so far. But the hoofprints we found along the back trail today all had the same kind of shoe, and you don't see that often with raider mounts."

"I imagine not," replies Baassyn.

Since Baassyn seems disinclined to say more, Alyiakal says, "We'll have to wait to see who's behind those tracks." Then he turns and enters his study.

He definitely needs to finish his letter to Saelora, as well as update his own map of Pemedra.

XXXI

Over the next eightdays, Alyiakal conducts daily formation drills with each company, excepting the company on patrol. The drills are designed to allow a squad or a company to use the greatest number of firelances in a given situation, to minimize the impact of an attack by archers or spear-throwers, and to attack against different formations or in differing circumstances.

While some of those formations had been taught at Kynstaar, most Mirror Lancer companies seldom encounter massed or disciplined forces. As a result, those skills lie somewhere between rusty and nonexistent. The remainder of formations are those that Alyiakal developed and used in the past.

That's likely why, on the third sevenday of Autumn, at the conclusion of a set of drills with Second Company, after dismissing the company to duties, Captain Chaem eases his mount up beside Alyiakal's gray.

"Might I have a word with you, ser?"

Alyiakal can tell that the senior captain is concerned about something, if not several matters, and he says, "Of course."

"Begging your pardon, Majer, but I've never seen some of these formations or heard those commands."

"You'd like to know why I'm insisting the officers and companies execute them?"

"Yes, ser."

"The simple answer is that I don't want what happened at Guarstyad to happen here."

"You think the Jeranyi or the Cerlynese will attack in force, like the Kyphrans?"

"The Cerlynese already did, a year ago, at Kraaslaen. They sent six, possibly seven companies against our three. If I hadn't spent two years training the companies at Lhaarat, the casualties would have been worse. As it was, we lost close to a complete squad with as many wounded. That was after a lot of training."

"What were their casualties, ser?"

"Roughly two squads' worth of armsmen survived."

Chaem says nothing for a long moment. "Ser? Less than a company survived?"

"Roughly. I don't like fighting the same people more than absolutely necessary. We don't have enough Mirror Lancers to lose many."

"Did you lead them personally?"

"I did, but I want all of you to have the tools to deal with a mass of trained armsmen if you're attacked on patrol. If either the Cerlynese or the Jeranyi attack en masse, or if we're ordered to deal with them, as was the case at Lhaarat, I will lead you personally."

"Headquarters ordered you to kill them all?"

Alyiakal shakes his head. "Headquarters ordered me to remove them from Cyadoran lands. They didn't want to be removed. We never entered Cerlynese lands."

"So it's true, then?"

"That's what happened in Kraaslaen."

"Wasn't what I meant, ser. Word is that you and your company gutted the Kyphrans pretty much by yourselves."

"We were in the right position, and my company was well-trained by then. We were able to do more than the others."

"In all these kinds of formations and maneuvers?"

"Not all of them. I developed some of them at Lhaarat."

"Do you really think we'll have to do that here?"

"I hope not," replies Alyiakal, "but I'm concerned. We aren't getting as many firelance replacements. We're getting more and more raw recruits. Both Cerlyn and Jerans appear to be building large forces, and most of the border posts aren't patrolling as aggressively as in past years." *And too many senior officers are playing internal politics rather than concerning themselves with threats from other lands.*

"Is that why headquarters sent you here?"

Alyiakal chuckles wryly. "I don't know why I was posted here. No one told me, and I received no instructions. The standing orders for Pemedra are to protect the borders from incursions and to deal with threats as effectively as possible with the least possible loss of lancers. That's what I'm planning for."

"I appreciate your sharing that, ser. Mind if I tell the other officers?"

"As long as you don't elaborate."

"Thank you, ser." Chaem turns his mount to head toward the stables.

From Chaem's last question, Alyiakal has no doubt the other officers persuaded the senior captain to ask Alyiakal about the drills. He smiles wryly and then follows Chaem.

Alyiakal has just finished dealing with the gray and is walking back to the headquarters building when he sees three dispatch riders enter the post. While he hopes for a letter from Saelora, he worries about what else the riders carry, because personal letters only arrive when there's something official being sent. He keeps walking.

Less than half a quint after he sits behind his desk, the duty ranker brings in two large envelopes and one smaller one, setting them on the desk. "Dispatches and personal envelope, ser."

"Thank you." Alyiakal instantly knows the smaller envelope is from Saelora and sets it to the side. He debates which envelope to open first, finally deciding on the heavier one, suspecting that it contains routine directives, which it does.

Alyiakal reads them through, finding yet another revision to post sanitary regulations and standards, a change to procurement practices, which on the surface doesn't seem any different from the present practices, and a new regulation stating that officers' sabres must be of the standard cupridium, without exception.

He frowns at the last. Why would an officer need an iron sabre? Or are matters so tense between the Magi'i and Mirror Lancer headquarters that the Magi'i don't want iron weapons near them? *Or is it as much symbolism as anything?*

He sets the directives aside, knowing that he'll have to compare the new directives word for word with the old ones, which will be time-consuming and tedious.

Then he opens the second envelope from Mirror Lancer headquarters, which contains a short letter written under the letterhead of the Captain-Commander and a note on a smaller sheet of paper.

Majer Alyiakal—

The Majer-Commander and I appreciate your expeditious diligence in completing the resolution of the accounting discrepancies previously uncovered at Pemedra Post.

You and Overcaptain Baassyn are to be commended for your action, especially at a time when the Emperor of Light has declared the need for effective safeguarding of Mirror Lancer resources.

The letter is signed by Laartol, as Captain-Commander.

The note is even shorter, saying that a copy of the letter has been sent directly to Baassyn, with only the letter "L" as signature. The cut-and-dried acceptance of the report and the wording tells Alyiakal that the matter is closed and that any future "discrepancies" will be attributed to him.

He's about to open Saelora's letter when Baassyn appears in the study doorway.

"Ser?"

"I take it that the Captain-Commander sent you your own copy of the letter declaring that the accounting discrepancies have been resolved?"

"Yes, ser."

"Keep it safe, just in case."

"Yes, ser." Baassyn pauses. "There is one thing . . . ?"

"The mention of effective safeguarding of Mirror Lancer resources? I'd say he's warning us that some supplies might be hard to come by in seasons to come. What do you think?"

"I'd have to agree. I just wondered if I read too much into the phrase."

Not with Laartol. "I don't think so. I get the feeling that with anything coming from headquarters, every word is carefully considered."

"Thank you, ser . . . and for insisting we send the report."

"You're welcome, but you did all the hard work."

After Baassyn returns to his own study, Alyiakal picks up Saelora's letter, knowing he'll have more than enough time to read it before evening mess. He smiles at the first words.

I can't tell you how glad I am that you arrived at your post safely. So was Hyrsaal, especially after I told him about your difficulties. I do hope that the rest of Autumn will be quieter. That's not likely, I know, but I can hope . . .

Hyrsaal was here because he stopped on his way to Fyrad. As you suggested, I gave him the notes I wrote up . . .

As you suggested? Then Alyiakal realizes that wording refers to the notes he wrote up for Hyrsaal and that Saelora had rewritten, but that she'd written it that way so that it appears she wrote the notes.

. . . He was pleased, and I can only hope he finds them helpful. He left for Fyrad yesterday, and it's unlikely that Gaaran, Mother, or I will see him until his next home leave.

That might be because Mother was rather cool . . .

How about icy?

I've made a few changes concerning Loraan House. First, whether you like it or not, I'm giving you the same honor as I did Vassyl.

The same honor? Abruptly, he understands. She's insisting that he has an actual ownership interest in Loraan House, but she doesn't want to put it that way in writing.

You'll be glad to know that I've been able to buy out Haansfel, and that will allow us to do more with outland traders, including sending cargo for sales in outland ports and taking interests in other cargoes . . .

Alyiakal reads every word carefully, including the warm closing, then tucks away the letter in the file that holds every letter she has written him.

XXXII

Few truly knew His Mightiness Kiedral'elth'alt'mer, Second Emperor of Light, and fewer still Kiedral Daloren, Vice Marshal of the Anglorian Unity, though scholars and few others pore over his words and aphorisms. As with many who are great in public stature, his sayings are accepted without understanding and consigned to history by those who believe that the present not only owes nothing to the past, but also that the hard-earned lessons of the past have no relevance to the present because the times have changed.

The times do change, if not as much as those who now lead us believe, but people do not. They make the same mistakes as their ancestors, if in different garb, and too often leaders claim to lead from the heart, as though there is special merit in such leadership. The heart is what powers the body, but that power must be directed and governed by the head, lest passion, or even excessive care, overwhelm reason and intellect.

That is true of Cyad and Cyador as well, for while Merchanters and trade are the heart of Cyador, Merchanters too often believe that they are the head and that their passion and desire, especially for golds, provide the best outcome. They forget that power guided only by the heart and without the rein of reason leads to corrupted wealth and continual bloodshed. That is why the Emperor of Light governs under the Rational Stars, and why the Mirror Lancers cannot ever forsake that guidance, lest Cyador fall . . .

Fragment, Mirror Lancer Archives
Zaenth'alt, Captain-Commander
Cyad, 45 A.F.

XXXIII

Although there are no signs of raiders or armsmen in the eightdays of mid-Autumn, Alyiakal continues to schedule patrols, if less frequently, and accompanies at least one each eightday. The first real snow—more than mere flurries—sweeps over Pemedra on the seventh sixday of Autumn, dropping perhaps four digits on the roads and weighing down the tall golden-tan grass enough to bend it before sliding off, but the air remains cold enough that, when a second and heavier storm follows less than an eightday later, the grass is pushed down to half its previous height.

At breakfast on the eighth fiveday of Autumn, as the officers finish eating, Alyiakal remarks, "For some reason, it appears that none of you have experienced thundersnow . . . or have I missed something?" He looks down the mess table, but no one responds. "Have any of you been caught in thundersnow?"

All five officers shake their heads.

"When I looked out across the valley this morning, I noticed a slight haze, but above the haze, there aren't any clouds, and the sky's a more intense green-blue. There's also a . . . stillness. That's exactly the way the weather is before a thundersnow. Now, not all mornings like this mean a thundersnow is coming, but it doesn't give much warning. You can head out on patrol, and the skies are clear. Then two glasses later a line of green-black clouds race over the hills to the northeast and the snowfall is so thick the clouds look like they have a black curtain beneath. Within a quint or two the wind is strong enough to blow you out of the saddle. The snow is falling so thickly that you can't see more than a few yards, and there's thunder and lightning everywhere. If you're out on patrol and this happens to you . . . you can't outrun it. That will make it worse. What you need to do is stay mounted, find a low rise that will block some of the wind, and pack your company together as tight as you can . . . and wait it out. You'll think it will last forever. It won't. The winds are so strong the thundersnow will pass over you in one to two glasses, and then the air will be cold enough to freeze you solid if you aren't wearing winter gear, which is also why you don't patrol without it, no matter how warm or quiet it seems to be. If the company is spread out, you could easily lose lancers, because an isolated rider is more likely to freeze or have an accident."

Alyiakal can sense a certain disbelief, especially from Suraat.

Chaem clears his throat, then asks, "You described that storm pretty well, ser. That because you got caught in one?"

"It is. I was a very green undercaptain. I was fortunate enough to have a very senior captain who told me about thundersnow. Even so, it was quite an experience. In those two glasses so much snow fell that it was more than calf-deep and the drifts were waist-high by the time the storm passed."

"That's . . . hard to believe, ser," says Suraat.

"Think of it as the Winter equivalent of a grass fire." Alyiakal laughs wryly, then adds, "I don't much care whether you believe me, only that you remember what to do if you're unlucky enough to be caught out in one. And if you are caught, and you lose anyone through failure to take the right steps, you won't be a lancer officer."

Chaem, Kessmyr, and Nolaan each nod. Baassyn doesn't quite hide a frown, while Suraat's face remains impassive.

The various reactions scarcely surprise Alyiakal, but all he says is, "That's all. Undercaptain Suraat, I'd like to see you in my study in about a quint."

"Yes, ser."

Alyiakal stands and leaves the mess, then makes his way through the quiet chill outside to the headquarters building and his study.

A quint later, Suraat arrives.

"Ser, you requested my presence."

Alyiakal motions for him to close the door and take a seat, then says, "I'm worried about you, Suraat. You're not overtly insubordinate, but I get the definite impression that you resent authority and that you have an underlying feeling that you know more than your superiors. At the same time, I haven't seen any evidence that you do."

"I believe you're surmising, ser."

"I'd have to disagree with that, Undercaptain. You may recall that I'm a qualified field healer, but I'm a bit more than that. I have order levels verging on Magi'i level. This isn't a secret. I've been examined several times by senior Magi'i, including the Third Magus. Close to someone, I can sense, fairly accurately, what they feel."

Suraat tries not to swallow.

"Now," continues Alyiakal, "it's clear to me that you come from something like a Magi'i background, and unlike some senior officers, I don't have a problem with that. What I care about is that you become a good officer, and while I can easily sense what comes across as condescension and arrogance, most other senior officers will feel that attitude sooner or later. That will make your life as an officer difficult." *If not short.*

"Ser—"

"Please don't tell me that I don't know or don't understand," says Alyiakal gently, projecting a sense of concern. "My mother died when I was nine. My father died on duty when I was at Kynstaar. I have no living relatives."

"Ser . . . what can I say?"

"You haven't said much at all," replies Alyiakal dryly, "except that I can't possibly know what you feel. Am I wrong in what I said?"

Suraat remains silent.

Alyiakal waits.

Finally, Suraat says, "I'm partly from a Magi'i background, and I was raised by another Magi'i family."

"All of the background and education, but without the ability to handle order and chaos."

"Yes, ser."

Alyiakal offers a pleasantly amused smile. "Do you know that a firelance holds more chaos than most Magi'i can use or release at one time?"

Suraat's forehead wrinkles in puzzlement.

"Or that the Majer-Commander has issued a directive that no lancer sabres can be forged of anything but cupridium?"

"Ser?"

"Think about it. The barbarians, raiders, or outland armsmen couldn't care less about the metal of our sabres. There's only one group in Cyador that would care."

After several silent moments, abruptly, Suraat laughs.

Alyiakal senses his bitter amusement without even trying. Then he stands. "I've given you a few things to think about. What I care most about, as far as you're concerned, is that you become the best officer you can. Bitterness, anger, arrogance, and condescension only get in the way. I'll see you at evening mess. You can leave the door open."

Suraat stands. "By your leave, ser."

Alyiakal nods and watches as the undercaptain leaves the study. While he senses no anger, he has no idea what effect his words have had . . . or will have.

But you can hope.

XXXIV

On midafternoon of the fourth twoday of Winter, Alyiakal sits behind the desk in his chill study, thinking over the lack of raiders or outland armsmen. He hasn't expected raids recently because, between the winds, cold, and snow, the hills to the north and west have been impassable since the beginning of Winter. There also hasn't been a Harvest or Autumn with as few raids or sightings of raiders as in the last two seasons, according to the patrol reports dating back to when he'd first been posted to Pemedra.

Because of the Winter weather, dispatch runs to Pemedra and back to Syadtar have been limited to every few eightdays. Still, Alyiakal has received two letters from Saelora since mid-Autumn, and sent two lengthy ones in return, given that he has had the time to write.

Late in the afternoon, the lookouts report dispatch riders approaching the south gates. Since the last dispatches arrived three eightdays earlier, Alyiakal suspects that the dispatches or official correspondence are likely routine, but he can at least hope another letter accompanies the official correspondence.

Slightly more than two quints later, he has two official envelopes, one from Mirror Lancer headquarters and one from Subcommander Zekkaat, as well as two letters, one from Saelora and one from Hyrsaal. He sets aside the personal letters and opens the larger envelope, which carries recent notices and directives.

Alyiakal begins with the notices. The first is an announcement that Third Magus Verinaar'elth has become Second Magus following the death of former Second Magus Kiataphi after a lingering illness, and that Astaalt'elth has been named as Third Magus. As Second Magus, Verinaar will be the Magus meeting with Captain-Commander Laartol on matters of mutual interest and concern in the defense of Cyador.

Alyiakal frowns. *Mutual interest and concern . . . defense of Cyador?* That suggests a threat, and there's been no previous mention of anything along those lines. He also wonders about the nature of the "lingering illness."

The second notice is an announcement that the Mirror Lancer horseshoe forges are in the process of being moved from Fyrad to Waabyn, a town fifteen kays south of Ilypsya, if on the main road, and that because of the transfer there may be significant delays in obtaining replacement horseshoes. In addition, all broken or damaged shoes that cannot be reforged on post need to be returned to Waabyn, not Fyrad.

Alyiakal wonders why the transfer was necessary unless the order created and dispersed in forging the iron is somehow disruptive to nearby processes requiring the use of chaos. *But wouldn't someone have known that years ago . . . or has something changed?*

There are only two directives, the first mandating a thorough cleaning of all water storage and handling systems at every post by the end of the fourth eightday of Spring. The second directive changes the procedures for home leave, limiting the amount that can be taken at the end of a full posting to four eightdays, and limiting the amount that can be carried over to one eightday's worth.

Alyiakal has to read that twice, because lancer officers only get four eightdays' home leave at the end of each posting. *In effect, if you don't take it, you lose it.*

He shakes his head and sets the directives aside, putting the one on leave on top, because he'll need to circulate that to all the officers, and get a signature from each. Otherwise, they could claim they weren't informed.

Then he opens the envelope from Syadtar, which has a letter from Subcommander Zekkaat, but signed, by direction, by Baertal. The key sentences are simple.

> *As instructed earlier, this letter orders you to provide an officer and a full squad to escort the Spring supply wagons from Syadtar Post to Pemedra Post. You are to provide all available wagons. Said supplies are scheduled to arrive at Syadtar at the beginning of the third eightday of Spring. You will be notified if that date changes.*

So far as Alyiakal knows, Zekkaat is the only regional commander requiring border posts to provide supply escorts. *And we're not even under his command.*

Even though Alyiakal doesn't report to Zekkaat operationally, he's not about to protest, despite the fact that Zekkaat's requirement will leave one company understrength for more than one eightday and possibly more than two. Protesting will only cause problems for Alyiakal, as Majer Moryah had obviously felt as well, and Alyiakal doesn't need any additional problems with Zekkaat and Baertal. He sets that letter aside and opens the letter from Hyrsaal.

> *Alyiakal—*
>
> *It's always good to hear from you. With all you have to deal with, you still take time to write.*
>
> *I have to say that I prefer Winter patrols along the Accursed Forest to another Winter in the freezing north of the Grass Hills. I'll take even icy rain over bitter wind and snow. My companies have only lost two lancers since I got here. That's far better than dealing with raiders and "misguided" Jeranyi armsmen. I wish you well, again, with those I won't name. The Rational Stars should deal with that, but they don't seem to help much unless we do most of the work . . .*
>
> *I can't believe how successful Saelora and Catriana have become. Catriana wrote me that the changes they made in Fyrad have been well-received and, better yet, made more silvers . . .*

She says that Haarlt is talking, really talking, and what he says usually makes sense, possibly unlike his father . . .

Alyiakal nods, recalling that Hyrsaal always had been leery of Baertal, but was careful enough only to allude to the problem. Then he smiles and goes on to finish reading the letter.

After he puts the letter with the others from Hyrsaal, he debates waiting until after evening mess to read Saelora's, but decides he has time . . . and he can always read it again later.

Alyiakal—

Your last letter was so poetic, in the way you described the wind and the snow. You made the cold seem so real that I had to put on a jacket to finish reading it. We haven't had any real cold, except for a few icy rains. We almost never get snow, but the towns twenty kays west of us do . . .

Alyiakal frowns. The Westhorns are east of Vaeyal, but the towns to the west get snow? *That has to be because of the Great Forest.*

I thought that the trading might slow down some now that we're in Winter. That hasn't happened, not for Loraan House, anyway. The new lands for greenberries finally produced a good crop all the way through Autumn, and we've been able to increase the production of the liqueur. We also were fortunate enough to be able to purchase additional maize so we could distill more Crystalflame, enough that we can offer Valtrad House more than we pledged . . . and possibly sell some to a trader out of Lydiar . . .

Oh . . . some time ago I asked Catriana to listen for anything she heard about trade problems with Suthya, but she didn't hear much until last eightday. You were right. Raiders from Cerlyn have been attacking the upland traders, more like brigands, looking for silvers, gold, and valuables. At least, that's what she heard.

I don't know what I'd do without Catriana. She's so organized and effective, and now that she's got Maerthe and Jael to help, they've totally redone the factorage in Fyrad so that they can stock a wider range of goods . . .

> *The only worrisome thing is that I don't think Mother is doing very well. Charissa says she's getting forgetful, and Mother never forgets anything. At least, she never used to. I can tell Gaaran's worried as well, but he won't say anything. She still dotes on Gaartyn and Rendara, and that's good, because it helps Charissa . . .*

Despite the references to Marenda's forgetfulness, and the rumor about Cerlynese raids on Suthyan merchants and traders, Alyiakal is smiling when he finishes the letter and gets ready to brave the wind and cold on his way to evening mess.

ALYIAKAL'ALT,

MAJER

Pemedra

Spring, 105 A.F.

XXXV

After breakfast on sevenday of the first eightday of Spring, Alyiakal stands in the doorway to Baassyn's study and says fatalistically, "We can't put it off any longer." *Not that it would be a good idea anyway.*

"Put off what?" asks the overcaptain.

"Cleaning the spring reservoir and the water system . . . and whatever else Majer Baertal might inspect. He's the one the subcommander would send."

"Headquarters sends that notice every year. No one ever follows up," replies Baassyn.

"Did headquarters ever send a follow-up notice declaring that inspections would be made at the discretion of the regional commanders? And do we want to risk getting a reprimand—or worse?"

"No, ser." Baassyn sighs. "I suppose you're right. Subcommander Zekkaat's the only one that's made outlying border posts send squads to escort their own supplies. You think Majer Baertal was behind that, too?"

"I doubt that it was his idea, but taking advantage of the provision in the regulations likely was." Alyiakal pauses, then says, "You know the water system. I've only looked at it. I assume we'd start by emptying the reservoir and cleaning the muck out, then cleaning the outlet pipe from the reservoir to the building cisterns, and then the cisterns, one by one. Once we get the reservoir and the outlet pipe cleaned out, we can start refilling the reservoir. After that . . . I don't see how we'd clean the pipes or how Baertal could inspect them. They're all buried deep enough that they won't freeze, and there's no sign of leaks."

"Clean the pipes where they enter and leave the cisterns," replies Baassyn. "That's the best we can do. Well, we can also clean out the outlet taps."

"We need to start on oneday. I'd like to have it all done by next sevenday, earlier if possible, even if it takes every ranker in every company. Right now, the ground's still frozen in the lower hills, and with snow still in the upper hills, there's little chance of raiders. Even so, I'd like to get all the Spring maintenance and other chores done well before we might see raiders, like escorting supply wagons."

"Ser . . . which officer are you thinking of sending to Syadtar to escort the supplies back?" asks Baassyn.

"I was considering sending Nolaan. He's had some experience and seems solid. Although he'll likely make captain later this year, he's also junior enough that if he upsets Majer Baertal, it won't be fatal for his career."

"I would have suggested him if you hadn't." The overcaptain pauses. "Majer Baertal doesn't seem to like you. Would you care to tell me why?"

"He tried to bully me at Kynstaar. That didn't work. So he set it up so we'd have to spar. He thought he could injure or maim me. I bruised him and disarmed him twice. The officer in charge of blade training told him that if we'd been using real blades and not wooden wands, I'd have killed him. He then courted the son of a senior commander and some of the captains and majers, suggesting that I was the kind of candidate that only did well in training, and not in the field. He can be quite persuasive, I discovered."

"That kind often is, and that gets them thinking that they're better than they are," says Baassyn. "I watched you instructing some of the lancers in blade training. None of them came close to touching you. Has anyone?"

"Not since halfway through Kynstaar," admits Alyiakal.

"From what Faaln told me, you're even better with a firelance."

"I've had a great deal of experience."

Alyiakal's wry tone elicits a chuckle from Baassyn.

"Right now," Alyiakal continues, "Majer Baertal's tactics merely annoy, and any response will hurt the post more than it will affect Baertal. All we can do is not make mistakes." *Until he does.* "Which means that Nolaan will have to be at Syadtar on the day before the third eightday of Spring and that we have an exceptionally clean reservoir."

"So Nolaan can tell Majer Baertal how hard everyone worked cleaning it all up?" asks Baassyn.

"Exactly. That way, Baertal can get the satisfaction of knowing he caused us extra work and he doesn't have to travel six days to find that out." *And we don't have to see him and put up with his frigging condescension.*

XXXVI

Less than a glass after breakfast on twoday Alyiakal stands at the top of the slime-covered stone steps leading to the mucky bottom of the reservoir just inside the northeast corner of the post walls.

Something about the reservoir nags at him.

Then he realizes what it is. The stone walls, even the floor under all the muck, hold a residue of chaos-glazed order. *Mirror Engineers built this.* That they had reinforces his feeling that the Emperor Kieffal had intended so much more for Pemedra.

Alyiakal wonders what else might be different and searches with his senses. After several moments, he discerns a long tube of order-reinforced and chaos-glazed stone running from the reservoir and angling deep into the ground to the northeast. *There wasn't a natural spring here! They created it.*

His second thought is that the Mirror Engineers who built the reservoir or the Magi'i who helped had to have had a geomancer. Yet Senior Magus Thiaphyl had stated that there were no current Magi'i with that ability. *An ability that you have—at least to some extent.*

"Ser?" asks Chaem politely.

Alyiakal wrenches his attention back to the older captain. "I'm sorry. I was just thinking how much better built this reservoir is."

"Better built or not," declares Chaem, "it doesn't look like it's been cleaned out in years. It's going to take some work to cart all that muck out, even with sixty men lugging those buckets. Might take well into the afternoon."

"Could be longer than that," declares Alyiakal. "Make sure they clean the steps first and that they do it well. The last thing we need is lancers breaking bones cleaning a reservoir."

"What do you want us to do with the slop they clean out?" asks Chaem.

"Will it help the grass in the pastures grow, or will it kill it?" returns Alyiakal.

"Couldn't tell you, ser."

"Then load it into the manure cart and dump it along the outside of the wall. One way or the other, it won't make a difference. Once the reservoir's clean, we'll need to see if there's any place where there's leakage before we put water back in." Not that Alyiakal thinks there will be any, given the reservoir's construction.

"We'll send for you when we've got it clean," says Chaem. "If we run into problems, we'll let you know."

"I'll see you one way or another." Alyiakal turns and walks along the north wall of the post until he reaches the central avenue. There, he turns south toward the various post buildings, looking at the fences and the short green sprouts of grass in the pastures they enclose. He doesn't see or sense anything out of order.

Each of the companies works on a different building, and Alyiakal hopes everything will be finished before Nolaan and his first squad have to leave for Syadtar on sixday.

When he returns to his study, he walks to the window, thinking, not so much about the water-system cleaning, which is overdue, but more about what attacks might come in late Spring or in Summer, or in the next year. Chaem has only a little more than a year left before he will either be reposted or be eligible to take a stipend. Kessmyr will be reposted in late Harvest or early Autumn and will likely be replaced by another fresh undercaptain.

Not the most experienced officers if you have to fight Jeranyi or Cerlynese armsmen, but then the Cerlynese can't be that much more experienced after what you did to them.

The biggest problem, Alyiakal knows, is that the Mirror Lancers will be outnumbered. While training and firelances can make a difference, the question is whether they'll be sufficient, whether they'll have enough chaos in the firelances, and whether they'll be able to obtain adequate chaos replenishment.

Worrying won't help. He moves from the window to his desk to deal with the various reports he needs to submit to headquarters on Pemedra Post's readiness.

By late afternoon a ranker from Second Company arrives with a report that the reservoir is ready for his inspection. Alyiakal leaves headquarters, where rankers from Third Company are finishing up with the water system as well as scrubbing down the interior of the building, which Alyiakal incorporated into their tasks, because there's much less plumbing in the building, unlike the quarters buildings, which include the kitchen, as well as showers, basins, and jakes.

Chaem waits for Alyiakal beside the entrance to the reservoir, while the lancers and their squad leaders, many in soiled work-duty uniforms, stand around the manure cart, waiting.

"Looks like it was even grimier than you thought," says Alyiakal.

"There was more than half a yard of muck at the bottom, ser," says Chaem. "We had to spread it a fair ways along the walls so it wouldn't build up."

"Good thought." Alyiakal turns and studies the stone steps, which are actually white, something he couldn't tell earlier in the day, all the way down to the stone floor, and then the sides, sensing that the Mirror Engineers who built the reservoir melted the surface of the stones together strongly enough that he can discern no cracks. "I don't see any cracks. Did you?"

"No, ser. We swabbed out the exit port to the main water line, and the overflow line that goes to the pasture pond," says Chaem, pointing to a circular opening in the south wall of the reservoir. "Least as far as we could go." He points to the entry port on the north wall. "Took a lot more to get that clean."

"This was designed so that any solids in the water would settle out," says Alyiakal. "It holds more water than we use so that the inflow doesn't churn up what's settled. You and the men did an excellent job. I'd like to tell them that myself, if you don't mind."

Chaem grins. "They'd like that."

Alyiakal turns and walks toward the grimy lancers, stopping several yards from them, then waits for them to realize he's there. "As you were." After a moment, he goes on. "I saw how much muck was in the reservoir this morning. It's clean enough now that you could eat off it . . . not that I'd suggest it. Sometimes, you have to do thankless tasks that have no glory and are just plain dirty and grimy, but you did an excellent job, and I appreciate it."

Alyiakal speaks quietly to Chaem. "There should be enough water in the barracks cisterns for them to clean up. I do appreciate how clean the reservoir is. You can dismiss them until evening mess . . . unless you have something else for them."

"No, ser." Chaem addresses the men. "Once you've got the manure cart back to the stables, you're free till evening mess, except for you, Jhaan. I'll need your help getting the water running into the reservoir and closing the doors."

Alyiakal watches as Chaem and the burly Jhaan open the heavy cupridium inlet valve and seal and lock the heavy access doors.

Then the ranker hurries off, and Alyiakal and Chaem walk toward the avenue.

"Have to say I'm glad that's done, ser."

"So am I," admits Alyiakal, "but the Mirror Engineers designed it so that it was easier than I feared."

"This is the best-designed post of all those where I served," says Chaem. "Ought to be a command post."

"That's what it was built to be, until Emperor Kieffal died."

"Last real emperor, if you ask me," says Chaem. "Not that anyone will."

"They won't be asking me, either," says Alyiakal, with a chuckle, pushing aside for the moment his worries about the coming seasons.

XXXVII

On sixday, Alyiakal sends off Undercaptain Nolaan with Fourth Company's first squad, along with three official letters reporting the successful cleaning of the post's water and sewage systems, the original to Mirror Lancer headquarters with copies to Subcommander Zekkaat and Majer Baertal. The squad also carries outgoing letters from Alyiakal and other officers and rankers.

For the next seven days, Alyiakal works on refresher formation training with all the companies. He also sends squads on reconnaissance patrols along the base of the hills bordering the valley to determine if either raiders or Jeranyi forces have been sending scouts . . . or if there are any signs of smugglers. While the squads find occasional tracks, most appear to have originated within the valley.

On the third sevenday of Spring, in early evening, Nolaan and Fourth Company's first squad return to Pemedra with four wagons of supplies, including another hundred and thirty replenished firelances. Once the late-arriving rankers and Nolaan are fed, Nolaan reports to Alyiakal in his study.

After Nolaan enters, he sets the dispatch pouch on the desk. "Thought you'd like to have this, ser."

"Thank you and welcome back. I'd like to hear how your supply run went, both to and from Syadtar."

Nolaan seats himself, then says, "I thought you might, ser. The ride down was routine. The weather was good, and we didn't see any raiders or outland armsmen. Didn't see much of anyone except locals planting. We reached Syadtar in late afternoon on eightday. Majer Baertal showed up within a quint. He wanted to know why we didn't have more wagons. I told him that the post only had three wagons, and I didn't know why we didn't have more. There's a letter to you from him. I imagine he'll want the wagon returned with the next dispatch riders." Nolaan grins. "You were right, ser. He wanted to know about cleaning out all the water and sewer pipes. When I told him how much we did, he seemed to lose interest."

Because he's looking to find fault. Alyiakal only nods.

"There are also some envelopes from Mirror Lancer headquarters."

Which will mean more work of some sort. "You were there a few days. Waiting for the supplies, then?"

"Not exactly. The last of the supplies got there late on oneday. We had to separate our supplies from those going to Isahl. The lancers from Isahl didn't show up until we'd finished separating and loading both our wagons and two of theirs."

"Did they have a full squad?" asks Alyiakal.

"No, ser. Just half a squad."

That also doesn't surprise Alyiakal. "Make sure all those matters are in your written report, but keep it strictly factual."

"Yes, ser."

"Did you learn anything interesting? Any reports of Jeranyi armsmen or anything happening in Cyad?"

"No raiders or brigands around Syadtar, but one of the undercaptains there told me that last Autumn scouts from Isahl saw Jeranyi armsmen, but the Jeranyi turned back. None of the junior officers said anything about Cyad or headquarters. Most of them didn't really say that much about anything."

"Were you dealing with Majer Baertal on the supply matters all the time? Or anything else?"

"No, ser. Except for the first time, we dealt with Sub-Majer Smaalt. He was organized and pleasant. Majer Baertal just added his letter to you with the dispatches and personal letters before I got the dispatch pouch. I found that out when I looked to see if any of the rankers with me had letters." Nolaan grins. "I think there might also be a personal letter for you."

"I appreciate the notice," replies Alyiakal, "but, if I were you, I'd be careful opening dispatch pouches, especially around officers like Subcommander Zekkaat or Majer Baertal. They're the type that gets sensitive about procedures."

"Ah . . . yes, ser."

"Did you talk to anyone from Isahl?"

"Not really. They only sent a squad leader."

Even more interesting. "I won't keep you, Nolaan. You've had a long eightday." Alyiakal stands.

"Thank you, ser."

After Nolaan leaves, Alyiakal opens the dispatch bag and sorts through the contents, replacing the personal letters in the bag, except for the two addressed to him, and setting the official envelopes on the desk.

He decides against opening the envelope from Syadtar immediately, since he wants to see what's arrived from headquarters first. That envelope contains a reminder that water and sewer systems need to be cleaned as well as a notice updating the specifications for sabres, which essentially codifies the ban on all blades not made of cupridium. The single directive states that all traders are prohibited from possessing or trading in copper unless they have a tariff receipt or an exemption certified by an Imperial tariff enumerator, and that any trader caught possessing copper unlawfully shall be detained and held in custody until a tariff examinator can be sent to adjudicate the occurrence.

Alyiakal reads the notice twice, thinking that it doesn't make that much sense when Cyador is short of copper. *Unless some clan or group of clans is using this to raise the price of copper exorbitantly.*

He shakes his head and sets the notices and directives to one side before opening the letter addressed to him from Syadtar. It's short and signed by Baertal.

> *Majer Alyiakal—*
>
> *In order to facilitate the timely delivery of supplies to Pemedra, Syadtar Post has sent one of its wagons to accompany Pemedra Post's three wagons. Subcommander Zekkaat would appreciate the return of the wagon with the next dispatch run to Syadtar. We trust that there will not be any great delay in accomplishing that return.*

Alyiakal considers the matter. Since he'd sent dispatches with Nolaan on the second sixday of Spring, he could delay sending the wagon back for another few days, but he'd rather get it out of the way, particularly since there's no reason to give Baertal something else to complain about or to use against Alyiakal's performance in commanding Pemedra. Certainly, Alyiakal can reasonably allow a day for unloading before sending the dispatch riders with additional lancers and the wagon back on oneday.

He nods, sets aside the letter from Baertal, and then opens the letter from Hyrsaal.

Alyiakal—

Not much has changed since I last wrote. It's not like Inividra where not much happens in Winter and there are problems from mid-Spring to mid-Autumn. Here there are little problems all the time, and occasionally a treefall that springs loose everything from stun lizards to the giant panthers. So far, we've only encountered one panther, but that one killed one lancer and mauled another . . .

Something else did happen you might find interesting. Last eightday I took Second Company on patrol, the one that ends up in Geliendra. At mess, I ran into Lydaal, another overcaptain. We got to talking, and he told me a story he'd heard about a young majer . . .

Alyiakal winces, knowing who that majer has to be and hoping that what Hyrsaal heard wasn't too bad. Then he keeps reading.

. . . who didn't think he was especially important and neglected to pay a courtesy call on the subcommander at Southpoint when he was on home leave and ordering new uniforms from the post tailor. I said I might know that majer, and we talked some more. He said that your modesty and apology to the subcommander and his predecessor had been well-received, especially since they'd had an unpleasant experience with another majer. That was how your name came up, but he wouldn't say who the other majer was. I can speculate but that will have to wait until the next time we get together . . .

It could have been worse, but it's still a reminder that from here on, everything you do or say is likely to get around and not necessarily in a favorable way.

The remainder of Hyrsaal's letter is about Catriana and Haarlt and how well Catriana is doing running the Loraan House factorage in Fyrad.

Then Alyiakal opens Saelora's letter and begins to read.

Alyiakal—

I'm always glad to hear from you and to learn how you're faring. Not much has changed here since I last wrote, except for one thing.

Last eightday, a well-dressed man spent a great deal of time at our factorage in Fyrad, talking mostly to Maerthe. He kept asking detailed questions.

Thankfully, Maerthe sensed that he wasn't up to much good, and played much dumber than she is. She kept saying that she didn't know this and that, and that the man really needed to talk to Catriana. The man didn't want to talk to Catriana and left after a brief conversation with her. Catriana's developed a wide-ranging group of friends and contacts, mostly women, but also a few influential local merchants and traders. She began asking around and found out that the man's job is to report on trade and traders in Fyrad for the Dyljani Clan . . .

Alyiakal nods. He's been worried that the success of Loraan House will not go unnoticed by the larger and more powerful trading houses in Cyad. In some ways, he's surprised it's taken so long, but that might be because Saelora's been so careful.

I have to say that I'm a little concerned. According to what Catriana found out, the Dyljani Clan is the second most powerful of the trading clans in Cyador and is looking for ways to increase their power in other ports, especially with the decline in trade with Suthya. Dyrkan's helped Catriana find and hire some guards for the factorage. I thought it was surprising that other factorages and traders in Fyrad have been offering information and help. That's partly because Catriana pointed out that if any of the Cyad clans got established in Fyrad, everyone there would suffer. They're all happier to have us be the target . . .

Of course . . .

Alyiakal can't help wondering if installing Donaajr as an Imperial tariff enumerator at Oldroad Post was part of that plan, and if the Dyljani Clan was also using the Imperial Tariff Enumerators in other ways to the clan's advantage. *Or it's more likely that all the clans infiltrate the Tariff Enumerators, and it balances out in a rough way, which might be why the Dyljani are looking at expanding into Fyrad.*

He returns to reading the letter and is grateful that the rest is cheerier and that matters in Vaeyal are far better than in Fyrad.

XXXVIII

Just before morning mess on the fifth oneday of Spring, Alyiakal is in his study thinking about Baertal and Zekkaat, particularly the fact that when the dispatch riders and the extra lancers returned from Syadtar, they'd brought an envelope with a directive from headquarters and personal correspondence for officers and rankers—if not for Alyiakal—but no acknowledgment of the prompt return of the borrowed wagon. While an acknowledgment certainly wasn't required, it was customary.

Alyiakal shakes his head and heads for the mess, also worrying about why he hasn't heard from Saelora, especially after her mention of the Dyljani Clan.

After breakfast, he's barely back in his study when a ranker rushes in. "Ser, there are raiders attacking the hamlet to the southwest, the one south of the midvalley road. One of the boys rode here to tell us."

"Find Captain Chaem and Undercaptain Suraat. Tell them to have their companies ready to ride out immediately. Tell them both that I'll be riding with Third Company."

"Yes, ser."

Alyiakal heads to the duty desk where a concerned-looking young man stands. "When did this happen?"

"Maybe a glass ago. Pa sent me out the back gate when he saw the raiders heading to the front. I had to outrun one of them, but Grazzie's the fastest horse we got."

"Did you see how many?"

"Not really. Had to be more than a half score. Some of them had bows."

"We're going after them. You stay here." Alyiakal looks to the duty squad leader. "Make sure he's taken care of."

"Yes, ser."

Alyiakal heads for his quarters to pick up his healer's satchel. From there he goes to the stable, where the gray nuzzles him for a carrot.

"Not this morning, fellow. Not this morning."

After saddling the gray and walking him outside, Alyiakal mounts and rides to where Second Company is forming, reining up beside Chaem.

"Your messenger said the raiders are attacking the hamlet to the west a little north of the midvalley road?"

"That's what the boy they sent says. At least a half score. You're to go after them directly. Use a fast trot on the way. The raiders might be gone before you get there. If they're still there, you know what to do. If they're not, I suspect they'll withdraw to the hidden trail to the west. Their tracks will tell you if that's where they're headed. You're to follow them. If they get into the hills on that trail, don't follow them, just stay there to make sure they don't come back that way. Wait there until you get word from me. If the tracks show they're heading to the northeast road, follow them that way. Third Company is going to take the northwest road toward Jeranyi and with some fortune, we might be able to catch them when they leave the trail. If you find them before they get into the hills or go somewhere else, let me know. I'll leave a squad where the road south splits from the northwest road."

"Yes, ser."

Alyiakal rides to join Suraat, reining up beside the undercaptain.

"Two companies, ser?"

"Captain Chaem's headed for the hamlet. We're going to try to trap the raiders on the back trail. We've got three chances—the road at the edge of the hills, the back hill road, or the west road to Jerans. We'll be moving at a trot, not a walk."

"Yes, ser."

Even with everyone hurrying, two quints pass from the time Alyiakal learns of the attack until Chaem leads Second Company out through the south gates, and Suraat and Alyiakal ride north from the post with Third Company. Alyiakal creates his unseen order funnel to collect chaos, almost out of habit.

Two more glasses pass before Third Company reaches the split in the road. There, Alyiakal and the scouts can see that the only hoofprints are those of cart horses.

Alyiakal turns to Suraat. "What does that tell us, Undercaptain?"

"That the raiders didn't come from the north road or the northeast road, ser. Not this part of them, anyway. If they're from the north, they took a back way we don't know, or they could be from the west."

After a very short break, Third Company resumes riding, and travels three kays, before halting where the road again splits, the right fork heading toward Jerans, and the trail to the left curving to the southwest along the base of the hills. Again, the only recent tracks are those of several carts, some heading west toward Jerans, and the others southwest.

"Detail third squad and a scout to wait here, to direct Second Company," Alyiakal orders Suraat, "or to take out any raiders who avoid the companies. First and second squads will head toward Jerans."

Three quints later, the company reaches the crest of the road before the descent into the vale holding the trail to the left. Alyiakal extends his senses, trying to discern whether the raiders have neared the main road, but he can't discern any large order/chaos patterns. As he rides closer, though, he can see more than a few hoofprints either entering or leaving the trail.

"Have the company halt," Alyiakal tells Suraat, "and have the scouts determine which way these riders were going."

"Yes, ser." Suraat then gives the order.

While the scouts investigate the tracks, Alyiakal continues scanning the area to the south. While he thinks he can sense something in the distance, it's too far away to determine whether it's a horse and rider or a red deer.

The scouts ride up, and the senior scout says, "Sers, the riders came from the west and went down that side trail. There's no sign of anyone coming back. They number at least a half score, and there might be more."

"Thank you." Alyiakal turns to Suraat. "Move the company west and set up with a five-man staggered front facing where the raiders will emerge from the trail." Before Suraat can question, he adds, "That way, any raiders who avoid our fire can only head back toward third squad. We'll hold fire as long as we can, until most of them are on the road."

"Won't they see our tracks?"

"Our tracks will show that we've headed farther west," Alyiakal points out. "Even if they see us, they're trapped, one way or the other. Second Company is at the other end of the trail." Alyiakal would prefer not to dig the raiders out of the narrow trail, but he can handle that, if necessary. "If we split the company, we risk firing through the raiders and hitting our own lancers."

After a moment, Suraat nods, then orders, "Company! Forward!"

In less than half a quint, the two squads are in position, with Alyiakal and Suraat on the side of the road opposite the trail, and twenty yards to the north.

Another half quint passes, and Alyiakal can definitely discern riders heading their way. "Silence in the company," he says quietly. "They'll appear suddenly. Arms ready. Pass it along."

As he waits, Alyiakal creates the illusion of the road west being empty, which conceals Third Company, creating the impression that the road is empty in both directions for the riders coming up the trail.

A quint passes before a single rider appears, looking both ways, then waving back to whoever is following before riding out into the road and looking back.

Alyiakal holds off on dropping the illusion until twelve raiders are on the road and the lead rider looks as though he's about to ride out. Then he orders, "Fire at will! Fire at will."

There's a brief hesitation before the firelances sweep the riders, and in moments all are down, as are some mounts.

Alyiakal targets the two raiders just about to ride onto the road, and senses another farther back. "Cease fire! Cease fire!"

The moment he is sure the firelances are still, he says to Suraat, "Take care of the cleanup. I'll be back in a moment." Then he rides across the road and onto the narrow trail, firing a short firebolt past the last raider, who's trying to turn his mount on the narrow trail.

"Stop right there or you're dead!" he snaps.

The raider freezes.

"Ride toward me, hands high."

The rider lifts his hands, then drops one, throwing a knife directly at Alyiakal, then glances to the side as if thinking about dismounting.

Alyiakal's next firebolt turns the raider's upper body to ash.

"Help!" comes a feminine shout from farther down the trail.

Alyiakal senses six more mounts.

Frig! You should have guessed!

Alyiakal eases the gray past the dead raider's mount, using order to bend back the evergreen branches on his left, getting just enough space to squeeze through by expanding his shields slightly.

Another twenty yards along the trail, four women are tied to mounts in a row with two raiders behind them. The raider nearest to the last woman holds a blade ready to strike the woman.

"You move forward, lancer, and I'll kill her."

Alyiakal uses a quick blast of personal chaos to remove the raider's hand and head, and a second blast on the last raider. He strongly doubts that any of the women will notice—or care—that the chaos didn't come from his firelance. He immediately scans the area with his senses but can find no other order/chaos patterns farther down the trail.

"If you four will follow me, we'll get you untied once we get on the road up ahead."

It takes some considerable care for Alyiakal to turn the gray before heading back along the trail, but the mount of the knife-throwing raider has proceeded along the path to the road, where it's been captured by the lancers.

Once he's on the road with the captive women, he asks, "Were there any others? Raiders that didn't come back this way?"

The first woman, a girl really, just looks at Alyiakal uncomprehendingly.

The second says, after a moment, "I don't think so."

The third ignores Alyiakal and stares blankly into the distance.

The fourth says, "No."

Alyiakal looks to Suraat. "Have someone untie them. Also, there are three dead raiders down the trail and two or three mounts. Send a few rankers to strip the bodies and dispose of them. Have the scouts see if the raider tracks look as though they came from Jerans."

"Yes, ser."

Alyiakal senses Suraat's discomfort, but that's scarcely surprising, since the encounter with the raiders is the first real action the undercaptain has seen.

In the end, unsurprisingly, all of the tack and weapons are from Jerans. What is surprising is that all the raiders wear the dark gray trousers of Jeranyi armsmen, although it appears that the muted colors of the surviving tunics differ from each other. Alyiakal has a ranker check the hooves of the surviving mounts, and all appear to be shod in the same fashion.

"That's rather interesting, don't you think?" Alyiakal says to Suraat.

"Why would the Jeranyi send armsmen disguised as raiders on a raid?" asks the undercaptain.

"I can think of several possibilities. They could have been raiders equipped by the Jeranyi to cause us trouble. Or they could have been Jeranyi armsmen raiding on their own to get women. Or possibly Jeranyi armsmen disguised as raiders to determine how well and quickly we respond." Alyiakal pauses, then adds, "Or raiders with Jeranyi gear supplied by someone else, like Cerlyn, designed to provoke us into attacking Jerans. What do you think?"

"I'd say the first or second are more likely," replies Suraat.

"So do I, but we don't know enough yet to dismiss the other possibilities."

The spoils are limited, consisting of a few simple gold or silver rings, twenty-three coppers, and a bag of flour. The only truly valuable loot was the women, apparently the main point of the raid. *Apparently . . . for now.*

Alyiakal wonders how many men the raiders killed in obtaining the women, and if that was where some of the coppers had come from.

Once the bodies of mounts and men are dragged well away from the road, and the gear and weapons loaded on the captured mounts, the two squads of Third Company ride back down the northwest road.

Suraat finally says, "Is it always like this?"

"No," replies Alyiakal, "it's very seldom like this, and you haven't seen the rest of what happened yet."

"What happened at the hamlet, you mean?"

Alyiakal nods. "I hope it wasn't too bad, but since they captured four women, it's not likely to be good."

Suraat says nothing, and Alyiakal doesn't press.

When they reach the junction of the northwest road and the trail south, where third squad waits, Alyiakal reins up beside the squad leader. "Have you seen any travelers or a scout from Second Company?"

"No, ser."

"Have your squad fall in at the rear. We're heading south to meet with Second Company. After that, if we don't run into more raiders, we'll head for the hamlet they raided."

Roughly a glass later, Alyiakal sights a scout ahead. Almost immediately, the scout rides toward Third Company.

When he reaches the company, he turns his mount alongside Alyiakal. "Ser, Second Company's just ahead. We couldn't catch the raiders before they got into the hills—except one. Captain Chaem's been worrying about whether to head north to meet you."

"He's done just fine," replies Alyiakal.

A half quint later, Alyiakal and Suraat rein up beside Chaem.

"I understand you chased the raiders into the rocks," says Alyiakal.

"Yes, ser. We couldn't quite get to them before most were in the rocks," says Chaem, "but we did bring down the mount of the trailing rider. Got him as well." He looks and sees the four women. "How did you manage that?"

Suraat looks to Alyiakal.

"They were strung out on the trail, and the women were near the end. We surprised them as they came off the trail onto the road." Alyiakal pauses. "We need to take the women back to their hamlet and find out how much damage the raiders did."

"Yes, ser."

Chaem momentarily glances at Suraat, and Alyiakal knows the older captain has questions for Suraat.

A glass later, the two companies near the hamlet. The usual mudbrick wall surrounds the houses and low barns. At slightly over three cubits high, it's more to confine and protect domestic animals than to deter raiders. The roofs of the dwellings are of mudbrick tiles, while the many low structures holding animals have turf roofs.

Alyiakal has Suraat call a halt short of the main gate to the hamlet. There's no sign of any raiders, except that the gate hangs to one side. Then he says to Suraat, "Hold here. I'm going to send Second Company back to the post. There's no need for another company now. Then we'll deal with the headman."

Once Alyiakal meets with Chaem and Second Company rides toward Pemedra, Alyiakal and Suraat, along with two lancers, escort the four women through the gate.

"Which is the headman's dwelling?" Alyiakal asks the women.

"The larger one on the square," answers the fourth woman.

The square is little more than an open area of packed earth and clay. Alyiakal rides up to the largest dwelling.

A black-haired and bearded man hurries toward the eight riders. Then he slows as he sees the women.

"We're returning the women the raiders took," Alyiakal says evenly. "Each can keep or trade the mount they ride. They deserve that."

"We're glad you could save them. Too bad you weren't here in time to save those they killed." The headman's words are bitter.

"How many did you lose?" asks Alyiakal.

"Three men . . . Oskaal, Paerdyn, and Ruustof. They injured two boys and another woman."

"Those raiders won't trouble you anymore."

"How can you say that?" demands the headman. "They'll be back."

"Not this group," replies Alyiakal. "They're dead."

"All of them?"

"Every last one."

"You're not a regular company officer."

"No. I'm the majer in command of Pemedra."

"And you ride patrols?"

"Only some of them. How badly hurt are the boys and the woman?"

"Bad enough."

"I'm a field healer," says Alyiakal. "I might be able to help."

"You're a man," says the woman who has edged up close to the headman.

Alyiakal's laugh is humorless. "That's one reason why the Magi'i wouldn't let me be a full healer." He dismounts and unstraps his healing satchel, then says, "While I see to your injured, I'd appreciate it if my lancers could water their mounts."

"Yes, ser. There's a trough over there." The headman points, then turns back to Alyiakal. "You're really a healer?"

"Let's see your wounded." Alyiakal turns to address Suraat. "Make sure all the horses are watered. Then stand down until I'm done."

The first of the injured is a boy about ten, Alyiakal judges. His face is bruised and cut, as if he'd been thrown into something, which he probably had been. There's a lump and a wide bruise on his forehead, and one arm is in a rough splint. The head lump and bruise concern Alyiakal, but he doesn't sense wound chaos inside the skull. The arm has already swollen, and the bone ends of the break in his forearm aren't aligned as well as they should be.

Alyiakal looks to the woman who has to be his mother. "His head will heal, but he should be quiet for an eightday. The arm isn't quite right." He looks to the boy. "Setting it so it will heal straight will hurt for a few moments. Do you understand?"

The boy nods.

Alyiakal removes clean cloth strips from the satchel, loosens the splint, and sees that there's no break in the skin. He gently uses order to immobilize what he can, and then repositions the bone ends, holding everything in place with order, as he re-splints the arm.

While Alyiakal does all that, the boy barely winces.

Then Alyiakal adds slight bits of order to the internal wound chaos before turning back to the mother. "He should wear the splint for six eightdays, and he shouldn't do any heavy lifting with that arm for another four eightdays after that."

The boy says quietly, "It doesn't hurt as much."

"It will keep hurting for a time, but the hurt should get less." Alyiakal stands.

The mother just looks at him, then at her son.

Alyiakal leaves the dwelling.

When he reaches the second dwelling, a woman gestures to a recessed bed, then turns away, tears in her eyes. In the bed lies a woman, immobile and likely fifteen years older than Alyiakal. He immediately senses the wound chaos on the side of her skull, as well as inside.

Now what do you do?

For several moments he just senses her skull and the depression on one side. He wonders whether, if he surrounded the depressed bone with order on both sides and lifted, that would help. There would still be the internal damage.

Alyiakal decides to try. It's delicate . . . and difficult. Then he removes some of the wound chaos. He steps back and watches. He's not sure but thinks she's breathing more deeply.

Then he walks over to the younger woman. "I've done what I could. Don't touch anywhere close to the hurt section of her head. Not for eightdays."

The third victim is an older boy who's taken a nasty slash to one arm. That's the kind of wound Alyiakal has seen all too many of, but there's not too much chaos, and while re-dressing the wound, he removes what wound chaos he can.

Then he walks out to find the headman waiting.

"I've done what I can."

"More than many."

"Good day, Headman."

"Good day, officer."

Alyiakal carries his satchel to where Third Company is resting and fastens it behind the saddle, then turns to Suraat. "Have the company mount up."

Alyiakal says little as the company leaves the hamlet and rides toward the midvalley road.

After a time, Suraat says, "You didn't have to try to heal their wounded, did you, ser?"

"But I could, and there was time. Besides, we're supposed to protect them."

"How did the healing go?"

"The two boys should recover. The older woman . . . it's possible, but less likely. She had a bad head wound. I did what I could."

Suraat nods, but Alyiakal senses some puzzlement.

Once Third Company is back at Pemedra and Suraat has dismissed the company to duties, Alyiakal turns to Suraat. "Even though I rode with Third Company, Undercaptain, you still need to write up the patrol report. I'll add anything I think necessary."

"Yes, ser."

Then Alyiakal rides to the stable, takes care of the gray, and heads back to his study, stopping briefly to leave his healer's satchel in his quarters.

Baassyn immediately appears and asks, "How did it go?"

Alyiakal gives him a brief summary.

"Twenty-odd raiders this early in the year," replies Baassyn, "that's more than I've heard of."

"The fact that all of the tack and trousers looked to be from Jerans is concerning. As is the fact that the raiding group was the size of a squad."

"You don't think they'll send more armsmen, do you?"

"Not yet. I'm guessing they're operating under the guise of raiders because it's a cheaper way to cause trouble and the Empire can't claim that Jerans is attacking." Alyiakal pauses. "No dispatches today?"

"None."

Alyiakal shakes his head. "I worry when there are dispatches, and I worry when there aren't."

"I'd prefer none," says Baassyn dryly.

Alyiakal laughs softly, then enters his office.

A quint before evening mess, Alyiakal walks to his quarters, then waits until the corridor outside his door is empty before emerging under a concealment and making his way to the officers' mess, where he waits for the junior officers to arrive.

The first is Nolaan, followed quickly by Chaem and Suraat.

"How were your patrols?" asks Nolaan.

"Second Company chased the frigging raiders up into that hidden trail," says Chaem. "Majer told us to guard that end and not to follow. He and Third Company caught them at the other end."

"More like a massacre," says Suraat. "They came out of that trail, didn't even see us until we opened fire, and most of them were dead in moments. The majer takes out two more coming out of the trail, leaves me in command, goes down the trail alone, kills three raiders, and brings back four captured women untouched."

"How'd he do that?" asks Kessmyr as he joins the other three.

"Black angels be damned if I know," replies Suraat. "I asked one of the women. She said he just killed 'em all with his firelance. He was so good he took out one who had a blade ready to lop off a woman's head. Firebolt didn't even touch her. Must have liquid ice instead of blood. A score of raiders, and they're all dead."

"That tell you something?" asks Chaem.

"He sure as sowshit doesn't like raiders," replies Suraat.

"Did you lose any men?" asks Chaem.

"No."

"Keep that in mind after you leave here," says the older captain.

"He's like that with blades, too," adds Nolaan.

"You sparred with him in blade training?" asks Kessmyr. "You never said anything."

"I asked him to. He taught me more this past Winter than I learned in three years at Kynstaar."

"Wager that hurt," says Suraat.

"Mostly my pride," replies Nolaan with an amused laugh.

Alyiakal slips out of the mess, retreats out of sight, drops the concealment, and then returns to the corridor outside the mess, where he waits for Baassyn to join him.

XXXIX

Another eightday comes and goes without any sign of raiders, and that worries Alyiakal. He's also a bit concerned because he's heard nothing from Saelora. While he can't do anything about Saelora's problems, he decides it's time to look into why nothing is happening to the northeast.

On threeday of the sixth eightday of Spring, Alyiakal joins Nolaan and Fourth Company for an extended patrol of the hills separating Pemedra's valley from the grasslands southeast of Cerlyn, the same grasslands he'd crossed to reach the border with Cerlyn years before. He also has three bottles of grass ale strapped to his saddle, as well as his satchel, bedroll, and trail provisions.

After Nolaan orders the company forward and toward the post's north gates, he turns in the saddle toward Alyiakal. "You haven't said much about this patrol, ser."

"That's because there's not too much I can say," admits Alyiakal. "I've checked the patrol records, and this Spring we've had the fewest raids ever—just one. That raid came out of the northwest by raiders or armsmen attired as raiders with tack and weapons supplied by the Jeranyi. In the past, all the raids came from the *north,* not from the northwest or the west."

"You're concerned because there haven't been any raids?"

"That's a considerable change from the past, and we need to know why. Has there been a plague? Have the Cerlynese wiped out the grassland barbarians? Or have they conscripted all of them?"

"Which do you think is likely?" asks Nolaan.

"I worry about Duke Taartyn building an army, but that doesn't mean he is. Also, it's possible that we won't learn anything from this patrol. One way or the other, I'd prefer to discover what's happening north of the hills before it affects us." Alyiakal offers a wry smile and adds, "At the very least, Fourth Company will get some extended training and much greater familiarity with the terrain in that area."

"That's true," says Nolaan warily.

"How do you think we trapped that last group of raiders?" asks Alyiakal quietly.

"Sorry, ser."

Since Nolaan sounds apologetic and feels upset, Alyiakal lets the matter pass and leans forward and pats the gray on the shoulder. "Long day ahead, fellow."

Once the company reaches the split in the road and takes a brief break, Alyiakal directs Nolaan to take the company up the narrower northeast road. While there are a few cart tracks for the first several kays, those vanish entirely as the company moves higher into the hills, suggesting to Alyiakal that the carts came from the valley looking for wood or foraging for food, such as the flat-eared cacti and wild quilla, which is even more vile than the domesticated variety, so far as Alyiakal is concerned.

"There's no sign that anyone's been this way recently," Nolaan finally says. "Not in the last few eightdays."

"Was there any time last year when there were no tracks, except grass antelope and the like?" asks Alyiakal.

"No, ser."

"When something feels wrong," says Alyiakal evenly, "you could be right . . . or you could just be imagining things. That was why I checked all the Spring patrol reports for the past ten years. There are reasons for those patrol reports. They're not just paperwork exercises. Reading those reports likely saved me and my company when I was an undercaptain."

"How was that, ser?" asks Nolaan politely, although Alyiakal senses the undercaptain is only moderately interested.

"I read them because no one would tell me much about my predecessor. I discovered that the last patrol report was written by the company's senior squad leader." Alyiakal waits.

"By the senior squad leader? Then something happened to the company officer?"

"It did. He was close to making captain, but he led a squad into an ambush.

He and a number of lancers were killed by a landslide started by barbarians. I'd never even thought of being attacked by landslide. It made me a lot more cautious about where I led the company, and several eightdays later . . ." Alyiakal relates how the report *and* his horse's reaction made him aware of the barbarians' location. Then he adds, "All the smallest details can tell you more than any one large fact. If you understand what they mean. Sometimes what you don't find is as important as what you do."

"Like the hoofprints we're *not* seeing now?"

"Also like the cart tracks we aren't seeing. Even in the worst of times some traders would sneak down into the grasslands from here."

"Why this way? Isn't it flatter from Cerlyn?"

"It is, but back then, the Cerlynese killed traders who came from the north and east without going through Cerlyn first. Even then, it was dangerous to go through Cerlyn because they often killed traders on a whim."

"Why does anyone deal with them, then?" asks Nolaan.

"They control the only large source of copper in Candar."

Nolaan nods slowly, as if he's not sure what to make of Alyiakal's information.

Before long, the slopes become rockier and more barren, containing only scattered evergreens, low bushes, and sparse spring grass that is not quite calf-high. Despite the clear sky, the air remains chill enough that Alyiakal is glad for his riding jacket and gloves. He's not about to complain, because he knows that in another few eightdays the hills will be almost as hot as the valleys.

After riding another glass, and still finding no hoofprints on the narrow road, he orders a break.

Is it going to be like this for the next two days? Or longer?

He's still pondering the lack of travelers and traders once Fourth Company continues riding northeast through the hills, wondering whether a plague has struck the grassland hamlets beyond or if a grass fire had burned them out the previous fall . . . or if the raider hamlet has decided not to raid anymore.

He shakes his head at the absurdity of the last explanation, but still wonders.

The remainder of threeday is no different. The company rides and takes breaks, but finds no hoofprints and no traders. Alyiakal occasionally sights grass antelopes and grass cats stalking them.

Given the barrenness of the hills and the seeming lack of travelers, Alyiakal keeps the company moving well into twilight.

On fourday not long after first light, he has the company back on the road, which has veered north, in agreement with both his map and memory. As the morning draws out, the only tracks in the road remain those of antelope, grass cats, and an occasional vulcrow. Alyiakal gets the feeling that no one has been on the road since the previous Autumn, if not before.

In late afternoon, the company reaches the point where the road begins to descend, although Alyiakal cannot yet see the grasslands to the north. Another glass passes, and a scout rides back toward the company, slowing as he nears Alyiakal and Nolaan.

"Sers . . . there's what's left of a body up ahead. No tracks. Might have been here for half a season, not much longer."

"Any sign of other bodies or hoofprints . . . even old ones?" asks Alyiakal, although he doesn't sense any large order/chaos patterns nearby, except for Fourth Company.

"No, ser."

"Halt the company," Alyiakal says to Nolaan, "and we'll take a look."

Once the company's halted, Alyiakal and Nolaan follow the scout around a gentle curve.

"At the base of that big stone, sers."

The remains lie just short of a squarish boulder some four yards uphill from the road. The bones are disarrayed and incomplete, even the skull, suggesting to Alyiakal that a grass cat, the only large predator in the area, had killed or scavenged the traveler. He rides closer, studying the incomplete bones and faded brown scraps of clothing. To one side is a strip of leather, what's left of a belt . . . and, surprisingly, a short knife in a sheath.

"Likely a man," says Alyiakal. "He wasn't killed by raiders or the Cerlynese. They would have taken the knife."

"Could he have been wounded and gotten away but died later?" asks Nolaan.

"Possibly," replies the scout. "No way to tell now."

"Or he could have been killed by a grass cat when he was too tired or weak to defend himself," adds Alyiakal. "The real questions are what he was doing and how he got here. What's left of his clothes suggest he came from the valley to the north, but traveling on foot would have taken more than a day. Also, there's no sign of a pack or any gear, and there'd likely be gouges in the ground if there had been horses around, even if he died at the start of Spring."

"Could he have come up here in the Winter and been frozen?" asks Nolaan.

"That's unlikely," says Alyiakal. "Getting this far from the valley in Winter on foot would be impossible, and there's no sign of a horse." He turns to the scout. "If you'd pick up the knife and a scrap of the brown cloth."

"Yes, ser."

Less than a quint later, Fourth Company resumes riding down the trail to the valley ahead, although Alyiakal still can't see anything but hills.

Very late in the afternoon, Fourth Company rides around a curve between two hills, revealing a clear view of the rolling plain of spring-green grass stretching for kays. Alyiakal calls a halt and rides out a short way on the ridge bordering the road, motioning for Nolaan to accompany him. Exactly as Alyiakal recalls, the Grass Hills to his right angle northeast while the wide expanse of grass before him widens to the north and northwest. He can make out the tree line to the north in the distance. Those trees mark the border between the grasslands and Cerlyn, with the fields and the small town immediately beyond.

Nearer to the ridge and below, he sees the brown lines of roads between the hamlets, and his eyes go right, toward the larger hamlet that hosted raiders in the past. He strains his vision, but can't see any signs of movement, nor even any smoke rising from the mudbrick dwellings. Frowning, he turns his attention to the nearest hamlet on the left, where he sees a single trail of smoke.

"Do you see anything moving?" he asks Nolaan.

"Just a few lines of smoke, ser."

What Alyiakal sees and doesn't see means that the patrol is going to take longer than he'd hoped. *But don't so many things?*

Because it will be dark before long and because there aren't any better sites to stop, he decides that they might as well stop for the night.

The next morning, Alyiakal has Fourth Company again moving at first light. Shortly after full sunrise, the company reaches the flat at the base of the lower hills. This sits north of the heights, where the road forks, with one route heading to the right, the other turning westward. Neither route shows hoofprints.

"We'll head right," Alyiakal tells Nolaan. "That leads toward the hamlet that held raiders, years ago."

Nolaan raises his eyebrows.

"If there are still raiders there," says Alyiakal, "and they attack, that solves one problem. If there aren't, that suggests another."

As Fourth Company turns onto the northeast road, Alyiakal checks his chaos-gathering funnel, then concentrates on sensing for anything ahead.

Although the grass flanking the road isn't high enough to hide much, the low rise farther on well might.

A quint later, topping the rise, Alyiakal sees the mudbrick dwellings of the hamlet a kay away. What he doesn't see is any movement. Even as the company draws nearer to the dwellings, he doesn't hear the alarm bell that rang the last time he'd approached.

"There's no one there," says Nolaan quietly.

Once the company nears the outlying buildings, Alyiakal also sees that the mudbrick dwellings are roofless, the straw-thatched roofs gone, with doors and windows blackened and charred. "Burned out and destroyed." He pauses. "Have third squad do a quick search for any remains."

While third squad begins the search, Alyiakal rides to the cleared area in the middle of the houses, the closest approximation to a central square the community had, and looks closely at the uneven ground. He sees depressions that might be the remains of hoofprints and some partly filled-in depressions that appear to be wagon tracks.

After making a circuit of the central area, he returns to where Nolaan and first squad have halted and asks, "What's your impression?"

"Someone didn't want them to return."

"I didn't see any signs of bodies, but we'll see what third squad finds." *Or doesn't.*

Two quints later, third squad and the scouts report no signs of remains, even of animals.

"How long ago do you think the fires were set?" Alyiakal asks the scouts.

"I'd say early Spring, ser. The fields weren't tilled, and the ashes haven't been that flattened. Close to the burned wood, you can smell just a hint of the charring. Likely wouldn't if it happened in Winter."

Alyiakal nods, then turns to Nolaan. "Order a break. After that, we'll start back."

"Yes, ser." After the undercaptain gives the orders, he looks to Alyiakal. "We're not looking any farther?"

"Right now, there's no reason to. There's no sign of bodies or dead livestock. Someone came in force. The people left without fighting. I'm guessing the Cerlynese made them an offer they couldn't refuse."

"An offer they couldn't refuse?" asks Nolaan.

"This was a raider hamlet. The only offer they wouldn't refuse was to move into Cerlyn and to be paid to fight for the Duke."

"Would they all accept?"

"Probably not," replies Alyiakal. "I'm guessing the body we found in the hills was someone who wouldn't. There are likely a few others scattered around, but that's a guess. I'm also guessing they pulled all the able-bodied men out of the other hamlets, and that's why we've only seen a few trails of smoke. The Cerlynese didn't want to leave any raiders behind, but by leaving women and children in the other hamlets, they can raid for young men again in another few years."

"You think the Duke's building up his forces?" asks Nolaan.

"I'd be surprised if it's otherwise. The question is how and where he intends to use them." *There are only two real possibilities.*

"What are you going to do, ser?"

"Ride back to Pemedra and report what we've discovered to headquarters. What we do after that depends on headquarters and Duke Taartyn. If he attacks us, we defend Cyador's territory however we can. If he doesn't, we keep patrolling until headquarters orders us to do something else."

"That's all?"

"Even majers who command border posts don't invade other lands, even if attacked, unless ordered. So far, neither an attack nor such an order has happened. So we'll ride back after a long and uneventful patrol."

And hope that your fear about what Taartyn will do doesn't happen.

XL

Alyiakal and Fourth Company return to Pemedra very late in the evening on eightday, having seen no traders and only their own tracks until they encounter evidence of carts coming from and returning to the valley in the hills north of the post. Alyiakal doesn't even enter his study until oneday morning before morning mess, where he's not surprised to find several unopened envelopes from Mirror Lancer headquarters and pleasantly surprised to find a letter from Saelora.

He immediately asks Baassyn when the dispatch riders arrived.

"Last night, ser."

"Have them wait and leave tomorrow morning. That way, they can take my report on what's happening in the grasslands south of Cerlyn."

"Yes, ser. I'll take care of that."

As Baassyn hurries off, Alyiakal decides that the directives or correspondence from headquarters can wait until after breakfast and immediately, carefully, slits open Saelora's letter and begins to read.

Alyiakal—

For some reason, both your previous letters were delayed at least several eightdays . . .

Several eightdays? Baertal or Zekkaat?

While Alyiakal could believe that Baertal might want to read or delay Alyiakal's letters, he can't see Baertal risking getting caught, especially since there would be little to gain from reading and/or delaying the letters.

. . . Both arrived a day apart—yesterday and today. I hope that doesn't mean that you, or other Mirror Lancers, are involved in matters like those in Lhaarat several years ago. Perhaps it's just because of bad weather or someone's carelessness, but I wanted you to know that I worried. I was about to start writing back today when your second letter arrived.

I understand that you can't say much about your duties, but even if you can't, I enjoy and appreciate every word, even if it's about the difference between the grass at Oldroad Post, Lhaarat, and Pemedra.

Catriana found out that the strange man at the factorage visited other factorages as well, but so far nothing else has happened. Gaaran and the twins have added bars to the distillery windows and reinforced the doors. They also made some improvements at Loraan House here. The trading house interested in distillery products has approached us about selling some goods for them on consignment. We'd get a small percentage, but there's almost no risk. Catriana and I are looking into perhaps more risk-sharing and a higher percentage. We'll see how that develops . . .

Mother definitely gets more tired more quickly these days. That's what Charissa tells me. Gaaran won't talk about it. Mother suggested that Faadyr might consider brewing ale to sell in Vaeyal. What he brews is far better than anything the inns, alehouses, and brothels have, and Faadyr can likely do it more cheaply.

Alyiakal reads through the rest of the letter quickly and then hurries down to the morning mess, where, after all the officers have served themselves, he gives a quick briefing on what Fourth Company discovered and what it didn't.

As soon as he finishes, Baassyn asks, "Why do you think Duke Taartyn would effectively kidnap an entire hamlet?"

"Because he tried grabbing young men three years ago, and forcing them to fight, because it didn't work all that well. The grassland raiders like to fight, and they'd be cheap at the price. His men likely destroyed the hamlet so the raiders didn't have second thoughts. He might be using similar tactics elsewhere. We have no way of finding out."

"What do you think headquarters will say, ser?" asks Suraat.

"They won't say anything until they receive my report. They may not say anything at all, except for a brief letter thanking me for the information. Right now, we don't know what Duke Taartyn is doing with those raider families. He could be moving them to his west border with Jerans to provide a buffer of sorts. He could be building a larger force of armsmen. Or it could be something else entirely. There's too much we don't know, and no way to find out without entering Cerlyn."

"Well . . ." begins Chaem, his voice warmly ironic as he speaks, "doesn't look like we'll see raiders from the north anytime soon."

Kessmyr half chokes on his ale at the understatement.

Alyiakal appreciates the way the older captain has ended the questions.

After breakfast, Alyiakal hurries back to his study, where he opens the first envelope from Mirror Lancer headquarters: a reminder about the need to clean post water and sewer systems and an updated directive on the procedures for handling horseshoes. Setting both aside, he opens the second envelope. The single sheet is from the Captain-Commander and signed by him, not, as is sometimes the case, signed on his behalf by another officer.

Majer Alyiakal,

This is to inform you, as one of the officers commanding a border post, that the recent directive dealing with the unlawful smuggling of copper into Cyador remains Imperial policy, contrary to any rumors to the contrary.

Given the nature of your responsibilities and the need to protect the borders of Cyador and the people of the Empire of Light living close within those borders, at times, you may have to choose between conflicting priorities.

> *This letter is to make clear that your duties to protect and defend the borders of Cyador and its people are a higher priority than any directive dealing with commerce.*

The signature is Laartol's.

Alyiakal offers a low whistle. Laartol is as much as saying that, if Alyiakal can justify it by operational necessity, he can largely ignore the copper directive. Laartol is also hinting that he doesn't think much of the Imperial edict.

While Alyiakal will need to circulate the edict to all officers, that can wait, and there's little he can do for Saelora at the moment, even given his worries about the Dyljani Clan trying to move into Fyrad.

He takes out paper and pen and begins to draft his report on Fourth Company's discovery north of the Grass Hills.

More than a glass later, finished with the draft, he carries it into Baassyn's study and hands the sheets to the overcaptain. "I'd like your thoughts. I want this to read as completely impartial."

Baassyn takes the draft but looks at Alyiakal. "Your reports are always impartial."

"This goes to headquarters. I need to dispatch it first thing tomorrow. I also have a gut feeling that there's going to be trouble with Cerlyn, especially after our findings. My past experiences there . . ."

Baassyn nods. "I can see why you want to be very impartial. I'll read it immediately."

Alyiakal returns to his study, where he drafts a cover note to the Captain-Commander's letter, telling each officer to read the letter and initial his note, signifying they've read it. Then he has the duty ranker carry the letter and cover note to the officers' study and place it in Chaem's box.

A quint later, Baassyn steps into Alyiakal's study. "I have a few thoughts, ser."

"Put the sheets on the desk and go through them." Alyiakal stands.

Baassyn lays the sheets side by side, then points and says, "Here, ser, I might suggest that you say . . . the lack of bodies, especially of women and children . . ."

"You're right. I'd thought about that, but somehow I didn't include it . . ."

In less than half a quint, Baassyn offers his remaining suggestions.

Alyiakal smiles wryly. "Thank you. I appreciate your comments and suggestions." After he rewrites the report, he writes two copies, one for his file and one for Subcommander Zekkaat. Then he drafts the cover letter to the Majer-Commander, as well as one to Zekkaat.

Thinking about Laartol's letter, he decides that he has even more to worry about—and there's not anything under the Rational Stars that he can do about any of it.

Not now, anyway, and maybe not ever. And that doesn't help, either.

XLI

The next three eightdays turn out to be relatively quiet. Suraat and Third Company discover three young men from a hamlet southwest of the mid-valley road facing off with the headman of the hamlet earlier raided over the youths' grazing their flock too far north. With the presence of the Mirror Lancer company, the young men decide that perhaps their flock has gone too far north and immediately drive their sheep south.

While patrolling the northwest road, Nolaan and Fourth Company sight four riders who immediately turn back before the company scouts can identify them. Nolaan suspects the riders were Jeranyi scouts, based on the number and their rapid departure, and Alyiakal shares the undercaptain's suspicion.

Alyiakal worries about what the Cerlynese may be doing, especially since he's had no response from either Subcommander Zekkaat or Mirror Lancer headquarters to his report about the situation in the grasslands.

Dispatch riders arrive in late afternoon on the tenth sixday of Spring, with two envelopes from Mirror Lancer headquarters, as well as personal correspondence for the post, including a letter from Saelora and one from Hyrsaal.

Alyiakal sets aside the personal letters and opens the official correspondence. The first envelope holds updates to existing directives, one of which is a change in how entries to post accounts for provisions obtained locally should be entered in the account ledgers. He sets that one aside so that he can call it to Baassyn's attention.

Then he opens the second envelope, containing a single sheet, a letter from Laartol as Captain-Commander of the Mirror Lancers, that is short and to the point.

Majer Alyiakal—

The Majer-Commander has received and reviewed your report on events recently occurring in the grasslands between the borders of Cerlyn and those of Cyador. Given the recent history of incursions by armsmen of Cerlyn, this information will be of value to post commanders who may be impacted by Cerlynese intrusions. For this reason, copies of your report have been forwarded to those post commanders.

The letter is signed with a single letter—"L"—unlike the letters usually sent from the Captain-Commander. Alyiakal has no way of knowing if that means something or if Laartol was rushed.

Although the letter appears to be a perfunctory acknowledgment of his report, the mention of "commanders who may be impacted" suggests that Laartol is as concerned as Alyiakal is. Since Laartol is likely in possession of more information than any post commander, that just adds to Alyiakal's worries.

Before turning to the personal correspondence, he takes the accounting directive to Baassyn.

The overcaptain accepts the directive with a quizzical expression.

"A change in accounting procedures for locally obtained provisions," says Alyiakal.

"All that will do is make comparing what we spent last year to this year more difficult," replies Baassyn. "Did you get anything interesting?"

"Apparently, the Majer-Commander actually read my report on the grasslands and is concerned enough that he's sending a copy to other border commanders."

"Nice of him to let you know, but most of them will read it and ignore it."

"If they do and the Cerlynese cause trouble in their areas, he'll at least be able to cashier or stipend them."

"If they survive," says Baassyn, "and if they're not well-connected in Cyad."

"They'll survive. That type seldom ventures into combat once they have command."

"There are dangers involved in taking any position once you're a majer, including taking no position," replies Baassyn.

"At least taking a position doesn't leave you as an immobile target." Alyiakal offers a crooked smile before turning and heading back into his own study.

Once there, he opens Hyrsaal's letter first.

Alyiakal—

One of my lancers had a question for me. He asked me if I knew an officer named Alyiakal. The way he asked it told me he'd never met you and had no idea of your rank. I said I did and asked him why he wanted to know. He said an older man he knew wanted to know if you were still an officer. I told him you were a majer in command at Pemedra and asked why the person was asking. He didn't know why the other man wanted to know. Since you spent some time in Jakaafra, I thought it might be someone you knew years ago. Maybe I shouldn't have said what I did, but now that you're a majer it wouldn't take much for someone to find out. Anyway, just in case, I thought you ought to know.

Who could that be? Triamon, in hiding but wanting to know how you turned out? Areya, wondering about the boy she'd fed for several years? Or Adayal? But why would Adayal be interested after so long? Or could it be someone else that you haven't seen or thought of in years? He can't think of any other likely possibilities, but regardless of who it might be, the larger question is why now?

He spends a few moments trying to come up with possibilities, then returns to reading.

The rest of Hyrsaal's letter has a few lines about Haarlt and Catriana and some generalities about patrolling the Accursed Forest. Hyrsaal doesn't mention his mother, and Alyiakal understands that.

Alyiakal is still wondering about who might be asking about him when he opens Saelora's letter.

I just got your latest letter. I'm so glad your letters are arriving more regularly. I loved your description of the grasslands, with the false dandelions in Spring, and about the grass antelope and how she kept her calf away from the grass cat.

We're still in talks with the outland trading company . . .

Alyiakal smiles. Saelora's never mentioned Elbarak or Valtrad House by name, which is wise, given that neither of them knows who's reading the letters and who else might find out. With the number of outland traders Loraan House deals with and how close-mouthed the outlanders tend to be, it's unlikely anyone will find out more from the letters than they could by visiting the factorages, and the odds are that the possible readers aren't in Fyrad.

. . . and matters are looking promising, although we can't count on anything until goods are delivered and paid for. That's always the way it is.

I did have dinner at Charissa and Gaaran's house, with Mother, last eightday, and, for the first time, she actually asked how you were doing, and said to send you her best. Both Gaaran and I had a hard time not gaping. Mother is a bit more forgetful, but not as bad as Gaaran had said. Maybe that was because I was there.

I hope it doesn't get too hot in Pemedra this Summer, and that you don't get one of those terrible grass fires . . .

Alyiakal smiles when he finishes the letter. Then he takes up pen and paper and starts a response so that he can send it back with the dispatch riders. He wants to let her know that someone has been asking Hyrsaal about him, for a number of reasons.

XLII

The second sevenday of Summer dawns extremely warm under a hazy green-blue sky. By midmorning, Alyiakal has no doubts it will be the hottest day of the year so far, and the days that follow won't be any cooler.

Late in the afternoon, just after Chaem finishes a northeastern patrol, dispatch riders arrive, surprising and concerning Alyiakal. A set of dispatch riders had arrived the day before and had left Pemedra just that morning—carrying his latest letter to Saelora.

The duty ranker appears in Alyiakal's study door holding a sealed dispatch bag. "An urgent dispatch from Mirror Lancer headquarters, ser."

While Alyiakal merely says "Thank you," he wonders what problem or disaster awaits inside the sealed dispatch pouch. He sits behind his desk and opens it, finding a large envelope, inside of which is a second, sealed envelope, containing a one-page letter from and signed by the Majer-Commander. The text is direct:

Patrol reports from Syadtar Post indicate possible fortifications are being placed at both the southeast and northeast entrance roads to the West Branch valley. Companies from Isahl are tasked with investigating and, if necessary, removing such fortifications from the southeast entrance before they become permanent. At the earliest feasible date, Pemedra Post is hereby ordered to investigate and, if necessary, remove any such fortifications and any armed forces from the northeast road leading into the West Branch valley.

A full report of all evolutions, once completed, shall be provided to Mirror Lancer Headquarters.

Why the frig didn't Zekkaat let me know about this! Alyiakal can understand the need to report possible fortifications immediately, but not to let Pemedra Post know at the same time seems unwise and almost inexcusable.

He takes a deep breath, then stands and walks from his study to Baassyn's, where he hands the directive to the overcaptain. "Your thoughts?"

The overcaptain reads the single sheet, hands it back to Alyiakal, then says, "We didn't get anything from Syadtar about this, I take it?"

"No. I'm not happy about that, either."

"I can see why. Majer Baertal, you think?"

"I'm guessing that. If Subcommander Zekkaat didn't specifically order him to inform us, he'd conveniently think it wasn't necessary. That is, if anyone ever gets around to asking him." *Which just might get overlooked in light of the larger problem, something that Baertal no doubt has already calculated.*

"Are you going to call the officers together or just tell them at evening mess?"

"Evening mess. It's not that long until then." Alyiakal pauses, then adds, "I'm thinking of heading out with First Company tomorrow to undertake that investigation. That way, whatever's going on, I can't be faulted for not giving the matter my immediate attention. While we're gone, I'd like you to work out what we might need if I have to take three companies there to deal with whoever's building what."

"The Jeranyi have to be behind it."

"It couldn't be anyone else, but I have a feeling Duke Taartyn's involved as well."

"Even after he removed that entire hamlet of raiders?"

"He didn't destroy them. He moved them somewhere else, with a purpose in mind."

"Do you have any idea what that might be?" asks Baassyn.

"Not specifically," *not that I'm willing to voice at the moment,* "but whatever it is, it's designed to strike back at Cyador and to demonstrate his power to Jerans."

"Rather ambitious for a duke who's barely above a barbarian lord, don't you think?" asks Baassyn.

"A barbarian lord who's building an army, I think, and who's paying it with golds he gets from selling copper to Cyadoran traders and possibly from raiding Suthyan traders."

Baassyn frowns. "You've never mentioned that before."

"A trader I ran into on home leave a while back told me that Suthya was having trouble with raiders. Given Duke Taartyn, I doubt that's changed."

"You think we're the ones who'll have to deal with it."

"It could be us. It could be Lhaarat, or it could be both."

"Not Isahl?"

"Not immediately, anyway. I need to draft a reply to headquarters to send back with the dispatch riders in the morning."

"To confirm receipt of the order and the fact that we had no advance knowledge?"

"Exactly." Alyiakal nods and then heads back to his study.

He has no trouble drafting the short response to the Majer-Commander.

> *Pemedra Post received the order to deal with possible fortifications at the northeast entrance to the West Branch valley late yesterday. We have immediately dispatched a company to investigate. What action Pemedra Post takes will be based on what the company discovers.*
>
> *For your information, for some reason, Pemedra Post was not informed of those findings prior to your directive but will act expeditiously, as required by your order.*

He makes a copy of the response, which he signs and places in a separate envelope to Laartol. He seals both envelopes, and places them in the dispatch pouch, then seals that as well.

Afterward, he and Baassyn walk from their studies to the officers' mess, where the other four officers are waiting. As Alyiakal enters, he says, "As you were," then adds, "Yes, there was an urgent message from Mirror Lancer headquarters, and you'll all hear about it momentarily."

He and Baassyn seat themselves, pour their wine, and Alyiakal takes a sip, then serves himself some of the breaded and fried fowl not quite drowned in a white sauce, along with cheesed near-potatoes, and the inevitable spring beans. He takes several mouthfuls, mostly of the highly peppered fowl, before taking a swallow of the barely passable white wine and clearing his throat.

"The message was directly from the Majer-Commander." Alyiakal repeats headquarters' message close to word for word. Even before he finishes, he sees puzzled surprise on the faces of both Chaem and Kessmyr.

Kessmyr immediately speaks. "Ser, you mean Syadtar knew about this and didn't tell you?"

"For whatever reason, we did not know of the possible fortifications until I received the order to investigate this afternoon. I have taken the liberty of mentioning that fact in my reply to the Majer-Commander which will go out tomorrow in the dispatch."

Chaem offers a faintly amused smile.

"Because the matter is urgent, I'll be accompanying First Company on an investigatory patrol leaving early tomorrow. Part of my reasoning is that I'm the only officer who's actually been in the West Branch valley, and that will make observing any changes much easier. The patrol will likely take four days, more or less, depending on the circumstances. In the meantime, Over-captain Baassyn will direct those remaining here in preparing to dispatch a larger force. While I hope that will not be necessary, events over the past several years lead me to believe that it will be."

"Ser," asks Nolaan, "could you tell us more?"

"Some ten years ago, the Jeranyi supported and encouraged local barbarians to build a town at the foot of the northwest entrance to the valley. They armed the locals with polished bronze shields, horn bows, and spear-throwers. The locals used those to ambush and inflict heavy casualties on at least two companies posted to Isahl." Alyiakal relates the role companies from Pemedra played in removing the barbarians, then adds, "This time, it's likely that the Jeranyi want to fortify both entrances to preclude an attack from the rear."

Alyiakal isn't about to mention his suspicions about the Cerlynese, because he has no facts on which to base them, except for the removal of the raiders from the grasslands.

"Why do you think they're doing this now?" asks Suraat.

"I'm guessing, in part, it's because a number of border posts have cut back on longer patrols. That might suggest Cyador can't defend its borders as strongly as it once did. That's only a guess."

"How does that fit with what you did at Lhaarat?" asks Chaem.

"They may think that was just one commander, given most other posts have cut back. If the Jeranyi have spies or contacts in Cyad, they might also have discovered that the Empire has cut back on the number of firelances at all posts."

"As if that was ever the best idea," replies Chaem sarcastically.

"There may have been reasons we don't know," declares Baassyn evenly.

"True," says Alyiakal, "but it doesn't change anything for us."

"Never does," murmurs Chaem.

Baassyn looks hard at the senior captain. Chaem returns the look with an iron coldness, and Baassyn is the one to look away.

Alyiakal clears his throat. "You know what I know about what headquarters has in mind." Then he grins, using a little order to project humor. "We should be able to manage a surprise or two." *Especially since we really don't have a choice.*

Baassyn is the only one who looks puzzled, but then, Alyiakal realizes, Baassyn's never been on a patrol with Alyiakal.

Alyiakal adds, "At least it's likely to be cooler there than here over the Summer," which is another way of hinting that what lies ahead will likely involve more than one patrol.

After dinner, Alyiakal returns to his study and writes a short letter to Saelora, telling her that he'll be leaving on a slightly longer patrol and that it might be a while before he can write again. He shakes his head. *Hinting at longer action will worry her, but if you don't tell her and this drags out, she'll worry more, besides which you've promised not to deceive her, even if you can't tell her the details until well after the fact.*

XLIII

By sunrise on eightday morning Alyiakal, Kessmyr, and First Company have passed the fork in the road north and ride toward the road to the West Branch valley. The last time Alyiakal had ridden into the valley had been years ago and in early Winter, and he suspects he'll be more uncomfortable in the heat of Summer than he had been in the chill back then.

The scouts detect no recent hoofprints when they near the road, nor are there any tracks to or from the back trail where Alyiakal and Suraat had encountered the Jeranyi-supplied raiders in Spring. As the company continues beyond the back trail, Alyiakal notices that not only are there no hoofprints, but there also aren't any signs of wagons or carts, definitely unusual for Summer.

"What does this road tell you?" he asks Kessmyr.

"No one seems to have traveled it lately."

Alyiakal waits to see if the young captain will say more.

"That seems unlikely in early Summer," Kessmyr finally adds. "Do you think the Jeranyi have blocked it with fortifications? Or stopped any traders? Or if traders have decided it's unsafe to come this way?"

"All those are possible, but smugglers can usually get around walls or armsmen. Sometimes, even traders will try. I don't think I've ever been on a road people usually travel in Summer where the only tracks belong to animals, and we're more than a day's travel from the valley entrance." Not that there are any hamlets along the rugged road through the Grass Hills.

By midafternoon, which Alyiakal admits is somewhat cooler than at Pemedra, the company still hasn't encountered any signs of travelers. That hasn't changed when Alyiakal calls a halt for the evening.

Oneday begins and continues no differently, until early afternoon, when the scouts report hoofprints in the road ahead.

"Sers, it's like a patrol. Four riders came this far and turned back. Not today, though. Most likely yesterday."

"Keep your eyes open," says Alyiakal.

"Yes, ser."

Although Alyiakal cannot yet sense any order/chaos patterns that could be armsmen or riders, he realizes that it's been quite some time since he's sensed either antelopes or grass cats. *Because the antelopes have been hunted out?*

Once the scouts return to their position ahead of the company, Alyiakal says to Kessmyr, "You can see ahead where the road turns more to the west. In a glass or so, we'll descend through a narrower valley, and it might be a good idea to send additional scouts along the higher ground on each side of the road."

Even when First Company begins to ride the road through the narrowed vale, neither the scouts nor Alyiakal discover anything amid the early-Summer grass, scattered clumps of bushes, and the occasional isolated evergreen. In time, the company halts at the top of a ridge overlooking the area where the road flattens out and enters the West Branch valley.

For a moment, Alyiakal misses what should be obvious—a set of mudbrick walls set in a square just north of the intersection of the road into the valley and another road heading west, clearly a fort of some sort. In the distance to the west, he can make out the town set just beyond the northwest road from

Isahl—where the previous town had been. He can't see if the town has a fort as well but surmises that it does.

His eyes go back to the nearer fort. It is roughly the size of the one the Cerlynese built in Kraaslaen, with corrals to the northeast. There are structures inside the fort, suggesting barracks or the equivalent, but he cannot see whether there's smoke coming from the fort, not in the afternoon heat. The longer he looks, the more he's amazed the Jeranyi have managed so much, given the lack of trees and how far the fort is from any large town in Jera. Then again, from the patrol reports, no lancer patrol has been this far since he and Thallyr had done so.

Even so, it had to have taken seasons, if not years.

After several moments, Alyiakal turns his gaze farther north at the hamlet holding perhaps a score of dwellings, rather than the single stead that stood there once before.

"The fort doesn't look that imposing," says Kessmyr.

"It's big enough to hold several companies, and that could be a problem," replies Alyiakal. "There are only a score of dwellings anywhere close, and that town to the west isn't all that large. What does that tell you about who's manning it?"

"They have to be from somewhere else, and most of them can't be raiders from this valley."

"That means Jeranyi armsmen to me." Alyiakal isn't about to mention the other possibility. While his companies can deal with the armsmen—assuming he doesn't do something foolish—and they can fire any wooden structure, he doesn't have the men and equipment to dismantle a large mudbrick fort.

"Well . . . one way or another, we need to head down there and find out more about the fort."

A glass later, First Company rides past a low ridge with a flattish top, bordering the narrow stream that flows out of the hills, before riding around a gentle curve that ends up heading straight north toward the fort.

Alyiakal calls a halt roughly a kay from the road behind which the fort stands. From there, he sees the fort is on the smallest of rises. The gate facing the road is closed, and the packed dirt or clay causeway from the gate to the road is only about thirty yards long. Thin trails of smoke rise from within the walls.

For a time, he studies the fort. Then he turns to Kessmyr. "Do you see anything unusual?"

"The tops of the walls are smooth. There aren't any crenellations. If they put archers there, they'd be exposed."

"True, but we'd have to cover at least a hundred and maybe two hundred yards before we'd get close enough to take out any archers on the wall. Probably only a hundred yards, because any archers they have are using horn riding bows. Do you think there's another gate?"

"There could be one in the rear or on the west side."

"That's possible, but gates are the weakest point of a fortification. I'd guess there might be a small gate, barely wide enough for a single armsman on one of the side walls." Alyiakal pauses. "We've seen enough for now. We'll ride back and set up camp on that low ridge. That's far enough away, and they can't see us without leaving the fort. I'll explain the rest to you after we get the horses and rankers settled."

While Alyiakal can sense slight puzzlement from the captain, Kessmyr merely says, "Yes, ser."

It's a glass later before the company's settled, with scouts posted midway between the fort and the encampment site, which Alyiakal picked because the steepest side of the ridge overlooks the road.

"Tonight, after it's full dark, I'm going to take four rankers and get closer to the fort to see what I can see."

"Shouldn't you leave that to the scouts, ser?"

"Some would say I should, and if I had five or six companies to waste, I might. I don't, and doing it that way wouldn't be fair to you or the men." Alyiakal ignores Kessmyr's momentary puzzlement and goes on. "There's always the possibility that the Jeranyi might see us and follow us back. That's why I want you to have a squad on foot spread across the part of the ridge facing the road, ready with firelances. A full squad should be more than sufficient, but make sure the other two squads have their firelances at hand, just in case."

"Do you have something else in mind, ser?"

"I always have something else in mind, Captain, just in case things don't go the way I've planned. So should you. Here, since I'm in overall command, you need to keep in mind how to keep the company together on high ground, and how to protect the horses if something happens to me. It shouldn't, but you need the practice."

After sunset, but while it's still light, Alyiakal meets with the four lancers who will accompany him. He also brings Kessmyr, so that the captain understands what he has in mind. *Most of what you have in mind.*

"This will be a nighttime reconnaissance. I need to know certain aspects of the fort, but getting close enough in daylight exposes us to archers. If we're quiet, we can get much closer before being spotted, possibly within yards of the wall. Even if we are spotted, they won't have as many archers on the wall, and we can get out of range before they can bring up more. One way or another, the longest part of this will be riding to and from where we'll start the reconnaissance. Once we get within range of the fort, I will order you to ready arms, just in case."

After going over a few more routine matters, Alyiakal and Kessmyr leave the four lancers, after which Alyiakal saddles the gray gelding.

Later, as twilight fades into night, Alyiakal checks the amount of sun-chaos he's collected over the past two days, then meets with the four lancers. The five walk their mounts from the back of the ridge to the road, where they mount and ride slowly down the last gentle slope. By the time they round the last curve, with the fort still a kay away, it's almost full dark, but Alyiakal reins up and waits another quint before urging the gray gelding forward.

Alyiakal creates a diffuse illusion of mist around his small group as they turn onto the road heading west toward the fort. Before long he can sense the outlines of the interior of the fort. Unlike the Cerlynese fort in Kraaslaen, which had quarters against just a wall and a half, the Jeranyi fort has wooden structures against every wall except the gate wall. He also discovers the Jeranyi horses are corralled directly behind the fort, suggesting a postern door in the rear wall to allow immediate access to the mounts.

Alyiakal reins up, and gestures for the four to move closer, then says quietly, "We're going to ride down the causeway closer to the fort. I'm going to use my firelance to set fires inside the fort. You're not to fire until my command. Then, you're to concentrate your fire on the middle of the main gate. When we've done enough damage, I'll give the order to withdraw. Now . . . forward . . . quietly."

Even before Alyiakal turns the gray north on the causeway, heading toward the fort, he can sense the sentries posted on the walls, one on each side of the gate.

He doesn't hear their voices until he's less than twenty yards from the gate.

"Someone's out there . . ."

"Where? Don't see anyone . . ."

Alyiakal lifts his firelance and fires two short bolts, order-guided to take out the sentries. Then he says, "Halt."

Concentrating, he begins to arc firebolts over the wall and into the wooden structures inside the fort, each firebolt order-guided and reinforced with his collected chaos. As he continues, he orders, "Fire at the gate. Now!"

From inside the fort, Alyiakal hears shouts and at least one cry of "Fire!"

He lofts a last few firebolts toward places not burning, then says, "Cease fire! Withdraw, now!"

Even while he turns the gray, he senses several black death mists, but he does not look back as he leads the four lancers down the causeway to the road at a fast trot, continuing toward the road into the hills for several hundred yards, before reining up, and turning to view the fort. Flames rise well above the walls.

"Ser?" asks one of the lancers.

"We're waiting to see if anyone comes after us. If they do, they'll be outlined by the flames, and we should be able to pick them off."

Although Alyiakal waits for more than a quint, he cannot see anyone in front of the fort, but he can sense that a number of armsmen have fled through the postern gate into the corral area and are trying to move the horses away from the flames.

Finally, he says, "No one's coming after us. Not tonight, anyway. We'll head back to the encampment."

None of the lancers say a word.

Alyiakal adds, "Would you rather attack during the day when their archers could loose shafts before you could ever get close enough to use your firelances?"

One of the lancers, Kassyn, says, "No, ser."

Alyiakal leaves it at that.

Kessmyr waits near the area where the mounts are picketed when Alyiakal and the four rankers return. He immediately looks at Alyiakal.

"I'll brief you as soon as I take care of my mount," Alyiakal says. *And as soon as we're away from the rankers.*

Roughly half a quint later and away from the others, Alyiakal says evenly, "We set the buildings inside the fort on fire, as well as the main gate. I have no idea how many Jeranyi got out of the fort, but I'm certain a number escaped through the rear postern door. Most of the mounts likely survived, but some may have escaped in the confusion. I think the four rankers who accompanied me were a little shocked. We were ordered to destroy whatever fortifications the Jeranyi built. Without siege machines, firing the interior of the fort is the best we can do. In the meantime, make sure that the forward sentries stay alert. I doubt the Jeranyi will attack in the dark, but they might at first light. In the morning we'll have to investigate and see just how much damage we did. The question is whether the Jeranyi are still around or whether they already withdrew to the town to the west and the fort there."

Kessmyr is silent for several moments, then asks, "Are there any other senior officers who use firelances that way?"

"I know of at least one other officer who did," replies Alyiakal, recalling Captain Thallyr's orders on his previous patrol to the West Branch valley. "Headquarters is well aware that I've used the tactic before. I frankly hope that the Jeranyi who survived have enough sense to withdraw."

"You sound like you feel sorry for them, ser."

"My first priority is to accomplish my orders with the least possible loss of lancers. Their priority was to draw us into an attack that would cost us lives. I can't afford to let that happen. The Mirror Lancers barely have enough men to defend our borders, and the Jeranyi and the Cerlynese know that. We're also not getting as many replacement firelances as in the past. So I try to employ our weapons in the most effective fashion, even if those tactics aren't usual. Sometimes firing a fort or a town is the best tactic. Sometimes, it's not. You have to know the best tactics for a given situation."

"How do you learn that, ser?"

"The least painful way is watching senior officers—emulate their successes and learn from their mistakes. The way most of us learn, unfortunately, is making mistakes and surviving them." Alyiakal takes a slow deep breath. "I need a little sleep, Kessmyr. Wake me if you need me, or at first light if I'm not already up."

"Yes, ser."

Alyiakal turns and walks toward his bedroll.

XLIV

Tired as he is, Alyiakal lies awake on his bedroll for what seems a long time. When he finally drops into sleep, it's an uneasy slumber, and he wakes before first light on twoday with vague memories of firebolts everywhere, screaming horses, and men being turned to ash.

Once on his feet, he checks with Kessmyr and then the sentries, but no one has heard or seen any sign of the Jeranyi or anyone else. He has some order-infused water and some trail biscuits before he saddles the gray. Kessmyr joins him as he finishes strapping his gear behind the gelding's saddle.

"Do you think the Jeranyi armsmen are still around?" asks the captain.

"They might be, and then they might not. They could have taken refuge in the houses to the north, or already left. Or some could have stayed and some left. We'll find out shortly, but for their sake, I hope they've headed west."

Kessmyr frowns. "After last night?"

"Especially after last night," replies Alyiakal. "But it's time to see whether any of them are left. At the least, I need to see the condition of the fort for the report to Mirror Lancer headquarters . . . and if there are any armsmen remaining here."

By daybreak, First Company rides around the last gentle curve to where Alyiakal can see the mudbrick walls of the fort. At first, he can't discern much damage, except that only blackened iron straps remain of the main gate. There's no one in sight, and the only order/chaos patterns Alyiakal senses are those of horses well behind the fort.

As First Company reaches the causeway leading to the burned-out main gate, a slight breeze carries the odors of charred wood and wisps of smoke from still-smoldering embers to Alyiakal, as well as a sickly odor of burned flesh.

Alyiakal rides up within a few yards of the remnants of the main gate, but all he sees are ashes, fallen and charred timbers, and partly blackened mudbrick walls. From the gate he rides to the left along the front wall and then along the side wall, where he sees a body sprawled facedown on the ash-strewn ground. Half the armsman's shoulder is charred.

When Alyiakal reaches the rear wall, he reins up opposite the smoke-blackened opening that had once held the postern door. Even from the saddle he can see through the opening ash-covered lumps, which could have been anything, including bodies or collapsed parts of the structures within the walls. Along the rest of the rear wall and the east wall are three other bodies, wearing maroon-and-gray Jeranyi uniforms.

Alyiakal turns his attention first to the corral closest to the fort, which holds no horses, but two saddles and possibly blankets and bridles set on the wooden fence, and then to the rear corral, which holds close to a score of mounts. After a moment, he looks to Kessmyr. "Have the scouts check the road west and see if they can tell how many riders left here . . . and anything else."

"Yes, ser."

Alyiakal doesn't even have to try to sense how appalled the young captain is.

When the scouts return, Alyiakal motions for Kessmyr to join him, then waits for the scouts to report.

"Sers," says the older scout, "the best we could tell was that there were maybe a score and a half of riders, possibly two score. No one walking, and no wagons. They likely left before midnight. From some of the hoofprints, at least a few riders led another horse, but that's a guess."

From what he's seen and sensed, and from the earlier raid, Alyiakal estimates that roughly two companies occupied the fort, although the fort likely could hold three to four, assuming the horses remained outside the walls. If . . . *if* his estimates are correct, between the raid and the fire the Jeranyi lost more than a company. There's also the possibility that some of the armsmen may be hiding in local houses.

Alyiakal nods. "Thank you."

Then he turns the gray and motions for Kessmyr to accompany him. After they're away from the scouts, he says, "We'll be starting back to Pemedra shortly once we round up the mounts the Jeranyi left. Taking them will make it harder for them to attack or raid Cyador for a while."

"You're not going to check any of the dwellings for armsmen, ser?"

Alyiakal shakes his head. "We were ordered to destroy the fortifications and remove any Jeranyi force here. We've done that. The orders didn't say anything about chasing down Jeranyi armsmen or breaking into houses of local people. It will take a season or longer just to replace the armsmen, and even longer to rebuild the interior of the fort, because there's not that much timber anywhere close. The same's true of weapons, horses, and tack."

A glass passes while the lancers get all the Jeranyi mounts on leads, including four for which the lancers had found tack, during which time Alyiakal neither sees nor senses any signs of anyone besides his lancers. As First Company leaves the fort behind, heading back to Pemedra, Alyiakal glances back a last time, hoping he doesn't have to return, and that the Jeranyi aren't stupid enough to try to repair or rebuild the fort.

XLV

First Company rides in through the north gates of Pemedra just before sunset on threeday, leading the twenty-four mounts taken from the Jeranyi fort. Surprisingly to Alyiakal, Baassyn appears at the stable as Alyiakal is unsaddling the gray.

He waits while Alyiakal finishes grooming, then asks, "How did it go? I didn't see any casualties."

"No casualties on our side. There was a fort, and we destroyed it—everything within the mudbrick walls, anyway—and we managed it without injuring anyone." Alyiakal gives a concise account, then ends by saying, "We'll have to see what headquarters has to say, but we accomplished what they ordered. For now, at least."

"You don't seem all that pleased," ventures Baassyn.

"I don't like burning armsmen alive, but it was the most effective way to accomplish the orders. The lancers from Isahl won't be as effective, if there is another fort to the west, and they decide to attack it. We'll get blamed for some of their casualties because the partial company that fled will likely reinforce the Jeranyi forces. Zekkaat won't send forces from Syadtar. The post commander at Isahl might not even have gotten his orders until we were on the way. I also suspect that the majer there would do a pure recon before deciding on how to attack."

"Then he should know the Jeranyi will have additional men there."

"There's no certain way to learn that from a recon, but I doubt that would weigh much in Majer Baertal's mind." *And possibly not in Zekkaat's mind, either.*

"Would you have done it any differently, ser?" asks Baassyn.

Alyiakal shakes his head. "We accomplished what was ordered. We killed a company of Jeranyi armsmen, possibly more, and rendered the fort unusable for at least a season, likely longer."

"Do you question the orders?"

Alyiakal takes a deep breath. "No, not after the Jeranyi raid this Spring. But I still can't see any other way I could have accomplished them without incurring casualties and deaths of Mirror Lancers."

"Maybe I'm missing something, ser, but I'm having trouble understanding your concerns."

"Contrary to the beliefs on the part of some of my officers, I don't enjoy killing people, especially burning them alive, and I don't like being put in positions where, to minimize deaths of my lancers, I need to adopt strategies that slaughter those who oppose us." Alyiakal laughs harshly, but quietly. "But then, that's the problem that every post commander faces."

"No, ser," replies Baassyn. "Only the effective post commanders."

"You have a good point. I wish it made me feel better, but that's my problem." Alyiakal picks up his satchel and bedroll. "I'm taking these to my quarters. I'll wash up a bit and see you at evening mess." He pauses. "Did we get any more directives while I was gone?"

Baassyn shakes his head.

"Good. I'll see you in a bit."

Alyiakal makes his way to his quarters, where he brushes the dust off his uniform and boots, washes up, and then heads for the officers' mess.

Baassyn stands alone in the corridor outside the mess doorway, waiting. "That didn't take you long."

"Not too long. It'll be good to have a hot meal." *Even barely passable wine will be a welcome change from order-infused water.* Alyiakal manages a brief smile as he follows Baassyn into the mess.

After Alyiakal seats himself and all the officers have been served, he gives a perfunctory toast, followed by a brief summary of the patrol, mostly about burning the Jeranyi fort and the withdrawal of the surviving Jeranyi. Then he turns to Kessmyr. "Did I leave out anything important, Captain?"

"No, ser." Kessmyr pauses. "Well, except for one thing. Most of us weren't directly involved and it happened so fast I didn't realize one thing until we were on our way back. We didn't suffer any casualties, and I don't think that would have been possible with any other kind of attack."

Chaem nods and says, "That's a good point. Sometimes, officers who aren't there overlook the casualties that other officers didn't suffer." He looks directly at Suraat, then adds, "Sometimes, the officers who don't realize that are even in headquarters. I've seen that happen before."

"Now that the majer's briefed us," says Baassyn cheerfully, "we ought to let him and Captain Kessmyr enjoy their first decent meal in days." He lifts his wineglass in what amounts to a toast.

Alyiakal manages a smile, then lifts his own wineglass and takes a small sip.

XLVI

Alyiakal dispatches his report on the successful attack on the northeast Jeranyi fort on fiveday morning, with a copy to Subcommander Zekkaat, knowing that it likely will be two eightdays before he hears anything from headquarters, if at all. He also doubts he'll hear anything from Zekkaat.

He writes and dispatches a brief letter to Saelora, with some description of the hills to the northwest of Pemedra, but only saying that the patrol had been as successful as possible and that he is well and in good health despite the daily heat that reminds him of an oven.

Over the course of the next two eightdays, he accompanies each of the companies on a routine patrol, but none of the patrols find any sign of travel from the grasslands to the north or from Jerans. Nor are there any signs of raiders. The lack of travelers and traders—and even smugglers—concerns Alyiakal. So does the lack of communication from Mirror Lancer headquarters.

Then, on the sixth twoday of Summer, dispatch riders bring several envelopes from Mirror Lancer headquarters and a letter from Saelora, along with a raft of personal letters for other officers and rankers.

The first official letter is from Captain-Commander Laartol.

> *Majer Alyiakal—*
>
> *The Majer-Commander and I appreciate your direct and timely action in dealing with the Jeranyi fort located at the northeast entry to the West Branch valley. At this time, no further action is required of Pemedra Post in that regard, other than normal patrolling duties.*

The signature beneath is that of Laartol, and there are no handwritten additions.

At least headquarters acknowledged your report.

The second envelope contains yet another revision to the directive dealing with horseshoes and an announcement celebrating the birth of the Emperor Kaartyn's second child, a healthy daughter, along with a few lines declaring that both mother and daughter were well.

Two daughters and no sons? Alyiakal wonders why that announcement was even sent, except to suggest the continued possibility of an heir.

Alyiakal wants to give that more thought, but that can wait, since there's nothing he can do about it, and he wants to read Saelora's letter, which has, predictably, been unsealed and resealed. He doesn't break the tampered seal but slits the envelope and begins to read.

> *I'm so glad to hear that your long patrol turned out successfully and that you're well. I know you plan and prepare carefully, but I still worry, as I know you do about me, but I'm doing well.*

So is Loraan House. We now have some more lands. I hadn't exactly planned on buying them, but Dyrkan came across them, and they're extremely well suited for maize on one part, with a small pearapple orchard in another. They weren't that costly because the larger third section is rugged and somewhat marshy, only suitable for greenberries. I did purchase the land with Dyrkan as an intermediary, which kept the price down . . .

Alyiakal shakes his head in amusement and appreciation.

The latest addition to the distillery is almost finished, and that will allow more production of Crystalflame. That's good because we have more interest in it than we can supply right now . . .

With the expansion of the distillery, Gaaran has recruited a number of former lancer rankers. We now have a modest guard force here and in Fyrad because a number of other smaller factorages have suffered rather unusual accidents . . .

Caused by the Dyljani trying to muscle into Fyrad, perhaps?

I think he's always missed being a lancer officer, and those abilities are likely to be helpful in the seasons ahead . . .

Alyiakal doesn't like that at all, but Gaaran is certainly levelheaded. The right kind of former lancers would make a good guard force. He just hopes it's good enough.

Catriana writes every eightday to update me on what is happening in Fyrad. I did take the wagon down there last eightday, and I got to see Haarlt. He's so like his father already. He's so happy and outgoing.

I haven't heard from Hyrsaal in several eightdays. He's never been the most regular in writing, and I'd rather that his few letters go to Catriana. I saw Mother yesterday. She's a bit quieter, and she stays in her cottage more, but she doesn't seem any more forgetful. She did say to send you her best.

Quite a change there.

The remainder of the letter deals with Laetilla, and Charissa and her children, and closes with warm words that Alyiakal treasures . . . and appreciates.

After setting Saelora's letter aside, Alyiakal considers what she's hinted at—that the situation in both Vaeyal and Fyrad requires guards, either because of Saelora's success or because of Dyljani efforts to drive out local traders, if not both. The fact that Saelora has been able to expand and pay for those guards implies success, but Alyiakal can't help worrying.

Not that you can do a black-angel-damned thing to help her right now.

He stands and walks to the doorway into Baassyn's study.

"Anything important in those envelopes?" asks the overcaptain.

"A brief acknowledgment of the report on the Jeranyi fort and a statement that no further action was necessary at present."

"That's better than it could be."

We also got another revision to the horseshoe directive . . ."

Baassyn laughs sardonically. "They'd do better to let us do our own smithing. Frig . . . the farrier almost has to, anyway."

". . . and there was a short announcement about the birth of the Emperor's second daughter."

The overcaptain straightens in his chair, frowning. "That's rather odd. It's like saying that his position isn't that secure unless he has a son."

"I had that thought as well. Do you think the Majer-Commander has certain . . . ambitions?"

Baassyn shakes his head. "He can't. He doesn't have elthage blood or, at the extreme, any magely talent. There's no way the Merchanters or the Magi'i would ever allow someone with either to serve as part of the high command, let alone as either Captain-Commander or Majer-Commander."

"Then it has to be a warning that there might be future unrest, possibly on the part of the Magi'i."

"That would be my guess as well," replies the overcaptain. "Anything else?"

Alyiakal laughs. "Isn't that enough?"

"For now, anyway."

Alyiakal turns and heads back to his study, considering Baassyn's words, and the fact that it's all too likely that even his healing ability will preclude promotion beyond subcommander—and even if he reached commander, he'd never be posted to Cyad.

You're thinking too far ahead . . . way too far.

He shakes his head and walks to the window but stands in the shade to one side to avoid the direct afternoon sun, thinking about all the uncertainties, but mostly about Saelora, hoping that she, Catriana, and Gaaran can deal with the Dyljani Clan.

In time, he and Baassyn walk from the headquarters building down and across the avenue to the officers' mess for the evening meal.

Once there and seated, Alyiakal says, "This afternoon, we received a brief dispatch from the Captain-Commander stating that he and the Majer-Commander appreciated our timely and direct action and that no further action was necessary, except to keep patrolling."

"Was that all, ser?" asks Suraat.

"That was all he needed to say," replies Baassyn. "Sometimes, headquarters doesn't even acknowledge reports."

"Have you heard anything about the other fort?" asks Kessmyr.

"Not a word," replies Alyiakal. "I wouldn't expect to unless we're required to support Isahl or Syadtar in some fashion."

"Is that likely?" asks Nolaan.

"It all depends on Isahl's success against the other fort," says Alyiakal. "If they're successful, we won't hear much of anything. If they're not, headquarters will decide whether Syadtar will be tasked with continuing against the fort or we will."

"If they weren't successful," asks Kessmyr, "wouldn't you have heard from someone already?"

"That would depend on headquarters," replies Alyiakal. "If we don't hear anything in the next eightday or so, it's likely we won't be involved." He's not about to comment on what Zekkaat might or might not do.

"Have you heard anything more about your report on the grasslands to the northeast, or about Cerlyn?" asks Nolaan.

"Only the one brief acknowledgment."

"Sometimes not hearing anything means nothing bad has happened," declares Baassyn.

Or that you haven't learned about it yet. Alyiakal just smiles and takes a bite of the lamb emburhka, which bears only the faintest resemblance to what Laetilla has prepared for him and Saelora.

XLVII

The sixth sixday of Summer dawns so hot that Alyiakal is sweating by the time he leaves morning mess, and he's sweating even more, when, in midafternoon, Alyiakal hears that dispatch riders have been sighted to the south. He blots his brow, stands, and walks to Baassyn's doorway.

"I don't think whatever news or directives they're bringing is anything we want to hear. What do you think?"

"I'd agree. Do you have any thoughts?"

"Most likely, the lancers at Isahl Post ran into trouble, and we'll have to deal with the other Jeranyi fort." *That's likely the best of what we could be tasked with.* Not that Alyiakal is about to say that yet. He worries that he'll be blamed for the additional armsmen who escaped from the eastern fort and may have reinforced the garrison to the west.

"I can hardly wait to find out," says Baassyn sarcastically.

"The same for me," Alyiakal comments before returning to his study.

Less than a quint later, the duty ranker hands off a sealed dispatch bag. "Ser, this is what the riders brought from headquarters. Also a few personal letters. That's all."

Alyiakal stands and takes the dispatch pouch, feeling how light it is. "Thank you." He waits for the ranker to leave before breaking the seal. Inside is a single sealed envelope. Alyiakal uses his belt knife to open it, taking out a single sheet with the letterhead of the Majer-Commander. He notes that there are no formalities or honorifics.

Alyiakal'alt
Majer
Post Commander, Pemedra

Mirror Lancer companies from Isahl suffered significant casualties in attacking the Jeranyi forces and the associated fortification located at the northwest entrance to the West Branch valley. Because of the terrain, the position of the fortification, and the number of Jeranyi armsmen, the companies from Isahl were required to withdraw without achieving the objective of removing the Jeranyi threat to the border of Cyador. Lancer companies from Syadtar will reinforce those companies from Isahl in dealing with the Jeranyi forces located there.

While it would have been optimal for companies from Pemedra to provide such support, the companies from Pemedra are required for a more urgent objective. Over the last eightdays of Spring and the first eightdays of Summer, Cerlynese forces entered the lands of Cyador, occupied the town of Kraaslaen, and engaged and significantly depleted the Mirror Lancer forces posted at Lhaarat. The last encounter, on the first sevenday of Summer, resulted in the loss of nearly two companies and the post commander . . .

Frig! They got Vordahl as well? Alyiakal just looks at the words for a moment before continuing to read.

An occurrence of this magnitude cannot be allowed to stand unchallenged. You are tasked with removing the Cerlynese from Kraaslaen and taking whatever additional measures you feel necessary to preclude a recurrence of such an attack. Such an evolution may, at your discretion, require the simultaneous involvement of all companies under your command.

At those words, and the fact that the letter-orders end there, Alyiakal feels a chill. Then he sees that the signature is that of Laartol, with the notation, "As directed by the Majer-Commander." That doesn't reassure Alyiakal. It suggests that Laartol is putting himself and Alyiakal out on a limb . . . one extending over a deep canyon, so to speak.

There are three words in the bottom corner—"Whatever it takes!"—followed by the initial "L."

Alyiakal wonders whether that emphasis is because Majer Vordahl is—or was—the son of Commander Dahlvor, who was and still might be one of the senior commanders in headquarters. Or because Laartol understands the danger Cerlyn poses. *Most likely both.*

Alyiakal rereads the orders, word by word. They don't change.

He looks up to see Baassyn standing in the doorway.

"That bad?" asks the overcaptain.

Alyiakal stands and extends the single sheet.

Baassyn takes it and begins to read. His face stiffens.

When he finishes, he hands it back to Alyiakal, then says sardonically, "Quite a reward for being effective when no one else seems to be."

"The Mirror Lancer posts on the border have been undermanned and undersupplied for years," replies Alyiakal.

"You seem to have managed," Baassyn says evenly.

"By doing the unconventional and not mentioning the details." That's true, but not quite in the way Alyiakal hopes Baassyn will take it.

The overcaptain frowns, then shakes his head, if with an amused expression. "I've read your reports. You're right. They don't mention certain details and emphasize the results without exaggerating." He pauses, then adds, "The Captain-Commander expects a great deal."

"He does. I think he always has."

"Has it always worked?"

"Sometimes, the costs have been high. We lost two companies and their officers against the Kyphrans . . . out of four companies."

"How many Kyphrans?"

"Around fifteen hundred. They had a mage and ten firelances."

"Just because I'm curious . . . how many Kyphrans survived?"

"A company or so."

"What about your company?"

"I lost a little less than a half a squad."

"And you were in the thick of the fight?"

Alyiakal nods.

"That might . . . just might . . . explain those orders," says Baassyn dryly, "along with what you did to the Cerlynese two years ago. You going to tell the officers at evening mess?"

"The sooner the better. This time, we'll take two days to load out. We'll be taking every possible firelance, and every spare wheel, as well as some long planks. You get to stay here and try to hold things together."

Baassyn frowns. "Planks?"

"There's a narrow stream to cross at the border, the way we're going. That could save time and a lot of effort."

After Baassyn leaves, Alyiakal begins a list of the various items his force might need, as well as what he doesn't know. When he finishes, for the moment, he takes out his book of maps and searches for any details about Cerlyn. There are few, and the map does show Kula, the town to the northeast beyond the grasslands and just over the hills from Kraaslaen. There's also a road from Kula along the River Yarth leading to Clynya, a distance of about three days' ride—if the map is accurate. He also notes a mark on the map to the east of Kula, and he wonders if that's where the copper mine or mines are. Retrieving his map of the roads around Kraaslaen, he starts to make plans for copies for each of the company officers.

When the time comes, Alyiakal and Baassyn walk from the headquarters building through the still-oppressive heat to the officers' mess. All the officers are waiting, looking expectant.

Alyiakal gestures to the table and says, "Yes . . . there is news from Mirror Lancer headquarters. I'll brief you on it after everyone's served." He takes his seat and pours some of the indifferent white wine into his glass and looks at the platter containing filled dumplings, spiced lamb or fowl, covered with a white sauce, as well as a bowl filled with roasted spring beans and a basket of bread. He serves himself and passes the platter to Baassyn, then waits until Suraat fills his plate.

"I said there was news," Alyiakal begins. "I can't say it's particularly good." He then quotes from memory, if not perfectly, Laartol's summary of the Jeranyi situation and the orders for Pemedra, after which he waits for questions.

No one speaks, but Chaem finally says, "It seems like the Majer-Commander has a lot of faith in us . . . or maybe not many options."

"Both, most likely," replies Baassyn.

"Have you decided how we're going to proceed, ser?" asks Kessmyr. "And when we'll leave?"

"We'll load out the wagons for the next two days, and all four companies will ride out early on oneday. We'll head directly for Kula, a Cerlynese town north of the grasslands. They had to have staged the attack on Kraaslaen from there. If there are armsmen, we'll remove them first before dealing with the Cerlynese forces in Kraaslaen. Then we'll return to Kula and evaluate the situation to determine if further action is necessary."

"Further action?" asks Suraat.

"There may be other Cerlynese armsmen on the way to Kula, or posted somewhere nearby," says Alyiakal evenly. "We won't have resolved the problem if they send more armsmen as soon as we leave. As events have shown, Duke Taartyn can be very vindictive. So we'll need to be prepared for anything."

"How long will this take?" asks Nolaan.

"As long as necessary. It will take close to three days to get to Kula, and it's at least another day from there to Kraaslaen."

"Well into Harvest, then, before it's over," suggests Baassyn.

"I'm not about to guess. Dealing with the northeast fort took less time than I thought, and dealing with the Kyphrans north of Guarstyad took longer than anyone expected. What's important is accomplishing the orders with the greatest effectiveness and fewest casualties." Alyiakal smiles wryly. "But then, commanders on both sides claim that, or something similar."

"Ser, how good are the Cerlynese?" asks Kessmyr.

"They were good enough to defeat two companies of Mirror Lancers. So we shouldn't take them lightly." Alyiakal pauses, then says, "That's about all I can say right now. Anything more would be guessing, and you all know how I feel about that." He picks up his wineglass and sips.

XLVIII

Over the next two days, Alyiakal checks every cubit of the three wagons with his senses and goes over every piece of gear and every spare weapon loaded into those wagons. He makes copies of the maps of Kraaslaen for each company officer. He also drafts a letter to Mirror Lancer headquarters informing the Majer-Commander that he has left with all four companies to deal with the Cerlynese, as per orders. Baassyn will send that letter via the next dispatch riders to arrive at Pemedra, because Alyiakal is not about to weaken his force in any way by using any of his lancers to deliver messages.

Alyiakal writes Saelora, congratulating her on her acumen and trading successes and telling her that he is leaving on another long patrol—one that might end up resembling the events following his discovery of the lost road to Guarstyad. He hopes that wording is vague enough not to have the letter delayed but accurate enough that she understands he won't be writing for some time.

Two quints after first light on oneday, Alyiakal rides out through the north gates with Kessmyr at the head of First Company, followed by Third and Fourth Companies, then the three supply wagons, and finally Chaem and Second Company. By leaving early, they'll at least be in the hills before the full heat of the day.

Alyiakal begins collecting chaos bits from the moment the sun clears the hills to the east, knowing that, uncomfortable as it makes him, he'll need to collect and use every possible scrap of chaos before the patrol, or whatever this all turns out to be, is over.

While there are cart tracks partway into the hills and returning to the valley, by midafternoon, neither Alyiakal nor the scouts find any recent traces of riders, wagons, or carts.

When the company halts for the night, and after the lancers have eaten their trail rations, Alyiakal gathers the officers, and his first words are, "Do any of you have any problems?"

One after another, the officers shake their heads, and, equally important, Alyiakal senses that none of them are hiding anything.

"Any questions?"

Chaem clears his throat. "Not a question exactly, ser. Have you ever been on a patrol like this where there's no sign of anyone traveling?"

"Only once before, and that was this Spring when I accompanied Nolaan and Fourth Company to see the grasslands north of here. I suspect that's because the Cerlynese conscripted all the raiders to fight for them and they don't allow traders or smugglers to enter the grasslands."

"Never heard of anything stopping smugglers," declares Chaem dryly.

"The Cerlynese torture and kill anyone who disobeys them," replies Alyiakal. "Since there are few hamlets in the valley north of Pemedra, and there are less dangerous ways into Cyador south of Pemedra, it's not worth the risk. That's my judgment, anyway."

Chaem nods. "Makes sense."

"You don't care much for the Cerlynese, do you, ser?" asks Suraat.

"I don't care much for Duke Taartyn and what he orders his people to do," replies Alyiakal. "I also don't have much respect for armsmen who assault and torture innocents, even if they're threatened with death if they don't. If people attack you, then you have to treat them the same as armsmen attacking. If they don't, leave them alone."

"Have you been attacked by people who weren't armsmen?" asks Suraat.

"I have . . . unfortunately. I wish they hadn't. It didn't turn out well for them." Alyiakal doesn't mention that he remembers every single incident, but he senses Suraat's unspoken disapproval and adds, "When a mage is about to throw a firebolt at you or a youth nocks a shaft directed at you, it's either you or them."

"And if it's them," adds Chaem, "you've left a company without a leader."

Kessmyr and Nolaan nod.

"Anything else?" asks Alyiakal.

"No, ser," replies Suraat, clearly chastened.

"Then I'll see you in the morning . . . unless the sentries wake me earlier," Alyiakal comments wryly.

While the sentries don't wake Alyiakal, he's up just before the first hint of dawn on twoday.

Twoday is the same as oneday, with no recent tracks in the road and the only other order/chaos patterns besides the Mirror Lancers being rodents, grass cats, and antelopes. When the companies ride past the site where Alyiakal and Nolaan had found the body, there appears to be nothing left. That night, they stop on the same ridge where Fourth Company camped on the earlier patrol.

By a glass after sunrise, Alyiakal and Kessmyr lead the force west through the grasslands toward the first hamlet Alyiakal entered so many years before.

Another quint passes before Alyiakal actually sees the houses through the gaps in the plains grass, replaced in part with small fields and plots, but those plots are fewer than his last patrol to the hamlet years ago. As First Company rides closer, Alyiakal sees that some of the mudbrick dwellings stand vacant.

While a few women are working in the plots, when they see the riders, they hurry into their small homes, closing doors and shutters. The company rides through the middle of the hamlet, continuing north, where, for the first time, Alyiakal sees a few hoofprints and the traces of a cart in the road dust.

For the next three glasses, the Mirror Lancers continue northward on the road through the prairie grass past two more slightly larger hamlets. Again they find a scattering of abandoned mudbrick dwellings, and the women immediately hide in their dwellings.

"We haven't seen a single man," notes Kessmyr after a time.

"I doubt that there are any except young boys and men too old to fight, and there won't be many of those," replies Alyiakal.

"Because they were forced into fighting earlier?"

"Those who weren't killed raiding. That would be my guess."

Another two quints pass.

Then, above the grass flanking the road ahead, Alyiakal sees the tops of the trees that mark the edge of the stream and the border with Cerlyn, with Kula on the north side of the stream. While the road had come to an end well short of the stream on Alyiakal's first patrol into the grassland, now it extends all the way to the streambed, where horses and wagons, in the recent past, have created what amounts to a ford.

Alyiakal calls a halt and studies the apparent ford, the fields immediately beyond, and the wider road leading to the dwellings perhaps a half kay farther north. "That's Kula."

"Usually, towns are closer to the water," says Kessmyr.

"A little west of here this line of trees turns north. It could be that the town extends to the water there. We'll see shortly." Alyiakal half expects someone to ring the warning bell, as had happened before, but the midday air is quiet. Then he realizes that there's no one in the fields beyond the stream, not that he would expect many in late Summer well before Harvest. He also can't sense any large order/chaos patterns nearby, not even cattle or sheep.

But people and no livestock? Has Taartyn impressed every man of fighting age? In a way the timing makes sense. The crops are established, and it's well before Harvest. *But don't jump to conclusions.*

"Captain, take First Company across the stream and form up five abreast to cover the rest of the companies as they cross the stream."

"Yes, ser."

Even though Alyiakal hasn't seen or sensed armsmen nearby, an attack is always possible, but no one appears even after First Company draws up in defense formation and Alyiakal crosses the stream.

Then, from the direction of the town comes the tolling of a bell, and as Third Company begins to cross, riders appear on the road from the town, moving toward First Company. When those armsmen near the company, Alyiakal notes they comprise little better than a half squad. They rein up more than a hundred yards from First Company before turning and withdrawing.

The bell keeps tolling.

Alyiakal sends a ranker from Third Company to Kessmyr with instructions to send scouts to recon without engaging anyone unless they're attacked. Then, once Third Company has fully crossed and Fourth Company starts crossing the narrow stream, he joins Kessmyr.

"What can you tell me about those armsmen?"

"They wore dark green uniforms, but it looked like some of them are graybeards, with one or two who look more like youths. When they saw us, they turned and withdrew." Kessmyr pauses. "How long do you think they'll keep tolling that bell?"

"For a while, one way or another."

Alyiakal glances back toward the stream, where Chaem works with lancers to position the planks to get the wagons over, then back in the direction of Kula, wondering how long it will be before the scouts return.

One wagon reaches the north side of the stream before the two scouts rein up in front of Alyiakal and Kessmyr.

"Sers, the town has close to a hundred houses, most of them to the northwest along the stream. No one's outside. Those armsmen must have withdrawn to the fort. It's on the east side of the town, where this road meets one heading east toward the hills. It's not that big, maybe thirty yards on a side. The gates are closed."

Alyiakal nods. "Head back to where you can watch the fort. Let us know if anyone enters or leaves."

"Yes, ser."

Alyiakal watches as the scouts head up the road, then looks back to the ford, where the second wagon struggles across.

Getting all three wagons across the now-muddy stream takes more than a glass, even using the planks, and another quint or so to remove most of the mud. Once that's accomplished, it's late afternoon before Alyiakal resumes leading his force toward Kula, where the bell has finally stopped tolling.

As First Company heads up the road, closer to the dwellings and their outbuildings, Alyiakal sees that most of the dwellings do hug the stream to his left, while the fort is directly ahead. As reported, the small fort has walls more than four yards high, but without crenellation, which will make it difficult for archers to fire without exposing themselves. It also stands well back from the side road, and its main gate faces east.

Alyiakal calls a halt two hundred yards from the walls and turns to Kessmyr. "Post scouts to watch the main road north and south to make sure we're not surprised. I'm taking first squad a little closer to the fort. I'd prefer that they surrender, but it might take some persuasion."

"I thought you said that they'd fight to the death or something like that."

"The regular armsmen will . . . so long as one of the Duke's officers is around, but it can't hurt to try, since the armsmen you saw might not be quite as willing to die."

"First squad, on the majer!" orders Kessmyr.

Alyiakal leads the squad forward toward the fort, watching and sensing along the top of the walls. No one appears, although Alyiakal can sense order/chaos patterns within the fort. He reins up a little less than fifty yards from the walls, calling out, "Hello, the fort!," boosting the force of his voice with order.

There is no response.

Alyiakal calls out again, with no response.

"We'd prefer that you open the gate and surrender," calls out Alyiakal a third time, "but we'll have to take stronger measures if you don't."

"No one here will surrender," comes back a voice.

"Not even if we spare everyone?" questions Alyiakal, trying to locate the speaker with his senses.

"The Duke will kill anyone who surrenders," returns the voice.

Alyiakal finds him, standing on a platform behind and to one side of the gate. "If we have to, we'll do the same to get control of the fort. Since you're going to lose the fort, regardless, wouldn't you prefer to live?"

"Do your worst!"

Alyiakal lifts his firelance and lofts a single bolt over the walls, guiding it down onto the order/chaos pattern of the speaker, which scatters into ash. After several long moments, Alyiakal calls out once more. "Open the gates. We won't harm anyone who doesn't resist."

Again, no one responds.

Alyiakal raises his voice. "First squad, five abreast, staggered formation. Ready arms!"

When first squad is in position, Alyiakal orders, "On my command, first two ranks, aim and fire at the center of the gate. Ready! Fire!"

As the firebolts strike the center of the gate, Alyiakal uses his firelance as well, but adds even more chaos from what he has collected over the past three days.

HHHSSSTT!

The center of the gate explodes in ash and flame.

"Cease fire! Cease fire!"

Alyiakal continues to sense order/chaos patterns within the fort, especially near the top of the walls, as the chaos-spurred flames consume the sides of the gate.

Then he senses someone climbing to the top of the wall near the gate, and he raises his firelance. The moment the archer appears, Alyiakal looses a quick chaos bolt, dropping the charred figure back into the fort.

Another quint passes, and the gate slowly becomes a charred opening dotted with ash and embers.

"Are you ready to surrender or do we fire the entire fort?" calls out Alyiakal. "We'll spare anyone who leaves his weapons behind and comes out with their hands up."

After several long moments, an older man in a green uniform edges through the gate, looking warily at the armsmen, and then at the larger force farther to the west.

"Just stand over there," commands Alyiakal, "until everyone who wants to leave is out here."

The second figure to leave is a scrawny youth, who joins the older man.

Over the next quint, seventeen others in green uniforms appear. The last one says, in a quavering voice, "There's no one left. That's alive, anyway. Your firebolts killed the Duke's headman, the head armsman, and two others."

"What do you want from us?" asks the older man.

"Very little," replies Alyiakal. "Some information and for you all to go home and never to raise arms against us. We won't be so generous a second time." He embodies those words with the cold certainty of order. He rides closer, then asks, "Are the Duke's armsmen still mostly in Kraaslaen?"

The captured armsmen exchange looks of puzzlement.

"The next town to the south, over the hills, did they go and stay there?" asks Alyiakal.

"Yes, ser," says the older man. "Most of them. Half a season ago. Another bunch came through here two eightdays ago."

"How long does it take to travel there?"

Most of the captives shrug, but one says, "A long day on a good horse."

"Has anyone come back since then?"

"Just the Duke's messengers," says one of the youths.

"Are most of the men who live here serving as armsmen with the Duke?"

"We had no choice," says another.

"How many armsmen rode through going south since the Spring?"

"Hundreds and hundreds," says one youth.

"More like six hundred," says the older man. "I heard tell there were ten companies."

"Did all of them carry shiny bronze shields?"

"Wouldn't say all of them, but most."

"What about strange weapons?"

"Didn't see any, but there was a mage, someone said."

"And the Duke's younger son . . ."

Alyiakal asks questions for another quint but learns little more. Then he says, "Go back to your homes. Stay there while we're here. If we catch anyone lurking around . . . you've seen what we can do."

In moments, all of those who surrendered are gone.

Alyiakal summons all the captains. "We need to clean up that gate and see if there's anything usable. Collect all the weapons as well. Nolaan, Fourth Company will handle sentries and security tonight." Alyiakal outlines the other details.

After he finishes, Kessmyr, Nolaan, and Suraat leave to handle their duties.

Chaem does not. "Might I have a moment, ser?"

"You can have all the time you need," replies Alyiakal.

"I was wondering, ser . . . about the armsmen here."

"Why I wasn't harder on them, you mean?"

"Yes, ser."

"What I can or can't do," says Alyiakal tiredly, "depends on the situation and my orders. The way I see it . . . First, we're on their land. Second, this group didn't attack us. Third, we're going to have to come back this way. Fourth, you can't get information from dead armsmen. Fifth, they aren't that much of a threat, especially after we take their weapons and some of their mounts with us. And sixth, I wasn't ordered to destroy *this* fort." Alyiakal offers a lopsided smile. "There are probably other reasons for and reasons against what I decided. Is there anything you think I haven't considered?"

"There's not much you don't consider, from what I've seen. What do you think will happen next?"

"Unless I'm mistaken, Duke Taartyn will expect what's happened in the past, and that the Mirror Lancers will attack from Lhaarat. We won't, however, and that will surprise them somewhat. Going against ten companies will be difficult, though. One thing in our favor is that they can't fit them all in that fort. We'll have to see if we can find a few other advantages."

"Ten companies . . . that's quite a few."

"If it were easy, headquarters wouldn't have sent us," replies Alyiakal dryly. "We'll have to make it work, and I have some ideas. Is there anything else, Chaem?"

"No, ser."

"Then I'll see you later."

As Chaem leaves, Alyiakal looks to the fort, where lancers are using axes from the wagons to remove the still-smoldering remnants of the gate, knowing nothing else will be anywhere close to this easy.

XLIX

Fourday comes quickly, and Alyiakal briefs the company officers early, including specific orders for dealing with any possible Cerlynese messengers, especially coming from the south. He doesn't want them turning back and warning the Cerlynese commander in Kraaslaen. There's little he can do about messengers coming from Clynya, but if a messenger or dispatch rider going through Kula discovers that Mirror Lancers have headed south, any reinforcements the Duke may send will not arrive until matters in Kraaslaen have been settled.

One way or another.

Shortly after first light, in the comparatively cooler morning air, the companies head out on the high road that, far to the south, ends in Jakaafra. The Kulan fort holds little in terms of supplies, most of which are questionable, but some grain is parceled out to the horses and a few palatable additions to the provisions carried by the three wagons.

By actual sunrise, Alyiakal, Kessmyr, and First Company ride up the lower part of the road into the hills separating Cerlyn from Cyador.

The hills aren't as extensive as those separating Pemedra from the grasslands. By close to midday, under the increasing heat of the white sun, Alyiakal sees that they're nearing the midpoint. Shortly, he senses that the scouts, half a kay ahead and around the curve of the road, have halted and moved sideways. *Likely waiting to get behind messengers from Kraaslaen.*

He discerns two other riders moving toward the scouts, however, and all he can do is hope the scouts are successful in keeping the riders from getting away. He tries not to hold his breath. Then he senses firelance blasts. One of the northbound riders halts, and the other turns, before another blast strikes him and his mount, followed by a black mist of death.

Alyiakal keeps riding, as if nothing has happened. He and Kessmyr cover another three hundred yards before they reach the scouts, riding back toward First Company with their firelances leveled at a third rider, wearing the dark green and brown of a Cerlynese armsman.

Once they get closer and rein up, Alyiakal halts the column and asks, "Only one dispatch rider?," although he knows otherwise.

"The other one thought he could outride a firelance," declares the lead scout. "The horse landed on him, and his head hit a rock. We'd appreciate some help getting the bodies out of sight, but we thought you'd like to see the dispatches, or whatever he's carrying."

Alyiakal turns to Kessmyr. "Detail some of first squad."

"Yes, ser."

The lead scout rides forward to hand the dispatch bag to Alyiakal, who takes it and turns to the surviving rider. "What dispatches are you carrying?"

The man swallows. "Hyaas had the dispatches."

"And you didn't have any?" Alyiakal offers a cold smile.

"Ah . . ."

"You wouldn't want to end up like your companion, would you?"

"Ah . . ."

"Dismount now or die!" Alyiakal gestures to a lancer behind him. "Get the horse."

The Cerlynese scrambles from the saddle.

"Search him and his saddlebags."

When Alyiakal opens the dispatch pouch, he finds a vague letter addressed to a Colonel Caarp that states that all is well in Laenkraas, apparently a decoy communication. The scouts' search turns up a concealed dispatch in a hidden section of the surviving rider's saddlebags. Alyiakal slits the envelope, careful to preserve the seal, then reads the dispatch before tucking it into one of his saddlebags.

"Ser?" asks Kessmyr.

"It doesn't say much. An Overcaptain Durrek reports, as directed, that they've seen no signs of Cyadoran armsmen and the surviving townspeople are appropriately obedient. He states that they will maintain control of the town as long as required and supporting his forces for an extended period of time will require enlarging and rebuilding the fort, especially if further maneuvers to the south are necessary."

As directed by whom? The Duke's younger son? Alyiakal has to wonder about that.

"It sounds like the Duke is interested in expanding Cerlyn," says Kessmyr.

Or retaining Kraaslaen permanently. Alyiakal only nods. "Tie up the messenger securely and stash him in a wagon until we have time to talk to him."

"Yes, ser," replies Kessmyr.

Over the next glass, the companies encounter no other riders, although the road holds more than a few hoofprints.

At the next break, Alyiakal rides back to the wagon to see what the Cerlynese messenger has to say—after he's set on the wagon seat and given some water.

"Before we start," Alyiakal says, "you need to know that I'm partly a healer, and I can tell when you're lying. What's your name?"

"Dagaar."

Alyiakal sighs loudly. "Try again." He projects cold hard order.

The man freezes for a moment, then says, "Lhomaal."

"Are you just a dispatch rider or do you fight with the armsmen as well?"

"Mostly a rider."

"How long were you in Kraaslaen?"

"If you mean Laenkraas . . . I was only there a few days. I brought a dispatch from Clynya. I got to Laenkraas on oneday."

"Are most of the armsmen posted there, or did the overcaptain send a company east to Lastop?"

"I heard there was a company in the hamlet to the east and scouts farther south."

"How many captains are in Laenkraas with the armsmen?"

"I don't know. I saw three or four, but there had to be more."

"Do all the armsmen carry polished shields?"

"I don't know."

"Guess," orders Alyiakal.

"Half . . . maybe a little more."

"How many times have you carried dispatches or other communications to Laenkraas?"

"Just this time."

"Where else?"

"Once to Kula and then back."

"Was that when armsmen were assembling for the attack on Laenkraas?"

"It was before the attack."

"How many armsmen were in Kula before they left for the attack?"

"I heard that there were five hundred. I was told others arrived later."

"Are any of the armsmen in Laenkraas quartered in the fort?"

Lhomaal shakes his head. "No one wanted to clean it up. They've taken all the houses. They're not much better."

Alyiakal continues the questioning for another half quint but doesn't learn much more. Still, he has a slightly better idea of what they face. *Which leaves a lot unknown.*

In late afternoon, even warmer than midday, the scouts signal that they see something, and Alyiakal rides ahead to join them. He sees, beyond them, that the road heads down toward Kraaslaen, little more than five kays ahead. He can't make out obvious movements or dust clouds that might indicate groups of mounted armsmen.

He turns to the scouts. "Pull back slightly, so you're not too obvious, and let me know if anyone's headed this way. If they are, handle them the same way you did the dispatch riders. The main body will be withdrawing to where we can set up for the night."

"Yes, ser."

By the time the four companies have withdrawn to the temporary encampment, near a small stream, and additional road sentries are posted and instructed, more than a glass has passed. The white sun hangs low in the west when Alyiakal finally meets with the four company officers.

"We'll head out at first light straight for Kraaslaen," he announces. "You need to study your maps after we're done here. You may not have time tomorrow."

"Won't they see us and be ready to attack?" asks Suraat.

"That's possible, but we'll face that problem no matter when we attack. Earlier, it's less likely that they'll see us." *Especially if I can hold an illusion of an empty road until we're largely across the bridge.* "Also, they're expecting an attack from the south, not the north. The only road they know about from the northwest runs through Jerans."

Alyiakal ignores the momentary frown from Suraat and continues. "I'll be with Kessmyr and First Company. We'll flush out and scatter the main body of the Cerlynese. Chaem . . . you and Second Company will take the road heading west after the bridge and ride to the second road into the town, where you'll form up to face any Cerlynese who flee that way. Nolaan, you and Fourth Company will follow Second Company, but you'll stop and form up at the first road. Suraat, you'll cross the bridge and form up, with the wagons behind you, just short of the open space leading to the fort."

"How accurate are these maps?" asks Suraat.

"They're the most accurate available. I've ridden every yard of the roads on the maps. I doubt they've changed much in the last year or so. The Cerlynese have never been much on roadbuilding. Also, none of the Cerlynese officers or squad leaders who saw how we used the roads when I was there were fortunate enough to survive."

Chaem offers the slightest nod.

"Now, we've drilled extensively, but I don't believe any of you have actually faced armsmen using the polished shields. Those shields will deflect most firebolts. If you're faced with armsmen who lead with the shields, aim for the legs of their mounts. I know you don't like that, but if you don't cut down their mounts, you're going to lose lancers, and maybe your life. I *cannot* emphasize that enough. The other possibility is that they'll lead with the polished shields and use archers behind the formation. What do you do then?" Alyiakal looks to Kessmyr.

"Try and get the shieldmen down and angle firebolts over them into the rear?"

"That's one way. If there are too many archers after you down the shieldmen, you can withdraw enough to mount a flank attack at speed. Don't charge head-on into a hail of shafts. Make them spread their firing pattern. You can also withdraw slowly, staying just out of range, forcing them to use bows to push you back—until they run out of arrows. Then you can charge, and they'll either break or die . . ."

After Alyiakal finishes, Suraat asks, "Begging your pardon, ser, but how many of these tactics have you used?"

"Over the years . . . all of them."

Nolaan smothers a smile, while Chaem manages to maintain a stoic expression.

"Now . . . I'll leave you to brief your men and look over the maps." Alyiakal steps back and moves around the wagon where, seeing no one nearby, he raises a concealment and eases back to where he can hear—assuming any of the officers will say anything.

"Suraat," says Chaem slowly, "why are you always trying to piss off the majer? Or are you too stupid to know that's what you're doing?"

"Ser . . . I just wanted to know—"

"Young as the majer is, he's likely forgotten more than you'll ever know. He's been in more pitched battles than you'll ever see, especially if you don't lose that attitude. You realize that he's gotten us within a few kays of the Cerlynese, and they don't even know we're here? *And* he's leading from the front. You know how few majers do that?"

"And how few are good enough to *survive* doing that?" adds Kessmyr.

Alyiakal has the sense that Suraat turns toward Nolaan.

"Don't look at me," says Nolaan, his voice showing a certain sense of amusement. "You're the one who watched him set up and destroy an entire Jeranyi squad without a single casualty in your company."

Alyiakal eases away and moves back toward his bedroll and gear, hoping he can sleep halfway decently, even though he worries about the next day, and about all the chaos he has gathered over the last four days.

L

At first light on fiveday morning, the Mirror Lancers start the advance on Kraaslaen, with Alyiakal and Kessmyr leading First Company, followed by Second Company, Fourth Company, Third Company, and then the wagons. Once the force starts down the slope toward the town, Alyiakal creates the illusion of haze, holding that until he and First Company near the flat, short bridge over the small river, when he replaces that with an illusion of an empty road leading up into the hills. The illusion won't fool anyone who's really looking, but it will still conceal his force. He doubts many will be looking for anyone coming out of the north just after sunrise.

As First Company starts across the bridge, Alyiakal still can't see any armsmen. Only when first squad forms up in a five-man, staggered front and Alyiakal calls in the scouts does a bell begin to clang.

"Company! Forward! Arms ready!"

Armsmen in green tunics and brown trousers begin to appear at the far side of the square as First Company rides past the ruined and deserted fort, in which Alyiakal can sense no order/chaos patterns.

"First squad! Targeted fire!"

The firebolts from the five-man front quickly remove the squad of armsmen on the other side of the square.

Someone shouts out, "Withdraw and re-form! Withdraw and re-form!"

While Alyiakal keeps the pace slow so that first squad can pick off Cerlynese armsmen attempting to form up, he has no doubt First Company will meet more resistance before long. He also suspects the main body of armsmen are quartered in the town's south side, where the Cerlynese expected an attack.

A sharp jab at his shields has him looking for archers, whom he locates a hundred yards ahead and to the right, behind a chest-high mudbrick wall.

He fires three quick firebolts to take out the archers there, then switches his attention to the left, loosing another firebolt.

He hears more orders being shouted farther ahead, and senses men and mounts withdrawing along the side streets.

Two hundred yards ahead, he sees a company forming up, a front rank of mounted shieldmen, with riders directly behind holding shields overhead. He also senses archers moving into place behind them.

"First Company! Re-form. Three-abreast column!" Alyiakal waits until he senses that the column is tight, then orders, "Forward! Fast trot!"

A handful of shafts sprays off Alyiakal's shields as he rides toward the hastily formed company ahead, each one feeling like a needle somewhere on his skin.

When he's less than twenty yards from their line, Alyiakal looses a chaos-boosted firebolt between the middle two shieldmen, and low enough to cut the legs off their mounts while thrusting them aside, providing a space for him to break through the line and spray chaos across the Cerlynese still holding their shields over their heads and then at the archers behind the mounted shield riders.

Instantly, the Cerlynese company begins to dissolve, but in the chaos First Company comes to a halt, and a quint passes before the lancers take out the armsmen who didn't immediately flee. Alyiakal almost feels sorry for the Cerlynese who keep trying to fight even as they're charred or turned to ashes. *Except I know what you've done to those who live here.*

"First Company! Re-form! Three abreast!"

Alyiakal scans the main street, but it is empty except for First Company and the fallen. He senses at least two Cerlynese companies riding west along the road leading to Fourth Company's position. Another company heads toward Second Company. Alyiakal decides that Chaem can handle a single company, and calls out, "First Company! On me! Fast trot!"

In a fraction of a quint, the company has turned onto the road west and ridden clear of the cluster of houses, continuing west between scattered dwellings little more than huts surrounded by small plots of land.

Alyiakal spies a lane roughly parallel to the road—and a field with low-growing crops that he could take to reach the lane. He turns in the saddle to Kessmyr. "I'm taking first squad to make a flank attack. Close on the rear of the force ahead and see if you can take out the archers. If they halt and start loosing shafts, fall back out of range until we attack."

"Yes, ser! First squad on the majer!"

As soon as Alyiakal reaches the plot with the low crops—potatoes, not well-tended, the holder likely a casualty—he turns the squad across the field. Once on the other side, they continue to close the gap. Alyiakal knows he needs to take out the archers before the Cerlynese can use them effectively against Fourth Company. As first squad draws closer to the Cerlynese rear, they ride past the trailing riders more than a hundred yards to the left. Alyiakal keeps looking for a suitable location to turn to the left and close on the archers, but there's only waist-high grass on the left, and very green grass at that.

You do have a lot of chaos. With that thought, he aims the firelance at an angle to his left, feeding a stream of chaos through the firelance to cut enough of a path to see obstacles otherwise concealed by the grass, and turns the gray onto the path he's creating.

He calls back over his shoulder. "Left file! Ready arms!"

As first squad closes on the rear Cerlynese company, Alyiakal sees most of the Cerlynese seem unaware of the squad.

Less than thirty yards from the Cerlynese, Alyiakal begins to pick off the leading riders and mounts. In a fraction of a quint most of the Cerlynese company has come to a stop.

"First squad! Halt! Left turn in place! Open fire!"

Some of the Cerlynese riders flee into the high grass on the far side of the road, but Alyiakal concentrates on the archers. Several of the Cerlynese riders with blades or spears initially turn toward Alyiakal and first squad, only to be taken out by the firelances before they can close on the Mirror Lancers.

Then Kessmyr arrives with the remainder of First Company.

In less than a quint, all that remains of the trailing Cerlynese company is a handful of riderless mounts and a few riders struggling through the high grass to the south.

"First Company! Close up and re-form!" orders Alyiakal.

As first squad moves through the last of the grass, some of which smolders from firebolts, and the company re-forms, Alyiakal sees Nolaan is withdrawing, slowly, to the south along the road around the town, to avoid the hail of shafts from the rear of the first Cerlynese company, which is less than half a kay ahead of First Company.

Alyiakal turns to Kessmyr. "We'll move out at a fast trot. If they start to target us, we'll do a full charge." Alyiakal hopes they can use firelances before the Cerlynese archers react and shift from targeting Fourth Company to targeting First Company.

"Yes, ser."

"First Company! Forward!"

When first squad is less than a hundred yards from the last ranks of the Cerlynese, Alyiakal moves to the shoulder of the road and orders, "First squad! Three abreast! Staggered formation! Ready arms!"

While several archers in the last ranks of the Cerlynese company see the oncoming Mirror Lancers, only a few turn and release shafts, and none of those shafts strike Alyiakal's shields.

"First squad! Fire at will!" orders Alyiakal.

In moments, most of the archers are down, one way or another, trapped between their own shield-bearers ahead, and First Company behind. With the high grass on each side of the road, the Cerlynese can't flee, and Alyiakal has no intention of letting any escape, not if he can do anything about it.

In the meantime, when the hail of Cerlynese arrows halts, Nolaan moves Fourth Company forward, taking out the mounts of the shield-bearers then the armsmen behind them.

Two quints later, the only survivors near the battle are Mirror Lancers.

"Re-form the company," Alyiakal tells Kessmyr. "I need to talk to Nolaan. I'll be right back." Then Alyiakal rides through the fallen and blackened figures to join Nolaan.

"Ser!"

"From what I saw, you handled the situation well."

The undercaptain grimaces. "I didn't like withdrawing, but I followed your advice. I don't know what would have happened if you hadn't showed up."

"You would have kept withdrawing until they ran out of shafts, and then you would have counterattacked, and they wouldn't have been able to do a thing. We just made it quicker. In the meantime, you kept your head and their attention, and they scarcely saw us coming." Alyiakal pauses. "Now I want you to head south on this road to reinforce Chaem. We're going to see if we can circle around and get behind the company attacking him."

"Yes, ser."

Alyiakal inclines his head, then turns and rides back to rejoin Kessmyr and First Company.

"Ser, company re-formed and ready to ride."

"Excellent. We're headed back toward the town to see if we can get behind the force attacking Chaem." *Or to deal with any other forces, since we haven't yet encountered all the armsmen supposedly here.*

For the first kay heading back toward the center of Kraaslaen, Alyiakal cannot sense any concentration of order/chaos patterns, although he can vaguely sense something ahead and to his right, which might be yet another Cerlynese company.

Might be? Could hardly be anything else.

A fraction of a kay later, he definitely discerns a force. He also senses that the force is realigning itself on the road leading out to Second Company's engagement with yet another company. That repositioning seems to be in order to face First Company. While Alyiakal hasn't seen any scouts, it's possible he missed one.

Alyiakal tries to sense a lane or a side street that will allow him to flank the force ahead, but he can't sense one. There are too many dwellings and other buildings for him to actually see any lanes or the other force.

When First Company turns right, onto the main street that leads to the side road, Alyiakal doesn't see the Cerlynese force until he is within a few yards of the side road, positioned between buildings that make any sort of flank attack close to impossible.

Not to mention the fact that you're facing at least two companies and don't have enough lancers for something like that.

The Cerlynese company has halted two hundred yards away, with a mounted shield wall across the road and riders behind the front rank with shields overhead. Alyiakal senses a modest concentration of chaos in several ranks back in the Cerlynese force that can only be a mage.

You knew that was possible.

"They're waiting for us to attack," says Kessmyr.

"Or to get in range of their archers," returns Alyiakal. "We'll have to do this the hard way." He raises his voice. "Forward! On me!" He urges the gray forward at a fast trot.

As First Company rides closer, a hail of shafts arches up from the rear of the Cerlynese forces above the shield-bearers in front, then slides off Alyiakal's extended shields, as First Company nears the point where the Mirror Lancer firelances can target the mounts of the front shield-bearers.

Then a firebolt arches from behind the foremost shield-bearers and sprays away from Alyiakal's shields.

Alyiakal ignores the mage and fires an order-bounded firebolt at the Cerlynese center, followed by a second bolt to wedge apart the shield wall.

Another firebolt flares toward Alyiakal, who has anticipated it and catches it with his shields, flinging it back with an additional firebolt, followed by a smaller order dart.

The center of the Cerlynese force is ripped apart by a wave of fire, and Alyiakal can barely remain in the saddle and hold his shields.

For a long moment, there is silence, or perhaps, Alyiakal thinks, he just can't hear after the chaos explosion. He can't see, either, and even after the temporary blindness passes, his vision is blurry because his eyes are still watering.

When he can see clearly, all he can see are ashes for the next fifty to seventy yards and stunned archers beyond that.

"First Company! Forward!" Alyiakal urges the gray forward, because the last thing he wants is to give the surviving archers a chance to recover.

At the sight of the charging Mirror Lancers, and the chaos bolts from Alyiakal's firelance, the archers break.

Another quint passes before First Company finishes dealing with the remnants of the mage's force and continues out the road past the last of the closely set dwellings, only to see Cerlynese armsmen riding toward them as if fleeing.

As the Cerlynese see the oncoming Mirror Lancers, they try to escape through the high grass. Most don't succeed.

A fraction of a quint later, Alyiakal can make out Chaem and Second Company riding toward him and calls a halt, surveying the lancers as they ride closer. Alyiakal doesn't see any obvious decrease in company size or any obvious casualties.

Once Chaem is closer, Alyiakal rides to join the senior captain, then says, "It looks like you didn't need much help."

"I split the company, put two squads behind outbuildings on one side of the road and one behind the house on the other side. Then we made running flank attacks. What settled it was Fourth Company's appearance. They just broke. We got a lot that way. Fourth Company's behind us." Chaem looks past Alyiakal, as if inquiring.

"We got most of the ones you didn't, and possibly two other companies before that."

Chaem frowns. "Possibly?"

"They had a mage. Something went wrong with his chaos, and the fireball incinerated at least two companies. We need to head back. Suraat's holding the bridge to keep stragglers and others from escaping." *And you just hope that there weren't too many for Third Company to handle.* "I'd appreciate it if you and Nolaan would keep an eye out for any other Cerlynese and take care of them."

"Yes, ser. We can do that."

Alyiakal adds, "Once we've dealt with all the Cerlynese, one way or another, I'll look at your wounded, but that will have to wait." He just hopes the wait won't be too long for some.

"I understand, ser."

Alyiakal nods, then turns the gray and rides back to Kessmyr. "We need to head back in case Suraat needs support."

"First Company! To the rear, ride!" orders Kessmyr.

He and Alyiakal ride along the shoulder of the road to third squad, which now leads the way back toward Kraaslaen's main street, moving at a fast trot.

While Alyiakal senses a few order/chaos patterns ahead, they're scattered, and most are individuals on foot. He suspects that the few riders heading north are survivors of the chaos explosion and the brief subsequent one-on-one fighting . . . and they're trying to escape back to Cerlyn. *Something we'll have to take care of later, as well.*

As Alyiakal continues toward the main street, he forces himself to look at the bodies strewing the road, most marked in some fashion by chaos flame, those not turned to ashes or black powder. Thinking of Duke Taartyn, he wants to shake his head, but doesn't, partly because his head throbs with dull aches, interspersed with occasional unseen needles that feel as though they're jabbing through his skull.

Just after Alyiakal turns the gray north on the main street, Kessmyr asks quietly, "Do you think we'll find any more, ser?"

"If there are any besides stragglers, they're likely attacking Third Company. I don't see any near us."

Before First Company reaches the square, beside one of the larger houses, Alyiakal sees two bodies hanging from a tree, both wearing the green and brown of Cerlyn. He notices that the fronts of their trousers have been cut open, and there's a great deal of blood on the trousers. He suspects that the two were caught unaware in the early moments of the attack. He also has no doubt that the two deserved their fate.

Kessmyr sees the bodies, looks hard for a moment, then turns away.

"With what they've done to the women before, and likely again this year," asks Alyiakal, "are you that surprised?"

"I suppose I shouldn't be, but . . ." Kessmyr pauses, then asks, "Why do the Cerlynese keep attacking? You'd think that losses like this would tell them something."

"Very few survive, and no one believes them. Besides, Duke Taartyn will keep doing this—probably in another three years—because he thinks we're weak for not attacking him. He doesn't care how many armsmen he loses so long as he wins in the long run."

"In three years, you won't be here," says Kessmyr.

"After this," replies Alyiakal dryly, "I may not be here next year . . . unless . . ." He breaks off his words, knowing he's already said too much. *Don't talk so much when you're tired. What you say gets repeated.*

"Unless?" presses Kessmyr.

"We'll leave it at that," Alyiakal says humorously. "Call it combat humor." He knows that makes little sense. Hopefully, that will distract Kessmyr. As it turns out, he's the distracted one because as he enters the square, heading toward the fort, he senses death mists that fade away. He can only hope that the dead are Cerlynese and not Mirror Lancers.

After riding a bit farther, he can see and sense the line of Mirror Lancers across the area before the bridge, and the slight wind out of the north carries the smell of ashes and burned flesh. The flat between the fort and the bridge is littered with ash and the charred bodies of mounts and men.

"Company! Halt!" Alyiakal orders before continuing toward Third Company and Suraat, letting the gray pick his way through the carnage. He studies where Third Company is still drawn up and can't help but nod. Suraat has his three squads stretched across the north end of the area, if only three deep, in a staggered formation that clearly allowed most of them to fire simultaneously.

Alyiakal reins up a yard or so from the undercaptain.

Suraat looks shaken.

"Excellent formation and tactics, Undercaptain," says Alyiakal, projecting a slight feeling of reassurance.

"There must have been more than three companies. They just kept coming. They didn't even try to loose shafts at us. It was as though they were fleeing the black angels. It didn't make any sense."

Alyiakal wonders if that was because of what happened to the companies surrounding the Cerlynese mage but doubts that he'll ever know for certain. After a moment, he continues in what he hopes is a quietly reassuring tone. "Sometimes, it doesn't. Just remember that they fight that way because the Duke would have killed them if they didn't. That doesn't leave you much choice if you and your men want to survive."

"Are pitched battles always like this?"

"All too often," admits Alyiakal. *Especially if you're the one who survives.* "That's why it's often better to avoid them, however you can."

After a moment, he glances toward the sun, absently realizing that fine black ash drifts around him, and that it's barely midafternoon. He looks back to Suraat. "Post a squad on the far side of the bridge to deal with any armsmen coming or leaving. Have the squad make sure no riders ford the stream and escape."

"Yes, ser."

"If you have any wounded, get them to the wagons. I'll do what I can. Also send a ranker to the other companies to let them know that."

Suraat nods, but still appears slightly dazed.

"It doesn't get any easier, not if you understand," adds Alyiakal, "and it shouldn't. Or you become like the Cerlynese." While that's unlikely to have been true for all too many of the dead armsmen, it's certainly true for those who commanded them.

Then he rides back to where First Company is drawn up. "Send any of the wounded to the wagons. I'll do what I can there. First Company and Second Company need to do a sweep of the town to make sure there aren't any armsmen lurking around. Fourth Company will deal with all the bodies. Pile them in places where they can be burned. They're not to go in the stream. If you'd convey those orders, that will allow me to get to the wounded sooner."

"Yes, ser," replies Kessmyr.

"And, later, I'd like a casualty report." Alyiakal turns the gray and rides to where the wagons are drawn up, ties the gray at the end, and unstraps his healer satchel. He looks to one of the teamsters. "Please get some water for my mount."

Walking to the middle wagon, Alyiakal finds one lancer is already lying on a crude pallet, and two others sit slumped beside the first. The prone lancer has taken an arrow to the chest, and Alyiakal feels that his chances aren't that good, given that there's also some matter from the arrow left behind. *But you've managed to save others with wounds this bad.* He opens the healer's satchel and kneels beside the wounded man. Alyiakal uses order to ease out the chaos-infused matter, re-dresses the wound, and seals it with order. Then he moves on to the next lancer.

He's worked with five wounded men when he senses two others walking toward him and he looks up.

"There's someone who wants to talk to you, ser," says the ranker. "She might be the town headwoman."

Alyiakal turns to see a thin black-haired woman with streaks of white in her short-cut black hair standing beside the ranker, one of the few women in

Kraaslaen with short hair, at least from the few Alyiakal has seen over the years. "You're the headwoman?"

"Only because no real men remain," replies the woman. "Do you intend to stay? Or will you leave like before and let the green bastards return?"

A very good question, unhappily.

"Well?" presses the headwoman, her voice firm but level.

"Staying will work only so long as we are here," replies Alyiakal. "We cannot stay here for years."

"You have forts elsewhere. Why not here?"

"That is not my decision. That lies with the Majer-Commander."

"Then you will abandon us once more?" She looks to the side as if to spit but does not.

"We cannot stay, but we will do what we can so that the Cerlynese do not return."

At Alyiakal's words, the headwoman offers a puzzled frown.

"I cannot promise more," replies Alyiakal, "but I will do what I can."

"Will that be enough?"

"I cannot say. I can only say that I will do what I can."

She studies him for a long moment, then says, "You are honest. We can hope."

Then she turns and walks away.

Alyiakal moves to the next wounded lancer, with a hastily and roughly dressed shoulder wound, most likely from an arrow.

LI

The aftermath of the battle over Kraaslaen takes far longer than the fighting did, lasting into the evening and extending into late afternoon on sixday. Alyiakal is frankly amazed at the comparatively few Mirror Lancer casualties. Out of the four companies, there are only six deaths—five of them dying before Alyiakal could even attend to them, and one being the first lancer he'd treated. There were also seven wounded, all likely to recover.

The four companies collect several hundred horn bows that Alyiakal has burned with the bodies and close to six hundred blades. Alyiakal knows the lancers didn't come close to finding all of the Cerlynese weapons.

One item of interest is a ring that Nolaan gives to Alyiakal. "One of the rankers found this where you . . . encountered that mage. I think he gave it to me because he knew there was no way he could hide something this valuable."

Alyiakal takes the ring, made of white gold, possibly platinum, with a large oval emerald. In the heavy metal setting on one side of the stone is the letter "L," with a small eight-pointed star on the other side.

"I'd say this belonged to someone important," Nolaan adds, "maybe the mage."

"More likely the Duke's younger son," replies Alyiakal. "One of the armsmen at Kula said that he was in Kraaslaen."

"The Duke definitely won't want to hear that."

As if he isn't already angry enough with Cyador. But Alyiakal only nods and places the ring in the small leather pouch attached to the inside of his belt.

After going through all the gear and captured horses, in the end Alyiakal decides they will only take twenty of the best captured mounts, leaving the rest to the people of Kraaslaen. Some of those twenty horses will carry the captured weapons. Alyiakal is well aware that without those, few will believe what his force accomplished, and he also doesn't want them in other hands.

Even with the weapons, there will be considerable doubts among the commanders at Mirror Lancer headquarters.

While Alyiakal can sense the order/chaos patterns of the surviving women and girls of Kraaslaen, he only glimpses them, briefly, on his inspection rides through the town, before they scurry out of sight. The late-Summer weather remains hot and dry, with little wind, and what wind there is stirs up the ashes that seem to be everywhere. Small bits cling to the heavy sweat on Alyiakal's face and forehead, another annoyance besides his scattered bruises and the persistent dull headache.

Later, after eating an actual meal, probably partly based on horsemeat, Alyiakal checks on the wounded again, adding bits of order to deal with wound chaos. Then, in the growing twilight, when he senses no one around, he raises a concealment and returns to where the four company officers sit on a low wall, talking.

"I'm not sure how we managed this," says Suraat.

"*We* didn't," says Chaem quietly. "The majer did. I've been around. He's trained us in formations I've never seen and used tactics I've never heard of. Some of them shouldn't succeed and wouldn't for anyone else. Somehow, he makes them work. Yesterday, he planned the attack so that the Cerlynese never could get organized. It would have been much harder if we'd had to face a larger force concentrated in one place."

"You think he'd do well at that?" asks Suraat.

"He would, but he'd lose more lancers, maybe lot more," says Chaem.

"He doesn't like losing men," says Suraat.

"That's something too many officers don't get," replies Chaem. "Trained officers and rankers are hard to replace. Casualties are higher among replacements, too."

"I still don't understand how he knows where everyone is," says Suraat. "The Cerlynese as well."

"It's like he knows where everyone is before he or anyone else can possibly see it," adds Nolaan.

"He does," says Kessmyr. "He tries not to show it, but I'm certain he does."

"Thank the Rational Stars he does," replies Chaem.

"I'll be glad to get back to Pemedra," declares Suraat.

"Don't get your hopes up," says Kessmyr.

"You think he has something else in mind?" asks Nolaan.

"I don't know," replies Kessmyr, "but yesterday he said that in another three years Duke Taartyn would be back doing the same thing. I said he wouldn't be here in three years—"

"He likely won't be," agrees Chaem.

"*But* he said that he likely wouldn't be here in another year unless . . . and then he wouldn't say more. He said it was combat humor."

Alyiakal waits as the momentary silence draws out.

Finally, Nolaan clears his throat. "You think it's because headquarters doesn't like the way he deals with problems?"

"Might be," says Chaem. "Sometimes seems like headquarters just wants to do enough to push off the problem for a year or so, if that. Majer wants to remove problems. The way he does it is better for us. We just wiped out something like eleven companies, and we only lost six men. Most posts lose more than that in a year on routine patrols."

"Too bad he's not Majer-Commander," says Nolaan.

"Don't wish that," declares Chaem. "Then we'd have the overcaptain in command."

Alyiakal slips away, mulling over what the four officers have said.

LII

Because everything takes longer than anticipated, especially after significant battles, including provisioning, Alyiakal puts off leaving until early on eightday. While the companies form, he meets with the company officers.

"As I told you last night, the plan is to ride to Kula. We should get there by late afternoon. That will give us time to send scouts toward Clynya and to discover if anything's changed in Kula. Then, I'll decide what we do next."

"We're not heading back to Pemedra from Kula?" asks Suraat.

"That depends on what we discover. If there's another Cerlynese force or reinforcements headed our way, we'll have to deal with them." Alyiakal smiles wryly. "I don't think headquarters would like us leaving Kraaslaen undefended when we know more companies are coming. I want to be very clear: What we do once we reach Kula depends on the situation." Alyiakal ignores Kessmyr and Chaem exchanging glances. "That's all for now. To your companies."

Little more than a quint later, Alyiakal rides out of Kraaslaen at the head of the force, now led by Nolaan and Fourth Company. As before, Chaem and Second Company provide the rear guard while Suraat and Third Company follow Fourth Company. The only spoils they take are those gathered from dead Cerlynese armsmen and already distributed to the Mirror Lancers—and one decent supply wagon, which carries most of the blades gathered as well as the three lancers unable to ride, and the captive dispatch rider.

The sentries Alyiakal had posted north and south of Kraaslaen haven't reported any Cerlynese armsmen or messengers, and he's relieved with the lack of new hoofprints in the road for the first ten kays north. Nor do the scouts discover any hoofprints belonging to Cerlynese armsmen over the course of the day, only scattered cart tracks and a few hoofprints coming from side trails and lanes.

Then, when Fourth Company is less than ten kays from Kula, Frasdyn, the lead scout, rides back and reports to Alyiakal.

"Ser, it looks like a squad came to a point just ahead and turned back."

"How recently? Could they have seen us and withdrawn?"

"They're at least several glasses old. Could even be a day ago."

Alyiakal frowns. "It might be that the Duke sent some armsmen to Kula and they heard about us and wanted to see if we were still close. Keep an eye out for Cerlynese scouts."

"Yes, ser."

When Fourth Company is only a few kays from Kula, Alyiakal sends out more scouts to learn if there are, indeed, additional Cerlynese armsmen in the town.

Less than two quints later, Frasdyn reports. "There looks to be half a company using the fort, ser. They haven't set scouts and they haven't replaced the gate, either."

"Sounds like they're garrison armsmen, maybe recovered or recovering wounded," replies Alyiakal. *Which might suggest that the Duke's better armsmen are stretched thin.*

Even when the Mirror Lancers reach the outskirts of Kula, no armsmen appear on the road or on the dusty street leading to the small fort. Three armsmen in green and brown, standing before the fort, turn as First Company rides toward them.

"Stay where you are!" calls out Alyiakal.

One man runs for the fort's ungated entry, but Alyiakal puts a firebolt in the dirt in front of him. "Halt or die!"

The armsman stops.

Alyiakal rides up on the man. "You have an undercaptain or a squad leader in command?"

"Squad leader."

"Go tell him that I'd like to talk to him. I'd rather not have to fill the fort with firebolts. So would you."

"Yes, ser." The armsman turns and walks swiftly toward the ungated entry, looking back over his shoulder the whole way.

In moments, another Cerlynese armsman appears, repeatedly glancing up the road toward the Mirror Lancer column as he walks to meet Alyiakal. His eyes widen as he takes in Alyiakal.

"We're not about to fight a whole company, ser."

"Four companies. Would you mind telling me why the Duke only sent a squad?"

"Just a squad, ser. We were sent to increase the complement here."

"Are any other armsmen being sent here or to . . ." Alyiakal pauses, then manages, "Laenkraas?"

The squad leader doesn't answer.

Alyiakal waits.

"I don't know, ser."

Alyiakal presses a touch of cold order at him.

"I really don't know."

"Did the Duke send armsmen to help the Jeranyi?"

"Not that any of us heard."

"How many armsmen are left in Clynya?" Alyiakal eases some order toward the squad leader, suggesting the need for truth.

"Couldn't be more than five companies there, not with the twelve . . ." The squad leader breaks off. "You came from the south . . ."

"There aren't any Cerlynese companies left in Laenkraas."

The man swallows.

"What about the companies attacking Suthya? How many are there? Ten?"

The unspoken reaction suggests to Alyiakal that he's close, and he asks, "Because the Duke got angry with the Suthyan traders?"

"I wouldn't know, ser. He just told us what towns to attack."

"And it was easy at first, but then you started losing more armsmen?"

"Lots more."

"So the Duke sent more. How many?"

"Four companies, maybe five. No one said, but that's what we figured." The squad leader pauses, then asks, "What are you going to do with us, ser?"

"Not much. Take your weapons and tack and leave you here. I wouldn't take up arms against Cyador any time soon, though."

"Don't know as I'd want to, any time."

"Call out your men with their arms. We'll take them. It would be most unwise not to turn over weapons. Just stay in the fort until we depart Kula. Anyone who tries to leave before that might just run into a firebolt."

"I'll make that clear. We'll be back shortly."

After the squad leader returns to the fort, Alyiakal turns to Nolaan. "Have first squad move up, five abreast, staggered formation, arms ready. Have second squad take the Cerlynese arms."

"Yes, ser."

After all the Cerlynese turn over their arms, Alyiakal looks to the squad leader. "Are there any armsmen or weapons that have been conveniently overlooked?"

"No, ser. That would be stupid."

Sensing the truth of the statement, Alyiakal says, "You can all return to the fort. Stay there until we depart."

Once the Cerlynese walk back into the fort, Alyiakal turns to Nolaan. "Set up four lancers as guards. Rotate them every two glasses."

"Yes, ser." Nolaan hesitates, then asks, "You had first squad show arms to make sure they didn't try anything, ser?"

"No. I did that so that the squad leader and his men could all say that they were faced with firelances and totally outnumbered."

Alyiakal dispatches scouts to the north and, over the next glass, watches as the companies set up for the night in the area around the fort. The returning scouts report no signs of armsmen nearby.

Then Alyiakal has Kessmyr and his squad go through the captured gear in hopes of finding maps, but that turns out to be unsuccessful. He instead spends the next glass and a half questioning the captured armsmen, particularly the squad leader, about the road and towns along the way to Clynya, a painstakingly difficult process requiring a certain amount of leading questions, discernment, and some order persuasion. He does discover that Cerlyn only has forts or posts near the borders—and in Clynya. He also learns that the copper mines are farther north. *Then what does the mark on the map signify?*

After the evening meal, such as it is, Alyiakal calls the officers together, standing quietly for several moments before he begins.

"I told you I'd decide what comes next after we got here. First, a bit of history. We destroyed two significant forces of Duke Taartyn's when I was at Lhaarat. His response has been to attack again, in even greater force, as soon as he is able. This time we destroyed twelve companies and likely killed his youngest son. I don't see him taking that lightly."

"You're suggesting we attack Clynya, ser?" asks Chaem evenly.

"If we don't, you'll all have a good chance of having to fight Cerlyn again, on the Duke's terms. That didn't go well for the Mirror Lancers at Lhaarat several eightdays ago." Alyiakal offers a crooked smile. "One way or another, I won't be here when that happens." *I may not be here after the Emperor discovers what I've already done, because Laartol can't protect me from the wrath of the Merchanter clans in Cyad once they discover we've disrupted the flow of copper from Cerlyn.*

"But the Majer-Commander—" Kessmyr stops short as Alyiakal looks at him.

"The orders were on the *letterhead* of the Majer-Commander, but they were *signed* by the Captain-Commander."

"To give the Majer-Commander a way out," says Suraat, surprisingly to Alyiakal.

Chaem nods slowly. "You're willing to lead us the way you did in Kraaslaen?"

Alyiakal laughs harshly. "For better or worse, I don't know any other way."

"Good enough for me," declares Chaem.

Suraat frowns. "I thought you said majers didn't invade other lands."

"I did. I should have added that majers don't do that except when they're ordered to, and those orders I received told me to do whatever it takes to put an end to what the Duke is doing. From what I've seen of the Duke, the only way to do that is to put an end to him." *And likely the whole black angel–cursed family.* "The Captain-Commander knows that. So does the Majer-Commander, but he can't say that." *Neither wants to keep losing lancers to the Cerlynese and the Jeranyi, and if what it takes is the removal or dismissal of a junior majer and an apology to the Emperor and the Merchanters . . .*

"When do we leave?" asks Kessmyr.

"Tomorrow morning. Early. As usual."

LIII

On eightday evening, after talking to the officers, Alyiakal draws a rough map for himself combining the earlier copy from his book of maps with the information he'd learned earlier in the day. It's rudimentary, but better than nothing, and apparently better than the maps.

Or at least better than what Cerlynese junior officers and squad leaders are given. But then, only Mirror Lancer officers at border posts are provided with maps—and not very good ones at that.

By sunrise on oneday, Alyiakal and the four companies head north from Kula, with Suraat and Third Company in the lead. Alyiakal also has his unseen order funnel in place gathering chaos to replace what he'd used in Kraaslaen.

For a glass, Suraat is quiet, but he finally asks, "Did you just decide this last night, ser, or did you have it planned from the beginning?"

"I didn't plan it from the beginning, but when I heard what happened to the companies at Lhaarat, I thought it might be necessary. I didn't decide until I knew more about where most of the remaining Cerlynese armsmen are posted. Most of them are a good five or six days' ride north of Clynya."

"Why would the Duke attack Kraaslaen and Suthya at the same time?" asks Suraat.

"You'd have to ask him, but I'd guess it's because the only time Cyador ever attacked in force beyond its own borders was when the Kyphrans tried to take Guarstyad. That's a long way from here. Duke Taartyn might not even know much about it. It was also six years ago."

"Why aren't we more aggressive with troublemakers like the Duke?"

"Partly because we rely on firelances, and the chaos needed to replenish them is limited. Firelances allow us to protect Cyador with fewer Mirror Lancers, but we really don't have enough men to conquer and hold much more land than we now have. That was one reason why more posts beyond Pemedra were never built after Emperor Kieffal's death."

"Are we trying to conquer Cerlyn?"

Alyiakal laughs, softly but harshly. "Right now, I'm only interested in removing Duke Taartyn and his family. I hope we can do it without dealing with his armsmen in Suthya. If those ten companies were *anywhere* near Clynya, we'd be on our way back to Pemedra." *Probably, anyway.*

After a moment, Alyiakal sees one of the scouts riding toward them.

In a fraction of a quint, the scout eases his mount alongside Alyiakal and reports, "There's a hamlet ahead, ser."

Alyiakal turns to Suraat. "Send out second squad, the way we discussed."

"Yes, ser."

Second squad and the scout depart at a fast trot toward the hamlet, where the squad rides straight through to the far side to prevent anyone from riding north to spread the news of their arrival. While Alyiakal thinks the probability is slight from such a small hamlet, he'd like to keep the Duke in the dark for as long as possible.

By midday, the Mirror Lancers have passed through two hamlets, continuing on the road to Clynya along the east side of the River Yarth. Alyiakal sweats profusely in the heat from the Summer sun, a humid heat that's required more frequent stops than he'd anticipated, but the fact that water is more available for men and mounts helps.

Alyiakal calls a halt for the evening some ten kays north of the third community through which they've ridden. It's a small town, rather than a hamlet, but a town without armsmen or a fort, and one where the locals look stunned to see Mirror Lancers—before they flee into dwellings and shops. The squad deployed to watch the road encounters two men, presumably trying to send word to Clynya. One refuses to halt and ends up dead. The other, seeing the fate of his comrade, decides to surrender.

Alyiakal interrogates him, but learns little, except that there's a hamlet another ten kays farther, and a larger town called Lound fifteen kays beyond that. While Alyiakal sees no point in keeping the man captive, he has him tied up and decides to take his mount and boots and leave him barefoot in the morning.

Twoday morning dawns cool and cloudy, and a glass before midmorning, as the lancers ride through the unnamed hamlet, a light rain begins to fall. The rain continues until close to noon before the clouds move south, leaving the warm air damper than ever.

A glass later, the lancers enter low rolling hills with scattered holdings that become more numerous. At the top of a rise in the road, Alyiakal sees a distant town, and notices a sizable lake to the east of the town extending several kays to where it's bounded by larger hills. He studies the town, situated on the river, and possibly half the size of Geliendra.

"That has to be Lound," Alyiakal tells Nolaan. While Alyiakal has concerns about riding through a larger town, there doesn't appear to be a feasible alternative that wouldn't add a glass or more, given the lake to the east and the river to the west.

He turns to Nolaan. "When we get to the edge of the town, we'll ride straight through at a trot, arms ready. Pass the order back."

The undercaptain raises his eyebrows.

"There's no fort or garrison here, and if we act like we belong here, we should be gone before anyone thinks too deeply about it." *Besides, most people won't attack an armsman who's not attacking them.* While Alyiakal may need to use magery, he'd rather not apply force if he doesn't have to. "Pass the order back."

"Yes, ser."

Over the next glass, Alyiakal sees several carts and riders, but all of them turn around or take side roads when they sight his force. Because they avoid the riders before getting close, Alyiakal suspects the locals don't want anything to do with any armsmen and doubts they have any idea who the riders really are. *That will change before long, but later is better.*

Once the lancers reach the flat, they follow the curve of the road toward the stream that has become a small river. Dwellings with small outbuildings are set along the way, but before long, the lancers reach the edge of the town.

"Ready arms! Forward!" Alyiakal urges the gray into a trot.

There aren't many people out in the midafternoon heat. Most just move away from the road and don't give the riders a second glance, but more than a few look surprised, especially when Alyiakal and Fourth Company ride along the west side of the market square, where many hurry away.

Alyiakal can see several older men pointing, and suspects they're former armsmen, but none make a move that could be considered threatening. Even so, Alyiakal doesn't breathe more easily until the entire column is well north of Lound and on the wider road following the river.

"No one did anything," says Nolaan.

"I thought they wouldn't," says Alyiakal, "but you never know. That's the last significant town until Clynya. Most of the larger towns are north of there."

In late afternoon, the company nears a stead, and Alyiakal thinks about purchasing some lambs, but shakes his head. It would take a good four glasses to roast them, and he'd need to buy at least four, if not more, depending on the size of the lamb.

In the end, the company makes camp near the river some three kays north of the stead.

Threeday begins the same as the previous two days, but by midmorning the lancers begin to see more people using the road. As before, no one wants to get close to the Mirror Lancers, although Alyiakal doesn't see any riders racing north, as if to report strange armsmen, and he doesn't know whether to be bitterly amused or more worried as people afoot, carters, and riders hurry down lanes or paths away from the main road.

By late midafternoon, Alyiakal spots a walled structure on a low hill overlooking the town or very small city in the distance, which can only be Clynya. While he suspects the Duke must have heard about a few companies of armsmen riding toward Clynya, he doubts that Cerlynese forces will attack immediately. *If they're smart, they won't attack at all.*

Even so, Alyiakal wants to find a camp location that can be easily defended, preferably a ridge or low rise near the river.

The Mirror Lancers ride another six kays before Alyiakal finds a site to his liking, on a rugged hill overlooking the river only about two kays from the outskirts of Clynya, but close to five kays from the walled area on the low hill.

As soon as Alyiakal calls a halt, he summons the company officers for a quick meeting.

"We'll need a squad ready to ride in moments, just in case the Cerlynese decide to try to surprise us. We'll change squads every two glasses." He orders sentry posts, the location and picketing arrangements for the mounts, and other details. When he finishes, he asks, "Any questions?"

"What do you think the Cerlynese will do?" asks Suraat.

"There are several possibilities. They might attack as soon as they find we're here, but late in the day as it is, I'd be surprised if they do. They might wait to see what we do. Or they might feign an attack early tomorrow to see how we react." Alyiakal gives an ironic half smile. "Or they might do something else entirely."

"What about the Duke?" asks Chaem.

"I'm guessing, but Cyadoran lancers this close to Clynya will upset him. At some time, they'll attack, and we need to be ready. For the moment, I'm going to send out more scouts and take Fourth Company's first squad and do some scouting myself. Second Company will remain ready to repulse any immediate attack while the other companies set up for the night. If there is one, it will be by one company or less." *Because there's no way the Cerlynese can find us and get many companies ready for an attack in the next two glasses, but there's always the possibility of a single company on patrol.*

Chaem just nods.

Alyiakal and Nolaan's first squad depart in less than a quint, riding toward Clynya. As the sun is close to setting, Alyiakal decides that he'll surround the squad with a dull greenish haze, hoping that most people won't look that closely, particularly in twilight. With that, he'll see how far he can take the squad into Clynya before anyone notices . . . *if* anyone does.

The main road follows the river until it reaches a point where the dwellings crowd closer together. Then the road becomes a street bearing right, heading generally toward the Duke's palace, while a narrower road continues to parallel the river. As Alyiakal and the lancers get closer, even in the late-day sunlight, he can clearly make out the palace. While probably modest in comparison to the Palace of Light, it's certainly the largest residence Alyiakal has ever seen, a whitestone edifice stretching a good hundred yards from one side to another and rising three stories. From what Alyiakal can tell, the palace itself is not fortified, except for the walls enclosing the grounds, and the wide gates are open. A number of larger dwellings sit on both sides of the walls.

The people on and in the street, for the most part, simply give way to Alyiakal and the lancers. Here and there, someone might stop with a puzzled expression, and once he sees an older man gape and hurry away.

The street becomes a broad avenue leading to the Duke's palace, but a block or so before what appears to be the market square, where a number of people and vendors still gather, Alyiakal turns to the right, leading the squad onto a street that parallels the broad avenue to the palace gates at the base of the hill.

Shops, and other establishments, most already closed for the day, line the side street but in the second block a man steps into the street and looks at the riders coming toward him. Shaking his head twice, he reenters the alehouse. Farther on, three ragged youths scurry down an alley when they see the riders.

After riding some five long blocks, Alyiakal halts the squad on the side street twenty yards short of the palace avenue beneath the walls surrounding the palace. He extends his senses for a better feel of the buildings within the walls. After several moments, he realizes, while the walls contain gardens and smaller buildings, there don't seem to be structures such as barracks or extensive stables. He continues to sense the surrounding area but only discerns larger dwellings near the walls of the palace compound.

He turns his attention west, toward the river, and nods. He discerns, if vaguely, just east of the river and downhill from the west side of the palace walls, something resembling an armsmen's post, much like the one at Luuval. Given its limited size, Alyiakal doubts there could be more than five or six companies posted there, if that. While other posts might be nearby, he thinks it unlikely, given most threats to Cerlyn lie well away from Clynya.

"Time to head back," he says to the squad leader. "We'll turn right at the street ahead and then down the adjoining street."

Once the squad is well away from the center of Clynya, Alyiakal can't help thinking about the open palace gates and the location of the armsmen's post.

It just might be possible . . .

In the growing twilight, they encounter no Cerlynese armsmen, or anyone inclined to look closely at the squad until they reach the first Mirror Lancer scouts and sentries.

Once Alyiakal returns to the camp, he meets with the men who scouted the main road, as well as other roads leading into the town, to learn what they discovered. Then he sketches a rough map illustrating the approaches and center of Clynya. Having done so, he summons all the officers.

"We've got a change of plans." Alyiakal relates what happened and what he learned on the scouting expedition.

"No one noticed you?" asks Suraat.

"They noticed a squad of armed riders, but with our firelances holstered, we didn't look that different from the Cerlynese armsmen, at least not in the dusk or deeper twilight." Alyiakal senses Suraat's puzzlement and adds,

"We're an eightday's ride from the border with Cyador. I doubt most people here have ever seen a Mirror Lancer, but they see the Duke's armsmen enough not to pay much attention. Also, people are afraid of the armsmen. Whenever they see armed riders, even at a distance, they move away. Since the only armsmen they've seen in recent years are the Duke's, I suspect Duke Taartyn isn't exactly beloved."

Chaem nods, followed by Kessmyr and Nolaan.

"The palace gates are wide and open with only four guards posted. I think we can take the palace and close the gates. We'll need one wagon, with the spare firelances, but the roads and streets are fairly good."

"That leaves the post and five companies of lancers," Nolaan points out.

"True, but I doubt they have anything to batter through the gates, and the palace walls aren't crenellated. Besides, not everyone will be inside the palace walls."

"You're thinking of having two companies hold back," says Chaem, "and then attack their rear?"

"The thought had occurred to me." Alyiakal smiles wryly. "You and Kessmyr could take the road closer to the river that leads to the post, and hang back to see if armsmen charge out. You might be able to take out nearly a company before they realize what's happened. Then you could withdraw. I doubt they'll pursue, not if we hold the palace."

"Then what, ser?" asks Chaem.

"One of two things will happen. They'll either make another attempt to retake the palace or they'll hole up in the post and wait for reinforcements."

"How far away are their reinforcements?" asks Kessmyr.

"North of the border with Suthya. That has to be at least a four-day ride." Alyiakal surveys the officers. "Any more questions?"

"What's the purpose of all this?" asks Suraat.

"To remove Duke Taartyn," *and all his heirs,* "and to reduce Cerlyn's power and inclination to invade our borders. And then to return to Pemedra." *Where there's a good likelihood that I'll be summarily removed from command.*

"Is there any point in remaining here?" asks Nolaan.

"Not that I can see. The Cerlynese wouldn't like us any better than the Duke. Someone will replace him, but we can hope that whoever it is will stay within their own borders. In any event, if we're successful, that problem will be years away."

"First light tomorrow, ser?" asks Chaem.

"First light," confirms Alyiakal.

LIV

At first light on fourday, Alyiakal leads Third and Fourth Companies and one lightly loaded wagon north on the road to Clynya, followed shortly by Second and First Companies. Leaving three wagons with the teamsters and the wounded, half of whom can handle firelances, shouldn't endanger the wounded or the wagons, given that there aren't any Cerlynese armsmen to the south.

Alyiakal briefly checks the amount of sun-chaos he's gathered over the past three days, before creating an illusion in front of Third Company. This time he tries to create the impression of a hazy fog spilling from the river, unlikely as that might be in Summer.

But stranger things have likely happened, and fog is more expected here than Mirror Lancers.

Alyiakal orders silent riding for all companies, and he half wonders if anyone glimpsing the lancers will dismiss them as angels or demons. A handful of scattered holders out early in their fields look up as they pass, more with puzzlement than alarm, from what Alyiakal can sense, then return to their work in order to get it done before the Summer heat descends. Even in the dawn light, the air is warm, as if it has barely cooled over the night.

When the companies reach the outskirts of Clynya, where only a few scattered souls are visible, Alyiakal leads the two companies onto the main street heading toward the palace, while Chaem, Kessmyr, and their companies continue on the river road toward the Cerlynese post.

As Alyiakal rides into the market square, largely empty except for a few carts in one corner, he urges the lancers into a trot through the right side of the square, past the statue in the middle. Either Taartyn or some forebearer, Alyiakal suspects but has no inclination to find out at the moment—then up the broad stone-paved avenue toward the palace gates.

After another two blocks, Alyiakal is certain that someone or some armsman will raise the alarm—the hooves impacting on the stone surface of the avenue sound like drums in his ears—but the city remains calm and silent.

At the end of five blocks, Alyiakal sees the four guards peering toward the hazy mist, doubtless concerned that it appears to be moving toward them as well as wondering why they hear hooves. Within twenty yards of the gate,

Alyiakal drops the illusion and uses four quick firebolts to drop bewildered guards who could only gape at the oncoming lancers in their last moments.

He continues through the open gates and up the long, gentle slope of the drive running to the arched entry of the palace. Behind him, once the wagon is scarcely within the palace gates, he senses half of Fourth Company's third squad moving to close the massive gates, while the remainder of the squad takes positions to cover them.

Riding closer to the palace doors, Alyiakal notes that the whitestone masonry shows a muted dinginess, particularly in the window casements, and there's a sense of age to the structure, suggesting it may well be older than any building in Cyador. The windows are all narrow and glazed with multiple small panes, except for a large, square, multi-paned window set several yards above the arch over the large bronze entry doors.

He glances at the long roofline three stories up but doesn't see any defensive walls on the palace roof or any guards posted there.

Alyiakal is less than fifteen yards from the main entrance when four guards rush out and sprint to close the heavy outer iron grates over the bronze doors. None of them survive Alyiakal's targeted firelance bolts, and two others appear from within the palace and pull the heavy bronze doors closed before Alyiakal can turn his firelance on them.

Alyiakal reins up, calling a halt, before glancing downhill where Fourth Company struggles to close the main gates, even using two mounts and ropes. Their difficulty suggests to Alyiakal that it may have been some time since those gates were last closed. He senses around the grounds but cannot discern any order/chaos patterns that might be armsmen anywhere outside the palace proper.

Why aren't there more armsmen or guards here? Or isn't the Duke here right now?

Hearing a rattling sound, Alyiakal looks up again, thinking someone must be closing shutters, only to note none of the windows have outside shutters.

Then he senses a large amount of chaos within the palace, more than he's sensed even from the Third Magus, and that chaos is coming toward the bronze doors . . . and him.

Definitely a powerful mage . . . and then some.

Alyiakal shifts his weight in the saddle and contracts his shields, strengthening them, then concentrates on the doors, ready to act or react, as necessary, trying not to be distracted as Suraat edges his mount away from Alyiakal.

The right-hand bronze door opens and a gray-haired figure, in dark green shimmersilk tunic and trousers, steps out and launches a chaos bolt.

Even as Alyiakal thinks, *That's the Duke,* he catches the chaos bolt and flings it back, only to see it spray off the Duke's shields.

Alyiakal senses the massive concentration of power being gathered by the Duke, and links to his own chaos store, while simultaneously concealing a significant spear of order within it.

An immense wall of chaos looms over Alyiakal, but he forces it back toward the Duke, now a figure glowing and illuminated by chaos, then adds his own store of chaos, followed by the carefully hidden spear of order that cuts through the combined forces and impales the shimmering green figure of the Duke.

As if each instant were a glass long, Alyiakal sees the amplified wall of chaos exploding in all directions, but he's unable to react, frozen in time as white stones, fragments of bronze, and shards of everything slowly but inexorably fly toward him, slamming into his shields, which contract under the enormous pressure.

A wall of flame and brilliant white chaos crushes those shields tighter and tighter . . . and then . . . there is nothing except blackness.

LV

Heat and light, then darkness, then more heat swirl around Alyiakal. He feels as though he's being crushed by an enormous oil press, the massive stones squeezing him into a thin paste. Then brilliant light sears his face, and he feels his skin peeling away before dropping into hot darkness.

When he emerges into the light, he knows someone is asking him something, and he answers, but he cannot recall what he says, or to whom, before everything fades. When he can see again, someone asks, and he cannot remember what they ask before he tumbles back into hot blackness.

At some point he opens his eyes to see some sort of roof above him, and the darkness does not claim him. "What happened . . . how many did we lose?"

"You'll be all right," says a voice, one Alyiakal finally recognizes as Nolaan's.

"What about the companies?" Alyiakal realizes he is lying on his back, and tries to sit up, but finds he cannot. "I can't move."

"You're strapped down, ser," says Nolaan. "You've been . . . rather restless."

"How many . . . did we lose?" Alyiakal tries to say more, but his mouth and throat are so dry. "Water . . . a little," he croaks, rather than speaks.

"Just a moment."

Alyiakal feels the pressure on his chest abate, and someone eases something behind his back and helps him into a half-sitting position. Every part of his body hurts, and he winces. That just momentarily adds to the pain. Someone puts a tin cup in front of him and helps him take several swallows. "Your men must have gotten the gates closed." He manages a smile, but the effort hurts his entire face.

"We did, but it turned out it didn't matter."

Alyiakal starts to frown, but that hurts as well. "How many did we lose?"

"So far eleven dead, ten injured."

"That's all?"

"So far."

"What about the companies outside the wall?"

"First Company's inside the wall. Second Company's on duty keeping the surviving Cerlynese from leaving their post."

"They're all still in there?"

"Those who are alive."

Alyiakal has so many questions, but he needs to take another sip or two of water, before he can say more. "What day is it?"

"It's still fourday, just after sunset."

After a slow careful breath, Alyiakal asks, "What happened?"

"After the big explosion . . . do you remember that, ser?"

"I remember a wall of flame hitting me . . . or I thought it did."

"Something hit you. When the palace exploded, I thought everyone in Third Company was dead, but when all the dust settled you and the first two squads were still there. Except for Suraat. The explosion . . . it pretty much shredded him and his mount . . ."

Alyiakal can vaguely remember Suraat moving away from him just before the Duke emerged from the palace, but he's still trying to make sense out of what Nolaan's telling him.

". . . three men in third squad were killed by stone fragments, and four others were bruised or cut, one got a broken arm. Took a lot to get you off your horse. Strange thing is your mount's fine, but you've got bruises everywhere, and I'd wager they'll get worse. And, ser, uh, your whole head's burned—sunburned, not fire-burned, and there's some sort of scrape or mark on the side of your forehead."

"What about the Duke?"

"The Duke? If he was in the palace, he must be dead. There's not much left of the palace, just a heap of stones. What happened? No one in Fourth Company was looking that way. We were working on the gates, and all anyone in Third Company knows is that you used your firelance and then there were brilliant lights and an explosion."

Alyiakal doesn't say anything for several moments, knowing that he's not thinking as clearly as he should be. *Simple is better.*

"Ser?"

"The Duke—he was a mage. He started to throw a huge fireball at me and Third Company. I pointed my firelance at him and tried to empty all the chaos at him, hoping it would block some of his firebolt. That was when I felt like I was hit with a wall of flame."

"Ser, how do you know the mage was the Duke?"

"He wore . . . dark green shimmersilk . . . head to foot, and he had gray hair. No one else . . . would be wearing that. I . . . could be wrong." Suddenly, Alyiakal feels slightly dizzy and very tired, and, despite his trying to find out more, his eyes close, but the blackness he falls into is only warm, and not searing.

When he wakes again, it's dark, although there's a faint light from a lantern.

"Ser? Are you awake?"

Alyiakal thinks the speaker is Kessmyr, but he's not certain. "Kessmyr?"

"Yes, ser."

"What happened to the Cerlynese in the river post?"

"Some of them are still there. Not that many, I think. After the palace exploded, about a company of greenshirts charged out of the post. They didn't have any archers, and Second Company pretty much carved them up from the rear before they knew what hit them. Then Second Company kept moving until Chaem re-formed in front of the palace gates. When Chaem withdrew, I moved First Company farther back and out of sight, then up a side street closer to the palace where the Cerlynese still couldn't see us. So they thought that Second Company was the only one outside the gate, and they went after Chaem with three companies. We came up behind. In the narrow streets, they couldn't really maneuver. It was a slaughter. There might be a company left in the fort. We posted scouts where archers couldn't see them and kept a company on the next street. They tried one sally at twilight. That didn't work well either, with all the bodies in the streets."

"You haven't lost too many men, have you?"

"Just a handful or so."

Alyiakal doesn't dispute that, although he thinks Nolaan had told him more than a handful, but he's still not certain.

"Sounds to me like we've done enough," says Alyiakal, who can feel his limbs and eyes getting heavy.

"We can talk about that in the morning, ser."

Alyiakal can only nod before his eyes close.

He wakes with the first glimmer of light, and his eyes actually focus. He discovers that he's stretched out on a pallet under what can only be a small pavilion in one of the Duke's gardens. Slowly and carefully, he rolls onto his side, although he feels sore all over and his face is still hot, then manages to get into a sitting position with his back against a saddle on top of blankets.

A ranker sitting on a garden bench starts awake, as if he's been half dozing. "You all right, ser?"

"I've been better, but it's . . . a definite improvement."

"Would you like some water, ser?"

"Please."

This time Alyiakal can hold the cup and drink without help. When he drinks what he can, he leans back against the blankets and saddle, neither quite awake nor asleep. When he becomes aware, he hears voices talking quietly, and he listens without moving.

". . . still can't believe he's alive, and not a broken bone anywhere . . ."

". . . sure looks like sowshit, though, bruises all over . . . nasty mark on his forehead . . ."

". . . all the rankers right behind him . . . not much more than cuts and bruises . . . worse for third squad . . ."

"And Suraat."

"One of the rankers in first squad said Suraat moved away from the majer when the Duke appeared . . . don't think of a duke as a mage . . ."

"Why not? The Emperor of Light has to have Magi'i blood."

". . . almost like the majer shielded the first two squads . . . maybe part of the third."

"He said he used his firelance just as the Duke threw a big firebolt . . . maybe his firelance deflected the firebolt to both sides . . ."

". . . probably won't ever know . . ."

"You know . . . lots of strange things around him . . . can't just be fortune or chance . . ."

"Frig if I care . . . leads from the front . . . knows what we face . . ."

Either the voices die away, or Alyiakal dozes off again.

When he wakes, it's full light, but still early morning. He eases into a more upright sitting position, and drinks more water, belatedly realizing he can barely sense the ranker a few yards away, and that small effort leaves him light-headed. *At least you can sense some.* Then his nose wrinkles at the faint odor of smoke.

He's still puzzling over the smoke when Kessmyr appears in the pavilion and says, "It's pleasant here in the gardens. The Duke definitely liked the finer things in life." He turns to where Alyiakal sits, propped against the saddle and blankets. "Do you think you can eat something?"

"I'd like to try."

The bread is stale, and Alyiakal has to eat it slowly with sips of water. After he finishes a chunk, the light-headedness recedes, and he asks, "What about the rest of the Cerlynese armsmen?"

"We lofted a few firebolts into the fort about a glass before dawn," says Kessmyr. "Some of them actually set other things on fire. A bunch of the greenshirts opened the gates and tried to escape, but we were ready. Maybe a handful got to the river. The fires in the fort are still burning."

"I smelled smoke. I wondered what was burning."

"Only the fort. The walls have kept the fire from spreading into the town."

"What about the people?" asks Alyiakal.

"They're staying away from us. Some look stunned. They keep looking at what's left of the palace, as if they can't believe what happened."

"Have you seen any other armsmen?"

"No. Chaem has scouts on all the roads so we won't be surprised. I've got a few lancers going through what's left of the palace. So far, no survivors. There are bodies, but not so many as I expected from the size of the palace."

"Those close to the Duke and the fireball were likely turned to ashes," Alyiakal says.

"Still amazes me, ser, that you and most of Third Company survived."

"It all amazes me, too," replies Alyiakal, holding back a cough until he finishes speaking.

"Are you all right, ser?"

"I will be, hopefully before too long."

The young captain offers a ragged smile. "Now . . . I'd say we're about ready to head back to Pemedra. Might take a day to finish salvaging what we can from the ruins and get enough provisions for the ride back. That's up to you, of course."

"And to all the company officers," replies Alyiakal. "You all know more than I do about your companies and what supplies and wounded we have." He also knows nearly getting himself killed isn't helping the wounded.

But how could you have known that Duke Taartyn was a mage? Except you should have considered the possibility once you suspected that the mage in Kraaslaen was Taartyn's son.

"By tomorrow or sevenday, I just might be able to ride," says Alyiakal. "Not much else, though."

"There's not much else you need to do, ser, as far as we can tell."

"That's a good thing because there's not that much else I can do. You three really took over after I was flattened." *In more ways than one.*

"Chaem, really, ser. Nolaan and I just finished what you set up and started."

"Finishing is what counts," replies Alyiakal. "All the planning and strategy aren't worth sowshit if you don't finish the task." He pauses. "I'd like a little more to eat, but I don't want to keep you."

"Yes, ser. I'll take care of that, and Chaem will be here in a while."

After Kessmyr leaves, a ranker returns with some warm porridge and a mug of ale.

"Where did we get the ale?" asks Alyiakal in surprise.

"Captain Kessmyr . . . requested . . . a few barrels from the local alehouse, ser. He said they were cooperative."

Hoping we wouldn't loot everything, no doubt.

Even if the ale was essentially, if politely, looted—Alyiakal can't imagine Kessmyr being other than polite—he enjoys it enormously, and definitely feels better after eating.

He rests, not quite dozing for perhaps half a glass before Chaem appears.

"You're looking better than the last time I saw you, ser," says Chaem. "How are you feeling?"

"My head feels like the worst sunburn ever. Every part of my body aches, but it doesn't feel like I broke anything. Eating helped . . . a lot."

Chaem shakes his head. "I still can't believe you and Third Company survived. There are pieces of stone everywhere around the palace, except a wedge where you all were."

"We were fortunate, and sometimes that counts more than skill." Because Alyiakal doesn't want to talk about how he shielded most of Third Company, he says, "I understand you and Kessmyr pretty much wiped out the Cerlynese garrison."

"Mostly Kessmyr. He did things the way you would. We just held firm, and First Company chewed up the Cerlynese from behind. He came up with using firelances to set the fort afire and had his company waiting."

Knowing that Chaem understates his own role, Alyiakal says, "It took both of you working together. Don't think I don't know that."

Chaem's smile is both amused and slightly embarrassed.

"From what I've heard from Kessmyr and Nolaan," Alyiakal continues, "and maybe you when I still wasn't altogether here, there's not much else we can or should do. Is that right? Or am I missing something?"

"Don't know what else we could do," replies Chaem. "The Duke and his heirs, likely most of his family, are dead, and there aren't any Cerlynese armsmen within kays, not any who want to get close to us."

"Then I'd say we ought to leave early tomorrow, unless there's something I don't know." Alyiakal looks directly at the senior captain and waits.

"Are you ready to ride, ser?"

"If I'm not, I can stand being in a wagon, but the sooner we're out of Cerlyn, the better."

Chaem nods. "Kessmyr thought you felt that way."

"And you?" asks Alyiakal.

Chaem chuckles sardonically. "I've seen more of Cerlyn than I ever wanted, and I'd rather not press our luck any further."

"Neither would I. If you have any questions, I can answer them, but getting us ready to leave is going to be mostly up to you company officers, especially you as the senior captain."

"Yes, ser. We'll take care of it."

"Good. Don't let me keep you."

Alyiakal holds his yawn until Chaem has left the pavilion.

LVI

On sevenday morning, Alyiakal visits the wounded, not that he can do much of any real healing, but he hopes he'll be able to deal with dangerous wound chaos in the next few days. He worries about three lancers especially, the most severely injured of whom he presses a tiny amount of order into, which is all he can physically do.

As he leaves, he hears one lancer murmur, ". . . majer doesn't look much better than some of us," and he doesn't know whether to be amused or appalled.

After that, he returns to where the lancers are forming up along the stone drive to the east of the palace's shattered ruins, where he finds his mount, already saddled by one of the rankers. He smiles briefly as he checks the water bottles and finds all three have been filled with ale. Then he senses someone behind him, not that he can sense all that far, perhaps fifty yards, but his sensing is improving. He turns to see Nolaan walking toward him.

The undercaptain smiles. "Still can't sneak up on you, Majer." He stops less than a yard away. "We went through the spoils last night. As you ordered, we split the coins and rings that weren't jeweled among the rankers. The heavier jewelry and other valuable pieces from the palace went in the strongbox. They're already in the wagon."

"I appreciate all of you handling that," says Alyiakal. "We'll have to write out a detailed inventory before looking into how to handle those pieces. I suspect the chest will have to go to headquarters. They'll take a cut, but we should still get more. If we try to deal with it, it's more likely that everything will get hacked up or melted down for a fraction of what it's worth. But that can wait until we get to Pemedra."

"We wondered about that, ser." Nolaan pauses. "There is one other thing." He extends a small leather pouch. "We thought it was better that you keep this."

Alyiakal takes the pouch, suspecting that he knows what's inside, which is, in fact, just that—a ring of white gold, holding a large oval emerald, with the letter "T" cut into the gold on one side of the stone and a small eight-pointed star on the other side. "It has to have been Duke Taartyn's."

"That's what we thought. You were already asleep when we got to it, and none of us wanted to wake you."

Alyiakal wants to protest that he's not fragile, but refrains, because he's definitely not back to where he was and he appreciates the courtesy. "Thank you. I'll keep custody of this and the other ring, but they'll also have to go to headquarters, for obvious reasons."

"We thought so, ser."

After Nolaan leaves and heads toward Fourth Company, Alyiakal places Taartyn's ring in the pouch, tucking it away with the other.

Another two quints pass before Alyiakal rides out at the head of the column beside Kessmyr. Chaem has insisted, politely, but firmly, that Second

Company will ride rearguard behind the five wagons, one of which was "claimed" from the Duke's stables, and which holds some of the wounded who cannot ride in addition to the spent firelances and some provisions. While, usually, Alyiakal would have taken command of Third Company, he's not in any shape for that, and for the present, Falkyr, the senior squad leader, is Third Company's acting company officer.

When Alyiakal rides past the open palace gates he looks right and toward the river, where a few wisps of smoke still rise from the Cerlynese armsmen's post.

A handful of locals scatter from the market square as the Mirror Lancers near, then stop and watch as the column rides past. From what Alyiakal observes, none of them speak, although their eyes remain on the lancers.

As First Company turns left onto the river road south toward Kula, Alyiakal looks back over his shoulder at the slumped ruins of the Duke's palace, vaguely surprised that the stones of the rubble still shine white in the light of the rising sun. *But then, the heat of the fireballs was so intense that anything that could burn went to ashes instantly.*

LVII

The ride back to Pemedra takes six days, every day as hot and as uneventful as the previous one, but Alyiakal is more than thankful for the routine, as his strength slowly returns and his bruises change from purple to yellow. By the time the Mirror Lancer companies enter the valley north of the post late on threeday afternoon, they are starting to fade. In addition, Alyiakal's ability to sense has almost returned to normal and he can maintain some shields without strain.

Alyiakal actually senses a grass cat concealed in the high grass a kay to the east as he and Kessmyr ride past the northernmost hamlet in the valley. "Not far to go."

"I'll be glad to get back," says Kessmyr. "I just hope there haven't been any raids."

"So do I." *I'd be surprised since there's no one left to raid anywhere near, unless we've overlooked some new barbarian hamlet.*

Neither says that much for the glass it takes to reach the post.

Baassyn is waiting on the avenue as Alyiakal and Kessmyr rein up. "It looks like most everyone returned."

"Not everyone," replies Alyiakal. "We lost Suraat and twenty men, and have twenty-one wounded—"

"Not counting the majer," interjects Kessmyr.

". . . and we wiped out thirteen Cerlynese companies at Kraaslaen, perhaps a squad at Kula and along the way, and six companies at Clynya—along with the Duke and most of his family. We can go over the details later because I'll need your help writing up the report."

"Clynya? You went *that* far?" asks Baassyn, surprise and concern mixing in his voice.

"After our discoveries in Kula and Kraaslaen, I didn't see there was much choice."

Baassyn looks to Kessmyr.

The captain merely nods.

Baassyn peers more closely at Alyiakal. "You do look the worse for wear, I have to say."

"Not as bad as some of the wounded, but it appears they'll all recover." *Except for the few you couldn't help immediately after the explosion.* Alyiakal turns to Kessmyr and says, "The company is yours, Captain," which is definitely a formality, but also signifies an end to the campaign.

"I have the company, ser."

Alyiakal offers a ragged smile as he looks back to Baassyn. "Now . . . I'm going to groom my mount and take a shower. We can talk after that."

"I've already let the cooks know," replies Baassyn. "I'll be in my study."

"Until then." Alyiakal turns his mount toward the stables, keeping to one side of the avenue to avoid the incoming companies and the wagons.

A glass passes before Alyiakal finishes with the gray, washes himself, and gets into a clean uniform, very carefully, because he remains sore in more than a few places.

Then he walks to the headquarters building. Only two steps into the anteroom to the studies, Baassyn hurries out, holding a sheet of paper. Alyiakal enters his own study, motions for Baassyn to close the door, and gingerly seats himself behind the desk.

"Are you sure you're all right?" asks the overcaptain.

"Bruises with more bruises over those and a few cuts."

"How exactly did you get that diamond mark on the side of your forehead?"

"That happened when the Duke tried to wipe out Third Company with a firebolt, but I'll get to that later. Let me explain it all in order." Alyiakal takes a quint to summarize all that happened. When he finishes, he looks at Baassyn.

"Well . . . the Majer-Commander did say 'whatever it takes.'"

"No," replies Alyiakal wryly, "he said to remove the Cerlynese from Kraaslaen and take whatever additional measures I felt necessary to preclude a recurrence. The Captain-Commander wrote 'whatever it takes.' I'm not sure either could publicly support the destruction of the Duke, his family, and the palace, although the fact that the Duke and his son were mages and engaged in the fighting might allow them not to be too hard on me."

"You knew that before you set out, didn't you?"

"I knew that what would be considered acceptable would be ruinous to the Mirror Lancers in time. When I found out that the Cerlynese commander in Kraaslaen was both a mage *and* the Duke's son, I thought there was only one way to resolve the situation. With the Duke and his mage-son removed and most of his armsmen dead, the Suthyans shouldn't have much trouble with the remaining Cerlynese invaders, but they won't be able to invade Cerlyn and likely wouldn't want to."

"So . . . what are you going to do?"

"Have a decent dinner, a better night's sleep, and, tomorrow, write up a report that you'll help me edit, and send off on fiveday."

Baassyn extends the sheet of paper he's been holding. "You might want to read this first. It came by headquarters dispatch messengers, so I took the liberty of opening it."

"As you should. You're deputy post commander." Alyiakal takes the sheet and begins to read. One section stands out.

> *. . . given the difficulties involved in obtaining adequate amounts of copper for cupridium, the Emperor of Light has requested to be informed immediately about the results of any encounters between Mirror Lancers and armsmen from Cerlyn.*
>
> *The Majer-Commander would appreciate a report on those activities immediately upon the return of any Mirror Lancer companies involved in such evolutions.*

Alyiakal nods. "Apparently, the Merchanters are applying a great deal of pressure on the Emperor."

"He's the Emperor," says Baassyn.

"The Imperial Tariff Enumerators are essentially ruled by the Merchanters; so the Merchanters effectively control the flow of golds available to him. It's long been rumored that Merchanters were behind the accident that killed Emperor Kieffal and all his heirs."

"I've heard that, but no one ever speaks of it publicly."

"The fact that they don't suggests that the rumor has some validity," Alyiakal points out.

"That doesn't bode well for you, ser. Did you consider that before you rode to Clynya?"

"I did. Regardless of what happens to me, it will likely be years before Mirror Lancers have to die fighting Cerlynese armsmen, and when they do, they won't be facing powerful mages."

"I wouldn't want to be in your boots."

"You may be in a worse position," says Alyiakal sardonically. "What if headquarters posts Majer Baertal here as my replacement? Or someone ineffectual?"

Baassyn shakes his head. "I don't know which would be worse."

"Baertal. There won't be many raids or any battles for some time. Someone ineffectual won't do anything except respond to a handful of raids, if that." Alyiakal pauses, then asks, "There wasn't anything else, was there?"

"Those dispatch riders were the only ones while you were gone. There were the usual not-quite-meaningless directives. A few letters. None for you."

Alyiakal nods. He hadn't expected anything from either Saelora or Hyrsaal. Then he stands. "We might as well head over to the mess. I could use an ale while we wait for dinner." *Even the slightly off Pemedran ale.*

LVIII

Alyiakal sleeps late enough on fourday morning that by the time he shaves, washes up, and gets dressed, he only has time to walk from his quarters to the officers' mess. Even so, the only officer there is Nolaan.

"Good morning, ser. How are you feeling?"

"Still sore in places, but better than yesterday. What about you?"

Nolaan smiles. "I never thought my bed here would feel so good."

Alyiakal laughs softly. "I felt the same way."

"Ser . . . what happens now?"

"Once everyone's had a few days' rest, you'll go back to riding patrols and looking for smugglers. I doubt that there will be many raiders, and there might be more smugglers by the middle of Harvest, once word gets out that there aren't that many Cerlynese armsmen around."

"That's all?"

"I have to send a detailed report to headquarters. Sooner or later, they'll decide whether they liked the way we dealt with the Cerlynese. They'll either say nothing except generalities that what we did was acceptable, meaning I acted in accord with their orders, if barely; *or* they'll relieve or repost me, which will amount to some degree of disapproval. That won't change anything affecting you. I'm certain you'll get that promotion sometime in Harvest."

"Why wouldn't they approve, after all the trouble Duke Taartyn caused?"

"I have no doubts that, no matter what the Majer-Commander or Captain-Commander *officially* say, they personally approve. I do have some doubts about whether the Emperor and the Merchanters will approve, since almost all the copper Cyador needs comes from Cerlyn, something I was reminded of by a letter from headquarters that awaited me when we returned yesterday."

"That doesn't seem right . . . to warn you afterwards."

"I don't think headquarters thought I'd act so quickly, but you don't have to worry about that," says Alyiakal cheerfully. "Not until you become a majer, anyway." He looks toward the mess door as Kessmyr and Chaem enter. "We might as well sit down. Overcaptain Baassyn won't be long, I'm sure."

In moments, Baassyn arrives and takes his seat at the table, turning to Alyiakal. "You look much better this morning."

"A good night's sleep in a real bed can do wonders."

"Definitely," adds Chaem, "especially when you're no longer quite so young."

The rest of the conversation at breakfast is light.

After eating, Alyiakal heads for the infirmary to check the wounded, which takes a good glass, given that there are more than a score. All are healing, and only a few require infusions of order to deal with stubborn wound chaos. Several look to be able to resume limited duties before long.

Then Alyiakal walks from the infirmary up the avenue to the headquarters building through the already hot early-morning air and makes his way to his study. There, he sits down and begins to write the first draft of his report to Mirror Lancer headquarters.

Two glasses later, he hands the draft to Baassyn. "Just mark anything you find questionable or poorly worded. Then I'll go over your marks, and we'll talk."

"I doubt I'll find much."

"Anything you find will help, not that it will change matters."

"You really think they'll relieve you? After you resolved problems no one else could?"

"They'll call it a reposting, but it will be where I won't have command of any lancers and where it can't be called a punishment."

"They won't cashier you," says Baassyn. "Not until they're sure they won't need you, and that could be years."

"I doubt they think that highly of me."

"From what I've seen, the Captain-Commander does."

"We'll see." Alyiakal half turns. "I need to write quite a few bereavement letters and death reports."

"Twenty-one, you said?"

Alyiakal nods, then heads back to his study.

He sits down behind his desk and begins with the letter to Suraat's "official" parents, writing that Suraat was a dedicated and outstanding officer, who always carried out his duties effectively, even to the last, and that his efforts were pivotal in the fighting against Cerlynese invaders. Then he continues with the rankers who were killed.

He finishes five more letters before Baassyn appears.

"I looked hard, ser, but I didn't find much." Baassyn hands back the sheets of the draft report. "You were totally impartial. I still don't see how they could see much fault, especially when you managed to prevail against two strong mages."

"Prevailing and removing a strong ruler may upset trade with Cerlyn," replies Alyiakal dryly, "not that the terms of that trade have been all that beneficial except to the Merchanter clans in Cyad."

"Do you think the Emperor will see it that way?"

"I hope not, but I suspect he will."

Baassyn just shakes his head. "Is there anything else you need?"

"Not at the moment, thank you."

Alyiakal spends the next glass rewriting the report, then goes back to writing bereavement letters. When he's finished those, he starts in on writing the death reports to send to headquarters.

He's not through all the death reports by evening mess, and he returns to his study after eating to finish those.

It's late twilight when he writes the last death report and turns to writing Hyrsaal a short letter that says little more than he was required to take all his companies to deal with Cerlynese armsmen who had attacked and decimated companies from Lhaarat. Although significantly outnumbered, his companies successfully resolved the problem, and there will be no further difficulties with Cerlyn.

Hyrsaal will understand, at least, in general terms.

Then, he takes a deep breath and begins the last letter, one that he definitely has to finish and send out with everything else in the morning.

My dear one—

As the mere arrival of this letter will tell you, I've returned from a long and arduous patrol that required all of my companies in order to deal with Cerlynese armsmen who had committed severe and murderous depredations against Cyadoran towns. We were successful in our efforts, not without casualties, but those were light compared to the numbers of companies we faced.

My tactics, successful as they were, will be considered by Headquarters over the next few eightdays, and we'll see whether they are judged acceptable in light of the scale of destruction and death caused by Cerlyn. There are doubtless many factors to consider, some of them similar to the difficulties you mentioned in previous letters. As always, I did my best to act in a way that benefits Cyador and the Empire of Light with the fewest casualties possible while accomplishing the mission with which we were entrusted.

Alyiakal pauses, trying to figure out how to convey the possibilities facing him—and her—in the seasons ahead. Finally, he continues writing.

At my next posting, whenever that might come, I think it might be best to consider the example of the officer whose map you allowed me to copy, although I will always defer to your extraordinary sensibilities. I must close now, although I would like to continue, because there may not be another dispatch run for days, if not longer.

All that's terribly oblique, but you still can't afford to be direct, not when it appears most of your letters might be read.

But Saelora knows that all too well.

He signs and seals the letter.

LIX

Early on fiveday morning, Alyiakal sends off the report to Mirror Lancer headquarters in a double-sealed dispatch bag containing the two rings, along with an explanation. There's a separate letter to Subcommander Zekkaat, informing him that the threat posed by Cerlynese armsmen has been removed and all companies are back at Pemedra. Alyiakal also tells the dispatch riders that, if they're questioned, they're simply to say that Majer Alyiakal wrote the subcommander and Mirror Lancer headquarters. He also sends off his letters to Saelora and Hyrsaal.

After that, all he can do is wait, recover, and slowly regain his full order/chaos abilities. He and Baassyn also need to create a complete inventory of the spoils recovered from the Duke's palace before they can dispatch the chest to Mirror Lancer headquarters, but Alyiakal knows it will take time to do that correctly. He cannot afford to delay the report, the bereavement letters, and the death reports.

By the next fourday his bruises have almost completely healed, and a copy of the spoils inventory he and Baassyn have compiled has been sent to headquarters, along with a request for two hundred forty replenished firelances. The companies are back into a regular patrol schedule, and, until Pemedra gets a replacement for Suraat, Alyiakal is commanding the slightly depleted Third Company.

Alyiakal's a little surprised to discover that he can sense even farther than before . . . and that his shields are stronger, considerably stronger. *Because of the confrontation with the Duke?* It seems to him that the more he's been forced to do with order and chaos, the more he *can* do. He has to wonder where the limit to his abilities lies, because trying to do more could easily result in doing himself in.

Late on sevenday afternoon, the lookouts report dispatch riders. Since his report on the expedition to Kraaslaen and Clynya couldn't have arrived at headquarters before threeday, there's no way the dispatch riders are carrying a response to the report. Whatever dispatches he receives will be routine.

Two quints later, a ranker hands a single large envelope from headquarters to Alyiakal. "I brought this up first, ser. They're still sorting out the letters."

"Thank you." Alyiakal doesn't worry about letters, since neither Saelora nor Hyrsaal will have had time to reply.

As soon as the ranker leaves, Alyiakal slits open the envelope and extracts the sheets of directives.

The first is a revision to the Mirror Lancer policy on wine for officers' messes, effectively stating that: while headquarters will still ship such wines, effective immediately, the cost of those wines will be borne entirely by the individual mess, rather than the half previously required. *Is this to cut down on drinking wine or because golds are getting tighter?*

Alyiakal shakes his head and sets that directive aside, turning to the second, which is more disturbing. It states that firelance replacement/replenishments will be limited to the equivalent of one half firelance per lancer per year, unless special circumstances apply, as determined by headquarters. Alyiakal knows that most of the lancers at Pemedra carry firelances less than half full, some even less than that, and there are no reserve firelances remaining.

That doesn't make sense. If they're that short on firelances and chaos, they ought to allocate the firelances based on which posts need them the most.

The third directive deals with standardization of post accounting procedures, and Alyiakal stands to take the directives to Baassyn for him to read when a ranker appears in his doorway.

"Majer, a letter for you."

"Thank you." As he takes the letter, Alyiakal frowns, wondering who could be writing him—and about what. He sets the directives on the desk and looks at the sender's address.

A.F.
Bakers Lane
Jakaafra

The seal imprint on the green wax is the outline of a great forest cat.

Alyiakal swallows, knowing that the letter has to be from Adayal. *But why now, after so many years?*

Moistening his lips, he checks the seal, which, expectedly, has been heated, removed, and replaced, then slits open the envelope, takes out the single sheet, and begins to read the graceful script.

Alyiakal—

With your father's death, and that of your former tutor, it has taken me a while to find your address. I hope this missive finds you well.

I've heard indirectly that you're a highly respected post commander. That reflects who you are and your willingness to learn from all who have knowledge and skills to offer, beginning even before you became a Mirror Lancer. While it remains for the best that you follow your own path, I would like to tell you that, whenever you are posted near Jakaafra or even Geliendra, I hope you will be able to visit and spend some time with your niece.

Niece . . . Niece? Alyiakal swallows and continues to read.

For better or worse, she seems to take after your side of the family, rather strongly, and especially in the practicality shown by you and your father. For this reason and others, it would be good for her to see you, if that is at all possible, since you're her only remaining relation. Those who accompanied you on your last visit, or their relations, can get word to us if you're anywhere nearby.

We know it may be some time before you're posted near here, if at all, but we wanted you to know that you're welcome at any time. If that is not possible, we do understand. You have your duty and commitments.

If you need to get in touch with us, you can write to us through Krimaan'mer, on Bakers Lane, Jakaafra.

The signature is simply "Adayal."

For several moments, Alyiakal is motionless.

Then he rereads Adayal's letter.

You had no idea. She never sent a word.

As he paces back and forth, he realizes why someone asked Hyrsaal about him, but, at the time, he'd dismissed the possibility that it might be Adayal, especially after so many years. *And a daughter? Who takes after you?*

After a time, Alyiakal carefully replaces the short letter in the envelope, wondering how Saelora will react, and later, to what could happen to him, especially given that he's very likely facing, at the very least, dismissal or ten years of insignificant postings.

LX

Slightly after first light on oneday morning, Alyiakal reads over the brief letter that has taken so much time to write, but one that has to leave with the dispatch riders shortly.

Saelora—

As you wrote me several years ago, there's no gentle way to let you know what has happened yesterday and in the previous eightdays. I have not yet heard from Headquarters regarding my last patrol, and it may be another eightday before I do, if not longer.

Yesterday, I received the attached letter. I'm sending you the original for reasons I trust you will understand. I had no idea I even had a niece. I fear that Adayal feels that my niece is not suited to the life that her mother planned for her and hopes that I will see that. I will not commit to anything without your understanding and your being with me if and when such a meeting occurs, but I wanted you to know about this totally unforeseen situation as soon as I could.

I'm as stunned as I'm sure you must be, but my love and care for you is stronger than ever, and I look forward to seeing you, as soon as possible, whenever that may be.

It's anything but perfect, but she has to know that you thought of her first and that you're not hiding anything. And at this point it doesn't matter who knows that you love her.

Not for the first time, he's glad he's told Saelora everything, even if he was a little hesitant at first. He's also angry with Adayal. *Why didn't she let you know earlier? Why now? Because her daughter has become inconvenient . . . or has asked too many questions about her father?*

He shakes his head, then seals the two letters into the envelope and carries them down to the duty desk where the outgoing pouch for letters is kept.

"You're here early, ser," says the duty ranker.

"I had no idea we'd have a chance to send letters so soon." *Or that you'd have to write one so important so quickly.*

"Funny about that, ser. Can't ever tell for sure."

"True enough." Alyiakal nods and then leaves the building, heading for the officers' mess.

Baassyn stands alone outside the door. "You were up even earlier than usual. Is something going on that I should know?"

"I have to say that I'm worried. It seems that every other directive we get is designed to undercut the Mirror Lancer border posts . . . and, of course, I can't help worrying about the possibility that I'll be dismissed or relegated to insignificant posts for the remainder of my career."

"You knew that was a possibility," says Baassyn evenly.

"I did. I just couldn't see any point in half measures that would get more lancers killed in the future."

"It might not be *that* bad, ser. I don't see them cashiering a post commander who carried out orders successfully when other post commanders failed. Three others, by my count."

"Three?"

"Word is that Majer Baertal took three companies to the West Branch valley and lost more than a company destroying that fort."

Alyiakal wonders how Baassyn knows that, even as he wonders if Baertal has learned anything from the attack, but only raises his eyebrows.

"Only a rumor, ser," says Baassyn. "One of the dispatch riders mentioned it to the duty ranker yesterday, and I found out later. If headquarters thinks that's a success, they'll have a hard time disciplining you."

"Even so, the Emperor certainly won't be happy, nor the Merchanters. Given that, what do you think will happen?"

"I don't know, ser, but they might do nothing, and let things quiet down. Or they might order you to headquarters for a thorough debriefing before reposting. They might even promote you."

"I don't see promotion. That would be a form of reprimand to the Emperor and Merchanters."

"We could both be wrong," declares Baassyn.

Alyiakal's laugh holds a touch of bitterness. "That's possible." He motions to the mess door. "I could use an ale, since it's too early for wine, and they're making it more costly for us."

"Like everything these days." Baassyn lowers his voice slightly as the two walk into the mess. "You think Emperor Kaartyn's turning out to be a disappointment?"

Alyiakal glances around, but they're the only officers. "Disappointment? More like he's under the thumb of his Merchanter Advisor."

"Be better if he listened to the Majer-Commander."

"Or the Captain-Commander." *Since the Majer-Commander also seems to be under that same thumb.* Alyiakal doesn't say more because he can sense Kessmyr and Chaem outside the mess. He just takes his seat at the head of the table.

In moments, all the other officers are seated.

"We had dispatch messengers yesterday," says Kessmyr, clearly pressing.

"It's too early for a response to our report on Cerlyn," replies Alyiakal. "We received a couple of directives. One said that we'll get fewer firelances, and the other said officers will have to pay more for mess wine."

"You should have set aside some of those spoils," says Chaem sardonically, "since headquarters doesn't seem to appreciate what we're doing."

"We already sent the inventory," replies Alyiakal. "Otherwise . . ." He shrugs, although he wouldn't have changed the inventory even if he had known about the directives.

"Makes you wonder," adds Nolaan. "Do they even know what's happening on the borders?"

"They know . . . and they don't," says Baassyn. "They read all the reports, but we've all become numbers."

"Except possibly to the Captain-Commander," adds Alyiakal.

"You can't fight raiders, the Jeranyi, or the greenshirts if you're counting every copper," says Chaem disgustedly. He looks to Alyiakal. "What do you think, ser?"

Alyiakal manages a wry grin. "I'd say that you do what it takes to get things done and figure out the coins later. Better yet, figure that holding Cyador together against outlanders takes more coins than the Merchanters think and put them aside so you have them when needed." He grins more widely. "But what do I know? I'm just a junior post commander." Then he takes a swallow of ale, and it tastes just as off as it always has.

LXI

While wondering when the next dispatch messengers will arrive, either with some word from Mirror Lancer headquarters or from Saelora or Hyrsaal, Alyiakal continues his routine, conducting training, making inspections, updating the records of the company officers, and taking two more patrols. Then, late on the afternoon of the first sevenday of Harvest, the duty ranker informs him that dispatch riders have been sighted.

After the ranker leaves, Baassyn appears in Alyiakal's study door. "Do you think we'll get an answer to your report, or that we'll get more useless directives?"

"We're into Harvest. That's when headquarters starts reposting officers. Whether any of the dispatches address my report on Cerlyn or not, we're likely to get information on a replacement for Suraat and possibly Nolaan's promotion to captain. Kessmyr's due for reposting as well."

"He'll do well anywhere," says Baassyn.

"I'd wager they'll send him to Inividra, Oldroad Post, or a Great Forest post."

The overcaptain nods. "I can see that, especially Inividra." He pauses. "Let me know, if you would."

"You'll know before anyone else."

More than three quints later, the duty ranker arrives with five envelopes addressed to Alyiakal, large envelopes only, no sealed pouches. Alyiakal doesn't know whether to be worried or relieved, but stands, takes the envelopes, and says, "Thank you."

"My pleasure, ser."

"Close the door on your way out, please."

"Yes, ser."

Once the door shuts, Alyiakal looks at the envelopes, seats himself behind the desk, and slits open the heaviest one, judging that it might hold Kessmyr's orders and information about his replacement. The cover letter is to Alyiakal as post commander and states that Captain Kessmyr is to be detached from Pemedra Post no earlier than the fifth eightday of Harvest and no later than the sixth eightday of Harvest, and, after no more than four eightdays of home leave, will report at Assyadt for subsequent duty at Inividra before the second eightday of Autumn. His replacement will be Captain Staalt from Lhaarat.

Staalt?

Alyiakal shakes his head in bitter amusement. Still, Pemedra could do worse than Staalt, and the fact that Staalt survived the mess that killed Vordahl at Kraaslaen means that Staalt won't have any illusions about either Cerlyn or Jerans.

Alyiakal then lifts the three remaining envelopes, choosing the next heaviest. It holds the official announcement of Nolaan's promotion to captain along with the appropriate insignia. The heaviest remaining envelope contains the notification that one Undercaptain Fraazt from Kynstaar will be the replacement for Suraat, along with a copy of his orders, indicating that Fraazt will report no later than the first eightday of Autumn.

The fourth envelope contains instructions for forwarding the chest of spoils to the post commander of Ilypsya for evaluation and monetization of the goods, with the notation that one-tenth of the value will be retained for associated services and requirements, the balance to be returned to Pemedra Post, with the post commander being responsible for distribution, including to rankers and officers reposted prior to the distribution, through attested vouchers.

Alyiakal smiles grimly at the use of the term "post commander," then opens the remaining envelope, which contains a single sheet.

Alyiakal'alt
Majer
Commander
Pemedra Post

You are hereby detached from Pemedra Post. You are to depart Pemedra Post no sooner than sixday of the second eightday of Harvest and no later than the third oneday of Harvest. You are to take three eightdays' home leave and to report to the Majer-Commander, Mirror Lancer Headquarters, Cyad, immediately upon completion of leave and travel to Cyad.

Majer Kortyl will report to Pemedra Post no later than the third eightday of Harvest, 105 A.F., to assume command.

Kortyl . . . far better than Baertyl. But then Captain-Commander Laartol knows Kortyl's abilities, as well as the fact that Kortyl is more than competent, if conventional, which will be fine for the post over the next few years.

Alyiakal takes a deep breath and stands, then makes his way to Baassyn's study, closing the door behind himself.

Baassyn immediately stands. "Is it that bad?"

"It could be much worse." Alyiakal manages a wry smile and goes on to tell Baassyn what he's received from Mirror Lancer headquarters.

"Kessmyr will do well at Inividra," Baassyn says after Alyiakal finishes, "and Nolaan certainly deserves the promotion. The new undercaptain will have time to learn something, and eventually, we'll all get a share of the spoils. What about Majer Kortyl?"

The way Baassyn has responded to what Alyiakal has said indicates that he wants to talk about the more routine matters first.

"I served with Kortyl when we were posted to Guarstyad. He's a very organized, solid, and conventional officer. He's also more insightful than it first appears and very fair. I suspect, but don't know, that the Captain-Commander selected him personally."

"From you, that's good to know, and it won't hurt to have a post commander who's known to headquarters."

That can be as much a liability as an asset. But Alyiakal only comments, "That likely won't make much difference for the next year or so. After that, it might."

Baassyn nods thoughtfully, pauses, and finally says, "Headquarters didn't mention anything about what you did in Cerlyn except for disposition of spoils?"

"Not a thing. The only hint was that they're granting the spoils, which suggests that they're not going to publicly disavow what we did."

"If that's so, what do you think your reporting to headquarters means?"

"I don't know. The fact that they're ordering me to take leave suggests that I'll be reposted, but senior officers are usually informed of that, even if headquarters doesn't know where. It could be that they want me to enjoy my last three eightdays before debriefing me and quietly relieving me from duty. Or they may give me routine paperwork tasks to do until I'm forgotten by the Emperor and the Merchanters." *Or suffer a convenient "accident."*

"Do you know yet what you're going to do?"

Alyiakal offers a sardonic smile. "I'm a loyal and faithful officer. I'll report as ordered"—*possibly with as much stored order and chaos as I can manage*—"and see what's in store for me."

"When are you going to tell the other officers?"

"At evening mess. A few glasses won't matter. I will summon Nolaan about his promotion and Kessmyr about his orders, but I won't tell them anything else except that I'll let them know what little I've heard at evening mess."

"They'll guess."

"That's always the privilege of junior officers . . . and even some senior officers." Alyiakal manages to keep his tone wry as he turns. "Now, I'll send for Nolaan."

In less than a quint, Nolaan arrives at Alyiakal's doorway. "Ser?"

Alyiakal stands. "Come on in. Close the door."

"Yes, ser."

Alyiakal laughs softly even as Nolaan closes the door and moves toward the desk.

"Congratulations, Captain Nolaan," declares Alyiakal, immediately sensing the new captain's palpable relief. He extends the envelope with the promotion letter and insignia. "You've actually been a captain since oneday, even if you didn't know it."

"Thank you, ser."

"No thanks necessary. You earned it. There are captain's insignia in the envelope."

Nolaan smiles. "I wasn't sure . . ."

"There's no doubt. You're now Captain Nolaan."

"I meant about the patrol to Cerlyn."

"I'll be briefing all the officers at evening mess. Again, my congratulations."

A fraction of a quint after Nolaan leaves, Kessmyr appears in the study doorway. "You asked for me, ser?"

"I did. Come in and close the door." Alyiakal remains seated and gestures toward the chair, waiting for Kessmyr to seat himself before saying, "I've received your orders, Captain. You're headed for Inividra after home leave, and you'll depart here sometime during the sixth eightday of Harvest."

"Inividra . . . another combat post?"

"Officers seen to have great potential have a tendency to get more potential combat postings," replies Alyiakal dryly.

"Great potential? I just tried to learn what I could and not make any obvious mistakes, ser."

"That's exactly what you were supposed to do . . . and what too many undercaptains fail to understand and do."

"But you, ser—"

"I didn't do much more than that in my first posting, Kessmyr." Alyiakal's not about to talk about subsequent postings. "First postings are where officers learn—or should learn. Unfortunately, some don't. Some do learn at second posting. Some never do." *One way or another.*

Kessmyr nods slowly. "What advice would you give me?"

"That would take days and still might not be applicable to your next posting. I'll give you a general approach. Question what you assume. You can't go around doubting or questioning everything, but don't blindly assume that past patterns will always repeat themselves." Alyiakal stands, not wanting to go further. Too much of what he did worked because of his order/chaos abilities. "I'll add one other point. We all have different abilities. What works for one officer won't necessarily work for another. Don't copy another officer just because an idea or tactic works for him. You have to learn what works for you."

"Thank you, ser."

After Kessmyr leaves, Alyiakal thinks about when he should leave Pemedra, then decides it should be on eightday because that will give the letter he needs to write to Saelora time to arrive before he does. *Not that it necessarily will, but you can hope.*

With that decision made, he takes out paper and pen and begins to write. Two quints later, after reading the letter, he tears it up, then decides to try again after the evening mess.

Alyiakal doesn't hurry getting to the mess, and takes his seat at the head of the table. He decides not to draw out the announcements and jumps in immediately. "I imagine you've all been guessing about what arrived with the dispatch messengers, besides Nolaan's promotion and Kessmyr's orders. Kessmyr's replacement will be a Captain Staalt from Lhaarat." Alyiakal pauses at the questioning look from Chaem. "Yes, Staalt served under me, through the battles at Kraaslaen, and continued there after my departure. Undercaptain Suraat's replacement will be an Undercaptain Fraazt straight from Kynstaar. He'll arrive the first eightday of Autumn. Headquarters also agreed that nine-tenths of the chest of spoils will go to officers and rankers of Pemedra Post, even if they're posted elsewhere before the silvers or golds are available."

"Is that all, ser?" asks Chaem politely.

"I've been ordered to take home leave and then to report to the Majer-Commander in Cyad. I'll be leaving an eightday from tomorrow. The orders don't say any more than that. My replacement is Majer Kortyl. We served together at Guarstyad. He's more traditional than I am, but he's competent and extremely fair in his judgments."

For a long moment, there's silence.

"No more than that, ser?" asks Kessmyr respectfully.

"Not a word," replies Alyiakal. "My guess is that they don't know what to do with me and have decided that a comparatively junior majer can't do much damage at Mirror Lancer headquarters." *Although that's a* very *optimistic guess.* Alyiakal lifts his wineglass. "To change. May we all survive it."

"To change" is the rather muted response.

No one says much until everyone is served. Then Nolaan asks, "Do you know why Majer Kortyl was chosen?"

"Headquarters doesn't tell departing commanders why their replacements are chosen, but Majer Kortyl distinguished himself against the Kyphrans, and likely after that. You're fortunate to have him." *Particularly since it could have been Baertal, or someone like him.*

The rest of the dinner conversation is unremarkable, and after eating, Alyiakal returns to his study, where he writes another letter to Saelora, one far simpler than his discarded and destroyed first attempt.

> *Dear one—*
>
> *This letter will be quick because I need to get it off immediately so you know what's happening. I've been reposted and ordered to take three eightdays' leave before reporting to the Majer-Commander in Cyad. Three eightdays is the usual leave for an officer after less than a full posting.*
>
> *I'll be leaving Pemedra on the second eightday of Harvest, and with good fortune should arrive in Vaeyal on the following fiveday or sixday depending on the firewagon schedules. I can't tell you how much I look forward to being with you before I go to Cyad.*
>
> *All my love*

The letter to Hyrsaal is even shorter.

Alyiakal seals both and leaves them in the dispatch pouch at the duty desk before returning to his quarters.

LXII

On the second eightday of Harvest, Alyiakal rides out of Pemedra, at first light, almost certainly for the last time. Just before sunset on twoday, he rides into Syadtar, where he personally stables and says farewell to the gray gelding, before making his way to the visiting officers' quarters and then to Subcommander Zekkaat's study.

"Ser?" asks the duty ranker.

"Majer Alyiakal to see the subcommander."

"Have him come in," Zekkaat calls out through the half-open doorway.

As Alyiakal enters the study, Zekkaat stands, motions for Alyiakal to close the door, and says warmly, "Good to see you, Majer." He gestures to the chairs and seats himself behind the desk. "Would you mind telling me what you actually did in Cerlyn? No one will say much."

"That's understandable," replies Alyiakal. "We wiped out fifteen or sixteen companies of Cerlynese armsmen—not all at once, of course—and took Clynya." Alyiakal summarizes what happened in general terms.

"I can't believe the Cerlynese were that inept, especially after what happened to the Mirror Lancers from Lhaarat earlier this Summer."

"We attacked through Kula, then attacked Kraaslaen from the north at first light. They were anticipating an attack from the south or west, and they weren't expecting an attack coming out of Cerlyn. After that, we discovered that there weren't any armsmen to speak of between us and Clynya, and not that many there."

"How many men did this expedition cost the Mirror Lancers?"

"One squad killed, and a squad of wounded."

"So far," says Zekkaat slowly, "you appear to have succeeded with unbridled audacity and by coming up with strategies that others have failed to anticipate. With such success, might I ask why you're here?"

"I've been detached, given home leave, and ordered to report to the Majer-Commander." Alyiakal decides on a slight gamble. "It might be that the removal of the Duke and much if not all of his immediate family might . . . jeopardize . . . certain trade arrangements dealing with copper."

Zekkaat fingers his chin. "That is possible. If you were aware of that, why did you proceed?"

"The Mirror Lancers removed the Duke's forces from Kraaslaen twice. That didn't do any good, and I couldn't see that removing them a third time would change his mind. So when I saw the possibility . . ."

The subcommander nods, then says, "It's too bad Majer Baertal isn't here at Syadtar at the moment."

"Is he at Isahl, then?"

Zekkaat nods. "Filling in until the late Majer Mozyn's replacement arrives, along with more than a company of rankers." After a moment, he stands. "It was good to see you. Dinner, I hope?"

Alyiakal stands as well. "I'll be there. I hope there will be a firewagon for Ilypsya in the morning."

"Early. I'll likely not see you then."

Alyiakal nods politely and leaves, making his way back to the visiting senior officers' quarters.

Dinner is pleasantly polite, with only Alyiakal and two overcaptains with Zekkaat at the senior officers' table, and what seem to be also fewer junior officers at that table.

At dawn on threeday, Alyiakal and his two duffels are waiting just inside the post gates. When the firewagon arrives, Alyiakal finds that the front compartment is empty, which is fine with him.

Although the firewagon makes several stops to load or unload cargo, no one joins him in the front compartment, and he arrives at Ilypsya in early evening, but well after evening mess. Once again, he discovers that he'll have to spend a day at Ilypsya because the next firewagon for Fyrad will not leave until fiveday morning.

So, before morning mess on fourday, Alyiakal makes his way to the post commander's study, wondering if Subcommander Bekkan is still in charge and if he'll be in his study.

"The subcommander's not here, ser," begins the ranker at the front desk, then says, "Oh . . . here he comes."

Alyiakal turns to see Bekkan hurry in.

"Alyiakal . . . the supply officer told me a Majer Alyiakal was here. Can you stay and have breakfast, or do you have to run off?"

"I have to leave early tomorrow morning."

"Then we can have breakfast, and you can tell me what happened in

Cerlyn. There are all sorts of stories flying around." Bekkan gestures toward the door.

On the walk to the officers' mess, Alyiakal only summarizes very generally what happened, and not all of that.

When he finishes, Bekkan smiles. "I think you left out a few parts, but I won't press."

"How did you know at all?" asks Alyiakal.

"I got a note from the Captain-Commander saying that you'd been unexpectedly successful, but that he couldn't say more at present. He specifically asked me not to press you when you came through."

Which is why Bekkan was informed you were here.

"I take it you're going on home leave and then to Cyad?"

"You don't know?" asks Alyiakal in honest curiosity.

"No. That's a guess, but what else can they do? They can't cashier the most successful field commander in years."

"You're right about leave. Then I report to the Majer-Commander."

"He and Laartol will want to know every detail before you talk to anyone else." When the two approach the mess door, Bekkan says, "No more about Cerlyn now."

Alyiakal doesn't recognize the sub-majer or the two overcaptains at the senior officers' table, but Bekkan stops just short of the table and says, "This is Majer Alyiakal, on home leave before reporting to headquarters." Then he gestures to the officers in turn. "Sub-Majer Jonquyt, Overcaptain Duultz, and Overcaptain Vornyt."

"Pleased to meet you all," replies Alyiakal before he seats himself to Bekkan's right.

"It's our pleasure," declares Jonquyt in a warm tone of voice that matches what Alyiakal senses and also makes him wonder what the sub-majer knows.

"You haven't said where you're taking your home leave," says Bekkan cheerfully.

"Vaeyal. It's a small town on the Great Canal not far from Geliendra. Since I have no living family"—*not that I knew about until an eightday or so ago*—"I've spent my leaves with friends there."

"You're wise to get away from everything on your leaves," says Jonquyt. "Too many officers don't realize that need."

The rest of the conversation at breakfast deals with ways to get away.

Once Bekkan and Alyiakal depart the mess, the subcommander stops outside the building and looks directly at Alyiakal. "Have you ever thought about consorting? You could now, and it might be helpful in Cyad."

"You mean remove me from being played by attractive women from various factions?" returns Alyiakal sardonically.

"There is that," admits Bekkan. "But I was thinking more that you might not find what suits you in Cyad."

"That I'd be happier with my own choice of someone not steeped in the intrigues of Cyad?"

"Exactly."

"I've more than considered it," Alyiakal says.

"Just think about it. Don't do it because I suggested it . . . *or* that anyone else did. But if you have someone in mind and have held off, as many junior senior officers do, one way or another, there's no reason to hold off now."

"For better or worse," says Alyiakal dryly.

"I don't think it will come to that, but I also can't promise anything."

"What don't I know that you can tell me?"

"I like your phrasing." Bekkan offers an amused smile. "I don't know the details, but I've gotten the impression that matters between the Triad leaders and the Emperor are . . . uneasy."

"You mean that the Merchanters' control of the Imperial Tariff Enumerators is cutting off funding to the Emperor and the Mirror Lancers."

Bekkan laughs. "Laartol told me that you see much more than most officers."

"I don't know that's exactly accurate. I happened to be in situations where I could determine what seemed to be happening."

"Fair enough, but other officers have had such opportunities and haven't."

"How unsettled are matters?"

"Unsettled enough that Laartol's requesting your presence. He could easily have left you at Pemedra. No one could have opposed that."

"Except the Merchanters."

"If they'd pressed to remove the most successful field commander in the Mirror Lancers, that would have openly revealed their motives and power."

"Pardon me if I have some doubts that a comparatively junior majer can have much impact in Cyad. I understand that even commanders don't seem to."

"You're right to have doubts, but I've learned that the Captain-Commander is an excellent judge of character and ability." Bekkan chuckles. "Didn't he place the only field officer who could be effective against the Cerlynese in the right place at the right time?"

Alyiakal shakes his head ruefully.

"Think it over. I'll see you at the evening mess."

"I'll be there . . . and thank you."

After Bekkan strides away, Alyiakal wants to shake his head—again.

ALYIAKAL'ALT, MAJER

Vaeyal

Harvest, 105 A.F.

LXIII

Late on fiveday afternoon, the firewagon slows to a halt at the Vaeyal waystop on the west side of the Great Canal, and Alyiakal steps out into the damp, late-summer-like heat, even warmer than the firewagon had been, wondering if Saelora even received his last letter. He doesn't see anyone nearby but lifts his two duffels out of the front compartment and sets them beside the bench, then watches the firewagon depart, quickly picking up speed.

He turns and looks east across the canal, although he cannot see Loraan House, before stretching various muscles and deciding to wait just a bit. He really doesn't want to carry both duffels half a kay unless he has to.

Less than half a quint passes before he sees the Loraan House wagon heading down Canal Street to the bridge over the canal, and he feels a certain tentative relief when he sees Saelora's mahogany-red hair.

Even before she slows the wagon, Alyiakal senses her joy at seeing him, and he finds his eyes burning. When the wagon stops, he looks up at her. "I wasn't sure if you'd get my letter in time . . ."

She smiles warmly. "I got the latest one yesterday afternoon. I got the two letters about an eightday ago. You do know how to surprise a woman."

"I had no idea—"

"I know that, dear one. We need to talk, but it can wait just a bit—until you load those duffels in the rear and get up here beside me."

Alyiakal just looks at her intently.

"You keep doing that," she says, "and we'll never get home."

He grins. "That wouldn't be all bad, Lady Merchanter." He picks up the duffels and carries them to the rear of the wagon, opens the doors, and lifts the duffels, one after the other, into the wagon and closes the doors. In moments, he's beside her on the wide teamster's seat, holding her one free hand and kissing her cheek.

She looks at him closely, then says, "I see a few more scars."

"Nothing too serious."

Saelora shakes her head, then says, "We do need to talk, and when we get home, I doubt you'll be listening."

"Maybe," Alyiakal says. "Where do we start?"

"After I get the wagon turned and headed back to the house."

Once Saelora turns the wagon, gets it over the bridge and headed up Canal Street, she says, "I've made arrangements for us to leave for Jakaafra on oneday. We'll take the wagon on a canal barge."

For an instant, Alyiakal is stunned. After a moment, he says, "You're the one with the surprises. That's good, though. It will give us a few days to be consorted." As he watches and senses Saelora, he can tell she's not surprised. "You knew I was going to ask?"

She smiles warmly, reaches out and squeezes his hand tightly. Then she murmurs, "I was going to ask you. I already hinted to Gaaran and Mother that it was likely. You don't really think I'd let you go to Cyad unconsorted, do you? Or Jakaafra?" Then she offers a mischievous smile.

"I hoped not, but I didn't want to assume." He scarcely notices as the wagon passes Loraan House, closed for the day. "I've done some thinking."

"I could tell that from your recent letters. I have the feeling that you were successful against the Cerlynese, possibly too successful for headquarters?"

"Too successful for the Merchanters and the Emperor, possibly for the Magi'i as well." Alyiakal tells her everything, including the aspects of magery that he's told no one else, as well as what Bekkan imparted, including the suggestion about consorting.

"I like the way that subcommander thinks," Saelora says as she turns the wagon onto the old road that leads to the distillery and her house.

"I was already leaning that way."

"It's a good thing you hinted at it in your letters," she teases.

"We might even be able to see Hyrsaal at Northpoint," muses Alyiakal, "and I'd wager you thought of that as well."

"Well . . . I did think that it would be nice to tell him personally that we were consorted. He won't be able to see you, otherwise. Also, since we're going there, we can take him some good wine, and some greenberry brandy."

"Perhaps some samples for local chandleries?"

"If any are interested."

Alyiakal hesitates, then says, "I didn't exactly plan on being relieved more than a year early."

"But you knew it was a possibility when you attacked Clynya," she says evenly.

"I didn't want to see more lancers die because of Taartyn's pride and the greed of the Merchanter clans."

"There's a price for everything, especially loyalty and duty. But you already knew that, dear man."

Alyiakal can't refute that and isn't about to try. He simply takes joy in sitting beside Saelora as she drives down the old road. When they near the distillery, he studies it, immediately noting that it has nearly doubled in size since his last visit, with heavy shutters that can be barred from inside and a small brick guardhouse set between the front loading dock and the iron-bound main door. The guard in the small house stands as the wagon approaches.

"This is Majer Alyiakal," Saelora calls out.

The man nods, then smiles as Saelora guides the wagon past the guardhouse and down the drive to the main house, to a stable that has also been expanded.

Surprisingly, Laetilla appears on the step outside the front door when Saelora halts the wagon in front of the stable. "Well?"

Saelora smiles broadly. "He did."

"You didn't hint, I hope."

"Not even once. He asked immediately."

"About time." Laetilla pauses, then says, "It'll be three quints before dinner's ready." She turns and reenters the house.

"I take it that Laetilla has offered a strong opinion about our getting consorted?" asks Alyiakal bemusedly, before climbing down from the wagon.

As Saelora descends gracefully, Alyiakal notes that she still wears the electrum and blue zargun bracelet.

With her boots on the ground Saelora says, "Laetilla's commented for some time. What's interesting is that Mother *hasn't.* She's been different about you ever since you made that comment about Vaeyal being home."

"I meant it."

"She knew you meant it."

"Since we have a little time before dinner, do you want the wagon in the stable?"

Saelora glances up at the cloudless but hazy sky. "I don't think so. The twins will be using it for the next two days since they'll be limited to the carts while we're gone."

"Carts? How many?"

"Three, but we can only use two at a time." She pauses. "If we want a hot dinner, and you want at least to wash up, then . . ."

"We need to block the wagon and unharness the horse," Alyiakal finishes.

Even with both of them, it takes close to a quint before they finish and close up the stable.

As they head for the door into the kitchen, each carrying one of his duffels, Alyiakal shakes his head.

"What's that for?"

"The huge addition to the distillery, three carts, and likely a lot more. You just keep expanding." Alyiakal opens the door to the kitchen.

"You should see what Catriana's done in Fyrad," says Saelora as she stops at the open door. "Well, partly with Dyrkan and Elina's help . . . and your golds."

"I have more if you need them. About the only thing I can spend them on is my mess bill." He pauses. "I do need a few new uniforms."

"We could go to Geliendra tomorrow, if you like."

Alyiakal recalls his last visit to get uniforms. "It might be better to get consorted first."

Saelora laughs. "That would mean getting consorted tomorrow."

"Is that even possible?"

She smiles enigmatically, then steps into the kitchen.

"Is there a recorder here in Vaeyal?" Alyiakal shakes his head. "Or a Recording Hall?"

"Vaeyal has both. Not grand, like Fyrad, but tasteful and adequate. Kharrl might have to squeeze us in, but he will."

"Possibly because you've revitalized Vaeyal?"

"She's done more than that," declares Laetilla, without turning from the stove. "More people work for her than for anyone else in town except for the Great Canal."

"From what I've seen," replies Alyiakal, "that doesn't surprise me. Has that outland trader been back?"

"Elbarak? Not here. He's visited Catriana. He'll deal with her as well because he knows she's one of the owners."

"There's warm water in the tub," interjects Laetilla, "and a kettle of hot water here. If you hurry, Majer, dinner won't get cold."

Alyiakal gets the message. "I'll be quick." He follows Saelora, marveling, far from the first time, at both her strength and grace, as she carries one duffel without any strain.

Not quite two quints later, much cleaner, and in a fresh uniform, he leaves the bedchamber, having cleaned up the bath chamber quickly before dressing. He heads for the front parlor.

Saelora emerges from the kitchen with two wineglasses and hands one to Alyiakal as he enters the parlor. "Laetilla says it will be half a quint. You surprised her . . . again."

"I trust that's good . . . in this instance, anyway?"

"It is." She sits in one of the blue upholstered armchairs.

Alyiakal takes the other, then sips the wine. "This is so good. When we get wine, at least in the border posts, we're fortunate if it's barely passable . . . and now headquarters, or the Emperor, or the Merchanters in Cyad, have decided to make it more expensive." He goes on to tell her why.

She nods. "From all your letters, it seems like headquarters is cutting back on all sorts of supplies."

"From wine to horseshoes, funds for local provisions, and lately even the number of replenished firelances."

"I'd think that would be dangerous."

"It won't be that dangerous for the next year or so, except possibly at Inividra."

"That's because you've removed the greatest threats."

"Not just me. The lancers at Isahl, Syadtar, and even at Lhaarat did their part." *And incurred far greater casualties.*

"Was Majer Baertal involved, or did he manage to get someone else to take the risks?" Saelora's tone is only mildly acidic.

"Subcommander Zekkaat sent him to deal with the Jeranyi who decimated the companies from Isahl. He prevailed, but he lost almost two companies. Then Zekkaat sent him to Isahl as temporary post commander for the late Majer Mozyn."

"Do you think he learned anything from that?"

"Doubtless, he did, but it may well have been the wrong thing."

Laetilla appears and says, "Dinner is ready."

Alyiakal is immediately on his feet, wineglass in hand, but he follows Saelora to the small dining room. They each seat themselves, and Laetilla places one of the Merchanter-blue platters Vassyl had given Saelora in front of her and a second in front of him, then leaves.

Alyiakal looks at the light golden pastry oval on his plate that is a good five digits high and surrounded by green beans mixed with sautéed mushrooms and toasted almond slivers. "I've definitely never had this before."

"Neither have I. I asked Laetilla to fix something different and special."

Alyiakal waits for Saelora to cut into her pastry, noticing that the pastry itself is a light crust that surrounds some form of meat, then follows her example, slicing off a bit of the meat with the crust. The beef is incredibly tender, and the sauce and pastry combine to create something that's hard to describe, except that it has hints of red Alafraan and a piquant butteriness, with the slightest hint of burhka and perhaps the tiniest hint of greenberry liqueur. He immediately takes another bite before saying, "This is amazing! It's likely better than anything the Emperor gets, not that we'll ever know that."

Even as he speaks, he can sense Laetilla just outside the dining room and her satisfaction at his comments before she returns to the kitchen. He smiles . . . and takes another bite, quickly followed by a third.

Neither he nor Saelora says much until they finish devouring the dinner. Then they look at each other and break into laughter.

The dessert is a variation on the greenberry egg custard that Alyiakal had eyed dubiously the first time Laetilla had presented it, until he tasted it, and this variation is even better. *Or maybe it's been so long since you've had anything this good that it seems that it's better.* Either way, it's delicious.

After Laetilla serves them the liqueur glasses holding greenberry brandy, she turns to Alyiakal. "How long will you be in Cyad?"

"I have no idea. It could be eightdays, seasons, or a posting for a year or two. I'm too junior to stay very long."

"You were too junior to be a post commander when they made you one, weren't you?" asks Laetilla.

"Several times," adds Saelora.

Alyiakal offers an embarrassed smile. "You're both right, but so was I. Maybe I should just have said, 'I don't know,' because I don't. I was guessing."

Saelora and Laetilla exchange amused smiles.

"I'm headed off for the night," says Laetilla. "I'll check the guard at the distillery. Don't stay up too late, not if you're serious about working in a consorting by tomorrow night. Especially with everything else you need to do." With that, she turns and leaves the dining room.

"She has a point," concedes Alyiakal, then takes a sip of the brandy, which is every bit as good as he recalls.

"You'll survive"—Saelora gives him a sly smile—"even if you miss a little sleep."

LXIV

Sixday morning, Alyiakal and Saelora are up a few quints after sunrise, if only in their dressing robes, and Alyiakal has to admit, if only to himself, that he certainly doesn't miss the sleep he didn't get. It does help that Laetilla has left almond rolls, fresh grapes, and apples for breakfast.

Neither says much until they've each had several bites of their almond rolls.

"Do we visit the recorder first?" asks Alyiakal.

"Well . . ." says Saelora with a smile, "we can't tell the family when to show up until we know when it will be."

"Then what? Since I've never been consorted or had to organize what happens, I'm a bit at a loss."

"We need to find out what else is necessary for the consorting dinner."

"You did say that your mother wouldn't come here until we consorted. She can't refuse that dinner invitation, can she?"

"We can't do that here," Saelora points out. "It has to be at Mother's house."

Alyiakal frowns. "On such short notice?"

"When I found out you had a shorter home leave, I mentioned the possibility to Charissa. It really is their house now."

Alyiakal isn't about to get into those particular family issues. Besides, Saelora's usually right in those cases, and he has another problem. "There's something we need to talk about. Adayal and my . . . niece . . ."

"Your daughter," Saelora says evenly. "I'm glad you brought it up. Adayal had the sense to offer you some protection by calling her your niece, even if most of those who read letters to you likely suspect that she's your daughter." Saelora frowns. "From what you told me, she has to be twelve, or thirteen a little after yearturn. Do you have any idea why Adayal wrote you? Beyond what she wrote?"

"I can only guess. She seduced me, and while I was definitely willing to be seduced, I never would have—"

"No, you wouldn't," says Saelora firmly, but not coldly.

"I'm just guessing, and it's in hindsight, but I think she wanted a child, and she wanted one with the talents to survive in the Great Forest."

Saelora adds, "You have those talents, and you were young and vulnerable. From her letter, it sounds like her daughter has quite a few of your traits. Do you think that Adayal hopes that seeing you will turn your daughter back toward the Forest?"

"Possibly, but I also think that she wouldn't force her daughter to stay against her will." Alyiakal frowns. "That feeling may be based on what I felt then and didn't see." He adds wryly, "There was a lot I didn't see."

"That's true of all of us."

"You're being generous. From what I've seen, young men tend to see less than young women."

Saelora laughs gently. "It's more likely that young women are better at hiding what they don't know."

"Anyway, she was quite clear that I didn't belong in the Great Forest."

"Perhaps she didn't want to be overshadowed."

"That's possible, but the Forest itself prefers I keep my distance."

"Mutual respect?"

"Probably, but what if my daughter really doesn't belong there?"

"She's too young to make a final decision," says Saelora. "She needs some time with you outside the Forest."

"I'm sure she's spent time outside the Forest."

"But not with her father."

"So she should spend some time with us while I'm on leave? That's not fair to you."

"It's also not fair to Adayal if her daughter chooses to leave the Forest. At least you and I can protect her."

"You'd do that?"

"If it comes to that."

Alyiakal senses both her firmness and lack of resentment. For a moment, he doesn't know what to say.

"You've been faithful to me and supportive for ten years. You've given me most of what you've saved over those years. You've never hidden anything from me, except military maneuvers, and you've told me about those as soon as you safely could. What happened between you and Adayal was over before we started writing." Saelora pauses. "I wouldn't ever want your daughter to suffer because of something *I* wouldn't do."

Alyiakal senses what she's not said as well, and he can feel his eyes burning and the tears seeping down his cheeks. *I so love you.*

She reaches out across the table and takes his hand, then says warmly and gently, "We do have a few things to do today."

After several long moments, Alyiakal asks, "How have you planned to get to Jakaafra?"

"I'd thought that we'd take the Great Canal to Northway and the road east from there. That's the usual way."

"It's also longer. We could leave the canal at Midway and take the road bordering the Great Forest straight to Northpoint and Jakaafra. You wouldn't be paying for the barge travel from Midway to Northway, and we'd get there and back sooner. We'd also likely run into less trouble."

Saelora laughs wryly. "With you there, you mean. Most traders won't travel that route."

"I do provide some advantages."

She shakes her head.

"There's one other thing. Last night, Laetilla said something—"

"About all we had to do. Yes, I told her. But she's the only one. She'll never break confidences."

"What did she say?" ask Alyiakal, half dreading what he might hear.

"She agrees with our decision. She thought you'd do the right thing, but while you were bathing, I told her that we'd be headed to Jakaafra after the consorting. She was pleased that you didn't disappoint her."

"In some ways, she's another mother."

Saelora smiles. "Is that so bad?"

Alyiakal laughs.

LXV

More than a glass passes before Alyiakal and Saelora can leave. They're just leading their mounts out of the stable when Kaasya and Kaastyl hurry down the drive past the distillery and toward the stable.

"You're headed south to Leftwall first." Saelora's words are anything but a question.

"If that's where you want us first," replies Kaastyl quickly.

"It'll work better that way, except for Hyleena," returns Saelora cheerfully.

Kaasya merely grins as she strides beside her brother toward the stable.

Once Alyiakal and Saelora mount and ride toward the center of Vaeyal on the old road, Alyiakal says, "I take it Kaastyl wanted to finish up where his girlfriend is?"

"Of course. Most times it doesn't matter that much, but they have a lot to do with the wagon before we leave on oneday, and they won't get much done on eightday."

"And we're taking the wagon because you only need one horse when it's not loaded, and that leaves two for the factorage?"

"Exactly," replies Saelora. "It's also much faster, because the canal boats don't stop at night."

"And mostly cheaper, because we don't have to pay for lodging, and once we're consorted, it's unlikely anyone will object to our using the visiting officers' quarters at Northpoint for a day or two."

"I wasn't sure about that," Saelora admits.

"Well, your brother is the overcaptain in command there, but if we don't want to impose, there used to be a decent inn in Jakaafra."

"That might be better."

Recalling when he took Saelora to Southpoint, Alyiakal just asks, "We're headed for the Recording Hall first?"

"Where else? Are you getting worried all of a sudden?"

Alyiakal senses and hears the teasing note and replies, "Hardly. What about you?"

"Not about being consorted. I do worry about all the complications."

"Putting off consorting will create even more complications." *Just a different kind.* "What do you think your mother will say?"

"It's about time, or something similar."

The Recording Hall in Vaeyal is tucked between two houses on Canal Street less than a block from what had been Vassyl's house. Alyiakal absently wonders if Elinjya has kept her father's house and rented it or sold it. The hall is indeed modest, no more than six yards across, but more than twice that deep, suggesting that the recorder's living quarters are in the rear.

The two dismount, tie their horses, and walk toward a graying man who is sweeping the walk from the front door to the street.

"Good morning, Kharrl," says Saelora cheerfully.

"What can I do for you, Lady Merchanter?" asks the recorder.

"This is Majer Alyiakal. We'd planned to be consorted on his next home leave, but he was suddenly reposted, and we decided not to wait any longer. Could you fit us in sometime today?"

The recorder nods slowly. "It is rather sudden, but you two have been seeing each other for years." He turns to Alyiakal. "Where is your home?"

Alyiakal laughs softly. "Vaeyal is the only home I have."

"He also owns a share of Loraan House," interjects Saelora, "and he has for years. That makes him a resident of Vaeyal."

"That makes it much simpler," says Kharrl. "I could fit you in just before noon or at fourth glass of the afternoon."

"Fourth glass of the afternoon," says Saelora. "It will just be immediate family and a few friends."

"I haven't seen Marenda for a while. I hope she'll be there." The recorder smiles pleasantly.

"That's up to her," replies Saelora, "but she should be."

"You know, she got consorted in much the same way. Everyone was quite surprised. Since Majer Alyiakal has been here often, your consorting won't be a surprise that way."

"More like surprise that we finally did it?" asks Alyiakal dryly.

"Well, it will remove some gossip," declares Kharrl with a hint of amusement in his voice.

"They'll find something else before long." Saelora pauses. "Half a quint before fourth glass?"

"That would be fine."

From the Recording Hall, the two ride to Loraan House, but tie their mounts in front.

When they walk in, Gaaran appears from the rear of the factorage. "I didn't expect to see you two this morning, especially this early."

"That's because I need to tell you to close at third glass this afternoon. That will allow you and the twins, if they want, to get to the consorting at fourth glass."

Gaaran shakes his head, as if he hasn't quite heard what Saelora's said. "Consorting? You and Alyiakal? So quickly?"

"He only has a short leave, and then he's being posted to Cyad. Now, we're headed to tell Charissa and Mother. Laetilla can help with the dinner if they need her. It's only for family here in town." Saelora pauses. "Can you get a message to Karola? Tell her, and say that we understand if they can't come, but events beyond Alyiakal's control made it necessary."

Gaaran frowns.

Alyiakal quickly explains.

"You two have always done things your way," replies Gaaran in an amused tone.

"And you haven't?" replies Saelora.

Gaaran grins. "Don't let me keep you."

"We won't," returns Saelora with a smile.

As Alyiakal and Saelora head back north on Canal Street, he asks, "Why is everyone so agreeable? Because they thought it would never happen? Or because you hinted that it might? Maybe they all think we should have done it earlier and are afraid that if they object we won't get around to it. Actually, there's another possibility, too. You've done so much for everyone that they all want the best for you." Alyiakal pauses. "That should have been my first thought."

"You did think of it . . . eventually," Saelora says sweetly.

Alyiakal winces.

When they near Gaaran and Charissa's house and Marenda's cottage, Saelora says, "We won't be long. We can tie the horses at the rail beside the side porch."

The two have barely tied their mounts when Charissa appears. "You two are here early."

"We have a lot to do today, and I have a large favor to ask. A *very* large favor."

Charissa looks from Saelora to Alyiakal and back to Saelora. "Might it be a consorting dinner?"

"Yes. Tonight. It doesn't have to be fancy. We're getting consorted at the fourth glass of the afternoon. Laetilla can help . . . only if you want."

"Does Gaaran know?"

"He does. He's closing the factorage at third glass."

Charissa shakes her head, then offers an amused smile. "We can do something."

"Who's there, Charissa?" Alyiakal recognizes Marenda's voice, although it sounds frailer than he recalls.

"Saelora and Alyiakal. They're getting consorted." Charissa then asks quietly, "Did you say fourth glass this afternoon?"

Saelora nods.

Charissa repeats the information.

Marenda hurries out onto the side porch and immediately looks to Saelora. "It's about time. Why so quickly, though?"

"Alyiakal's only got a short leave, and he's being posted to Mirror Lancer headquarters in Cyad."

Marenda immediately looks to Alyiakal. "What in the name of the Rational Stars did you do this time?"

"Headquarters told me to stop Cerlynese raids. So I did the only thing that might permanently solve the problem. We invaded Cerlyn and wiped out the Duke and most of his family and armsmen."

"Someone should have done that years ago. Kayral recommended something similar, you know. Headquarters said they couldn't spare the men. After that, he took his stipend." Marenda pauses. "It's too bad Hyrsaal can't be here."

"We're going traveling to Jakaafra after the consorting," says Saelora. "That's the best we'll be able to do."

"Why?" asks Marenda.

"Because I want to," replies Saelora. "And that's the last place Alyiakal was with his father."

Alyiakal manages not to show any surprise at Saelora's response.

Marenda turns to Alyiakal. "Was that your idea?"

"I knew I needed to go there sometime. Saelora decided when."

Marenda shakes her head. "I can't say I understand, but there are some things I likely never will. Well, it's *your* life together." She pauses, then asks, "You are getting consorted in the Recording Hall, aren't you?"

"We are," replies Saelora, repeating, "At fourth glass."

"We'll be there," declares Marenda.

"If you could spare Laetilla," murmurs Charissa quietly.

"She'll be here shortly."

"Karola?" asks Charissa.

"Gaaran's sending word. Who knows?"

"You're right about that," declares Charissa sarcastically. "Don't worry. We'll handle the dinner."

"And no presents. *None,*" replies Saelora. "We're asking a lot of everyone on such short notice, especially with the dinner."

"You always try to make it easy, Saelora," replies Charissa. "We'll see you at fourth glass."

Once Saelora and Alyiakal are riding back to Saelora's house, Alyiakal says, "I take it Karola's been more distant lately?"

"She's declined invitations to dinner, both from me and from Charissa, for the past year."

"You didn't mention that. Do you know why?"

"There wasn't anything you could do. I asked around. So far as any of us can discover, she and Faadyr are doing well, and he's selling his ale to some of the inns. I even rode out there three eightdays ago. She looked healthy, and was pleasantly distant. She just said that, with the children and the demands on Faadyr, they didn't have much time to spare."

"I wonder what they're hiding."

"I don't know that they're hiding anything. I think they just don't like being around us. I've made the effort, for years. None of us have ever been invited there."

That was something that Alyiakal did recall. "It seems like a shame."

"They'll either come to the consorting or dinner, or they won't."

"It sounds like you're wagering they won't."

"I'd like it if she would, but if she won't respond to invitations with more than an eightday's notice, I have some doubts."

"Do we need to rent or borrow a coach? I did notice that you extended the stable."

Saelora shakes her head. "There's no point. We'll both ride to the Recording Hall, and from there to Gaaran and Charissa's house. The extension is for an extra cart horse and a mount for Laetilla."

"That's good for her."

"It's also good for me," Saelora points out.

Alyiakal and Saelora have almost reached the distillery when Laetilla emerges and waits for them, before asking, "What time?"

"Fourth glass of the afternoon, and Charissa would appreciate any help you can provide. She said she'd be happy to do the dinner." Saelora pauses, then adds, "I'm certain Mother will be mostly with the children."

"She won't be a problem, not at your consorting and dinner. Just don't be late for your own ceremony," replies Laetilla. "I'll be on my way shortly."

"Then we'll see you later," says Saelora, turning her mount down the drive toward the stable. Alyiakal follows.

Since it will be some time before the ceremony, the two unsaddle, groom, and stall the horses before returning to the house.

"I don't have a dress uniform," says Alyiakal, "but I did save my best uniform. You're going to wear your good blues, I take it?"

"Since I don't have shimmersilk blues like the Cyad clan Merchanters, I'll make do with the best I have."

"You'll be stunning," Alyiakal insists.

"To you."

"To everyone who's there," he returns.

"Not that there will be anyone but family." Saelora offers a bemused smile. "But I wouldn't want Mother to think I slighted my appearance because those present are only family."

"You always look good."

"Thank you." She pauses. "We need to eat a little, and then you dress first. After that, I'll need some time to make myself presentable."

When the two finish eating some sliced apples and cheese, Alyiakal readies himself, with the exception of his tunic, which he won't don until after he saddles the horses. He sits in the front parlor, waiting, occasionally pacing, and wondering exactly how much Saelora needs to do.

It's close to third glass when she reappears in a set of Merchanter blues he knows he's never seen, perfectly tailored to her, her hair shimmering. All Alyiakal can do is stare.

"Well?" she asks.

"You're more than stunning. You're absolutely gorgeous."

"That's because you love me."

"That's true, but you look gorgeous." He continues to look. Finally, he says, "I'll saddle the horses, then be back."

"This time, I'll let you."

Roughly two quints later, the two mount their horses and ride down the drive toward the old road.

When Saelora and Alyiakal near the Recording Hall, he sees a group he doesn't recognize standing near the building, including several women he's certain he's never seen before. There are enough people that he has to look around for a moment to find Charissa and Gaaran—and Marenda—standing directly in front of the hall. With them is a white-haired man that Alyiakal doesn't immediately recognize before recalling that he must be Traybett—Charissa's father. Farther to one side is Kaastyl . . . and Laetilla. Alyiakal doesn't see any sign of Kaasya, Karola, or Faadyr, then realizes that Kaasya is likely holding everything down at Charissa and Gaaran's house so that Charissa and Laetilla could come to the consorting ceremony. *Another thoughtful young woman.*

"Who are all these people?" Alyiakal asks Saelora quietly.

"Townspeople I know through Loraan House . . . but I never told anyone."

"Someone did," replies Alyiakal. "Likely Gaaran or the recorder."

"Gaaran. Kharrl wouldn't do that."

As they ride closer, Alyiakal doesn't need to sense to know that most eyes are on Saelora as they rein up outside the Recording Hall, where they dismount and tie the horses. Alyiakal takes a quick look at the graystone building, which, like the hall in Fyrad, is devoid of any adornment, as are the oak doors.

Saelora turns to Gaaran and asks, "Did you announce it to the whole town?"

Gaaran flushes. "Cheslya asked why we were closing early. She must have spread the word."

Cheslya? Then Alyiakal remembers that she's the owner of the only reputable brothel in Vaeyal.

Charissa stifles a smile, and Marenda shakes her head, then says, "You are the most important person in Vaeyal these days, dear, and you're consorting the most dashing of Mirror Lancer officers."

Dashing? Alyiakal refrains from shaking his head as he takes Saelora's arm and guides her toward the hall doors.

After Saelora and Alyiakal step into the Recording Hall, family and friends follow. Alyiakal senses Kaastyl is the last and he closes the door. Each side wall holds a single narrow window with frosted glass and no wall sconces, sculptures, or other adornments.

Saelora and Alyiakal walk slowly toward Kharrl, who wears the traditional brown tunic and trousers, and a wide, white shimmersilk scarf, and stands behind the white sunstone pedestal that holds the recorder's open book.

Marenda takes her place on the left side of the hall, closest to the pedestal, with Gaaran and Charissa beside her, while Traybett, Laetilla, and Kaastyl are on the right side, opposite Marenda.

Alyiakal and Saelora stop several yards short of the pedestal. The recorder looks at the two and intones, "I am Kharrl, recorder of consortings in Vaeyal. Approach the book."

Saelora and Alyiakal step up to the open book.

"Do you, Majer Alyiakal of the Mirror Lancers, and Saelora, Lady Merchanter of Vaeyal, declare your intentions to take each other as consorts?"

"I do," declares Alyiakal.

"I do," says Saelora.

"Then each of you inscribe your name in the book before you, signifying that such is your choice of your own free will, in the prosperity of chaos and light and under the oversight of the Emperor of Light." Kharrl extends a shimmering white pen.

Saelora takes the cupridium-tipped pen, dips it in the inkwell in the pedestal, and signs her name. Then she hands the pen to Alyiakal, who also signs.

Kharrl takes the pen from Alyiakal, replaces it in the ceremonial holder of the pedestal, and then declares for all to hear, "As entered in the book of Vaeyal, you are hereafter consorts. May you always be fulfilled in the light and in the fullness of time."

Alyiakal completes the rite by placing a single shiny silver in the book just below their signatures. Then he turns and kisses Saelora, gently, but intensely, then murmurs, "I've wanted this for so long."

"Almost as long as I have," she murmurs back with a mischievous smile.

Then the two turn toward the doors, which Kaastyl has begun to open.

Alyiakal glances to Marenda and sees that tears streak her face and that her eyes are on Saelora. His eyes go again to Saelora, and he murmurs, "Somehow, you made your mother very happy."

"That's as much your doing as mine," she murmurs in return.

"Then it's very good we're consorted." He laughs softly and happily as they step out through the open doors. Somewhat, but not completely, to Alyiakal's surprise, the townspeople remain outside, watching as he and Saelora leave the Recording Hall and walk toward their mounts. "You've made quite an impression on people."

"I couldn't have done it without you and everyone else."

Alyiakal suspects she could have done quite well without him, but he's not about to contradict her. "You have a great ability to get people to work together."

Saelora just squeezes his hand before letting go and untying her horse.

In moments, they're riding north on Canal Street, leading a small family procession. Bringing up the rear are Charissa and Marenda in the chaise that Gaaran drives.

Less than a quint later, Saelora and Alyiakal have stabled their mounts and walk toward the side porch of Gaaran and Charissa's house, accompanied by Charissa and Gaaran.

"Just enjoy yourselves in the parlor," says Charissa. "Dinner won't be ready for more than a glass."

"I'll have drinks for you both in just a few moments . . . and Mother," says Gaaran. "She's already in the parlor."

Once in the parlor, Charissa heads for the kitchen, followed by Gaaran.

Marenda has taken her usual dark green upholstered armchair, but motions for Saelora and Alyiakal to take the adjoining settee, then glances around, as if to make sure that no one else is nearby before she says to Saelora, "You know, in some ways, you take after your father. He wasn't much for unnecessary ceremony or the display of emotion, but behind that pleasant front he could feel very deeply."

"I always thought that," replies Saelora.

Alyiakal smiles and asks Marenda, "Aren't you a bit the same way?"

"A bit, but Kayral felt more deeply."

The honesty behind her words momentarily stuns Alyiakal, even though he's suspected that Marenda isn't the most affectionate of people.

Marenda looks to Saelora. "He would have been so proud of you." Then she adds, "And of you, Alyiakal." Then she glances to the porch door as Traybett and Kaastyl step into the parlor.

"I hope we aren't intruding," says Traybett.

"Not at all," declares Saelora. "We're glad you're here."

Gaaran returns with an ale for Marenda, and white wine for Saelora and Alyiakal, then leaves, returning immediately with pale ales for Kaastyl and Traybett.

Marenda lifts her beaker. "To Saelora and Alyiakal."

Once everyone has sipped, Alyiakal raises his wineglass. "To the mother of the most successful Lady Merchanter in Vaeyal, who was kind enough to let an officer she'd never met take years to court her daughter, and in the process, give me the only home I've had since my mother died."

After sipping, Marenda replies warmly, "No consort-son could have treated me better than you, even if I had doubts at first."

More than just at first. But Alyiakal smiles and inclines his head to Marenda. Then he senses two other people approaching the porch.

In moments, Karola and Faadyr enter the parlor.

"We're sorry we had to miss the ceremony," Karola says, "but Faadyr had already left for Geliendra by the time I got Gaaran's message. We came as soon as we could."

"We're just glad you could be here," declares Marenda.

"Very glad," adds Saelora.

"I didn't think you were due for home leave quite this soon," ventures Faadyr.

"I'm not," replies Alyiakal. "I'm being reposted to Cyad, and that would mean no home leave for another two years. So . . ." He leaves the sentence unfinished.

"That makes sense," declares Karola, "even if it means a small consorting."

Alyiakal chuckles. "Everyone we'd invite is here, except for Hyrsaal and

Catriana, and no matter what we plan, there'd be no certainty that he could attend."

"Exactly," declares Gaaran firmly, looking at Faadyr. "Ale for the two of you?"

"Please."

Karola turns to Alyiakal. "When did you arrive here in Vaeyal?"

"Late yesterday afternoon."

"His letter saying he was coming only arrived on fourday afternoon," Saelora adds, her tone slightly sweet.

"So this was a surprise for everyone?" says Faadyr.

"It was. I asked her if we could manage it," replies Alyiakal, "on the ride from the waystop to her house."

He can sense the surprise from both but doesn't have to say more because Gaaran reappears with two ales, hands one to Karola and the other to Faadyr, and says, "Make yourselves comfortable. Dinner won't be for a glass."

Karola and Faadyr find the last seats in the parlor—on the padded bench that clearly has been brought from another room for the occasion. Karola takes a healthy swallow of her ale, while Faadyr surveys the room.

For a moment, there's a silence. Then Kaastyl says, "I've never seen that many people in one place on Canal Street, not ever."

"Well . . ." drawls Traybett, "that might be because it's been years since there was a consorting of two such distinguished people here in Vaeyal, and lots of folks wanted to be able to say that they saw it." He laughs. "Doesn't hurt that Saelora's strikingly gorgeous and Alyiakal's handsome, and that they're both tall enough to stand out."

"It'll certainly give folks something to talk about," returns Kaastyl.

"There'll be gossip for years," adds Marenda, her voice only lightly tinged with acid, "and none of it will be close to the truth."

Which is all for the best, a thought Alyiakal isn't about to utter.

"That's the whole point of gossip, isn't it?" asks Karola. "People find the truth boring."

From there the conversation moves into what people talk about and why, and Alyiakal is relieved when Charissa appears and announces that the dinner is ready.

Although it's slightly crowded, Alyiakal and Saelora sit side by side at the head of the table in the dining room, with Gaaran next to Saelora, and Marenda beside Alyiakal.

The menu is simple, but good—rosemary roasted fowl, rather than the traditional lamb, likely because there hadn't been time for lamb, with cheesed lace potatoes, and green beans with both sautéed mushrooms and toasted almonds, along with baskets of rosemary-garlic bread and a platter of pickled cucumbers, beets, and carrots—and no quilla in any form.

Once everyone's plate is full, Marenda turns to Gaaran. "You're her oldest male relative."

Gaaran stands, grinning. "It's been a long time since I could call Saelora my little sister, and because I'm now the one working for her, I'll just say that she's my youngest sister. She's always wanted to be the best she could be, and we all know how that's turned out. I worried that she'd never consort, not because there haven't been men eyeing her for a long time, but because none of them were worthy of her. Then this friend of Hyrsaal's kept writing, for more than five years before they met, and we all worried, until Alyiakal turned out not only to be utterly devoted to Saelora, but just incidentally, the most acclaimed and accomplished majer in the Mirror Lancers. To the perfect pair—Saelora and Alyiakal." With that, Gaaran raises his beaker.

"To Saelora and Alyiakal!"

Once everyone has finished drinking the toast, except Alyiakal and Saelora, Alyiakal stands. "Many years ago, I wrote the sister of a friend, who became, first, my friend, then my love, and now my consort, and through her, I've found not only love, but a home and family. I wish Hyrsaal were here so that I could thank him in front of all of you, but I have told him so before and will again. Thank you all."

"You can't sit down yet," says Saelora as she stands beside Alyiakal. "I've never said much about this before, but from the first Alyiakal encouraged me, counseled me, and believed in me. He listened and supported me, and he's saved my life when I doubt anyone else could have. In his quiet way, he's partly responsible for the success of Loraan House, but never asked anything of me. How could I not love him and consort him?" Her smile is open and joyous.

Then they both seat themselves.

"I worried that I'd never see this, and I'm so glad I have," says Marenda. "It won't get any easier you know."

"We know," replies Saelora.

Alyiakal nods, knowing that what lies before them will be even harder than what they've dealt with before—the attempts of the Merchanter clans of Cyad to take over in Fyrad and even Vaeyal, all the intrigue and dangers awaiting him in Cyad, not to mention meeting with Adayal, the Great

Forest . . . and his own daughter. And that doesn't include his irritation and anger at Adayal for never telling him that he has a daughter.

Alyiakal has several bites of the fowl and the cheesed lace potatoes before Faadyr clears his throat and says, "You haven't said what you'll be doing in Cyad."

"My orders just say to report to the Majer-Commander. In all likelihood, that means the Captain-Commander will assign my duties. I have no idea what those duties might entail."

"Isn't that a bit worrisome?" asks Charissa, her voice showing concern.

"So far," replies Alyiakal wryly, "I've never had a posting that wasn't worrisome."

Gaaran laughs. "Neither has any lancer officer."

Before long, the serving girl clears the plates and Charissa stands and waits for the conversations to die away. "While the traditional consort dessert is seedcake, Saelora and Alyiakal are anything but traditional, and dessert will be excellent but very untraditional greenberry-almond tarts."

Gaaran nods approvingly, while Traybett appears puzzled.

Once everyone has a tart, Alyiakal waits for Saelora to sample hers before beginning on his. "Excellent," he says after several bites, "but not quite as good as some I've been served." He smiles.

No one says much as they eat the tarts, but after a time, Traybett declares, "I could get very used to these."

After a time, Saelora smiles shyly at Alyiakal, then leans toward him and murmurs, "The consorted couple always leaves first."

"Are we ready to leave?" he murmurs back.

She nods, just slightly.

Alyiakal taps his glass, then waits. "This has been a wonderful dinner." He nods to Charissa, then to Marenda, and then gestures to Laetilla, sitting next to Kaasya at the foot of the table. "We appreciate all the effort, especially given the lack of notice, and the excellent fare, which, as you all have to know, is not something I often taste." Alyiakal pauses for the smiles and expressions of amusement. "I doubt we could have had much better, no matter how much notice we gave, and we're both grateful for everything. As I've said before, if quietly, Vaeyal has been my home almost from the day I met Saelora, and you've certainly made it so. For newly consorted couples, I've been reminded, there comes a time . . ." He smiles broadly, then stands, and extends his hand to Saelora, who stands.

Then the two walk from the dining room through the parlor, out onto the porch, and then toward their waiting horses.

LXVI

On sevenday morning, Saelora and Alyiakal don't rise at dawn, but they also don't sleep very late, and when Alyiakal wakes, he just watches Saelora.

She slowly opens her eyes but says nothing for several moments.

He waits.

"I still can feel it when you look at me."

"Is that bad?"

She smiles warmly. "Not the way you look at me."

"How could I look at you any other way?"

"You could, but I'm glad you don't."

"Do you have any plans for today?"

"I think you're the one who has plans."

Alyiakal flushes, then says, "I do need to get new uniforms. You don't have to come if you have things you need to do at the factorage."

"We don't have that much time together. I'd rather be with you."

"I'd like that, but I wanted to make sure." He pauses, then asks, "Breakfast?"

"You go to the kitchen. I'll join you shortly."

Alyiakal smiles as he stands, then pulls on the lancer-green robe she'd given him years before and heads for the kitchen, where he finds more almond rolls, some early grapes, and a quarter round of cheese, from which he cuts several slices. He makes up two plates and carries them to the dining room, before returning to the kitchen and pouring two beakers of ale and bringing them as well, just as Saelora emerges from the bedchamber in her robe.

They both take their seats and begin to eat.

After several mouthfuls, Alyiakal asks, "Do you need to stop by the factorage this morning?"

"Not this morning, but I should when we come back from Geliendra, or I suppose I should say Southpoint."

"You can say either. No one will mind."

Within a glass, Saelora and Alyiakal have dressed, left the house, and ride south on Canal Street. In less than a quint, they're on the main road east toward Geliendra.

Close to two glasses pass before the road turns into the avenue through the town to Southpoint, and, as before, a number of people look at them with more than a passing interest, as if it's unusual for a senior officer to be riding with a Lady Merchanter.

Before long, Alyiakal points to the tall shimmering sunstone gateposts ahead. "We're almost there. This time, I'll pay a courtesy call on the subcommander first. That shouldn't take too long." *You hope.*

As they near the gates, Alyiakal slows his mount as he nears one of the lancers on guard duty, extending order and a sense of command. "I'm Majer Alyiakal on reposting leave, but I need to obtain some uniforms. The lady is my consort. I'll be paying my respects to the post commander first, however."

"Yes, ser. Do you know—"

"I do, thank you." Alyiakal urges his mount forward and through the gates, Saelora beside him. After they've half circled the entry square with the statue of the second Emperor of Light, Alyiakal reins up outside the headquarters building, where he dismounts, then says, "You can wait here, or you can wait inside at the duty desk."

"I'll come with you as far as I can." Saelora dismounts, and the two enter the building.

The duty ranker looks surprised to see Saelora.

"I'm on reposting leave," Alyiakal says, "but I wanted to pay a courtesy call on the subcommander, if he's available. I brought my consort because I didn't wish to leave her out in the sun."

"Ah . . . yes, ser."

"If you'd tell him that Majer Alyiakal is here to see him."

"Yes, ser."

As the slightly bewildered ranker hurries off, Alyiakal says, "The post commander I met the last time was Subcommander Hurtaal. I don't know if he'll still be in command."

In moments, the ranker returns, with Subcommander Hurtaal just behind him, a bit of a surprise to Alyiakal. So is the broad smile that the graying and thin-faced Hurtaal bestows on Alyiakal and Saelora.

"Majer, I'm so glad to see you . . . and your consort."

"Once more, I need to replace uniforms, and I wasn't about not to see you first." Alyiakal inclines his head. "Subcommander Hurtaal, Lady Merchanter Saelora'mer, the head of Loraan House." Alyiakal senses the momentary surprise that Hurtaal immediately suppresses.

Hurtaal offers an amused headshake. "Given your reputation and achievements, Alyiakal, I shouldn't be surprised that your consort is so accomplished in her field."

"She's also tied to Mirror Lancers," Alyiakal adds, "through her brother, Overcaptain Hyrsaal at Northpoint. We'll be heading there to see him tomorrow."

"Do you have other family there?"

"No. Northpoint was the last post where I stayed with my father before I went to Kynstaar."

"Then you should stay with Overcaptain Hyrsaal or at the visiting officers' quarters."

"That's very kind of you, Subcommander," says Saelora warmly.

"It's little enough," replies Hurtaal, "given what your consort has done." The subcommander turns to Alyiakal. "I heard that you wiped out something like sixteen companies, and only lost two squads. Is that accurate?"

"Not quite. We lost a squad of lancers and one undercaptain, with a little more than a squad of wounded, but they all survived and are either back or duty or will be soon."

"Might I ask . . . ?"

"We attacked from unexpected places at unexpected times, and we managed to avoid facing their combined forces at any one time."

"I suspect that it wasn't easy, not with only four companies."

"It never is, ser, but I had well-trained lancers and good officers."

"I notice recent scars." The subcommander gestures at his forehead. "You don't get those except in the front."

Alyiakal smiles wryly. "I didn't say it was easy, ser."

"Where are you being reposted, if I might ask?"

"Mirror Lancer headquarters, at least initially. My orders just say to report to the Majer-Commander."

Hurtaal nods slowly. "I wish you well." Then he turns to give Saelora a warm smile. "A definite pleasure to meet you. I've never met a Lady Merchanter who holds her own house before."

"Thank you, Subcommander. It was my pleasure as well."

"I wish you both the best," Hurtaal says, "and I won't keep you."

"Thank you, ser," replies Alyiakal, inclining his head politely.

Neither Saelora nor Alyiakal says much until they're riding to the tailor's shop.

"After you told him about your orders," Saelora offers, "he looked worried."

"I sensed that. I don't think he has the highest opinion of Mirror Lancer headquarters." Then Alyiakal smiles. "But we don't have to worry about where to stay in Northpoint."

"You handled that well, also."

"Sometimes I do think ahead."

Saelora laughs.

LXVII

Late midmorning on eightday, Saelora guides the Loraan House wagon onto a barge moored on the east side of the Great Canal. An upper deck rises to the rear of an open-well deck stacked with barrels, boxes, and pallets. A waist-high bulwark, designed to handle wagons and other items unsuited to being stacked or lashed in place, surrounds the aft section's flat deck.

Alyiakal watches as she follows the loader's directions to the outboard space on the starboard side, clearly left vacant for the wagon. The moment the wagon is blocked in place, the small crew raises the loading gangway, and by the time Saelora has the horse in its designated stall, the firetow begins to pull the barge away from the loading dock.

"They didn't stop long," says Alyiakal as Saelora rejoins him on the teamster's seat.

"They seldom do. That's why I had to make arrangements in advance. We were fortunate they had a space."

"Fortunate . . . or because you're one of the better customers in Vaeyal? Or the only regular one?"

"A little of each," Saelora replies with a smile. "Now . . . since we have plenty of time, will you tell me all the details of how you managed to destroy a force five times your size and slaughter a duke and most of his family?"

"You deserve that, but much of it consists of boring details."

"Solid details aren't boring."

"Spoken like a successful Merchanter," returns Alyiakal. "You already know the first part of what happened, because what I did at Lhaarat led to Taartyn's later attacks on the Mirror Lancers at Lhaarat after I left." From there, Alyiakal fills in all that happened after, beginning with the Jeranyi attacks, while including how he used magery.

He finishes well past noon, and they've long since abandoned the teamster's seat for the shade of the open rear of the wagon.

"I can see why you thought nothing less would stop the Duke," she says. "I can also see why Mirror Lancer headquarters is concerned. You've succeeded too many times where it wasn't possible. Look what happened at Lhaarat after you left, and how you destroyed a Jeranyi fort with no casualties, when it cost another post close to two companies. To any commander with brains, it has to be clear that you're the difference. From what you've told me, Captain-Commander Laartol is quite perceptive."

"I can see why Laartol might want to post me to Isahl or Assyadt to deal with the Jeranyi. I'm a good post commander, but what good can I do in Cyad—except be put on the shelf as an ornament or kept around to get assassinated?"

"I have no idea," Saelora replies, "but I'd wager that Laartol does. He doesn't sound like he'd favor either ornamentation or assassination."

Alyiakal smiles crookedly. "Then I'll just have to see."

"You don't like trusting people you don't really know or can't sense. Most of us know even less about people."

Saelora's quiet comment brings Alyiakal up short. He shakes his head. "You're right. Compared to most people, I don't have much to complain about on that." Then he quickly adds, ruefully, "Or on a number of other things, either."

She offers an amused smile and asks, "Such as?"

"Your love, especially. I doubt that there's another lancer officer as fortunate as I am in that regard . . . well, except possibly Hyrsaal."

"Why do you think I was willing to write you?"

"Because of Hyrsaal. That's another area where I'm fortunate."

"Sometimes, dear man, we need to remember that. We've both worked hard, but without our fortune in other people—and each other—we wouldn't be where we are."

Alyiakal chuckles. "You're kind, but you already knew that. I'm the one who needed the reminder."

She reaches out and takes his hand, squeezing it gently. "We both do."

But I need it more, because you see those parts of life more clearly. He tightens his fingers around hers.

Conversation and catching up, on both their parts, fills the rest of the afternoon and evening.

At roughly a glass past dawn on oneday, the firetow slows, and ahead on the right, Alyiakal sees buildings and dwellings. "I'm guessing that's Midpoint."

As if to reinforce his impression, the loading clerk appears and addresses Saelora. "It'll be about a quint before we're ready to offload, Lady Merchanter." Then he adds, awkwardly, "Majer."

"Thank you," says Saelora.

"She's the important one," adds Alyiakal cheerfully, almost simultaneously with Saelora.

Once the loading clerk hurries off, Alyiakal asks, "Do you have any customers you should visit?"

"There's a small factorage here. They've bought brandy occasionally."

"Would it be wise to stop, early as it is?"

"It can't hurt. Someone's either there or they're not. Besides, it'll be more than a quint before we're off the barge."

Saelora's prediction turns out to be more accurate than the loading clerk's, because more than two quints pass before she guides the wagon across the heavy gangway and onto the whitestone cargo-handling area. From there she turns the wagon north onto the main street of Midpoint, a town that turns out to be smaller than Vaeyal.

Although Alyiakal knows there has to be a road east to the Mirror Lancer post at Westend, and his maps suggest that the road is on the north end of the town, he doesn't immediately see any side streets wide enough to lead to such a road, let alone any that are paved.

"I think that must be the factorage ahead on the right." Saelora nods toward a building.

Alyiakal concentrates on the modest one-story, redbrick establishment with a slightly pitched roof, and a single door flanked by narrow barred windows.

Even before Saelora brings the wagon to a stop in front of the factorage, a man emerges, his eyes taking in the Loraan House wagon and Saelora's Merchanter blues, his expression turning to puzzlement as he sees Alyiakal's uniform.

"He's my consort," says Saelora, "and he's on leave. Since we were coming this way, I thought we should stop and meet you. I don't get here often. Oh . . . I'm Saelora'mer."

"You're the head of Loraan House?"

"For better or worse," says Saelora, handing the lines to Alyiakal, and then climbing down from the wagon.

"Rhynal, Lady Merchanter," replies the factor, pausing for several moments before saying, "Midpoint isn't really on the way to anywhere, except the Accursed Forest and the Mirror Lancer post."

"It's the shortest way to get to Jakaafra," Saelora points out.

"Also the riskiest." Rhynal looks to Alyiakal. "You must know that. Or are you taking command somewhere?"

"No. Along the way, we'll visit Saelora's brother, who's in command at Northpoint, but don't let me keep you two from any business."

Rhynal frowns momentarily, then looks back to Saelora.

"You've purchased some of the Greenberry brandy before," she says, "and we have Crystalflame liquor as well."

The factor shakes his head at the mention of Crystalflame, but says, "I could use a little more of the brandy, especially if I don't have to pay for shipping."

"I do have some in the wagon," admits Saelora, "but there will be a shipping charge, just less of one."

Alyiakal merely listens, and, in the end, the factor purchases a case of the brandy, with a promise to order more near the end of Harvest.

After the factor has paid and received the case of brandy, she asks, "The road to Westend . . . up ahead?"

"You can't miss it. It's the only stone road heading east."

"Thank you."

"Best of fortune."

Saelora climbs back into the teamster's seat, as gracefully as always, and he hands the lines back to her. Once they're well away from the factorage, he asks, "Was the stop worth it?"

"He'll likely buy more. He didn't have any brandy left, and he can't sell what he doesn't have."

"I'd think it would be worth it to have met with him."

"Usually, but not always. Some of the older shopkeepers prefer to deal with Gaaran."

"Leery of powerful women?"

"Aren't most older men?"

"That's certainly true of the Magi'i. I'm not so sure it's true of lancer officers, but then, those who are consorted, from what little I've seen, usually have strong consorts, because they have to take care of everything most of the time. Certainly, neither you nor Catriana are weak in any way, and neither is your mother."

"I hadn't thought of it quite that way," muses Saelora.

After she turns the wagon east on the graystone road, Alyiakal immediately sees a kaystone with the inscription: WESTEND 4 K. "Well, we're on the right road."

"You thought otherwise?"

"I like confirmations cut in stone. There are so few."

"Especially in what you do."

"Merchanting isn't all that certain, either," Alyiakal points out.

"No, but generally Merchanters don't get killed if trading doesn't work out. Sometimes ruined, but usually not killed."

"Except, perhaps, in Cyad?" asks Alyiakal.

"I've heard of it happening. That's another reason Catriana and I want to keep the Dyljani Clan out of Fyrad."

"How are you managing with that?"

"That's why Catriana has expanded so much. Some of the smaller merchants who discovered they owed to the Dyljani were able to sell out to us, and escape with at least something." Saelora pauses. "We couldn't have done all we did without your help." Then she laughs softly. "The fact that we paid in golds left the local trader fronting for the Dyljani thinking another clan or an outland trader was backing us. We've said nothing."

"But because you work with Valtrad . . ."

"No one's sure, and Catriana's good at keeping it that way."

Neither says much more as they leave the scattered houses on the outskirts of Midpoint and ride past small fields and a few woodlots.

Before long, Alyiakal sees the Mirror Lancer post ahead, which isn't fortified, although it's surrounded by a graystone wall two and a half yards high, within which are the stables, barracks, and officers' quarters. He also doesn't sense large numbers of men about, which means that the lancers posted there have already left on patrol.

"The post looks quiet," says Saelora. "Are all the Great Forest posts like this? I mean, except for Southpoint?"

"It's quiet now. Westend and Eastend are about the same. Northpoint is a little larger. Jakaafra is bigger than Midpoint. It used to be about the same size as Vaeyal."

"Used to be?"

"I haven't been here in thirteen years. I don't know what it's like now. Vaeyal's grown even since I met you." Alyiakal chuckles. "But that might just be because of a certain Lady Merchanter."

As Saelora and Alyiakal ride past the wall surrounding the post, he sees no one outside, then looks ahead where, less than half a kay away, the gray paving stones end at the whitestone road paralleling the five-cubit-high whitestone walls enclosing the Great Forest. Just west of the corner where the two walls meet stands a tall stone structure. Alyiakal points. "There's one of the chaos towers that power the wall wards."

"It looks rather plain, except there's something about it."

"A great deal of chaos going from it to the walls," says Alyiakal.

When the wagon reaches the wall road, Saelora turns the wagon northeast. "The ground between the wall and the road is bare."

"It's salted so that it's harder for seeds from the Great Forest to grow." He pauses, then says cheerfully, "Less than a hundred kays to Northpoint."

"A mere three days," replies Saelora dryly.

After a time, she asks, "Does the Great Forest sense you?"

"I don't know. It hasn't reached out to me, but then it never has. I always had to go to it, but I suspect it could sense me if it wanted to."

"Would it tell Adayal that you're coming?"

"The way she wrote indicated that I'd have to at least climb the wall and get inside the wards to let the tawny cougars carry word to her. There's not much point in that until we're close to Northpoint."

"Sometimes . . ." Saelora offers an amused half smile.

"Sometimes?" prompts Alyiakal.

"Sometimes, dear man, the things you take for granted would be impossible for anyone else—except perhaps the Great Forest itself."

"I'm sorry. I don't really take them for granted. I worry about them a great deal. You know that I don't always sleep easily. I've told you about the last time I was in the Forest, and I had all those . . . visions or images, and one of them was how the greatest of the First gathered chaos bits from the sun. I never even thought of that, and I've wondered if that wasn't just a vision, but more."

"But wasn't that First magus an enemy of the Great Forest? So he had to have that ability without getting it from the Forest."

"They were opponents. I'm not sure they were enemies. Opponent or enemy, I can't help worrying, and I wonder, more than a little, if in trying to do things, sooner or later, I'll overreach."

"I'm very glad you think about that." Saelora's voice is firm, but not cold.

"I also worry about the First Magus and the other Magi'i in Cyad. Except for Duke Taartyn, I've never had to deal with really powerful mages."

"You mean one stronger than you?"

Alyiakal nods. "That's a definite possibility."

"Wasn't the Duke powerful? How did you best him?"

"By using order cloaked in chaos."

"You've often said that most Magi'i you've met avoid order. Why wouldn't that work against them?"

"It might, but there's no way to tell."

"Isn't that true of much in life?" Saelora's tone is amusedly acidic.

Alyiakal laughs.

"Now that you realize you're only an extremely talented man, and not one of the Rational Stars . . ."

"We need to talk about more immediately practical matters?"

"Exactly, like what you expect from Adayal or your daughter."

"I don't know what to expect, except that Adayal wouldn't have written if she could have handled her . . . our . . . daughter without writing."

"I'd agree with that, even without having met her. What else?"

"I'm still angry with her for not letting me know. I couldn't have done anything for the first six years, but . . . well . . . I can't help it."

"I understand. There's more of an edge to your voice when you mention her name now."

"Am I wrong to be angry?"

"No, but—"

". . . it won't do any good. I know that, but I had to tell you."

"I understand that, dear man. But we can't change the situation, and you shouldn't deny your daughter, and I wouldn't want you to."

"I do love you."

"I love you."

That's never been more obvious.

"Is there anything else?" asks Saelora.

"I'm guessing that our daughter has healing talents, and possibly . . . more."

Saelora frowns momentarily. "Why do you think that?"

"Because I tried to heal birds and cats and dogs when I wasn't much older than she is, and I have the feeling—I don't know, it's just a feeling—that Adayal doesn't have that skill."

"You didn't mention about your trying to heal animals."

"I'd sort of forgotten. I didn't hurt them, but I'm not sure I helped them that much. It came up with Triamon, and he said healing would be a valuable skill for a lancer officer. That might have been another reason why he didn't think I belonged among the Magi'i."

"I wish I could have met him. He sounds like a remarkable man."

"He was. When I heard he'd vanished, I was . . . upset, but I tried not to think about it too much." He laughs, nervously, then adds, "As you know I often do."

"You're better now, at least with me." After a moment, Saelora asks, "What else do you think about why Adayal contacted you?"

"If our daughter is really unsuited to staying in the Great Forest, who else could protect her?"

"That would be any mother's greatest worry, the fact that her daughter might have to live where she can no longer protect her. So she needs to find someone she can trust who can. You're trustworthy and, even if she doesn't know how much you've developed as a magus, as just a Mirror Lancer majer, you have more power than most. She also knows you're responsible to a fault."

"Even if I had no idea I'd become a father?"

"Isn't that also life?" asks Saelora.

LXVIII

In late afternoon on threeday, Alyiakal sees a house on a low hill off to his left, thinking that it's almost, but not quite, familiar. Then he realizes that there are two outbuildings instead of the one he recalls.

"What's the nod for?" asks Saelora.

"Northpoint can't be that far. That house on the hill is part of the Zhaim dairy farm. My father didn't want me to walk any further than there."

"You *walked* this road?"

"Not all of it. Just a few kays on each side of the post. Father said that there had never been any attacks by Forest creatures within two kays of a post."

"What about brigands?"

"They don't like lancer posts, either."

Slightly more than a quint later, Alyiakal sees Northpoint, located just east of where the whitestone Forest walls meet to form the northernmost point of the Great Forest.

When Saelora slows the wagon to a stop at the open gate, the ranker on guard duty looks at Alyiakal, who senses the man's puzzlement.

"I'm Majer Alyiakal, and we're here to see Overcaptain Hyrsaal. Subcommander Hurtaal is aware that we're visiting. Is the overcaptain here or out on patrol?"

"He got back yesterday, ser."

"Is he in his quarters, do you know?"

"I don't know, ser."

"Then we'll start there. I know where they are."

"I'd better announce you, ser."

"Excellent. We'll follow you."

The ranker hurries down the narrow stone lane and makes his way to the commanding officer's quarters, which don't look any different to Alyiakal. Saelora brings the wagon to a halt, and the two wait while the ranker raps sharply on the door.

After a moment, he announces, "Ser, there's a majer and a Lady Merchanter here to see you."

The door opens, and Alyiakal immediately sees Hyrsaal's flame-red hair as he hurries out toward the wagon. "Saelora! Alyiakal! I never thought I'd see you both here." He stops below the teamster's seat.

"Well," says Alyiakal, "since there was no way you could make the consorting, Saelora thought we should come visit you."

"Finally! It's about time." Abruptly, Hyrsaal turns to the perplexed ranker. "Thank you. You can return to your duties." Then he grins and adds, "Someday, this will be a story you can tell."

Even more perplexed, the ranker says, "Yes, ser," then turns and hurries back toward the gate.

"By the way," Alyiakal says before Hyrsaal can speak, "Subcommander Hurtaal knows we're here, and said we could stay on post."

"Do I want to know how you managed that?"

"I merely gave him the opportunity to give us permission, and he did."

Hyrsaal looks up to Saelora, questioningly.

"He did. I was there."

Hyrsaal shakes his head. "Well, let's get the wagon and the horse settled. I do have a spare room . . ." He breaks off momentarily, then says, "But you already knew that."

"I thought you might," replies Alyiakal, "but the quarters could have changed."

"The spare room is probably better than the visiting officers' quarters, and you'll definitely have more privacy, especially if anyone finds out you're newly consorted. Since you have the subcommander's permission, you can eat in the officers' mess. On the way back from the stable, I'll stop by and make sure the cooks know. While there's a kitchen in the quarters, I rarely use it, and you don't want to eat my cooking."

"Or mine," says Saelora sweetly.

While Alyiakal knows that Saelora cooks better than he does and suspects the same of Hyrsaal, he decides to say nothing.

"Now," says Hyrsaal, "let's take care of the horse and wagon."

Two quints later, after carrying personal gear to Hyrsaal's quarters as well as a case of Greenberry brandy, and then washing up, Alyiakal and Saelora sit down in the small parlor with Hyrsaal.

"How did you get here?" asks Hyrsaal, looking to Saelora.

"We took a canal barge to Midpoint and then the wall road," replies Saelora.

"You didn't have any trouble with the Accursed Forest?" asks Hyrsaal.

"No," replies Alyiakal.

"You're telling me that you traveled from Westend here and encountered no difficulties?"

"Well," Alyiakal smiles ruefully, "I did have to persuade an undercaptain that we'd be perfectly safe. He was most doubtful, but he didn't want to order a majer off the road, which was sensible on his part, since lancers don't have that authority. I did give him my name and told him that Subcommander Hurtaal knew we were traveling to Northpoint to visit you."

Hyrsaal shakes his head. "Before you're done, every officer in the Mirror Lancers will know about you."

"If they don't already," says Saelora.

"Right now," says Alyiakal, "I'm afraid most of the senior officers already know, for better or worse, and most of the junior officers couldn't care less, except for the few handfuls who've served under me."

"I'm sure that a few more junior officers know about you," says Hyrsaal, "if only that you're the post commander who put the Cerlynese in their place." He looks to Saelora. "Have you heard anything recently from Catriana?"

"Other than trading, you mean?" asks Saelora. "The last letter I had said that Haarlt is looking and acting more like his father, and that he charms every woman he sees."

"I never . . ." Hyrsaal breaks off.

"No, you never had eyes for anyone but Catriana," says Saelora, her tone

one of amusement, "but that didn't mean you didn't charm most of the girls in Vaeyal . . . and in a few other towns."

"Sisters . . ." Hyrsaal looks to Alyiakal, with an exaggerated expression of being wronged.

Alyiakal laughs, then says, "I've found your sister most charming . . . and honest."

"You're her consort, not her brother," mock-protests Hyrsaal.

This time, both Saelora and Alyiakal laugh.

Then Saelora says, "I know it's not what you're most interested in, but Catriana managed to buy out another factorage in Fyrad in a way most advantageous for us and for the seller—and it kept the Dyljani from getting a foothold in Fyrad. So far, anyway." Then Saelora relays more tidbits about Haarlt.

Then Hyrsaal turns to Alyiakal. "What do you think your orders to Cyad mean? You only wrote that you were being posted there."

"I don't know. I could be there to debrief the Majer-Commander before being sent to another posting, and that posting could be Isahl or Inividra or some not particularly distinguished destination, or as second-in-command at a large post. Or I could end up writing directives at headquarters."

"They'd be stupid to waste you, but some of the directives are stupid, especially about horseshoes and firelances. We can live with the firelance restrictions here, *if* the men are careful, but those limitations would never work at Inividra. I can't imagine the situation in Pemedra after what you did." Hyrsaal pauses. "You didn't say much in your letter. How bad was it?"

Alyiakal tells Hyrsaal what his lancers did but leaves out most of the order/chaos details, except saying that his firelance bolts blocked Taartyn's magery and resulted in destroying most of the Duke's palace.

"Casualties?" asks Hyrsaal.

"One officer, and twenty lancers dead, roughly a squad wounded."

Hyrsaal shakes his head. "You make it sound like everyone you fight is hapless, but anyone else who fights them takes a beating."

"I do my best to surprise them and strike where they're weakest."

"There's a lot more to it than that, but I won't press, except to say that headquarters is going to want to know how you keep doing the seemingly impossible." Hyrsaal stands. "We probably should head for the mess."

The three leave the quarters, walking down the lane to the officers' mess, part of the main quarters building.

The small chamber holds a table set for four, and a young undercaptain stiffens as he sees the two officers, even as his eyes focus on Saelora.

"As you were," says Alyiakal cheerfully. "I'm not here on an inspection."

"Wraasyn, this is Majer Alyiakal. You may have heard of him. He's an old friend. The Lady Merchanter with him is his consort. She's also my sister, and her name is Saelora."

"I'm pleased to meet you, ser . . . Lady."

"We're happy to meet you," replies Alyiakal.

Hyrsaal gestures toward the table. "We're not being formal."

Once the four are seated, and the wineglasses filled, Hyrsaal lifts his glass. "To our welcome, if unexpected, guests."

The dinner consists of beef slices with brown gravy, mashed potatoes, and boiled quilla, the combination of which makes Alyiakal certain that Saelora, for all her protests, could have done better. *But it's acceptable, and she didn't have to cook it.*

After several moments, Wraasyn asks, "Majer, is it true that you've already commanded three posts?"

"Four, if you count temporary duty closing Luuval. My first command was Oldroad Post on the Kyphran border. Just two companies. My last was Pemedra. I'm headed to Cyad for duties yet to be determined."

Wraasyn nods.

Alyiakal senses his unease and adds, "My consort's achievements are much more impressive. More than a few officers have prevailed in combat. She's one of the few women not born into the Merchanters who's founded her own house, not to mention building a sizable distillery in the process."

"Might I ask how you accomplished that, Lady?" asks Wraasyn.

"I started out as a scrivener, then became an enumerator for a small factorage." Saelora cheerfully summarizes the building of Loraan House.

When she finishes, Hyrsaal chuckles and says, "So we're dining with distinguished company, Wraasyn."

"Where are you from?" Alyiakal asks the undercaptain.

"Ilypsya, ser. My grandsire was a lancer officer."

"So, all of us have lancer forebears," says Saelora warmly. "I suppose that's hardly surprising."

"What's surprising is your rise as a Merchanter," declares Hyrsaal.

The remainder of the conversation at dinner is about why some children follow family occupations and why some don't.

After dinner, Saelora, Alyiakal, and Hyrsaal return to Hyrsaal's quarters and settle into the small parlor.

"I'm flattered that you two came all this way," says Hyrsaal carefully, "but

I suspect I'm not the only reason." He looks to Saelora. "Perhaps some merchanting?"

"I'm not neglecting that," replies Saelora, "and we did bring you some brandy, but there's another reason." She turns to Alyiakal.

"What I'm about to tell you," Alyiakal begins, "is something that Saelora has known from the days when we first met—except for one thing I learned just before being reposted." He outlines his relationship with Adayal and the daughter he never knew he had.

When Alyiakal finishes, Hyrsaal looks stunned. Finally, he asks, "You were how old?"

"Sixteen."

"And she never wrote or said anything?"

"Never. I thought about writing her when I was first at Kynstaar, but there was no way I could, and the only person I could trust in Jakaafra who knew her was a mage who vanished."

"Do you think she's telling the truth?"

"She never lied to me. There were certainly things she didn't reveal, but she also knows that she can't lie to me face-to-face."

"You always know when someone is lying, don't you?"

Alyiakal nods. "I can also tell when they're evading."

Hyrsaal turns back to Saelora. "What do you think about it all?"

"She arranged this trip without telling me," interjects Alyiakal quietly, "and told me we were coming to Jakaafra."

"You got consorted knowing this?" Hyrsaal asks his sister.

"Alyiakal asked me before I could ask him." Saelora smiles. "He was hinting before that, though."

"You two amaze me. Most women . . ."

"I'm not most women. I never have been, and Alyiakal isn't most men."

"You're right about that," says Hyrsaal with a touch of sardonic humor.

"We don't know what will come of this meeting," adds Alyiakal. "My daughter might not care for us at all, or it just may be passing curiosity, but she deserves to meet us." He adds wryly, "For all I know, in the flesh, I might be a great disappointment."

"That's not likely," declares Saelora. "Not if Adayal or your daughter have any sense at all."

"I'd tend to agree with Saelora," says Hyrsaal.

"If you don't mind, we need to take a walk." Alyiakal stands.

"All that sitting on a wagon seat," replies Hyrsaal, "of course."

Alyiakal senses Saelora's momentary confusion and smiles. "You don't have to come, but I'd like your company."

She smiles back. "A walk won't hurt me."

Once Saelora and Alyiakal walk down the stone lane toward the gate in early twilight, she asks, "Why do you need to take a walk?"

"We need to go to the Great Forest and let it know we're here. We can't count on showing up at that Merchanter's shop on Bakers Lane and being able to find her. Not quickly. I know where her dwelling was in the Great Forest, but whether she's still there after thirteen years and a child is problematical, but if she's still there, I'd definitely prefer not to appear unannounced."

"She certainly surprised you."

"True, but this way I hope we'll spend less time waiting. I don't have that much leave, and waiting around is to no one's benefit."

"True."

"Also, I haven't been near the Great Forest in years, not counting that brief encounter outside the walls on my last leave."

"That was a bit of a shock," replies Saelora.

"It might not hurt to have you see it and for me to get reacquainted when Adayal's nowhere near."

"You're being very cautious."

"Whether the Great Forest knows it or not, it contains enough order and chaos to flatten a large part of Cyador. With that much power, it's wise to be cautious."

"Then why has it helped you, or not tried to destroy you?"

"It did try, but only enough to determine . . . something. I think it wants something from me, but what that might be, I have no idea."

Saelora shivers, although the early evening is pleasantly warm. "And you trust it?"

"So far it's been more trustworthy than most Imperial tariff enumerators. And most of the Magi'i I've encountered."

"That's not saying much."

"Agreed," replies Alyiakal dryly.

As they approach the gate guard, Alyiakal says, "We're just taking a walk. We won't be that long."

"Yes, ser."

Alyiakal turns to the southeast, and they walk another hundred yards. Then he asks, "Are you up for climbing the wall?"

"You want to enter the Great Forest *now*?"

Alyiakal shakes his head. "We're just going to sit on the wall. I have to get inside the wards."

"Won't the guard see us?" asks Saelora.

"I've created an illusion behind us that just shows the empty road and the wall."

"You've mention illusions, but you speak of creating one as if it's easy."

"It's easy now, but it took years before I could do it quickly and effectively. Just like it's taken you years to become a formidable Lady Merchanter." He guides her toward the whitestone wall.

Saelora looks up at the massive trees that tower before her, none of which have any limbs crossing the wall.

Alyiakal senses her discomfort. "You can stay at the base of the wall if you want. I'll be just above you."

"The Great Forest . . ." Saelora looks up again. "How can you talk so casually about something so powerful?"

He laughs softly. "What else can I do? A number of those nightmares you've heard about and witnessed were about the Forest. I may talk about it casually, but I still worry. I respect it greatly, and so far, it's respected me." He adds sardonically, "Far more than most of my Mirror Lancer superiors."

"Still . . . I have trouble . . . understanding . . ."

"Why it's communicated with me . . . and given me insights?"

Saelora nods.

"I'm just guessing, but . . . maybe it's lonely."

"Lonely?"

"Who else has it been able to . . . talk to since the first great magus?"

A momentarily puzzled expression crosses Saelora's face. Then she slowly nods. "I never thought about that." After a pause, she asks, "What about Adayal?"

"If she could, I don't think we'd be here. But that's a guess. You can decide for yourself when you meet her." Alyiakal gestures to the wall. "Do you want to join me?"

"It still worries me, but I might never have another chance to look at the Great Forest safely."

In moments, the two sit on the flat whitestones capping the wall, looking into the shadowed green understory of trees and far beneath the arboreal behemoths towering into the darkening greenish-blue sky.

Alyiakal senses the massive power of the Great Forest; its combination of order and chaos and something else beyond. As with his last experience, he discerns the feeling of inquiry, and he replies with the best mental image he can create of Adayal and of a smaller version of her. He follows that with the image of the two tawny cougars who had escorted him from the Forest before, but this time he does his best to convey the image of the cougars bringing Adayal and her daughter to him and Saelora.

For a time, there is no response, although the massive unseen presence does not vanish.

Then, abruptly, he senses something briefly touching Saelora and then withdrawing, followed by an image of a shop before the presence vanishes as if it had never been there.

Alyiakal turns to Saelora, and, as he does, he realizes that early twilight has become late twilight—and that his illusion has vanished, although he doubts the post guard could have seen them anyway.

"Something . . . was here." Saelora frowns. "There's a gray haze around you . . . except there's no light to it. No darkness, either."

"I think you're sensing my shields."

"How can . . ." Saelora breaks off. "Because of the Great Forest?"

"That would be my guess. You're sensing the order/chaos flow around me, but my shields keep you from sensing more."

Abruptly, she shakes her head. "How did it get dark so quickly?"

"It didn't. Somehow, when I've dealt with the Great Forest, time passes more slowly without seeming to. Maybe because the Forest takes longer to convey things. Did you get any feelings from it?"

"Just a feeling of power."

"I suspect you'll be able to sense Magi'i and healers from now on."

"Why do you think so?"

"Because my abilities got stronger after my first meeting with the Forest."

"Why did it do that to me?"

"I don't know, but I'd guess it somehow thinks that will benefit the Great Forest . . . or perhaps it wants us together. Or maybe it respects your respect."

"That's . . . frightening."

"It is," Alyiakal agrees. "Why do you think I've had nightmares where the Forest plays a part?"

After several moments, Saelora asks, "Did you learn anything?"

"I got the image of a shop. I'd wager that it's the one on Bakers Lane. All we can do is go there tomorrow and see."

"I never thought . . ."

"Neither did I when I really met with the Great Forest for the first time," replies Alyiakal, adding wryly, "but I do think we should climb down and walk back to the post."

LXIX

Alyiakal and Saelora wake early on fourday, and she looks at him. "I still sense that grayness around you."

"I didn't think it would go away. Whatever I've gotten from the Great Forest hasn't," he says dryly. "Try not to look surprised if you sense order/chaos flows around Hyrsaal."

"You think I will?"

"Perhaps, but you'll have to see."

Little more than a quint later, the two are in the parlor waiting for Hyrsaal.

When Hyrsaal appears, Saelora gives the smallest of nods to Alyiakal as Hyrsaal says, "Good morning. I heard you two come in last night, but I was tied up reviewing squad leader reports, and by the time I finished I didn't want to disturb you."

"The walk took longer than we thought," says Alyiakal, "but you looked busy when we got back. Since we surprised you by arriving unexpectedly, I thought you might have some pressing reports."

"I should have done them earlier, but I admit I didn't expect company, especially you two. Still, I'm so glad you came. What are your plans for the day?"

"Have breakfast, and see if we can meet with Adayal," replies Alyiakal.

Hyrsaal nods. "I told the duty ostler that you could have two mounts for the day. That way you won't have to use the wagon."

"That's very thoughtful of you," declares Saelora. "You're sure it's not against some regulation?"

"All officers on leave are allowed to use mounts, as available. Your mounts will be logged out that way. Distinguished majers and heads of trading house certainly fit the criteria." Hyrsaal grins.

Saelora shakes her head.

"I have another question, with greater imposition," says Alyiakal.

"Go ahead," says Hyrsaal cheerfully.

"If . . . if my daughter wants to come to Vaeyal with us for a time, is there any possibility that I can ride a horse from here to Geliendra and leave it there at the post stables?"

Hyrsaal frowns for a moment, then says, "I don't see why not. Longer loans of mounts are allowed, and sometimes mounts go lame and are switched. We have some spares."

"That will make matters much easier, *if* it comes to that. I don't know that it will."

Hyrsaal shakes his head and turns to his sister. "That's why he's a majer and I'm an overcaptain. He's thinking about and arranging possibilities before he knows the outcome."

"That's also why she's a Lady Merchanter," replies Alyiakal. "She does exactly the same thing in trading."

"I'm definitely outmatched," says Hyrsaal.

"Hardly," declares Saelora. "You consorted Catriana when no one but you knew what a gem she is."

"I think it's time to head for the officers' mess," says Hyrsaal, grinning again as he walks toward the door.

Breakfast with Hyrsaal and Wraasyn is pleasant and quick, and before long, Hyrsaal escorts Alyiakal and Saelora to the stable. Both mounts are saddled, but Alyiakal checks both just to make sure the girth straps are tight enough before he and Saelora lead the horses out and mount up.

"Enjoy yourselves if you can," says Hyrsaal.

"We'll do our best," replies Alyiakal wryly.

Once Alyiakal and Saelora ride out past the gate, she eases closer and says, "I could sense the flows around both Hyrsaal and Wraasyn, but how do you know what they mean?"

"A lot of practice," replies Alyiakal. "When the flows are smooth, that usually means no one's excited or upset. Right now, your other senses are likely more reliable, but you'll sense more and learn more every day."

"I wish this had happened earlier, well before we meet Adayal. What does she look like?"

"When I knew her, she had black hair and black eyes. She was about the same size as Catriana."

"Petite, in other words."

"As I recall." Alyiakal offers an embarrassed smile. "When I first met her,

I was awed by the fact that she could walk the Great Forest. Then . . . well . . . I had other things on my mind."

"And elsewhere," replies Saelora with an amused smile. "I'm just glad that your first look at me was in my eyes."

"I was older and at least a little wiser." *And we'd been writing for years.*

"More than a little. Hyrsaal was likely just as bad at sixteen."

Although Alyiakal doubts that, since Hyrsaal grew up with sisters, he decides not to comment more on his youthful blindness.

They don't encounter anyone, either riding, on foot, or with a cart, until they're on the short side road to Jakaafra. No one pays much attention to Alyiakal, but several men and women look intently at Saelora, no doubt because Lady Merchanters are very rare, especially riding.

While Jakaafra hasn't changed much, Alyiakal never paid much attention to street names, and since there are no signs, they ride past Bakers Lane once before he asks an older woman.

They turn back and start up the lane, and almost immediately, Alyiakal points to a cabinetmaker's shop. "That's the shop."

"The image from the Great Forest?" asks Saelora quietly.

"It's exactly the same."

"That's . . . eerie."

"You can see why I'm careful with the Great Forest."

"I can, especially now."

The two tie their mounts at the railing beside the door, and Alyiakal raps, not wanting to barge in, even if most customers might, early as it is. Within the building, he can already sense two people embodying the mixture of order and chaos reflective of the Great Forest, one of whom is definitely younger.

An older white-haired man opens the door. "Majer Alyiakal?"

Alyiakal nods.

"Adayal's in the showroom. She thought you'd be early. I'm Krimaan."

"Thank you for allowing her to use your address."

"It was my pleasure. She's my late older brother's daughter." Krimaan gestures to his left.

She never mentioned that, but there was a lot she never mentioned, and you never asked. Alyiakal leads the way to the small showroom.

Adayal turns from the small side window and stands waiting, wearing a simple forest-green tunic with matching trousers, but when he enters and looks at her, she inadvertently steps back. She appears much as he recalls, for a moment, until he sees beyond the illusion. She is far older than he had thought, and likely had been as well when he first met her, although her hair and eyes remain jet black. She manifests an integrated order and chaos balance that he has never seen outside the Great Forest. Yet that balance also seems unbalanced, though he cannot immediately discern why.

Adayal does not address Alyiakal but turns to Saelora. “I’m Adayal. I take it that you’re Alyiakal’s consort?”

“I am.”

“Saelora’s also the head of Loraan House, a substantial trading house that she founded,” says Alyiakal, adding, “This was the soonest we could get here. I see you brought our daughter but wanted to talk to us first.”

Adayal’s smile is both sad and wry. “You’ve become far more powerful than I ever imagined. The Forest tried to warn me.”

“We only want to do what’s best for her.” Alyiakal pauses, sensing that Saelora’s attention is on Adayal. “I didn’t know, and I have the feeling you never meant to tell me. Might we know her name?”

“You weren’t meant to know about her. Her name is Saryalth.”

“Saryalth,” says Saelora. “That’s lovely. I imagine she is as well.”

Adayal again turns to Saelora. “I was going to ask your feelings, but I don’t need to, do I?”

“No. You can sense what I feel, and I can sense enough to know what you feel.”

“How?” asks Adayal.

“Call it a gift from the Great Forest, although some would call it a curse.” After a pause, Saelora adds, “I imagine it’s for Saryalth’s sake.”

For the first time, Adayal looks stunned.

“It’s recent,” adds Saelora, “from when the Great Forest learned we were seeking you and Saryalth. The Forest wants her protected.”

“I didn’t expect . . .”

“Neither did we,” answers Alyiakal, waiting. After several moments, he asks, “Did you want this meeting, or did Saryalth?”

“She wanted to meet her father, and I decided it was necessary. I’ll get her now. There’s no point in waiting.” Adayal turns and leaves the showroom, returning with Saryalth within moments.

Saryalth is several digits taller than her mother, with broader shoulders and eyes of the same intense green as Alyiakal’s, as well as the silver hair that suggests the real but unrecognized elthage background of her parents. Her forest-green garb is similar to her mother’s, if more loosely fitting.

Adayal makes the introductions. "Your father, Majer Alyiakal, and his consort, the Lady Merchanter Saelora."

Saryalth looks straight at her father.

Alyiakal meets that piercing gaze and smiles gently. "You're most impressive, Saryalth, not that I thought otherwise."

"You're not what I expected," Saryalth replies. "You're more impressive, and you feel a little like the Great Forest."

"That's because the Great Forest has shared some of what it is with me. What would you like from us?" asks Alyiakal.

"I'd like to spend a little time with you."

"A little time is possible," replies Alyiakal, "but I have to travel to report to Mirror Lancer headquarters starting on the fifth sevenday of Harvest. Since our home is in Vaeyal, near Geliendra, we cannot stay here for more than a few days." Alyiakal looks to Adayal.

She turns to her daughter. "If you would like to spend more time with your father and Saelora, I can meet you in Geliendra and we can travel back through the Great Forest."

"That's a long trip for you," says Alyiakal.

"It's easier for us than for you, and you've been thoughtful enough to come all the way here on short notice."

Alyiakal looks to his daughter. "It's six days by wagon back to Vaeyal, and you'll be quite close to us all that time."

Saryalth says nothing for several moments. "After we get to Vaeyal, I'd like one eightday." She looks to Saelora.

"You can have as much time with your father as he has, if you wish. It will be slightly less than an eightday."

Alyiakal notes Adayal's surprise at Saelora's genuineness.

Adayal says quietly, "You're kind, but I should have known that. Thank you." Her eyes go to Saryalth.

"We have no real place for Saryalth tonight," says Alyiakal, "but we can meet you here early tomorrow morning and depart then. We'll need to make some arrangements." He looks back to Saryalth. "You can spend today with us, though, if you like. Or we can stay here and talk for a while."

Adayal says quietly, "If she's to be gone for almost two eightdays, we'll need the rest of the day to prepare." She looks to Saryalth. "Do you have any questions for your father or Saelora?"

"Where will I stay?"

"In our house," says Saelora. "You'll have a choice. There's a guest suite in the building next to the house, or there's a small room in the house you can have to yourself."

"Are there any forests nearby?"

"There are woods, and a swamp nearby. Also, there's the Great Canal."

"If you get lonely for the Great Forest," adds Alyiakal, "we can ride there. It takes about two glasses."

"Your father can keep you perfectly safe in the Great Forest," says Adayal.

"I can tell that," declares Saryalth politely, but firmly, before asking Alyiakal, "Will you teach me more about magery?"

"I can teach you how to learn the basic skills you don't already know. How well you master them depends on you."

"What about healing?"

"I can teach you the basics of healing. We won't have time for more than that."

After another half quint of questions, Adayal says, "Saryalth, if you want to be ready to depart tomorrow, we should leave now and get together what you'll need."

"Yes, Mother." Saryalth inclines her head to Saelora. "Thank you for having me. I'll try not to be too much of a bother."

"You won't be a bother," replies Saelora, adding with a warm smile, "A challenge, perhaps, but not a bother."

Saelora's reply startles Saryalth, but then she says, "You're honest."

"She always has been," Alyiakal adds fondly.

"Thank you both," declares Adayal. "Tomorrow about this time?"

"We'll be here," says Saelora.

Adayal and Saryalth leave the showroom immediately. Alyiakal and Saelora follow, but Alyiakal stops and says to Krimaan, "Thank you."

"You're welcome, Majer."

Once Alyiakal and Saelora leave the shop, she says, "We're going to have our hands full. I'm guessing, but I get the sense that she's almost as strong as her mother in her abilities with order and chaos."

"In raw power, she may be stronger. For her own sake, I hope I can train some of that ability while she's with us."

"Will that be dangerous?"

"Not nearly so dangerous as not training her."

Saelora laughs wryly. "I was afraid you'd say something like that. We also need to get some provisions for the trip home, and we might as well do that while we're in town."

LXX

Alyiakal knows that Saelora is mulling over more than a few things while they shop for provisions, but he doesn't press, knowing she'll speak when she's ready, and if she doesn't, in time, he'll ask.

After they've obtained what they can from the shops in Jakaafra and start the ride back to Northpoint, Saelora says, "I've been thinking . . ."

"About what in particular?"

"Adayal uses an illusion to look younger, doesn't she?"

"You sensed that?" *So quickly?* But that's not a question he wants to verbalize.

Saelora nods. "I could also sense that she's *much* older than you."

"I knew she was older, but not as much as I realized today."

"How much older, do you think?"

"It could be as much as twenty years," replies Alyiakal.

"Closer to thirty. She was desperate for a child when she seduced you, I'd guess."

"I did figure that out." Alyiakal pauses, thinking about the strangeness of the balance of order and chaos he'd sensed in Adayal. *Could she be somehow drawing order from the Great Forest to keep that balance?* "Do you think she's not well, or worried that she won't be and wants to make sure Saryalth has a protector?"

"I couldn't tell, but why else would she write after all these years?"

"She told the truth when she said Saryalth wanted the meeting."

"But she never answered the question about whether *she* wanted the meeting," Saelora points out.

"You're right," says Alyiakal ruefully.

"From what little I've seen and what you've said, she's someone who tells the truth, but not always all of it."

"Looking back, that's obvious," Alyiakal admits.

"You see that with other people," says Saelora gently.

"I suppose I don't like to admit how gullible I was."

"How innocent as well. She played on that."

Rather well . . . but . . . "I think she was desperate."

"I believe I said that," replies Saelora with a touch of humor. "It could be that she's even older than we think, and she wanted a child. Any other man in Jakaafra or at Northpoint would have created problems. You were perfect. You have order/chaos talents that she wanted the child to have. You were fairly inexperienced—"

"*Completely* inexperienced in terms of women," interjects Alyiakal.

". . . and you were headed for Kynstaar and becoming a Mirror Lancer officer. You'd never even know."

"Until something came up," says Alyiakal. "If it's all Saryalth's doing, we'll know that before she returns to the Great Forest."

"She may think it is," replies Saelora.

"You'll know the difference," declares Alyiakal. "I have no doubt about that."

Saelora just smiles.

When the two return to Northpoint, they unsaddle and stall the horses, then load the various stores in the Loraan House wagon before returning to Hyrsaal's quarters, where they settle in the parlor and talk over the details of the return trip to Vaeyal and other matters.

When Hyrsaal enters the quarters late in the day, he asks, "Did you meet with Adayal and your daughter? How did it go?"

"We did," replies Alyiakal. "Her name is Saryalth."

"And she's definitely Alyiakal's daughter," adds Saelora. "She's more like him than her mother, and she has his eyes."

"She also has the elthage silver hair," says Alyiakal.

"That means . . ." begins Hyrsaal.

"Why do you think I'm such a good field healer?" asks Alyiakal. "The Captain-Commander already knows that, and so do the Magi'i." *Not that any of them like it.* "As long as they think all I can do is heal, I'm not a problem."

"But you once said there weren't any mages in your family," says Hyrsaal in a puzzled tone.

"I was wrong. I found out a year or so ago that my great-aunt, the one I stayed with after Mother died, was a healer. Father never told me. Perhaps he didn't know."

"Or didn't want you to," counters Hyrsaal.

Alyiakal shakes his head. "I don't think so. He had me tutored by a mage before I went to Kynstaar. The mage taught me the basics of healing, and Father knew that. There would have been no reason not to mention that my great-aunt was a healer."

"So what are you going to do about your daughter?"

"She's coming back to Vaeyal with us, and she'll stay an eightday before we return her to her mother in Geliendra. I will need to borrow a mount, if that's still possible."

"Of course. No one can fault a majer riding a mount from one post to another under the same command." Hyrsaal clears his throat. "What are you going to tell everyone in Vaeyal?"

"That she's our daughter," says Saelora.

"No," declares Alyiakal. "That will reflect badly on you. She's my daughter, a daughter I didn't even know I had, and she's visiting us. We'll leave it at that."

"Mother will be beside herself," Hyrsaal points out.

"She might not be," says Saelora. "Adayal was much older and took advantage of Alyiakal, and he never knew he had a daughter. Now he's doing the right thing."

"She'll want to know why you consorted when you knew that," Hyrsaal points out.

"One reason is because Alyiakal let me know about Saryalth immediately. I already knew about Adayal. He's never misled me or hidden anything."

"Except I didn't tell you everything until after we met in person."

"Not many men can say that." Hyrsaal laughs softly, adding, "Not truthfully, anyway."

"Why do you think I consorted him?" asks Saelora, adding with a smile, "Or why Catriana waited to consort you?"

Hyrsaal winces, then says, "Now that you've analyzed us both, after I wash up, we ought to head to the officers' mess, but no talk about Adayal or Saryalth, I promise."

Both Alyiakal and Saelora nod.

LXXI

Immediately after breakfast on fiveday, Alyiakal and Saelora ready the wagon, right after Hyrsaal has handed Alyiakal the letter authorizing him to turn over the roan gelding to the Mirror Lancer supply officer at Southpoint.

Standing beside the gelding, Alyiakal turns to Hyrsaal. "Thank you for everything."

"It was more than a pleasure to have you here, and especially to learn you two are consorted. I've worried about that for years."

"So have I," admits Alyiakal.

"I hope all goes well with Saryalth as well."

"Thank you." Saelora grins and adds, "Effectively you're her uncle."

"I'm too young to be her uncle," protests Hyrsaal.

"I'm too young to be her father," returns Alyiakal, "but here we are."

Hyrsaal laughs, shaking his head as he does.

Saelora looks hard at her brother. "Just take care."

"I always do."

"Then take more care," she replies.

Alyiakal mounts. "Thank you, again."

"Have a good journey," replies Hyrsaal as Saelora eases the wagon forward.

When the two are away from Northpoint and on the road to Jakaafra and Alyiakal is riding beside the wagon, he says, "I'm not sure I'm ready for this."

"Neither of us is, dear man. That doesn't matter. We need to learn about Saryalth, and she needs to learn about us. If anything ever happens to her mother, we'll be all she has. Her great-uncle isn't young. Better we know something, and that she knows about us and how to reach us, just in case. You'll do fine. You seem to handle young lancers well."

"I have the feeling that handling young women is rather harder."

Saelora looks at him and grins. "That's a good start."

Alyiakal chuckles ruefully.

Close to three quints later, when Saelora brings the wagon to a halt outside Krimaan's cabinetry shop, Alyiakal dismounts and ties the roan to the hitching rail. He's barely finished when Adayal and Saryalth appear. Saryalth wears a tan long-sleeved shirt and brown trousers and carries a small pack.

Alyiakal concentrates on his daughter. Saryalth looks and feels composed, possibly a little worried and a little excited. He doesn't detect shields, but she is still young. He momentarily shifts his attention to Adayal, whose shields are close to nonexistent. Then he says, "Good morning, Saryalth. Are you ready for a long trip?"

"I hope so." Her smile is shy.

"You'll be close to the Great Forest for most of the journey. That might help." Then Alyiakal turns to Adayal. "It will take six days to reach Vaeyal. An eightday after that will be the fifth threeday of Harvest."

"Then that's when I'll be in Geliendra," says Adayal.

"Have you been to Geliendra?" asks Alyiakal. "It's quite a bit larger than Jakaafra."

"No."

"The north gates of Southpoint Post are only about a quarter kay from the southern point of the Great Forest walls," says Alyiakal, "but the gates are restricted to Mirror Lancers. We could meet you under the northwest corner of the post walls. From there it wouldn't be far to the Forest. Would you like to meet two glasses before sunset?" Alyiakal asks the last question because it would likely be easier for Adayal and Saryalth to enter the Great Forest undetected in low light or darkness, but he also doesn't want Saelora driving back to Vaeyal in darkness.

"That would be acceptable."

"One other thing." Alyiakal hands Adayal a card with the address and location of Loraan House. "If you cannot make it, Saryalth will be with Saelora in Vaeyal. This is also the best place to write to make other arrangements or to contact us for any reason."

"I'm almost always available," says Saelora. "Alyiakal obviously isn't. I also have family there, who can be helpful."

"I'll be at the post walls on the fifth threeday of Harvest."

The sense of certainty behind Adayal's words gives Alyiakal relief. "I know you will be, but it's best to be prepared for the unexpected. This way, you and Saryalth will always have a way to get in touch with me."

"You're being thoughtful, again." Adayal's smile is faint and slightly sad.

This worries Alyiakal, as well, but he has sensed her determination to be at Geliendra. He is about to speak, when Adayal shakes her head, and says to Saryalth, "Be good for your father, and listen to both him and Saelora. They can help you learn a great deal that I cannot teach you."

While Alyiakal remains worried, all he says to Saryalth is, "Let me put your pack in the wagon while you join Saelora on the teamster's seat."

"Thank you." Saryalth hands the pack to her father.

Alyiakal takes the pack and walks to the rear of the wagon.

Adayal follows and asks quietly, "You don't have any other children, do you?"

"No, but you had to know that," replies Alyiakal as he opens the rear doors and places the pack inside. "We've been together for years but only consorted recently. Saelora's known about you from the first."

"Give Saryalth the same consideration, if you would."

"How could I not?"

"Thank you." Adayal turns and walks up the right side of the wagon and stops below where Saryalth sits. "I'll see you in a little less than two eightdays."

"Promise?"

"I promise. Be good."

As Alyiakal turns toward his mount, he notices that Saryalth sits perfectly in the middle of the right side of the teamster's bench, closer neither to Saelora nor to the outside edge of the seat.

Adayal walks to the steps of the shop and stops, watching as Alyiakal unties the roan and mounts, then accompanies the wagon down the lane toward the street that leads to the Great Forest.

Because Alyiakal senses a trace of what might be sadness in Saryalth as well as a bit of concern, he rides beside his daughter.

After a time, once the three are on the whitestone road headed southwest, Saryalth asks, "What's in the wagon?"

"Not much," answers Saelora. "A half a case of the brandy Loraan House sells, provisions and water, clothes, and some pads and blankets to sleep on."

"That's all?" asks Saryalth.

"The wagon is also a cleaner and safer place to sleep," says Saelora, "at least with Alyiakal here."

"You sense what I feel, don't you?" Saryalth asks Saelora. "Like Mother?"

"I'm not as good as your mother. Alyiakal is far better at that than I am. You can sense feelings as well, can't you?"

"Not really," replies Saryalth. "I can sense what flows around people, sort of, but except when people are really happy or really angry, it's hard to tell what the flows mean. With the animals in the Forest, it's easier."

"I imagine their feelings are simpler. What can you sense about Alyiakal?"

"Just a gray wall."

"Those are his shields."

"He has more than one?" asks Saryalth.

"Two, actually," interjects Alyiakal. "That's what you should have when you're older."

For several moments, Saryalth is quiet.

Then Saelora asks, "Do you live in the Great Forest most of the time?"

"Except when I have my lessons with Great-Uncle Krimaan or when we visit him. Or when we go to the market square. That's not always comfortable. People move away from us."

They always treated your mother that way. "Do you go other places outside the Great Forest?" asks Alyiakal.

"More often, we trade at steads where Mother knows the people. They're nicer."

"I've found that when I trade often with people," says Saelora, "they're nicer because they get to know me, and I get to know them."

Saryalth doesn't speak for a while, then asks, "You're a majer. You must have been in some battles?"

"A few. That's what Mirror Lancers do. We stop people who want to take things from people or hurt them. Sometimes, that means we fight."

"I know *that.* Have you fought much?"

"More than most officers," Saelora interjects. "Alyiakal is a majer because he's been effective when and where other officers weren't."

"When you've killed people," asks Saryalth, "do you feel it?"

"Yes. It's a bitter cold black mist that chills my bones."

"Like when a red deer or a cougar dies."

"It's stronger than that."

Surprisingly, Saryalth shivers, but says nothing for a moment. "How can you keep doing it?"

"Because the people we fight have killed others and would keep doing so if they aren't stopped."

Again, Saryalth is silent.

Saelora says gently, "Your father isn't heartless or cruel. He has nightmares about it. Often. But more people would die without what he does."

"Like when the Great Forest calls the lightning to kill a rogue stun lizard?"

"I've never seen that," says Alyiakal, "but I'd say it's similar."

"Mother said you're the most powerful mage she's ever seen."

"Maybe," replies Alyiakal with an amused laugh, "but there are powerful mages in Cyad. They could be stronger than I am. That's something I'll find out after I get there."

"You haven't been to Cyad before?" asks Saryalth.

"No. Most Mirror Lancers and most lancer officers aren't ever posted in Cyad, only the most senior officers. There's no need for us there. Where we're needed most is along the borders or in port cities away from Cyad where there's trading and in places where there are smugglers."

"Then why are you going to Cyad?"

Alyiakal laughs wryly. "No one's told me. I think Mirror Lancer headquarters wants to know why the Duke of Cerlyn attacked our borders and how my force at Pemedra managed to defeat all his forces."

"He's leaving out quite a bit, Saryalth," says Saelora. "He had four companies, and the Duke had sixteen or seventeen and two strong mages. You also might notice that your father has a few scars on his forehead, and others elsewhere on his body. He's come close to dying more than once."

After several moments, Saryalth asks, "Do senior officers in headquarters think you're lying?"

"No," replies Alyiakal. "They know what happened. They likely want to know more about how we managed it."

Saryalth frowns. "You're not telling me everything."

"No, I'm not, but everything I've said is true, so far as I've been able to find out."

"When will you tell me more?"

"When you've learned more about the world beyond the Great Forest, and about who rules it and how they rule it."

"How can I learn more—"

"Saryalth," interjects Saelora, "you have a lot to learn, but we'll both teach you what we can while you're with us. Did you learn everything about the Great Forest all at once?"

"No." Saryalth pauses. "When can I start learning more?"

Saelora laughs softly. "You already are. Why don't I start by telling you about how I became a Merchanter? We'll start there because trading touches everything outside the Great Forest. Then your father can tell you how he grew up and became a Mirror Lancer officer."

As Saelora begins to talk, Alyiakal extends his perceptions to the left, toward the whitestone walls surrounding the Great Forest, but can sense only the power of the Forest, without any specifics, which is as it usually has been.

Saryalth seems to enjoy what Saelora has to say, occasionally asking questions, about why Saelora became an apprentice scrivener and why she decided to write Alyiakal.

To that question, Saelora replies, "My brother Hyrsaal became friends with Alyiakal when they were in training at Kynstaar, and since Alyiakal had little family, my brother said that your father would appreciate a letter. So I wrote him."

"And I wrote her back," adds Alyiakal, "and we exchanged letters for years before we met."

Later, Saryalth asks, "Why did Factor Vassyl help you so much?"

"Partly because I helped him make the factorage more successful and partly because he regarded me as a daughter."

"Didn't he have other children?"

"His son and his consort died of a flux, and his daughter didn't like factoring. She consorted a smallholder. After I'd been working with Vassyl for a while, Elinjya and I became friends, partly because her father had someone to help him, and she didn't have to worry about not wanting to work at the factorage."

Saryalth pauses, then says, "Will you ever become friends with Mother?"

"Your mother and I don't live very close to each other, and we're very different," says Saelora cautiously.

"You don't look at all alike," replies Saryalth, "but you don't feel that different."

Alyiakal stiffens. He's never really thought of comparing Saelora and Adayal. *Are they similar in some ways, or is that just what Saryalth wants to believe . . . or is she just sensing what the Great Forest gave Saelora?*

He's still pondering that sometime later when Saryalth asks, "Couldn't my father have healed Vassyl?"

"Alyiakal tried very hard, but the best he could do was to make Vassyl more comfortable for a while."

"Some chaos-sicknesses, even the greatest of healers can't heal," adds Alyiakal. "I spent a little time working as an apprentice healer under one of the greatest healers in Cyador, and she couldn't keep a lancer from dying when he had the same kind of illness as Vassyl."

Saelora talks some, listens a great deal, and gives Saryalth time to think, look around, and comment on what she sees.

Later, in the early afternoon, Saelora finishes and says to Saryalth, "That's enough about me, perhaps too much. Tomorrow, you can hear what your father can tell you. For the rest of the afternoon, we need to hear about you."

"I haven't done anything," protests Saryalth.

"You've done more than you think," replies Alyiakal, "and you're the best person to tell us about you."

Saryalth flushes slightly.

"What's the most beautiful thing you've seen in the Great Forest?" asks Saelora.

Saryalth frowns. "I don't know. I've seen a cougar cub, and she's beautiful. But so is a pond turtle's shell in the sun. Or a tree lily . . ."

Alyiakal just listens.

Later, after Saryalth has gone to bed in the wagon, and Alyiakal has set wards around their de facto campsite in a small grove west of the whitestone road, Saelora says quietly, "You didn't say much today."

"I liked your approach. I also thought it would be better if she heard from you first. She's still wary."

"She'll be wary for some time, possibly the whole time she's with us."

"That's hardly surprising," says Alyiakal.

"When you did talk, you were rather honest and direct."

"Adayal asked me to be honest with her."

"It's probably better for her. I'm not sure it is for you. She's awfully young and hasn't been that exposed to much outside of the Great Forest."

"I thought about that. Even if she can't sense behind my shields, she reads us fairly well, and I'm not comfortable with half-truths."

"Oh?" Saelora infuses the single word with sardonic doubt.

"I meant with you, and I don't want to start off that way with her. I'm more comfortable in using half-truths with senior officers because often I don't even get that from them, and I often can't tell lancers under me the whole truth for a number of reasons."

"Like revealing what you really are?"

"Partly . . . and partly because they'd have trouble believing matters will work the way I've planned them, and doubt erodes trust. Since what I've planned has usually worked, if not always as planned, if what I have told them is true and matters work out, they trust me more in the future."

"Something's still bothering you."

"Adayal. As you said, she's much older than I thought, and there's a sadness and worry there. I also think she manipulated Saryalth to be curious about me. After all, she made it quite clear years ago that we had totally separate lives to live."

"That worries me, too."

"She was absolutely firm that she'll meet us in Geliendra."

"Do you think . . ." Saelora pauses, then continues, "do you think that she sees something in the future?"

"I thought about that. If the Great Forest foresees the future, it might well have shown her something disturbing, like the images the Forest showed me." Even before Alyiakal finishes, he can sense Saelora's apprehension and fear, and he adds, "I could be wrong, but I don't think it's about me. She might feel regret and want Saryalth to know something about me, but it just didn't *feel* that way." Alyiakal offers a short sardonic laugh. "I could be rationalizing. I don't think so, but . . ." He pauses. "We always find ways to deceive ourselves."

"That's true, but I'm glad you're considering it. Maybe that way, you won't carry things as far as you did in Cerlyn in the future. Now you have two people to think about, and if something happens to Adayal, who will Saryalth have?"

Right now, I'm more worried about who you might have.

Saelora shakes her head. "I'd survive. It might be harder on Saryalth."

"Am I that obvious?" asks Alyiakal, chagrined.

"Only to me, dear man." She reaches out and takes his hand. "And I am glad you feel that way."

"I suppose we should get some sleep."

"We should, but when we get home, she'll be in her own room."

For that, Alyiakal has to admit, he will be grateful.

LXXII

Sixday morning is much like fiveday, with Alyiakal riding beside the wagon, alternating sides every half glass or so. Saryalth asks fewer questions of Alyiakal than she had of Saelora, and Saelora often asks follow-up questions when she senses that Saryalth is puzzled or reluctant.

In late midmorning, Alyiakal tells Saryalth about his first meeting with the Great Forest, and the images presented by the Forest, from that of the first great magus to the future images of a time when the white walls have been overgrown. When he finishes, he waits.

"Do you think those images are real?"

"Except for the time when the Forest overgrows the walls, which has to be in the future, the other events have already taken place," replies Alyiakal. "So I'd say they're real. The Forest showed me ways to use order and chaos more effectively . . . and a few other things I didn't know before."

"What are those?" Saryalth's voice sharpens.

"When you have strong shields, I'll show you. They're too dangerous if you don't."

"How strong is that?"

"Strong enough to stop chaos bolts and arrows," replies Alyiakal.

Saryalth turns to Saelora. "Are his shields *that* strong?"

"They're even stronger."

"Have you seen that?"

"I saw an arrow shatter against his shields."

"You saw him in a battle?"

Saelora shakes her head. "Brigands. Alyiakal was escorting the wagon. Four brigands attacked us."

Saryalth turns to Alyiakal. "What happened?"

"I killed all four. Brigands who'd kill people don't deserve to live."

Saryalth looks to Saelora, who nods.

After several moments, Saryalth says, quietly, "Mother said I'd be safe with you."

"And you weren't so sure?" asks Saelora.

"I wondered," admits Saryalth.

"I never worry when I'm with Alyiakal," says Saelora.

Saryalth nods, then asks Alyiakal, "Why did the Great Forest show you those images?"

"I don't know. Perhaps because I respect it, or because it feels I can help it in some way."

Saryalth frowns, shifting her weight on the teamster's seat. "Have you been in the Great Forest since then?"

"Twice. The last time was the day before we came to meet you. We can talk about that later." Alyiakal changes the subject and talks about how he finally met Saelora.

By the end of sixday, Saryalth has heard more than enough about Alyiakal and Saelora, and on sevenday, riding beside the wagon, he says to Saryalth, "Now we're going to see what you can do with order and chaos."

"Really?"

Neither Saelora nor Alyiakal can miss the enthusiasm in the young woman's voice, and they exchange amused glances.

"It's going to be work, and some of it won't be easy. First, we'll do some exercises to see what you can do. In a few moments, I'm going to ask you to close your eyes, and I'll create two small balls of chaos in front of you. You're to keep your eyes closed and point to the one that holds more chaos." Alyiakal pauses. "Are you ready?"

Saryalth nods.

"Then close your eyes."

When Saryalth does, Alyiakal creates two small balls of chaos, one twice the size of the other, and places them in the air a yard in front of his daughter. "Point to the one with more chaos."

She points to the one on the left.

"Good." Alyiakal compresses the chaos in the larger ball until it's half the size of the chaos in the other, then switches their positions. "Now, which one has more chaos?"

"The one on the right is smaller, but it has more chaos."

"Excellent! I couldn't tell that at your age. You can open your eyes now." Alyiakal next gathers some free order and creates two small balls, both of order and chaos, but containing differing amounts of each. Again, he suspends them in front of Saryalth. "Which one has more order?"

"The one on the left."

"That's right." Alyiakal suspends a tiny bit of chaos before Saryalth. "Can you push this away from you, just by thinking about it?"

"I don't know. I've never tried."

Alyiakal nods and lets the chaos disperse, instead gathering a small ball of free order. "Try it with this."

Saryalth concentrates.

Alyiakal can sense a certain amount of pressure, but not enough to move the order. "Stop for a moment. Take a deep breath."

After several breaths, he says, "This time I'm going to put the tiniest bit of order in front of you. Can you sense it?"

"Yes."

"Good. Try to move it."

Saryalth again concentrates, and the tiny point of order trembles . . . and moves perhaps a digit.

"Good," declares Alyiakal.

"But it barely moved." Saryalth's voice is despairing.

Alyiakal smiles broadly. "You moved it. That means you have the ability to handle order and chaos. What we'll need to work on is building up your strength and perceptions. I couldn't do any of that at all when I was your age."

"Really?"

"Really," confirms Alyiakal.

Over the next glass, Alyiakal goes through more exercises with his daughter, then says, "You're getting tired. That's enough for now."

"Do we have to?"

"We have to. You're not doing as well, and you're getting sloppy."

"Can we do more tomorrow?"

"We can, but only for a glass in the morning and a glass in the afternoon," Alyiakal says firmly. "There are other things you need to learn about Cyador and the world."

Later in the evening, after Saryalth has dropped off to sleep, and just before Alyiakal and Saelora are about to join her, Saelora whispers, "I could sense the strength of the chaos and the order/chaos mixtures."

"I'm not surprised. You can sense my shields. Do you want to try to see if you can influence order or chaos?"

"That might be a bit much," says Saelora, "but I might as well try."

Alyiakal places a tiny bit of order in the air before her.

"I can sense it," says Saelora, "but nothing happens."

"Maybe you'll be able to later," he suggests.

"I have the feeling that I can sense those flows and forces, but nothing more."

"Well, perhaps for *now,*" returns Alyiakal.

"You're always looking on the bright side, dear man, and I love you for it, but for now I can't, and we'll just have to see."

Once again, at those words, Alyiakal gives a sardonic smile in the dark, and nods.

LXXIII

By midafternoon on threeday, Alyiakal is more than ready to be in Vaeyal. It's not that Saryalth has been a problem, or that they have run into any difficulties, but more that Alyiakal is a little tired of his leave resembling, however slightly, a Mirror Lancer patrol. When he sees the walls of Southpoint ahead, he takes a quiet deep breath, and looks to Saelora.

"When we get closer, we'll need to take a street heading south parallel to the walls. You and Saryalth can wait by the south gates with the wagon, while I return the gelding. It'll be quicker that way." *Not to mention safer.* Alyiakal hasn't ever forgotten the brigands who targeted Saelora and the wagon in Geliendra.

Saelora nods in a way that says she knows very well why he wants her and Saryalth to wait by the south gates. "That makes sense. You might want to stop by the tailor's shop, though."

"Thank you for the reminder."

When they're less than half a kay from the post walls, Saryalth says, "The walls look immense. Is there more there than the post?"

"Just the post," Alyiakal confirms. "The walls run a kay on each side. There aren't that many more lancers there, but this is one of the few posts that has quarters for families, and sometimes Mirror Engineers are here."

"What are Mirror Engineers?"

Saryalth's question reminds Alyiakal how sheltered his daughter has been. "Mirror Engineers work with machines powered by order/chaos flows. They keep the chaos towers and the wall wards working properly. They also work on the firewagons that travel the great highways, the firetows on the Great Canal, and the fireships that protect Merchanter ships on the ocean. Magus Triamon thought at one time I might be suited to be a Mirror Engineer officer."

"The magus who taught Mother?"

"He taught us both—at different times." Alyiakal pauses. "Did your mother ever tell you what happened to him? All my father could tell me was that he vanished."

"Mother only said he disappeared one night and that the mages in Cyad might have been behind it."

"I thought that as well, but I doubt we'll ever know exactly what happened. That was one reason I couldn't write your mother. He was the only one I knew who could get a message to her." *Safely for both of us, anyway.*

Before long, Saelora turns the wagon down the side street nearest the post walls. A little more than a quint later, she turns east on the avenue leading to the south gates, and brings the wagon to a halt just west of the gates. "We'll wait here."

"I'll be as quick as I can."

Saelora nods.

The guards barely note Alyiakal as he rides through the gates, heading toward the main stables. Once there, he dismounts, then walks the gelding into the stable.

An ostler hurries up. "Ser?"

"This mount is from Northpoint. I'm to turn it over to the supply officer, or to someone with authority to accept it."

"I'd better get the captain, ser."

A fraction of a quint later, the ostler returns with an older captain who gives Alyiakal a quizzical look.

"Majer . . . what can I do for you?"

Alyiakal extends the transfer letter. "The gelding and the tack are from Northpoint."

The captain reads, frowning slightly, then looks up. "Don't see many of these, but that's not your concern, ser. Any problems with him?"

"None, but there's a fair amount of wear on his hoofs. You might want to check them before sending him out on patrol."

"Thank you, ser." The captain looks at the gelding. "No gear, ser?"

"I dropped it off before I came here, thank you." Alyiakal smiles, then turns and makes his way from the stable, heading to the tailor's shop.

While his uniforms are ready, the walk back to the main gates seems more than a little longer. He ruefully shakes his head. *That might be because you're carrying five complete uniforms.* He debates paying Subcommander Hurtaal another courtesy call but decides against it. He's alone, and a second visit seems unnecessary within two eightdays.

Once he walks out the gates and reaches the wagon, he carefully loads the uniforms in the rear of the wagon, then closes the doors. Walking up the right side of the wagon, he addresses his daughter. "You'll have to move over, Saryalth. It's going to be crowded up there for the next glass or so."

"Why didn't you bring another horse?" asks Saryalth as Alyiakal settles at the edge of the teamster's seat.

"Because we didn't know you'd want to come back with us," replies Alyiakal, "and Saelora needed to leave enough horses for the factorage while she was gone. We took the wagon so that we only needed one horse for us both. That left another horse for Gaaran, the twins, and Laetilla." Alyiakal looks past Saryalth to Saelora. "You can explain that better."

"It's harvest season. They need to collect pearapples from the orchard Loraan House owns and from other growers, as well as maize and greenberries. They all have to be carted to the distillery."

Alyiakal listens as Saelora explains in painstaking detail. What he finds intriguing, and a little depressing, is that Saryalth actually shows great interest in those details, as if they come from another land, which, for Saryalth, they do.

By the time Saelora finishes, the cart has passed through Geliendra and is on the road to Vaeyal, and Saryalth asks, "How did you learn all that?"

"By doing most of it or working with people who did. My brother Hyrsaal—the one who's the overcaptain at Northpoint—suggested that a combination of pearapples and greenberries might make a good brandy. He was right, but it took several years before we got the mixture and distilling right."

After a time, Saelora glances at Saryalth, and asks, "What did your mother tell you about your father when you were growing up?"

"She said that he was a Mirror Lancer officer and wasn't suited to living in Jakaafra or the Great Forest, but she wanted me, and he helped her. I didn't understand exactly what she meant until I was older."

"I didn't even know I had a daughter until your mother's letter came almost a season ago," Alyiakal says quietly. "Do you know why she waited to write me?"

"I asked her why you never wrote me. She said she didn't know. Last year I realized she wasn't telling me everything." Saryalth offers an embarrassed smile. "I told her so. She said she'd written you and you never wrote back. She lied about that, too. I didn't say anything, but she knew I knew. In Spring, I asked if she'd write you again. That way I didn't have to tell her that she'd lied to me." Saryalth pauses. "You both don't mind, do you?"

"Not at all," says Alyiakal.

"Of course not," declares Saelora almost simultaneously.

"Just before we met you, Mother admitted she hadn't written before, but she thought things might have worked out better because she hadn't."

"I don't know about that," replies Alyiakal. "They would have worked out differently, yes, and that could have been better or worse. *But* they worked out the way they have, and we have to go on from here in the best way we can."

"You really don't mind?" asks Saryalth anxiously.

"I'm glad you got your mother to write me," replies Alyiakal. "Otherwise, I would never have known I had a daughter." He smiles wryly. "I do have to say that I was a little irritated at your mother." *More than a little and for more than one reason.* "I would have liked to know that I had a daughter."

"She was worried you wouldn't come."

"How could I not come?"

"Some men wouldn't," says Saelora gently. "I think Saryalth knows that."

And if she doesn't, you're going to make sure she does. Alyiakal doesn't show the wry amusement he feels at his consort's unspoken meaning.

"I hoped you would," declares Saryalth, "but Mother said you might not be able to come soon."

"She was right," admits Alyiakal. "As I told you the other day, I was supposed to spend another year at Pemedra. Once that changed, Saelora immediately arranged for us to come."

Saryalth frowns and addresses Saelora. "You made the arrangements without telling him?"

"I knew he'd want to see you, and he doesn't have much leave. We left Vaeyal less than three days after he arrived, and he'll have to leave for Cyad soon after you meet your mother in Geliendra."

"Oh." Saryalth's tone of voice is quietly subdued.

Alyiakal is slightly surprised that she realizes that most of his leave revolves around her.

"Is there anything you'd like to do in Vaeyal?" asks Saelora.

"I don't know." Saryalth sighs. "There's so much I don't know."

"Then we'll take things day by day," says Alyiakal.

"There are a few things you do need to know," says Saelora. "First, it makes people nervous if they think a Mirror Lancer officer is a mage. They know your father is a healer. That's *all* they need to know. Is that clear?"

Saryalth nods. "Mother says the same thing."

"Second, the first person you'll meet at the house is Laetilla." Saelora explains Laetilla's duties and the fact that while she occasionally cooks, she does that as a favor. Her main job is to run the distillery.

Before long, Saelora turns the wagon north on Canal Street.

Alyiakal points west to the white stonework. "That's the Great Canal. You might be able to sense the order holding the stones together. There's also a deeper order farther below the canal similar to the Great Forest."

"I can sense the canal," says Saryalth. "It's hard, like it's been forced together."

"It most likely was," replies Alyiakal. "The deeper order is just as strong but feels unforced."

"I can't sense beneath the ground," says Saryalth. "Not more than a few digits. Mother can't at all. Why can you do it, and we can't?"

"I don't know," admits Alyiakal. "I realized I could do it about the time I found the dissidents' old road between Guarstyad and Kyphros." He pauses. "If you can sense into the ground a little, you might be able to do more when you're older." Not wanting to say more, he gestures. "In the next block, the large building on the right is Saelora's first factorage, the one she bought with the silvers she made from the distillery."

Saryalth studies the building, which is closed and shuttered for the day. "That's much bigger than anything in Jakaafra."

"It's only one of several buildings belonging to Loraan House." Alyiakal doesn't know exactly how many buildings Saelora owns, not with what she and Catriana have bought in Fyrad and at least two pearapple orchards and some lands growing maize.

The young woman looks to Saelora. "You really are a Lady Merchanter."

Alyiakal grins at his daughter. "You thought I might be exaggerating?"

"You *are* consorts," replies Saryalth primly, but Alyiakal can sense the hidden smile.

When Saelora turns the wagon east toward the house and distillery, Alyiakal explains to Saryalth, "This used to be the main road to Geliendra, but the swamp east of the distillery expanded and is so deep that they had to reroute the road. I'll tell you more when we show you the swamp."

"Is it a big swamp?"

"Not compared to the Great Forest, but it's definitely too deep and wide to build a road through it."

Two quints pass before the wagon nears the distillery, where a guard steps out of the brick-walled guard post, and nods as he recognizes the wagon and Saelora.

Saelora slows and asks, "Have you had trouble?"

"Some, Lady, but nothing Captain Gaaran and the rest of us couldn't handle. He'd know more than I do."

"Thank you for taking care of it," replies Saelora.

"That sounds like it was more than a casual intruder," says Alyiakal quietly.

"We'll find out soon enough." Saelora turns the wagon down the drive. She has barely brought the wagon to a stop outside the stable when Laetilla steps out from the front door and hurries to the wagon before any of the three can climb down from the teamster's seat.

"Laetilla, this is my daughter Saryalth." Alyiakal turns to his daughter. "Saryalth, this is Laetilla. As I told you earlier, she runs the distillery and helps Saelora with other things, as necessary."

"I'm pleased to meet you, Saryalth. You definitely have some of your father's looks."

"Thank you," replies Saryalth.

Laetilla looks to Saelora. "I didn't know exactly when you'd be back or whether Saryalth would be with you, but I can have a modest dinner ready in a little more than a glass. There won't be any dessert."

"We can certainly do without dessert," says Alyiakal, adding with a grin, "no matter how much I appreciate it."

"You've made that known, Majer," replies Laetilla with an amused smile. "I also have the big kettle on the stove for warm water, and the small bedroom is ready. I thought it was better to be prepared."

"That would be wonderful," says Saelora. "We'll take care of the horse and wagon, get Saryalth settled, and then wash up."

Alyiakal immediately climbs down, then gives Saryalth a hand.

Two quints later, the horse is unhitched, groomed, and stalled, and the wagon unloaded and blocked in place. Saelora leads Saryalth to the small room that had been a study. Alyiakal isn't totally surprised to see that one desk has been moved out and a single bed put in its place, already made up. A washbasin, a small bar of soap, and towels are set on the remaining desk, with a chamber pot in one corner.

Saryalth sets her pack on one end of the desk.

"The desk has some drawers where you can put a few things," Saelora says. "You'll need to wash up before dinner, but you don't have to change clothes."

"I don't have many clothes," says Saryalth apologetically.

"That's all right," replies Saelora. "We have a woman who comes in every few days who can wash what you have. You'll only be here an eightday, but we might be able to have another pair of trousers and a tunic sewed for you. We'll see about that tomorrow."

"This is my room?"

"For whenever you're here. When you're several years older, when you visit, if you want, you can have the larger chambers on one end of the distillery. Right now, we'd prefer to have you closer to us."

"I like this."

"Good," says Alyiakal from the doorway.

"What would you like to drink with dinner?" asks Saelora.

"Juice or water. I can only drink watered ale when we're at Great-Uncle Krimaan's house."

"You can have watered ale tonight," says Saelora.

"Right now," adds Alyiakal, "we're going to wash up as well. Once you're cleaned up, you can stay here, or you can sit in the parlor." He steps back to allow Saelora to leave, then closes the door, and the two enter the main bedchamber. Alyiakal closes that door as well.

"She's only got three sets of clothing and undergarments," says Saelora.

"That may be all she has."

"Most likely. The cloth is good and sturdy, but tan and brown hardly suit her. Forest green is better."

"With the time she spends in the Great Forest," replies Alyiakal, "I suspect sturdiness is more important than color, and the choice of fabric in Jakaafra has to be limited."

"From what I saw when we got provisions, you're being charitable." She glances toward the kitchen.

Alyiakal grins. "I'll get the kettle, and you can bathe first."

Over three quints later, wearing an old, clean uniform, Alyiakal walks into the front parlor, where Saryalth stands looking out the window.

She turns and points. "Is that whole building the distillery?"

"Not quite. There are guest quarters at the east end, and quarters for Laetilla at the west end. There's a storeroom on the west end as well, but the distillery takes up most of the building."

"Did Saelora have all this when you met?"

"When I started writing her, she didn't have anything. She was living with her mother in Vaeyal. When we finally met, she'd become an enumerator for Vassyl. She'd just started the distillery and began to have this house repaired and rebuilt. The distillery then was maybe a third the size it is now."

"If that," Saelora adds as she walks into the parlor, wearing informal Merchanter blues.

"Do you always wear blue?" asks Saryalth.

"Most of the time, just like your father always wears cream and green-edged uniforms. The Magi'i usually wear white, except for healers, who wear green."

Saryalth frowns, then asks, "To show they're different?"

"That's partly it," replies Alyiakal, "but white and green are the colors of the Empire of Light—the Malachite Throne and the light of the Rational Stars. So Mirror Lancers wear white and green because we support the Emperor. So do the Magi'i. Merchanters wear blue because they trade on rivers and oceans."

"Even though we also trade on roads of different colors," adds Saelora dryly.

"Don't Merchanters support the Emperor?" asks Saryalth.

"They're supposed to," answers Saelora.

"But some don't?" presses Saryalth.

"Well, outland merchants and traders have no reason to support the Emperor," replies Saelora. "Merchanters in Cyad are supposed to. Some are not particularly enthusiastic."

"What about you?"

"I support the Emperor. He holds Cyador together. Too many people don't see that."

"They certainly don't, and they're foolish not to," adds Laetilla as she enters the parlor. "It's also time for dinner."

When the three enter the small dining room, Alyiakal gestures for Saelora to sit at the head of the table with Saryalth at her left.

Saelora raises her eyebrows, but Alyiakal only says quietly, "You're the Lady Merchanter, and it's your house." Then, sensing Saryalth's puzzlement, he turns to her. "In Cyador, the most important person sits at the head of the table. Often, as a courtesy, the oldest or most important person in the house is accorded that honor, even if someone more important is at the table. Here, there's no question. Saelora is important as the head of a Merchanter house and this is her house."

"Exactly," adds Laetilla as she sets a plate in front of Saelora, and then a second before Alyiakal, returning in moments with a third plate for Saryalth.

Alyiakal looks at his plate, which holds fried lace potatoes, fried fowl, and green beans covered with sautéed mushrooms, in addition to the basket of bread already on the table, and he senses Saryalth's surprise as she speaks.

"We don't get dinners this special except when we eat at Great-Uncle Krimaan's, and that's not often."

"What do you eat most of the time?" asks Saelora.

"Porridge and fruit, other things. There's always some fruit or green thing that's good to eat. We get cheese from some of the steads, sometimes cold cooked meats." Saryalth tries the fried lace potatoes tentatively, then eats another mouthful without hesitation.

"We won't have as many fruits as you have in the Great Forest," says Alyiakal, "but we have more cooked food. Breakfast will be similar, except we usually have some type of sweet pastries with fruit, and, sometimes, cheese."

After the lace potatoes, Saryalth finishes off the mushrooms and beans on her plate, then cuts a bit of the fowl, clearly copying Saelora, and eats it slowly, as if trying to determine what it is and whether she likes it. Then she cuts a larger piece and eats it without hesitation, before asking, "Can I see the swamp tomorrow?"

"There's not much to see," replies Alyiakal, "especially compared to the Great Forest, but we can manage that sometime tomorrow. It might not be until afternoon. Saelora needs to go to the factorage first thing tomorrow."

"You could show Saryalth around here first thing in the morning," says Saelora, "while I deal with what has to be done at the factorage."

Alyiakal nods. "That might be best."

In the end, Saryalth leaves nothing on her plate, and she struggles to keep her eyes open.

Saelora stands and turns to Saryalth. "I think it's time for you to get a good night's sleep."

"Would you mind?"

"We won't be that much longer," replies Saelora. "It's been a long trip for us as well. Let me help you."

While Saelora deals with Saryalth, Alyiakal carries the dishes to the kitchen and helps Laetilla, as he can.

"She seems to be a good child," says Laetilla.

"She is. We'll just have to do our best and see how things work out."

"I'd wager she's your daughter more than her mother's."

"Why do you think that?" asks Alyiakal, honestly surprised by Laetilla's words.

"She wouldn't be here if she weren't. She's meant for more than the Great Forest, just like you're meant for more than being just a middling lancer officer."

"Like Saelora was meant to be more than a simple consort or a scrivener," adds Alyiakal.

"Nice to hear you say that, Majer."

"I've always told her as much, and I mean it."

"Still nice to hear." Laetilla gestures toward the parlor. "You've done what you can to help. Go sit down. I'll be done in a few moments."

"If you say so." Alyiakal smiles briefly, then withdraws to the parlor.

Once Laetilla leaves the kitchen and retires to her quarters and Saelora settles Saryalth in for the night, Saelora joins Alyiakal in the parlor.

"Did you find out from Laetilla what the 'trouble' was?" he asks.

"A crew of brigands, likely from Fyrad. Cheslya warned Kaasya that she'd heard something might happen on eightday evening. Gaaran had the guards and a few others he'd gathered ready. Laetilla said the doors were barely scratched. All the bodies went into the swamp, weighted."

"The Dyljani, you think?"

"Most likely. They probably thought there wouldn't be guards here."

"They won't stop," predicts Alyiakal.

"No, but Kaasya conveyed our thanks to Cheslya, in 'golden' terms, and said that we'd appreciate further information."

"So you'll have much of the town watching for strangers."

"That's the idea. That won't be as effective in Fyrad, but it will work here." Saelora pauses, then says, "I thought dinner went well."

"I worried that she might be a picky eater," says Alyiakal.

"That's unlikely. She's your daughter. The only thing you don't like is quilla, but you'll still eat it. Even I could sense that she liked everything."

"Even you?" Alyiakal shakes his head. "Before the Great Forest touched you, you generally knew what people felt. Now, there's no doubt."

"I still don't understand why the Forest did that."

"I don't know that we'll ever know, but one thing I'm fairly certain of is that it can't, or doesn't, take things back. It didn't with the great magus of the First, and it hasn't with me."

"But it could, couldn't it?"

"I don't think so. It opens abilities we have the potential for, and it's impossible to unlearn abilities." *Unless you're dead.* "You're already sensitive to feelings, and this just makes you better at discerning them. You might be able to detect people working for the Dyljani Clan with greater certainty."

"I could use that. Catriana could use it even more. She's the one who deals with most of that."

"I doubt that the Great Forest will bestow sensing on her."

"I didn't think it would."

After a moment, Alyiakal comments, "Tomorrow is going to be interesting."

"In several ways," replies Saelora. "In what way were you thinking?"

"I don't want to hide Saryalth, and that means we have to tell your mother. Since my actions created the situation, I should tell her."

"Only if I'm there."

"That would be best," Alyiakal admits, with relief.

Saelora laughs softly. "You were hoping I'd say that, weren't you?"

"You know the answer," he admits.

"I still like you to reassure me sometimes."

"Believe me. I'd much rather face your mother about Saryalth with you there."

"I appreciate that you're willing to talk to her without me."

Saelora sets her empty wineglass on the side table and looks at Alyiakal.

"Are you ready for bed?" he asks warily.

Saelora smiles. "I thought you'd never ask."

And it has been almost an eightday since we could be that close.

LXXIV

Alyiakal, Saelora, and Saryalth all rise early on fourday, although Saryalth doesn't leave her room until she hears Alyiakal and Saelora in the kitchen. She wears a dark gray shirt and dark gray trousers that don't quite match the shirt, and she's surprised to find them wearing robes, rather than being fully dressed.

"I can do this when I'm at home on leave," declares Alyiakal. "On duty, I'm fully dressed when I leave my quarters."

"That's our choice," says Saelora, turning to Saryalth and asking, "You didn't bring a robe, did you?"

"No, but—"

Before Saryalth can say that she doesn't have one, Saelora continues, "I have a robe I don't use anymore. I'll leave it in your room so that, if you want, you can use it."

"Thank you."

"You'll have to have water this morning. We don't have any juice," says Alyiakal, *except what's fermenting in the distillery,* "but I've made sure that the water's chaos-free."

"You can do that?" asks Saryalth.

"Among other things," says Saelora, "but it's best if you keep that between us. You can tell your mother if you want, but we'd appreciate it if you didn't tell anyone else."

"I won't. We don't talk about order and chaos to anyone."

"That's a very good practice," says Alyiakal. "Now . . . we have almond rolls and grapes and summer apples, and some cheese."

Shortly, all three are at the dining room table, eating, and less than a glass later, after dressing, Saelora gives instruction to Kaasya and Kaastyl before each heads off with a horse and cart. Then Saelora rides off to the factorage.

Standing just inside the front door, since Alyiakal hasn't wanted the twins to see Saryalth until he and Saelora have talked to Marenda, Saryalth looks to her father. "Do you always wear a uniform?"

"I've never bothered to get other clothes. If I have dirty work to do, I wear an old uniform."

Saryalth tilts her head, as if pondering, then asks, "What are we going to do today?"

"I thought we'd walk to the swamp first. Later, we'll be visiting Saelora's mother, and if there's time in between, and Laetilla has a moment, she can show you around the distillery and explain how it works."

Saryalth wrinkles her nose.

"You don't have to like going through the distillery," says Alyiakal firmly, "but you need to know about it and how it generally works. Why do you have to know about stun lizards or the giant serpents? Or what fruits of the Great Forest are safe to eat? Aren't you better off the more you know about the Forest?"

"Yes," Saryalth admits, grudgingly.

"The same is true outside the Forest, but there's more to learn, and many things that don't seem important now may be important in the future. It won't hurt to learn as much as you can. Now . . . I promised you could see the swamp." Alyiakal opens the front door, follows his daughter out, and closes it.

He walks swiftly up the slight slope of the drive to the old road, then turns left and walks east along what remains of the roadbed. Saryalth matches his steps.

"What do you sense beneath your shoes?" he asks.

"The ground is different."

"It is. How is it different?"

"I don't know."

Alyiakal refrains from sighing, possibly because he's heard, or overheard, that phrase from green lancers all too often. "Is there more chaos there than in the Great Forest?"

"I don't think so."

"What about order?"

"The order is different."

"Different in what way?

"It's linked like it's forced together."

"Excellent. What does that tell you?"

"That some magus did it?"

"Most likely one of the First." Alyiakal doesn't say anything more until they near the dark water of the swamp. He stops several yards short of the rocky edge. While he doesn't sense any weakness in the ground, as he had at Luuval, he prefers caution. "I want you to do something else. Try to sense what lies beneath the water. That should be easier than sensing through the ground."

After several moments, Saryalth says, "There are swirls of order and chaos, more chaos than order." She pauses. "There isn't that much of each . . . oh, and a frog, and some fish, but not many."

"No . . . there's not much free order or chaos. Why might that be so?"

Saryalth shrugs and shakes her head.

"I'll give you a hint. Deeper beneath the ground lies very ordered rock that was most likely once part of the Great Forest."

"Why isn't there any Forest here now, then?"

Alyiakal reminds her about the First and the struggle between the first great magus and the Great Forest.

"Mother never told me that. She just said that the First built the walls around the Forest." Abruptly, Saryalth says, "That's what the Great Forest showed you, wasn't it?"

Alyiakal nods.

She shivers. "No one else talks with the Great Forest."

"I've only done it a few times." Alyiakal pauses, then asks, "Can you sense anything besides frogs or fish in the water?"

She shakes her head.

Alyiakal points to the tangled greenery less than a yard away. "Do you know what those are?"

"No. I've never seen them before."

"Those are all greenberry bushes. The berries are very bitter."

"And Saelora makes brandy from the berries?"

"From the berries and pearapple juice."

"Sweet and bitter." She nods. "That makes sense."

For the next glass or so Alyiakal draws out Saryalth, while also trying to impart some information and having her try various exercises to improve her order/chaos skills, including gathering tiny bits of free order. When she finishes her morning practice, he accompanies her as Laetilla explains the distillery and its processes.

Shortly afterward, Saelora returns to the house, along with Kaasya, who returns a cart and horse. Alyiakal has Saryalth stay in the house until Kaasya leaves, and then Saryalth watches as Alyiakal and Saelora harness the cart horse to the wagon.

After that, Alyiakal and Saelora motion for Saryalth to join them.

"You know that none of us even knew you existed a season ago?" asks Alyiakal.

Saryalth nods.

"We also didn't know that you'd want to come to Vaeyal with us," adds Alyiakal. "Because we didn't know what to expect, we didn't want to tell anyone else about you until we knew more, but now you need to meet the rest of Saelora's family, beginning with her mother."

"Because she's the oldest in the family," asks Saryalth, "and needs to know first?"

"That's right," says Saelora. "She's older, and we don't want to surprise her too much. So we'll tell her about you, and then you'll meet her. Now, hop up on the wagon."

Saryalth does just that, asking, "Won't people be asking when they see me with you?"

"They might, but they won't be able to until after you've met my mother. Then it won't make any difference."

Alyiakal rides alongside the wagon on the right, so that he's closer to Saryalth, in case she has questions, but she says nothing until Saelora turns the wagon onto the short drive toward Gaaran and Charissa's dwelling.

"Is this where your mother lives? It's bigger than all the houses in Jakaafra."

"She used to. Now my brother Gaaran and his consort live here. Mother lives in the cottage to the rear, but she spends some of the day in the house." Saelora brings the wagon to a halt at the railing next to the side porch and sets the wagon brakes, while Alyiakal dismounts and ties both horses. Saelora enters the house through the door on the porch.

She returns in a fraction of a quint. "Mother's in the parlor, and Charissa has the children in the kitchen." She then turns to Saryalth, who stands beside Alyiakal at the side of the wagon.

"You want me to wait here, then?" asks Saryalth.

"On the side porch where it's shady," says Saelora.

"It won't be long," says Alyiakal. *One way or another.* He and Saelora step up onto the porch and then enter the parlor.

Marenda doesn't rise from the dark green upholstered armchair. "So you've returned from your mysterious trip."

"It was mysterious for several reasons," begins Alyiakal. "You wanted to know why we had to go to Jakaafra. The first reason was to see Hyrsaal. The other reason was because I discovered that I have a daughter."

Marenda doesn't appear terribly upset, only somewhat irritated. All she says, if cuttingly, is, "Oh, and when were you going to tell me? Did your first wife die before you could consort Saelora?"

"No. I never had a first wife. Until half a season ago, I didn't know I had a daughter . . ." Alyiakal goes on to explain, adding, "I told Saelora about Adayal the first time we met."

"He's never kept anything from me," adds Saelora.

"You're the second in the family to know," says Alyiakal.

"Hyrsaal was the first?" asks Marenda.

"We told him, but he's never met her. You'll be the first to meet Saryalth."

"Saryalth . . . not an unpleasant name." Marenda shakes her head. "With all the secrecy about going to Jakaafra, I'd imagined much, much worse. I'm not thrilled, you understand, but very young men do make mistakes, and you've handled it as well as you could. Does your daughter know exactly what happened?"

"Actually, she does, in general terms," replies Saelora. "She knows her mother wanted her and that she got Alyiakal to help her, and that Alyiakal never knew. She figured out on her own that he didn't know and got her mother to write."

"Sounds like she has some brains. Is she coming to live with you?" Marenda asks Saelora.

"In the future, if she wants, she can, but she's only staying with us for an eightday. She asked to spend some time with her father. Her mother will meet us at Geliendra on the coming threeday."

"That's something. Not much, but something." Marenda looks at Alyiakal. "Won't having a daughter this way affect your career?"

"Possibly, but likely not as much as what I did in Cerlyn. Besides," he adds wryly, "Kaartyn became emperor even though his father never consorted his mother, and there was a more legitimate heir. If that's acceptable for the Emperor, why should anyone make a fuss about Saryalth?"

"Just possibly," returns Marenda tartly, "because you're not emperor."

"True," admits Alyiakal, "so why would anyone bother?"

"Given your reputation, and what happens to obstacles you meet, it might not be worth the bother." Marenda shakes her head again. "Well, I might as well meet her."

Alyiakal walks to the porch door and motions for Saryalth to join him, then escorts Saryalth to Marenda.

"Saryalth, this is Lady Marenda. She's Saelora's mother."

Saryalth inclines her head. "I'm pleased to meet you, Lady."

Marenda snorts. "I'm no lady, Saryalth, but I appreciate the courtesy." She surveys Saryalth for several moments, then says, "You definitely take after your father. With that hair, are you a healer, too?"

"Father says I likely could be if I work hard."

"He's right about that. Anything worth doing takes hard work." Marenda pauses, then asks, "You know that you can't see your father that often, don't you?"

"I know. He's not here much at all. But I had to meet him. I just had to."

"You know you can't learn enough to be a healer if you spend most of your time in the Great Forest?" Marenda asks coolly.

"I know. But I'm not old enough to leave Mother yet. Father's already working with me."

Marenda looks to Alyiakal. "Her attitude is like someone else's I know." She pauses. "Two others, in fact." She turns back to Saryalth. "You have a lot to learn and a great deal of work ahead."

"Yes, Lady."

"We won't take any more of your time," says Alyiakal, "but we both wanted you to be the first to meet Saryalth."

"I appreciate your courtesy, Alyiakal." Marenda offers an amused smile and adds, "It is refreshing to learn that you actually do make mistakes. I did wonder about that."

"I've made more than a few," admits Alyiakal, "but I was smart enough to hang on to Saelora."

"You suit one another," says Marenda, "but then, I'm not sure anyone else would be comfortable with either of you."

Alyiakal chuckles ruefully. "I won't speak for Saelora, but I'm afraid you might be right as far as I'm concerned."

"I won't keep you three, but I enjoyed meeting you, Saryalth. Make sure your father teaches you everything you need."

Saryalth inclines her head respectfully.

As the three leave the parlor and step out onto the side porch, Alyiakal senses that Marenda remains amused. He also discerns that Saryalth is definitely puzzled, but he says nothing because Charissa appears on the side porch.

Saelora smiles. "Charissa, you should meet Saryalth. She's Alyiakal's daughter, and, no, he wasn't ever consorted before. She's twelve and won't be thirteen until after yearturn. Saryalth, this is Charissa. She's the consort of my oldest brother, Gaaran."

"I'm pleased to meet you, Saryalth." Charissa's voice is warm and friendly. "Will you be here long?"

"Just for an eightday. Then I have to go back to Jakaafra."

"Then I'll likely see you around. Be good for your father and Saelora."

"I will, thank you."

Neither Alyiakal nor Saelora say much more until Saelora has the wagon moving south on Canal Street. Alyiakal rides beside the wagon, next to his daughter, and asks, "Saryalth, you were puzzled when we left Marenda. Can you tell me why?"

"Lady Marenda was trying not to laugh."

Alyiakal laughs softly. "Sometimes, adults laugh at things that younger people don't find amusing, and sometimes, it's the other way around. I could try to explain, but you wouldn't find it amusing. In ten years, you might. In fifteen you definitely will."

Saryalth immediately turns to Saelora. "Do you know why your mother wanted to laugh?"

"I do, but I agree with your father. Sometimes other people find things amusing when you don't. That amusement is fine so long as no one gets hurt."

"By the way," Alyiakal asks Saelora, "where are we headed?"

"To the factorage. Saryalth needs to meet Gaaran and the twins." Saelora turns. "Gaaran is my oldest brother. He helps me run the factorage here in Vaeyal. He's older than Hyrsaal, and Hyrsaal's older than my sister Karola and me."

Saelora drives the wagon to the back-alley entrance to the factorage, where Alyiakal blocks it in place and stalls the horse he's been riding. Then the three walk through the warehouse section of the building.

Alyiakal easily senses Saryalth's amazement at the size of the factorage and the rows of shelving that rise almost to the high ceiling, and he says, "This is just one of Saelora's factorages."

"It's not just mine," Saelora adds. "Part belongs to your father and part belongs to Catriana. She's Hyrsaal's consort."

"You have quite a family," says Saryalth.

"That makes up for us," says Alyiakal cheerfully. "You're the only living blood relative I have."

"So far," declares Saelora.

"Are you—" Alyiakal breaks off his words.

"No." Saelora grins, then says to Saryalth, "I love your father, but once in a while he gets too serious."

Saryalth grins back at Saelora.

When the three reach the area of the factorage holding the desks, filing chests, and conference tables, Gaaran rises, looking at Saryalth and then at Saelora.

"Gaaran," says Alyiakal, "I'd like you to meet Saryalth. She's the daughter I never knew I had until less than a season ago. She's very determined and got her mother to track me down."

Gaaran fails to conceal his shock, but manages a shaky smile.

"Don't worry," says Saelora. "I knew about Saryalth's mother from the time I first met Alyiakal, but neither of us knew about Saryalth . . . and Mother and Charissa have already met her."

"So that was why you two had to go to Jakaafra?"

Saelora nods. "It took some arranging, but Saryalth wanted to meet Alyiakal, and I wanted to meet Saryalth. She's spending an eightday here with us before returning to her mother."

Gaaran looks to Saryalth. "You are quite a surprise, but I'm pleased to meet you. How are you finding Vaeyal?"

"We just got here late yesterday. Everyone's been nice. This morning I visited the swamp and the distillery. Then, I met Saelora's mother and Charissa. She's very, very nice. I could tell."

Gaaran smiles more broadly. "Yes, she is."

Saryalth frowns, momentarily, then asks, "You were a Mirror Lancer officer, weren't you?"

Surprised as he is by her question, Alyiakal decides not to speak.

"Why yes, I was," answers Gaaran.

Saryalth nods slightly.

"We won't keep you," Saelora tells Gaaran, "but I wanted you to meet Saryalth."

Gaaran looks to Saryalth. "I'm sure I'll see you again." Then he says to Alyiakal, "She looks a lot like you. In a few years, you'll have your hands full."

"I've discovered that I already do," replies Alyiakal.

Saelora leads the way back to the rear of the factorage, where Alyiakal unblocks the wagon and unstalls the horse.

"Where are we going now?" he asks.

"South to the pearapple orchard. Since we needed the extra horse, Kaasya didn't have time for a second run to pick up all the baskets of spoiled and dropped pearapples. We'll pick them up and drop them at the distillery."

Once Saelora has the wagon headed south, Alyiakal rides alongside Saryalth and asks, "How did you know that Gaaran was a Mirror Lancer officer?"

"Yesterday, when we got to the distillery, the guard said that Captain Gaaran had stopped some trouble. You both feel different, except there's a tightness. Your tightness is in your shields, but it's like his."

Saelora gives Alyiakal a quick glance of amusement.

Alyiakal shrugs and smiles ruefully.

At the pearapple orchard, the baskets of fallen and bruised pearapples are lined up outside a storage building, and, even with all three of them working, it takes more than a quint to load the wagon. Saryalth has no trouble lifting and carrying a basket, turning out to be stronger than Alyiakal had thought.

But then, living in the Great Forest can't be the easiest of lives.

More than a glass passes before the three reach the distillery and Saelora halts the wagon at the loading dock, sets the brakes, and then says to Alyiakal, "Once we unload and carry the baskets to the preparation area, I'd appreciate it if you'd take care of the wagon and horses while Saryalth helps me."

"And that includes cleaning up all the juice that oozed out of the baskets?"

"If you would," replies Saelora pleasantly.

"Consider it done, Lady Merchanter."

"We'll need clean clothes more than you will, Mirror Lancer Majer," returns Saelora in an excessively sweet tone.

Alyiakal winces. "Will you accept my apology?"

She grins. "Of course."

Once the three lug the pearapples to the initial vat area, and Saelora takes off her outer Merchanter tunic, Alyiakal leaves to stable the horse he rode, then returns to deal with the cart horse and then the wagon, which requires several buckets of water and more than a few rags to clean.

By the time the three finish their tasks and make themselves reasonably presentable, they make their way to the dining room, where they have no trouble enjoying a fowl and noodle casserole, followed by a simple egg custard for dessert.

After dinner Saelora helps Saryalth with a bath, and afterward the three gather in the parlor, sitting in a semicircle, with Saryalth wearing Saelora's old robe.

"Do you work that hard all the time?" Saryalth asks Saelora.

"Not always that hard physically, but most days are long. I try not to work as much when your father's here, because we have so little time together. That's not always possible. The pearapples wouldn't wait, not if we want to get the best must possible for the brandy."

Since Saryalth nods at that and isn't in the slightest puzzled, Alyiakal can tell she's remembered what Saelora and Laetilla have told her. He gets the impression that she forgets very little. *Which is something you need to remember about her.*

"Have you ever played Fyrr?" asks Alyiakal.

"What's that?"

"It's a pastecard game."

"I don't know many pastecard games."

Meaning that you don't know any. "Well, Fyrr is a game played by Magi'i, Merchanters, and Mirror Lancer officers."

"You mean it's a game for important people," says Saryalth dryly.

Saelora smiles. "Exactly."

"What about healers?"

"Healers, too," says Alyiakal.

"Once you know how to play it," adds Saelora, "it can be fun. That is, if you don't take it too seriously."

"Does Father take it too seriously?"

"No. He's fun to play with. For my father, playing Fyrr was a battle." Saelora stands. "I'll get the pastecards and the board and tokens. We'll play in the dining room."

For the next glass, the three are absorbed in the game, and by the time Saelora tells Saryalth it's time for bed, the young woman definitely understands the game.

As Saryalth stands, she asks, "Can we play again?"

"We can," say Alyiakal and Saelora almost simultaneously.

Once Saryalth is in her room, and the pastecards, board, and tokens are put away, Alyiakal and Saelora return to the parlor.

"Do you think she could be a healer?" asks Saelora.

"If she wants it enough. She already senses more than some healers." Alyiakal pauses. "I might be able to get her instruction, in another year or so, if Adayal allows it."

Saelora frowns, then asks, "That healer you worked with years ago?"

"Vayidra. She's in Cyad, and I have the feeling she was the reason Taezyl lasted as long as he did. Whether she's still alive or would even be willing . . ." He shrugs.

"Don't mention it to Saryalth," says Saelora firmly.

"By the Rational Stars, no. There are too many unknowns. I don't even know if I'll be in Cyad long enough to find out if Vayidra's still there, or alive."

"You said she's an outstanding healer. She'll likely be alive."

"But who knows where . . . and whether she will be in a year or two. Or where I'll be."

"I have the feeling you'll be in Cyad."

"Why do you think that?"

"You're too valuable not to keep, and if you're there for a little while, you'll work it out, somehow."

"You have great faith in me."

She smiles. "That's only fair. You had great faith in me."

LXXV

On fiveday morning, after Saelora leaves for the factorage, Alyiakal takes out his book of maps and begins to tutor Saryalth on the geography of Cyador, beginning with maps of the area holding the Great Forest, then the sparser maps of Kynstaar. He does his best to tie the geography first to the area she knows and then to the areas where he's been posted. At the same time, he adds some historical facts.

When he opens the book to the map of the area around Pemedra, she asks, "Why are there more places and marks on this map?"

"Because I was posted there, and the original map had almost nothing on it. As I learned about the area, I added details."

"Why? You know them, and the book is yours. If you take it with you, no one else will learn from it, and you already know all that."

"I may not remember all those details in years to come. When I went back to Pemedra, I made copies of the map for the company officers to help them learn more."

"Why do you want me to know this?"

"To learn more about Cyador. Too many people only know about where they live and where they've been. They often don't know little things, like the grain needed for ale doesn't grow in the lands around Pemedra, and neither do real potatoes."

"That sounds awful. But do they really need to know those things?"

"Most of them probably don't, but *you* do. You want to become a healer. Healers can be sent anywhere, and if you know about where you're sent, you can often avoid trouble—and you never know. I learned a bit about healing from Magus Triamon. Without that, I wouldn't have gotten training in healing at Kynstaar. Without that training, I wouldn't have been given more training in healing at Syadtar when I was on my way to Pemedra. I learned more there from an older Magi'i healer who'd been sent to Syadtar. That meant that I could save more of my rankers after skirmishes and battles."

"What happened to the healer?"

"She was recalled to Cyad to tend the Emperor Taezyl before he died."

"Are you as good as she was?"

Alyiakal shakes his head. "I know a fair amount about broken bones and wounds, but nothing about surgery or childbirth or other ailments. I can sometimes use order to help heal wounds or some head injuries."

Alyiakal returns to the geography tutoring but calls a halt after little more than a glass and takes Saryalth to the stable. At the stall that holds Laetilla's horse, he spends a few moments trying to discern any small wounds, then nods.

"Can you sense any wound chaos?"

"Wound chaos? You mean the grayish-red chaos?" Saryalth wrinkles her forehead, then looks at the mare.

Alyiakal waits.

Finally, she says, "There's a little patch just above the hoof of her right front leg."

"Do you sense anything else?"

"Maybe at the corner of her mouth on the left side. I'm not sure."

"Good. That's pretty much healed." Alyiakal pauses. "Have you ever sensed a whitish bright red chaos in an animal or person?"

"Not that I remember."

"You'd remember. If something that bright appears in a wound, and it's more than a pinpoint in size, there's usually a serious problem. A sting from a fruit wasp can appear as a tiny white-red point, but it will fade to a dull red in a day or so, but that sting can kill a small bird, not that fruit wasps usually sting birds."

"How do you know that?"

"Because I sensed a bird with such a sting when I was a few years older than you, and I asked Magus Triamon about it."

As Alyiakal turns from the stall and motions for Saryalth to accompany him, she asks, "What was he like?"

"Didn't your mother tell you anything about him?"

"She said he was a good person, but she didn't want to talk about him. She wasn't lying. I can tell when she is or isn't saying everything."

"So far as I know, he was a very good man, and a truthful one. He let me know that I wouldn't make a good magus because I was too ordered. He also said that having healing skills would help me as a lancer officer. He taught me some of the order/chaos exercises I've showed you." Alyiakal shares what he knows about Triamon with Saryalth.

Less than a quint after he finishes, he says, "Saelora's on her way."

"How far away can you sense her?"

"Saelora? Sometimes, almost a kay."

"Mother and I can only sense people fifty yards away, maybe a little farther. How far away can the First Magus sense people?"

"I don't know. Years ago, the Third Magus sensed me from over a hundred yards away."

"How strong a mage is he?"

"I couldn't sense behind his shields, so I have no idea, but his shields appeared strong."

"Can we play Fyrr tonight?"

"If Saelora doesn't have anything else planned. And that's if you finish your order/chaos exercises."

"Then I'll start on them before she gets here."

Alyiakal conceals a smile.

LXXVI

For Alyiakal, Saelora, and Saryalth, sixday and sevenday follow a pattern similar to fiveday, except for Saelora's trip with Saryalth to the local seamstress. She orders two more shirts, each with matching trousers, if in different shades of gray, as well as a black vest.

Since Loraan House is closed on eightday, Alyiakal and Saelora sleep late. Saryalth does not, and when Alyiakal and Saelora rise, they find her sitting in the parlor in her robe reading a short history of Cyador belonging to Saelora, one that she's been perusing for the last few days.

"How are you finding the history?" asks Alyiakal.

"It's not very long, and it doesn't say very much."

"Cyador isn't very old," replies Alyiakal, "only little more than a century. Most of the important events happened in the first twenty years." *Except for the death—or likely disguised assassination—of the Emperor Kieffal.*

"It doesn't say much about the Great Forest or the dissidents."

"The first emperors tried to keep details about both quiet."

"If Alyiakal hadn't rediscovered the old road and their hidden refuge," adds Saelora, "the dissidents would have been totally forgotten."

"In time, they will be anyway," says Alyiakal. "Most everything disconcerting is. Now, we need breakfast. After that and getting dressed, you and I are going to work on something you haven't tried before."

"What?"

"You'll find out." Alyiakal gestures to the kitchen, then joins Saelora in fixing their simple breakfast, which now includes redberry juice for Saryalth.

Once both he and Saryalth have finished breakfast and dressed, Alyiakal leads her outside to the small patch of open ground between the house and the greenberries covering the ground to the north and down to the swamp.

"Why are we here?" she asks.

"It's a good place for you to get started on building and carrying shields."

"Mother won't like that."

"Probably not," replies Alyiakal cheerfully. "That will make it harder for her to tell how you feel, but she'll know anyway, at least for a while. You need to start working on shields now, so that they'll be strong enough to protect you when you need them."

"Were yours?"

"No, they weren't, and I didn't know it until Healer Vayidra pointed that out to me at Syadtar. Her warning gave me three years to build them up."

"But she wasn't a magus."

"All women of the Magi'i who have order/chaos talents are officially restricted to healing, but that doesn't mean that they can't have shields. I suspect Vayidra was as much a magus as many of the Magi'i men. She was careful not to let them know that, and so will you, too, in time. Now, concentrate on what I'm doing with these tiny bits of order and chaos." Alyiakal surrounds a tiny bit of chaos with a shell of order, then says, "You try it."

"I don't know how."

Alyiakal suspends a tiny bit of chaos in front of Saryalth, then forms a slightly larger bit of order beside it. "Do you sense the bits of order and chaos?"

"Yes, Father."

"Push the chaos toward the order."

Alyiakal senses the small push that barely moves the chaos. "You keep trying, and I'll help you just a little bit."

Saryalth's second attempt is stronger, even without Alyiakal's aid, but the chaos bit fragments into nothingness when it strikes the order.

"What happened?" asks Saryalth.

"That was my fault. I've done things for so long without having to think about them that I forget some of the little steps. First, you pull together the free chaos, and then you surround it with a shell of order. Then, you can either push the order-shelled chaos into the order or create a larger order shell around the chaos."

"How does that make a shield?"

"You can link the order shells with chaos inside them together. Chaos doesn't stick together very well or for very long unless it's contained in some way. Most Magi'i just use their will to force chaos together. Using order is harder to begin with, but once you learn how, it's much, much less tiring."

"Is that why you're a strong magus?" asks Saryalth.

"I'm not sure anyone would call me a magus, but it's why I can handle more chaos and order than many Magi'i. Now . . . we need to work on what I forgot—creating a thin layer of order that you can shape around free chaos."

After a glass of effort, Saryalth is flushed and sweating, but she can finally surround small bits of chaos with order . . . several times in a row.

Alyiakal smiles broadly. "You did well."

"It's so little," she protests.

He shakes his head. "It's a great deal. We'll work on it again later. What you've learned today is the hardest part. It's the basic tool of handling order and chaos. As you get stronger, you'll be amazed at what you can do. It will take time, but if you keep at it, you'll get better and better." Alyiakal turns toward the old road leading to the swamp. "We can take a few moments for you to cool off before we go back to the house for a short history and geography lesson."

"You want me to learn a lot in an eightday."

"I do. The more you learn about Cyad away from the Great Forest, the more you'll be able to make a better decision about your life. We could play more games—"

"Can we play Fyrr later?"

"After your geography and history lesson, and after dinner. But, as I was saying, Saelora and I could play more games and not ask much of you, but that wouldn't be fair to you. You wouldn't know as much about our life or what your life outside the Forest might be . . . if you choose that in the future."

"Do I have to choose?"

"Saryalth, not making a choice is in fact making a choice."

She frowns, then nods.

"Let's see if you can sense more fish farther away in the swamp."

"There aren't ever very many."

"Are there that many in the ponds and lakes in the Great Forest?"

"There's only one lake in the north part. Mother says there's a smaller lake in the southeast. They all have more fish than the swamp. That's because there's not much order in the swamp, isn't it?"

"More likely because there's not that much chaos." Alyiakal explains briefly about how life requires both.

At the swamp, Saryalth's prediction proves correct, but she's cheerful as they walk back to the house.

When they enter the parlor, Saelora looks up from her armchair. "How did the practice go?"

"Saryalth did well, even if she didn't think so."

"She sounds like her father," replies Saelora, turning to Saryalth. "He's always saying how he should have done things better."

"As if I'm the only one guilty of that," says Alyiakal dryly.

Both Saryalth and Saelora laugh.

LXXVII

On oneday evening, Alyiakal and Saelora have just entered their bedchamber when Alyiakal says quietly, "We have to take her back to Geliendra the day after tomorrow. Do you think she'll want to come back?"

"You can sense her. What do you think?" Saelora stops in front of her armoire, removes her Merchanter vest, then hangs it up.

"She really enjoyed playing Fyrr with us. I wonder about that."

"I feel Adayal is lonely. Saryalth is old enough to sense that, and it's not lonely when we're together, not that she's about to leave her mother anytime soon."

"You speak as if she will."

"Given Adayal's age, Saryalth will be fairly young when her mother dies, but Saryalth is also your daughter." Saelora sits on the edge of the bed and pulls off her boots. "According to Adayal, and even from what little we've seen, Saryalth is already showing signs that she may want more than the Great Forest can give her."

"So Adayal wants her to see the other side before she gets older?" Alyiakal glances at the closed door, then slips out of his boots and puts them in the bottom of his armoire.

"Were I in her boots, I'd want that. There's always the chance that, if she didn't meet you, she'd create an unrealistic dream and flee the Forest into something very different from what she's dreamed. This way, she has a better idea of what our life is like."

"What she's seen still isn't realistic," Alyiakal points out, shedding his tunic.

"It is, and it isn't. What she's seen of me isn't that unrealistic. What's unrealistic about you is that you're not here that often, but she's gotten hints of that. If she comes again, she'll learn more."

"Do you think she will?" Alyiakal asks, sitting down on the bed beside Saelora.

"Right now, she wants to. After she returns to her mother and the Great Forest, who knows?" Saelora pauses. "You still have something on your mind, don't you?"

"I'd like to give her a few silvers, perhaps five and a few coppers, just for her."

"If you do that, it might be best to provide a gold or two to Adayal, especially since she didn't have to write you."

Given what Alyiakal has seen of his daughter and what he senses as her quiet perseverance, he wonders how much choice Adayal had. "Are five silvers too much or too little for Saryalth?"

"She doesn't seem like she'd waste them, but I'd tell Adayal you gave Saryalth a few silvers and coppers for her own use, for the little things a father might provide were he more present."

"That's a good way of putting it. Thank you for that, and for being so good to Saryalth." He puts his arm around her shoulders, then leans closer and brushes her cheek with his lips.

"I've truly enjoyed it, and it's been good to see you with her." Saelora lowers her eyes. "I've wondered . . ."

Alyiakal understands instantly. "When do you think we—"

"Not quite yet . . . not quite." She rises from the bed, smiling. "But it is time for us."

LXXVIII

Between Saelora's work at the factorage, and Alyiakal's tutoring and training of Saryalth, and the time Alyiakal and Saelora both spend in games and conversation with Saryalth, not to mention picking up Saryalth's new clothes, threeday morning comes more quickly than Alyiakal has anticipated.

At breakfast, Alyiakal asks Saryalth, "Which of your new clothes are you going to wear today?"

"Could I wear the light gray with the black vest?" Saryalth looks to Saelora.

"Of course."

Alyiakal nods, although he knows that his approval means far less than Saelora's where clothes are concerned.

After a moment, he asks Saelora, "Is there anything else you need to do in Geliendra besides pick up more barrels from Doerst?"

"Nothing that can't wait. The barrels will take up most of the wagon, and we're going to need every barrel we can get."

"For Crystalflame or for brandy?"

"Mainly Crystalflame. Valtrad will take as much as we can produce."

"Why do you sell so much to the outland traders?" asks Saryalth.

"Because they're willing to pay more." Saelora sees or senses Saryalth's coming question and adds, "It's easier and cheaper to grow maize here than in Nordla or Austra. So we can produce and sell Crystalflame at a lower price, even after shipping costs."

"Why don't other traders here do that?"

"They could, but they'd have to grow or buy the maize and build a distillery, and then to take the trade from us, they'd have to sell for less, and it wouldn't be as profitable for them. We already had the distillery and because it's cheaper to build and grow maize here, it costs us less."

When Saelora finishes explaining, Saryalth looks slightly dazed.

Alyiakal laughs softly and says, "You're beginning to see why she's so good. Now you need to finish your breakfast and get cleaned up and dressed. Then put all your things in your pack. We'll be leaving for Geliendra in early midafternoon."

"Can I leave the robe here? I won't use it in the Great Forest, but I'd like to have it when I come again."

"Of course," replies Saelora. "It will be here for you."

"Thank you."

After both Alyiakal and Saryalth are dressed, Alyiakal takes Saryalth on a walk to the end of the old road, partly to give Saelora some time to herself. They stop a few yards short of the swamp. Once there, Alyiakal hands Saryalth a small leather pouch.

She looks at him quizzically.

"It's for you, not for your mother. There will also be something for her. There are five silvers and five coppers inside."

"Thank you. I didn't come here for silvers."

"I know, but I can't be with you that often. These are for times when I could get you something if I were there." After a pause, he asks, "How has your time here been?"

"I'm glad I came. It was a little scary at first. I liked Saelora right away. I'm glad you consorted her. She feels like Mother, but different."

"Different how?"

"Just different," replies Saryalth in a tone that borders on exasperation.

Deciding not to press his daughter about Saelora, Alyiakal asks, "Is there anything else you'd like to know?"

"Not really."

"You mean that we told you more than you ever wanted to know?" Alyiakal asks in a cheerful tone.

"Pretty much." Saryalth pauses. "Except . . . Saelora said you have nightmares . . . and . . . well . . ."

"You want to know what they're about?"

"Sort of."

"They're usually about things I had to do but wish could have been otherwise."

"Did you really have to do them?"

"I'll tell you about one, and you can tell me what you think." Alyiakal pauses. "When I was an undercaptain at my first posting, before my shields were very strong, I was on a patrol against some raiders in Jerans who'd attacked and killed a company of lancers from another post. There were raiders everywhere, and someone stepped out from behind the corner of a house with a bow, with the arrow nocked and pointed at me. I loosed a firebolt from my lance. The archer turned out to be a girl about the age you are now, but I didn't see that until just before the firebolt hit her. I still have that nightmare, and I can still sense the black mist of her death."

After a long moment, Saryalth asks, "Are all the nightmares like that?"

"Some are. Some are about battles or skirmishes. None of them are pleasant."

"I don't think I'd like to be a Mirror Lancer."

"You don't have to be one. But if you're a healer, you'll likely have bad dreams about people you can't heal. Most people have nightmares of one sort or another. We make mistakes, or we're put in positions where any choice we make isn't good."

Alyiakal senses Saryalth's dismay, and adds, "That doesn't happen often, but I'd be lying if I said you can always avoid hard choices."

"Why did you tell me that nightmare?"

"You asked, and it's the one I have the most often."

"Couldn't you have done something else?"

"When you're in a situation like that, you have to react faster than you can think, or you might not survive. Or if you're an officer, the rankers with you might not."

Saryalth offers a dubious half nod.

After another silence, Alyiakal asks, "What one thing did you like the best?"

"Playing Fyrr with you and Saelora. We were all together."

"Anything else?"

"The dinners were so good."

"I like them, too. They're so much better than what I get at the officers' mess, and field rations are even worse."

The two are quiet on the walk back to the house, and Alyiakal doesn't sense any strong emotions from Saryalth. While he decides not to intrude, he wonders if he should have been so direct, except, for better or worse, he'd promised Adayal he'd be honest. *But did you have to be that honest?*

He's still wondering about it in midafternoon when he, Saelora, and Saryalth leave the house, heading for Geliendra to meet with Adayal.

He rides beside the wagon on the side closest to Saryalth, who occasionally asks questions, then says, "Why is the road to Vaeyal gray part of the way and white the rest?"

"The part that is the main road to Fyrad and the Great Canal is white and smoother in order to allow the Imperial firewagons to move faster."

"You ride a firewagon to where you're posted, don't you?"

"Most of the way, but usually, I have to ride the last part. When I go to Cyad, that will be the first time ever I won't have to ride partway."

"Why don't the white roads go all the way?"

"That would take too much chaos. The amount of chaos created by the chaos towers is limited."

That leads to a discussion on what chaos from the towers is used for and why, which lasts until Saelora turns down a narrow lane, barely wide enough for two wagons, to Doerst's cooperage.

As she brings the wagon to a halt, centering the flatbed on the small loading dock, the burly, white-bearded cooper appears.

"Thought it wouldn't be long before you or your brother showed up." The cooper looks to Saryalth and then to Alyiakal. "You were here once before, ser, weren't you?"

"Alyiakal is a friend of my brother's," says Saelora. "Now, we're consorted. We don't have much time before he leaves for his next post. So he came with me. Gaaran said you might have a half score tight barrels."

"Actually have twelve, if you can take them. They're even toasted the way you like. Only a little extra for that." Doerst offers a broad smile.

"How much is a little extra?" asks Saelora cheerfully.

"A copper a barrel."

"How about a silver for all the toasting," counters Saelora, "and we'll take all twelve."

Alyiakal can sense that Doerst worries that he may have gambled on toasting all the barrels, while Saelora is only bargaining because it's expected.

"For you only."

"We appreciate it," replies Saelora.

Alyiakal dismounts and ties the gelding to a post at the end of the loading dock, then takes the barrels from the cooper and places them in the wagon. When they're finished, the wagon holds eight barrels upright, and four lashed sideways on top.

Once Saelora pays the cooper and drives back down the lane, at the main avenue she turns the wagon east toward Southpoint.

When they near the northwest corner of the post walls, Alyiakal senses Adayal and tells Saryalth, "Your mother's already here."

"You can sense her that far away?"

Alyiakal nods. He's sensed *someone* from even farther but hasn't been able to discern the feeling of the Great Forest that shadows Adayal until they are closer.

Alyiakal can definitely sense Adayal's relief as she catches sight of the Loraan House wagon as well as a burst of affection and love for her daughter. At the same time, he notes again what feels like an imbalance in Adayal's order/chaos flows, but when he concentrates more intensely it's as though her order is comprised of two flows, although he can't discern any difference between the two.

As soon as Saelora brings the wagon to a halt opposite Adayal, Alyiakal dismounts and ties the gelding to the wagon, then retrieves Saryalth's pack and walks toward Adayal.

She takes the pack and turns to Saryalth. "Say goodbye to Saelora. I need a few moments with your father."

"Yes, Mother." Saryalth moves back toward Saelora.

Adayal steps farther from the wagon, then says, "You've always been a man of your word. It's good to see that you still are."

"How could I not be?"

"You're powerful, well beyond your position and rank. Power changes some people."

"If I were that type, Saelora never would have consorted me."

"For that, Saryalth and I are grateful."

"And for what you taught me, I'm grateful. It made a difference." Alyiakal extends the leather pouch. "There are a few golds there in case of need. I also gave Saryalth five silvers and a few coppers, for whatever she might like."

Adayal takes the pouch and tucks it away. "I see she has a new outfit as well."

"Two, actually, in different shades of gray."

"I'd ask if you attempted to entice her, but it's clear you didn't."

"That wouldn't have been right. We did our best to show her what our lives are like. I was honest with her, as you requested, about what I do, and the costs of doing so. So was Saelora. I did work with her on some of the basics of healing and shields. One way or another, those skills should be useful."

"You're a healer, too, aren't you?"

"More than a field healer and less than a full healer."

"You said you're going to Cyad. For what?"

"I have no idea, but likely because I've been improbably successful, and that concerns senior commanders."

"You were improbable at sixteen." After a slight hesitation Adayal goes on. "We have Saelora's address. If she wishes to write, I'll have her write as your niece."

Alyiakal shakes his head. "She's my daughter. I won't hide that." He laughs softly and ironically. "Besides, the current emperor is from an unconsorted union. I doubt anyone will care, but if they do, that shows them for what they are. I can deal with that."

"I imagine you can. Is there anything else?"

"Just take care of yourself," replies Alyiakal. "Saryalth loves you and needs you to be there very much."

"I'll ask the same of you, for the same reason." Then Adayal turns and walks toward Saryalth, saying with a cheer she doesn't totally feel, "We mustn't keep your father and Saelora any longer, or they'll be returning to Vaeyal in the dark."

Saryalth turns and gives Alyiakal a fierce hug, the first physical embrace she's given him. "Thank you! And Saelora." Then she steps away and takes her mother's hand.

Alyiakal isn't sure but thinks he might have seen a brightness in Saryalth's eyes.

After he unties the gelding and mounts, he watches for a few moments as Adayal and Saryalth walk toward the whitestone road that borders the Great Forest, then turns to ride alongside Saelora.

"Did Adayal say anything interesting?"

"More what she didn't say." Alyiakal relates what Adayal said.

When he finishes, Saelora is silent for a few moments, then says, "She really didn't get to know you well."

"I'm sure I've changed since then."

"Not in the ways that count. You've learned more and make fewer mistakes, but you're responsible, and fiercely loyal to those you love and those you command. Regardless of the cost to you, you won't disavow your daughter, and I love you for that." Saelora adds, "Your loyalty doesn't extend to gross incompetence."

"Not if it endangers others."

"That goes without saying. From what I could sense, Adayal seemed sad. Do you have any idea why?"

"I sensed that as well, but I'm fairly certain it doesn't have much, if anything, to do with me. There is something odd about her order, as if she has two linked order flows. I've never sensed anything like that before."

"Could it be something having to do with the Great Forest? Perhaps, because she's spent so much time there?"

"I'd wager it is, but I don't know what it means."

"You've often worried that the Great Forest wanted something from you. What if Saryalth is that something? Or if it has plans for the two of you?"

Alyiakal laughs sardonically. "I'm not sure it thinks that way, but if it does, you're part of it. You're getting able to sense more about what people feel every day, aren't you?"

Saelora nods. "I could also sense what you were doing in teaching Saryalth, but I couldn't do any of it."

"That's odd, too. From what Triamon told me, being able to sense feelings was linked to power."

"You mean the more you can sense, the more ability to manipulate order and chaos?"

"That's what he said, but I haven't been around enough Magi'i to know if it works that way."

"You may get that chance in Cyad."

"I can't say I'm looking forward to it."

"Don't. We only have three full days before you leave, and I intend to take up every moment of those days."

"I'm yours."

"That you are, and don't forget it."

They both laugh, and then Saelora turns the wagon west on the road to Vaeyal.

LXXIX

The next three days are far too short, but Alyiakal and Saelora spend almost every moment together. Then, on sevenday morning Saelora uses the wagon to take Alyiakal to the Vaeyal waystop, where he unloads his two duffels, then climbs back up to the teamster's bench to talk to her until the firewagon arrives.

Before he can say a word, she speaks. "I've been thinking. Most, if not all, of the Mirror Lancer post commanders know what you did at Lhaarat and Pemedra. You said that most company officers probably didn't."

"A few know."

"If the subject comes up with other officers on your way to Cyad, don't demur. Don't boast, either. Just say that you were in command and did what was necessary or something like that. If someone asks questions, answer, but make the answer short. It can't hurt to have more officers knowing what you did."

Alyiakal smiles. "You're right. It won't help me any to be silent, but boasting will be equally detrimental."

She smiles in return. "Sometimes, I do have a good idea."

"More than sometimes. Much more."

He's about to say more about her good ideas when he catches sight of the firewagon coming from the south.

Saelora puts her arms around him and gives him a lingering, gentle, but passionate kiss, then says, "Let me know as soon as you can."

"Given the way the Mirror Lancers seem to be working, I might have to leave it at letting you know I arrived in Cyad. Anything else may have to wait."

She smiles. "I won't mind two letters."

"Then you'll get two," he says as he leaves the teamster's seat. He almost makes it to the firewagon before the firewagon comes to a stop and the driver's assistant opens the door to the front compartment.

"Majer Alyiakal?"

Alyiakal shows his ring seal and his travel authorization.

"Cyad. Not many officers go there unless they live there."

"Or if they have orders," Alyiakal replies dryly, as he loads his duffels into the front compartment of the firewagon. He stuffs them under and behind the one vacant seat before taking a last, long look at Saelora and climbing inside to take the seat, one of the two facing forward.

Alyiakal suspects that one of the two captains moved to a rear-facing seat beside an undercaptain to allow him that courtesy, and he says, "Thank you," not being more specific because he doesn't know that for certain.

As the driver's assistant closes the compartment door, the younger of the two captains says, "My pleasure, ser," then asks, "Did I hear that you're headed to Cyad under orders?"

"I am." Alyiakal tries to get a last glimpse of Saelora but can only see the lower part of the Loraan House wagon, then finishes, "For duties to be determined by the Majer-Commander."

The older captain comments in a politely sardonic tone, "Better you than me, ser. By the way, I'm Aalstyd, heading to Chulbyn."

"And I'm Laaskyl, reporting to Lhaarat," adds the younger captain.

"Alyiakal, coming from Pemedra to Cyad."

Alyiakal senses a certain surprise from Aalstyd but waits to see what the older captain might say or ask.

"You weren't the one—"

"Who removed the Duke of Cerlyn and destroyed most of his armsmen? Yes. For better or worse."

"I didn't hear about the Duke," says Aalstyd.

"And at least one of his sons and possibly more of his family."

"My last recollection," says Aalstyd carefully, "was that Pemedra only has four companies."

"Your recollection is correct. We used all four."

"Heavy losses?"

"Not really, considering what we faced. One officer and twenty rankers killed. A squad's worth of wounded, but all of them are recovering and expected to return to duty."

Aalstyd nods and inclines his head. "My apologies for intruding, Majer, but there have been rumors."

"I'd like to dispel them, but it's best I don't say more until I report to the Majer-Commander."

"I understand."

Alyiakal notes how his words have unsettled Aalstyd, but Laaskyl seems more puzzled than unsettled and says, "I saw a rather elaborate Merchanter wagon at the waystop."

"That belongs to my consort. She's a Merchanter and the head of Loraan House."

Aalstyd looks hard at the younger captain, and Laaskyl quickly adds, "No offense meant, ser."

Alyiakal offers an amused smile. "But it's rare to see a senior officer in the company of Merchanters? She is rare, but her entire family is altage. Her father was a majer. Her older brother is a wound-stipended captain, and her other brother is an overcaptain at Northpoint. And, of course, she consorted me."

"But how . . ." The so-far-silent undercaptain breaks off his involuntary question.

"She built it herself," replies Alyiakal, sensing the surprise from all three officers. Before any can ask more, he looks to the undercaptain. "I don't believe you introduced yourself."

"Zaabyrt, ser, posted to Isahl from Eastpoint."

"Where are you from, Undercaptain?"

"Sollend, ser."

Alyiakal nods, thinking it more than likely that Zaabyrt is from an elthage background, although he shows no signs of either greater than normal order or chaos levels. "Just a year at Kynstaar?"

"Ah . . . yes, ser."

"I imagine Kynstaar wasn't quite what you expected, but you obviously persevered."

"No, ser. It was more difficult than I anticipated, and I worked harder than I ever had."

Sensing the truth of Zaabyrt's words, Alyiakal says, "Good for you."

"Begging your pardon, ser, but can you tell me anything about Lhaarat? Neither of the captains has been posted there."

Alyiakal smiles. "You'll have to switch firewagons at Ilypsya and catch one to a supply post called Terimot. From there, it's a hard, and long, three-or-four-day ride if you're accompanying supplies." Alyiakal limits his descriptions to the post itself, the geography, hamlets, the main roads, and the need for extended patrols to Kraaslaen.

When he finishes, Zaabyrt says, "Thank you so much, ser. That was a briefing, and I appreciate it."

Laaskyl says, "From what you know, you have to have been posted there."

"I was posted there as deputy post commander, then promoted to post commander after a year."

While Aalstyd looks intently at Laaskyl, the younger captain remains oblivious, and Aalstyd says nothing.

Since no one else has any questions, and Alyiakal could use a nap, he leans back, trying to find a marginally comfortable position, and wonders what awaits him at Cyad. His mind also wanders to how Saryalth will see the Great Forest after her time with him and Saelora, what he was able to teach her. *Less than you would have liked, but more than Adayal could, and hopefully enough to open her eyes and perceptions a little wider.* He knows that, more than he'd prefer, is up to Saryalth, and that worries him, along with his concerns that something is not quite right with Adayal.

But then, right now there are far too many things he doesn't know and far too many factors are beyond his control.

As if that's anything new.

ALYIAKAL'ALT,

Majer

Cyad

Harvest, 105 A.F.

LXXX

As on Alyiakal's previous journeys from Vaeyal, the firewagon reaches Ilypsya well after dark. Because the firewagon to Chulbyn leaves at first light, Alyiakal obtains some refreshment from the officers' mess, then writes and leaves a brief note for Majer Bekkan with the duty squad leader regretting the lack of time to meet. After that, he retires and manages to get some sleep before arising early on eightday and readying himself for the next part of his travels.

When he reaches the firewagon on eightday morning, he finds that two captains and a sub-majer are traveling with him, with Sub-Majer Kaen heading for Assyadt as deputy post commander, Captain Joult for training duty at Kynstaar, and Captain Kaellyt returning to Cyad on home leave prior to reposting to Guarstyad.

Once the firewagon is headed west on the whitestone road, Kaen, who is clearly at least ten years older than Alyiakal, turns and asks, "Might I ask the reason for your travel to Cyad?"

Alyiakal offers an amused smile, since he hasn't mentioned anything more than his destination being Cyad when he'd introduced himself prior to entering the firewagon. "Orders to report to the Majer-Commander, duties unspecified. I was previously post commander at Pemedra, and commander at Lhaarat before that."

"Then you were the one . . ."

"I was."

Kaen shakes his head. "Someone should have dealt with Cerlyn long ago, but headquarters would never provide the lancers. How did you manage to get them?"

"I didn't. I wagered and took all four companies on a back trail. We ambushed and destroyed ten companies at Kraaslaen, then rode to Clynya and attacked the Duke's palace, killed the Duke and most of his family, bottled the remaining armsmen in their garrison, fired it, and killed most of them when they tried to escape. Then we rode back to Pemedra with what spoils we gathered from the palace."

"With four companies?"

"That's all I had."

"Casualties?"

"One company officer, twenty deaths, and roughly twenty wounded, all of whom survived."

Kaen looks unbelievingly at Alyiakal. "Am I supposed to believe you did that with only four companies?"

"The Captain-Commander, the Majer-Commander, and those four companies do. Besides which, it happens to be accurate."

The sub-majer frowns. "Several years ago, a sub-majer at Lharaat wiped out Cerlynese forces at Kraaslaen two years running."

"That was when I was deputy post commander and then post commander there. It took three companies each time."

"How in the Rational Stars . . . ?" Kaen shakes his head once more. "And to ride to Clynya . . ."

"Good strategy, good officers, well-trained rankers, and considerable audacity," replies Alyiakal. "The Duke couldn't believe it when I took a company up through the palace gate a little after first light."

"One company?"

"The other three were bottling up his armsmen."

"How did you get authorization?"

"I just followed orders. Earlier this year, the Cerlynese wiped out two companies from Lhaarat, including the post commander. I was ordered to remedy the situation. I decided that the only way to do that was to remove all the Cerlynese armsmen we could and, if possible, the Duke. We were fortunate to accomplish it."

"I have the feeling fortune had little to do with it," comments Kaen dryly. "You had to know you were exceeding your orders."

"Actually, I wasn't. I was told to do whatever it took with the resources I had."

Kaen chuckles, sardonically. "I can see why you're being ordered to Cyad."

By now, Alyiakal can tell that both captains are listening intently. The older Joult is clearly amused, while Kaellyt is somewhere between appalled and amazed.

Alyiakal decides to stir the pot just a bit more and asks, "Captain Kaellyt, you don't happen to be from an old altage heritage, do you?"

Kaellyt swallows, then says, "Yes, ser."

"I thought you might be. Best of fortune."

"Kaellyt," adds the sub-majer, "think about what you've heard, and about the majer's question."

The younger captain frowns.

"Try harder," adds Kaen, murmuring, "not that it will help." Then he says to Alyiakal, politely, "I trust you'll use your skills only when necessary, Majer."

"So far as I've been able, I never have done otherwise. I just didn't see the point in losing large numbers of lancers continually and unnecessarily."

For the remainder of the travel to Chulbyn, conversation deals with various matters not pertaining directly to Mirror Lancer policies or orders, although in a discussion of ales, Alyiakal does mention Pemedra's grass ale.

When he arrives in Chulbyn, again well after the evening mess, he accompanies the porter, and his gear, to the visiting officers' quarters, then obtains some nourishment from the officers' mess. Apparently the officers who accompanied him to Chulbyn had either come before or would be in after him, and he retires to his temporary quarters.

He leaves Chulbyn at first light, but Kaellyt isn't in the forward compartment, possibly because the others with him are a commander and two senior overcaptains, none of whom have said much in boarding the firewagon.

Alyiakal sits beside the commander and across from the overcaptains.

Once the firewagon leaves Chulbyn, the sandy-haired commander turns and asks, "You wouldn't be Majer Alyiakal, would you?"

Although Alyiakal feels the question is largely rhetorical, he answers, "I am."

One of the overcaptains looks more intently at Alyiakal, while the other appears and feels disinterested.

The commander nods and says, "Coeryn. You're even younger-looking than I expected. How do you know the Captain-Commander?"

"He was my commanding officer at Guarstyad, years back."

"During the Kyphran mess, I presume?"

"Yes, ser."

"Have you ever had a purely administrative duty?"

"The closest was in closing Luuval Post, ser. Some administrative duties as deputy post commander at Lhaarat before I became post commander."

Coeryn nods. "You'll find headquarters combines all your duties, except field command." He pauses. "What do you know about merchanting?"

"I was acting Imperial tariff enumerator when I was the officer in charge at Oldroad Post and had to deal with the Imperial tariff enumerator in closing Luuval. I'm also consorted to a Lady Merchanter who has her own moderately sized house."

"Very interesting. Does the Captain-Commander know this?"

"I assume that he has access to all the reports I made dealing with Merchanters and enumerators."

"You speak as if you haven't met with him recently."

"Not after my first year at Guarstyad."

"Most interesting. I'm sure I'll see you at headquarters." Coeryn leans back in his seat and pulls his visor cap down to shade his eyes. Before long, he is dozing.

Alyiakal considers the commander and his questions, which were more than idle curiosity. They were certainly calculated, although Alyiakal couldn't sense any immediate malign intent, but wonders at a deeper purpose.

To gain information other headquarters commanders don't know for immediate benefit or for use in the future, as necessary?

Both, probably, Alyiakal decides. It's also clear that the brief interaction was a barely polite reminder of how junior, and insignificant, Alyiakal will be when he arrives at Mirror Lancer headquarters.

As if you didn't know that.

LXXXI

In midafternoon, the firewagon leisurely descends from the low hills toward an expanse of whitestone structures that comprise Cyad. An imposing shimmering white edifice that has to be the Palace of Eternal Light dominates the city from its location on a low rise overlooking whitestone buildings, the white piers, and the blue-gray waters of the harbor.

Another quint passes before the firewagon reaches the far less imposing, if still largely stone, dwellings and assorted structures at the edge of Cyad, and yet another quint elapses before the firewagon comes to a halt.

Commander Coeryn leaves the firewagon first, followed by Alyiakal, who can't help glancing up at the five-story white granite building that, from the crossed firelances over the entry, is Mirror Lancer headquarters. Each story above the first has a terrace on the east side, surrounded by a low wall, so that each story is smaller than the one beneath.

Coeryn glances at Alyiakal with an expression of vague amusement.

Alyiakal ignores the amusement and says, politely, "Ser, since I've never been in Cyad before, and headquarters isn't a standard post, where do I report?"

"To wherever your orders say, Majer."

"Then, if you could direct me to the Majer-Commander, ser?"

"Is that what your orders say, precisely?"

"Yes, ser."

For the first time, Commander Coeryn appears momentarily concerned. "His study is on the fifth floor, but I'd suggest telling the duty squad leader just inside first. He'll likely wish to verify that."

"Thank you, ser." Alyiakal lifts his duffels and makes his way through the entrance and into the building's entry foyer, where he sees a senior squad leader seated behind a golden-oak table desk, flanked by two Mirror Lancers in spotless cream dress uniforms, each armed with a short firelance and a sabre.

Alyiakal stops short of the table, retrieves his orders from one of the duffels, and presents them to the senior squad leader. "I have orders to report to the Majer-Commander directly."

The squad leader peruses the orders, frowning momentarily. "Yes, ser. You'll need to present your orders to the squad leader at his study on the fifth level." He gestures toward the square arch flanked by green tapestries, through which Alyiakal can see a set of wide stone steps.

Alyiakal smiles wryly. "Could I leave my gear here?"

"No, ser." The squad leader offers a smile and adds, "But I can have it carried to the quarters building behind headquarters to be held there for you."

"Thank you. I appreciate it." Alyiakal inclines his head, then makes his way to and through the arch and begins to climb the steps, which rise a half flight to a landing. From each end of the landing another set of steps rises to the next floor, a pattern that continues for four flights.

In the open space beyond the steps on the fifth floor, Alyiakal finds a squad leader seated behind yet another golden-oak table desk. Beyond the desk are three doorways. Those at the far left and right are closed. The middle double doors are open, revealing an anteroom.

Alyiakal again tenders his orders and presents his ring seal. "Majer Alyiakal, reporting."

"Yes, ser. The Captain-Commander has been expecting you. At the moment, he's engaged." The squad leader gestures to the middle doors. "You can wait there." He does not return Alyiakal's orders.

"Thank you." Alyiakal makes his way past the squad leader to the anteroom, where he walks to the windows, both of which are open, bringing a slight breeze into the chamber, and looks out over the white and green of the city, taking in the late-afternoon shadows. Then he sits in one of the cushioned wooden armchairs and waits.

More than a quint passes before the squad leader appears in the anteroom doorway. "He'll see you now, ser."

Alyiakal follows the squad leader to the Captain-Commander's study—a rectangle of fifteen by thirty cubits, containing a conference table for eight, a wide and polished table desk with a comfortable desk chair, with one wall comprised entirely of bookshelves and one mostly of narrow windows overlooking Cyad.

Laartol stands from behind the desk as Alyiakal enters and the squad leader closes the door behind him. Alyiakal senses a certain weariness and sees that Laartol's once-silver-shot black hair is now largely silver, and there are circles under his hazel eyes.

"Captain-Commander," offers Alyiakal, with a deferential head bow.

"It's good to see you, Alyiakal," declares Laartol, his voice warm and welcoming, as are the feelings behind the words. "Have a seat."

Alyiakal takes the single seat across from the Captain-Commander, who resumes his place behind the desk. Then Alyiakal waits to see what Laartol has to say.

"Why do you think you're here?"

Alyiakal can't sense anything cold or malign behind the question, but possibly a little warmth and amusement. "Because you want me here, but there are several possibilities as to why."

"I'd like to hear what you think those might be."

Alyiakal decides to gamble. "I've proven that I'm likely one of the Mirror Lancers' best field commanders. Given that the Jeranyi appear to be the greatest remaining threat on the border, and given that I wasn't sent to Assyadt or Inividra, that suggests that either you have a greater need for me here or you've been pressured by the Emperor and/or the Merchanters to remove me from command."

Laartol smiles with wry warmth, and he takes a pouch from somewhere and hands it across the desk to Alyiakal. "Both. Congratulations, Subcommander."

Alyiakal doesn't have to feign surprise, not at being correct in his assumptions, but at the immediate promotion.

"You earned the promotion, effective on the first oneday of Harvest, by the way. Also, while your success has disconcerted a number of influential individuals in the Triad, we'll talk more about that later after you're more settled. I say 'more settled' advisedly, because no one with any intelligence is ever completely settled here in Cyad. Now, I'd like to know exactly how you came to your conclusion and what facts and experiences support it."

"Yes, ser. One: When Overcaptain Tygael, the acting post commander at Pemedra, ordered me on a patrol beyond the Grass Hills to the border of Cerlyn. At the time, I had no idea that what I learned would be so important." After that, Alyiakal discusses what he learned about the Merchanters from his experience as an acting Imperial tariff enumerator, his difficulties with the enumerator in closing Luuval Post, the subsequent interrogation by a senior magus, and then his further experiences at both Lhaarat and Pemedra.

He's about to mention what he learned from Saelora when Laartol says, "There are reports that you're romantically involved with a Lady Merchanter. How accurate are those reports?"

Alyiakal can tell that Laartol has an interest, but he can't discern why. "I was about to get to that, ser. She's the sister of my best friend, Overcaptain Hyrsaal, and I've been seeing and writing her for years. She's taught me a great deal about trade and Merchanters, in general. The reports you mention are likely accurate as far as they go, but they don't go far enough. We were consorted during my reposting leave."

Laartol's laughter is both warm and amused. "Excellent, excellent. I'd hoped for something along those lines, but that's even better."

"Because it becomes more difficult for those unhappy with my dealing with Duke Taartyn to accuse me of being biased against Merchanters when I'm consorted to one who's created her own house?"

"Her own house?"

Laartol's modest surprise concerns Alyiakal. "Yes, ser. Loraan House. She bought out another factor around six years ago and has factorages in both Vaeyal and Fyrad, as well as a moderately large distillery. She also has ongoing trading with several large outland trading houses. I would think that anyone who looked into her would have discovered that."

"There are more than a few matters about which I'm less informed than I should be," replies Laartol dryly. "That's another reason you're here." He smiles and asks, "How are you coming with your maps?"

"I've kept up with updating and drawing new maps for every posting."

Laartol nods. "I'd appreciate it if you'd entrust those maps to me for an eightday or so. I'd like to have them copied. I have no doubt that they're more accurate than what headquarters currently has."

"I'd be happy to do that, ser. They're in my gear, which I understand has been carried to the quarters building."

"Have you shared them with others?"

Laartol's question seems more of curiosity, so Alyiakal answers easily, "When necessary. Guarstyad was my only posting where the maps were comparable to mine. The copies of the maps I made and left at Pemedra were never used to update the company maps; so I updated them when I took command. I did that on a continuing basis at Lhaarat because there weren't any maps."

"I'd appreciate it if you'd keep what we discussed to yourself, for now. It will be more useful shortly."

Alyiakal nods.

"I've wandered a bit," Laartol continues, "but I need to get to the point. Your official duty title is Tactical and Regional Information Officer. The maps figure into that, naturally. I have another question. A number of reports state that you usually led from the front and accounted personally for a disproportionate number of enemy casualties. One lancer stated that he'd never seen you miss. How accurate is that?"

"After . . . after my first year at Pemedra, it's close to accurate."

"I trust you noticed the guards at the headquarters building entrance carry smaller short firelances. Would you be equally accurate with one of those?"

Alyiakal manages not to frown. "Probably more accurate. A number of times, I used firelances in battle at the limit of effective range."

"From those reports, you're being conservative, and we won't discuss that further. Is that understood?"

"Yes, ser."

Laartol clearly knows that Alyiakal can do things no lancer officer should be able to do and wants Alyiakal to understand that he does. *But he doesn't ever want to talk about it again. Why?*

"You've obviously used tactics in ways no other post commander has managed. Part of your duties is to write out those tactics so that they can be disseminated to post commanders."

"Some were strategies; others were tactics," Alyiakal says.

"Better yet. That will make it a two-part document. Don't rush its completion; it has to be well-written and absolutely clear."

So that the densest field-grade or senior officer can't misconstrue anything, and also because this needs to take a while. "Yes, ser."

"The strategy and tactics document will take longer than you might think because you'll likely be accompanying me a great deal. There's already a small study set up for you on the fourth level. If you need supplies, just ask Senior Squad Leader Taysaan—he's the one who took your orders. In your capacity as the senior information officer, you'll be included in most meetings, but you have no standing unless addressed. Even if you have questions, you may not bring them up at the meeting unless asked. However, I expect you to bring such questions to me in private later. Is that clear?"

"Perfectly clear, ser."

Laartol smiles, again with amusement. "One of the reasons your promotion is backdated is so that you'll immediately have the additional pay in addition to your uniform allowance to purchase two formal uniforms. How are you set for uniforms?"

"I had five made in Geliendra while I was on leave. I have two others in good condition, and two best used for cleaning or other unobserved uses."

"I'd suggest ordering two more standard uniforms in addition to the formal uniforms. The tailor in the quarters building is a bit more expensive, but worth it."

Alyiakal nods.

"Now, we'll get into your understood but never mentioned additional duties. There have been some . . . disturbing . . . events near the Majer-Commander and me over the past season or so. They appear accidental, but we both have our doubts. Because my attention will often be on those with whom I'm meeting, I'd feel a great deal more comfortable with someone else watching for 'unusual events.'"

Because Alyiakal has been acquiescing all too frequently, if necessarily, he replies, "Perhaps it's another way to ostensibly show that the unpredictable post commander who destroyed a Duke, his palace, and most of his armsmen and family, is under tight rein?"

Laartol's smile is rueful. "You haven't changed much, Alyiakal, except that you're more polished and almost unreadable—and that will definitely be useful in Cyad." He pauses. "You'll be issued a short firelance tomorrow. Do you have any questions?"

"Are the threats aimed largely at you and the Majer-Commander?"

"More at me, I suspect, but that's not certain, and it may change."

"Where do the Magi'i stand with regard to headquarters and the Merchanters?"

"Where do you think they stand?" counters Laartol.

"I'd guess, and it's only a guess, that they're polite to both in public and quietly contemptuous in private."

"That's fairly accurate, except the contempt in private isn't quiet enough."

"How strong is the Emperor?"

"He's physically healthy, but doesn't want to offend the Merchanters, many of whom have private guards that, in total, outnumber the palace guards."

"And the lack of ostensible revenue makes hiring and training more impractical."

"Why did you say impractical?" asks Laartol.

"The Merchanters have the golds. If the Emperor hires more guards, he has fewer golds for other purposes, and then the Merchanters can hire more guards for their private forces."

"That's about right," agrees the Captain-Commander. "I can see you understand the basics of the situation. In the eightdays ahead, a great deal more will become clearer. There's one other capability you possess that could prove useful in your duties here." Laartol pauses.

"Ser?"

"You seem able to find and implement solutions to problems in ways no one else has considered. That's a rare talent, and while best used sparingly, it may be necessary to carry out your duties."

Alyiakal understands the words, but decides that asking for amplification would be unwise at the moment. Instead, he asks, "Since this doesn't appear to be a normal post, what is the daily routine and schedule here?"

"The duty glasses are the same, but there's no morning muster here. After the morning mess, there's always a senior staff meeting in the Majer-Commander's study. You'll be there, but silent as we discussed. You'll often be the senior officer in the mess because the other senior staff, except Commander Coeryn, have houses or private quarters for their families here in Cyad."

"I met the commander on my trip here."

"He mentioned that."

Alyiakal manages not to frown, but says, "I did tell him in passing I was consorted to a Lady Merchanter who heads her own moderate house."

Laartol nods. "I'm not surprised, but keep that between us." Then he smiles. "You need to get settled. Skip the senior staff meeting tomorrow morning and take care of the uniforms and other necessities. I'd appreciate your being available by noon. On your way out, see Senior Squad Leader Taysaan for your back pay and quarters authorization—and have him show you your study." With those words, Laartol stands, and adds, "I'll see you tomorrow, and put on the new insignia before you leave the fifth floor."

Alyiakal is on his feet even as he says, "Yes, ser." He closes the study door quietly as he leaves, then pauses to change his rank insignia.

"Congratulations, Subcommander," says Taysaan, standing as Alyiakal approaches his desk.

"Thank you. It was rather unexpected."

"But deserved, I'm sure." Taysaan hands Alyiakal a large, unsealed envelope and a leather pouch. "Your uniform allowance and back pay are in the pouch, along with the key to your study. The envelope holds your senior officers' quarters authorization, your statement of duties, and the crossed firelances pin identifying you as headquarters senior staff. It's worn just back of your left collar insignia. If you'll follow me, I'll take you down to your study."

"I'd appreciate that."

Alyiakal follows the senior squad leader down the steps to the fourth level and into a small foyer, beyond which stretches a corridor floored with the same pinkish-white granite as the rest of headquarters.

Taysaan walks through the foyer and stops at the first door on the left, some two yards along the corridor. "Here you are, ser."

"That's convenient, especially for an officer junior to a number of commanders."

"Not that many, ser. Five at present. Their studies are farther along the corridor. This is the smallest and the least quiet."

Alyiakal laughs softly. "Of course."

Taysaan gestures. "The first door on the right is the large conference room, ser. Your key will unlock it as well." The senior squad leader opens the door to Alyiakal's study and moves aside.

Alyiakal steps forward and takes in the chamber, roughly the same size as his deputy post commander's study in Lhaarat. As he suspected from the building's structure, the study has no windows, but has several air shafts with vented covers and a cupridium oil lamp mounted on the wall beside one end of the desk, adjacent to one of the air shafts. The golden-oak desk is well-polished and anything but new, as is the leather-upholstered chair behind it. There are two file chests on a low table and two straight-backed chairs, along with a narrow bookcase. The cream plaster walls are bare.

"The inkwells and pens and paper are in the desk drawers, ser. If you need anything else, you're to let me know."

"Thank you, Taysaan. I will. I don't doubt that I'll also have a few questions."

"Everyone does, ser, after they get here." The senior squad leader's voice holds a hint of amusement. "If there's anything else, ser?"

"No, thank you. I won't keep you."

After Taysaan leaves, Alyiakal inspects the chamber, but finds nothing unexpected. He pins the staff collar insignia in place and then locks the study before making his way down three flights to the main floor.

The squad leader in the foyer looks at Alyiakal quizzically.

"You aren't imagining things. I didn't know that I'd already been promoted."

"Congratulations, ser."

"The best way to the quarters building?"

"Take the corridor under the staircase to the back of the building and the rear door. Then walk through the garden to the other side."

"Thank you." Alyiakal turns and heads back to the staircase, where, in addition to the corridor, he discovers that there's a narrower staircase heading to a lower level, although it's blocked with a floor-to-ceiling iron-grated door, suggesting the lower level is for storage. The corridor to the rear of the headquarters building is punctuated by a number of doors, one of which is open, revealing two clerks and rows of filing chests on shelves.

No lancers guard the rear door, and Alyiakal exits into a high-walled garden whose foliage and reduced light momentarily brings to mind the Great Forest. The garden isn't all that large, perhaps fifteen yards by twenty, and is presently empty except for Alyiakal. The single exit, on a narrow lane separating it from the quarters building, is guarded by a pair of lancer rankers, both of whom stiffen as Alyiakal steps through the open iron gate.

He crosses the lane and enters the quarters building.

"Subcommander?" asks the ranker at the table desk in the foyer. Several yards behind the desk is a moderately wide staircase.

"Formerly Majer Alyiakal. I was promoted when I met with the Captain-Commander." Alyiakal draws out the quarters authorization and presents it.

The ranker looks at it, then says, "Oh . . . yes, ser, we have your gear. We'll move it to your new quarters immediately. They're on the second level with Commander Coeryn." He opens a small chest, extracts a key, and hands it to Alyiakal.

"Where is the officers' mess?"

"On this level about halfway back on the left."

"And the tailor?"

"One level down. I believe he's left for the day, ser."

"Thank you." Alyiakal walks back along the corridor to find the door to the mess, then retraces his steps to the front and takes the stairs to the second level, where he notices a ranker closing a door and locking it, then heading for the rear of the building and presumably to a service staircase.

Alyiakal makes his way to the door, discovering that it is in fact the entry to his new quarters. After he unlocks the door and steps into the foyer of his new quarters, he sees his two duffels awaiting him. He can't help smiling as he takes in the parlor/study, the bedchamber with an armoire, and the bathing chamber/jakes. *Definitely for a higher-ranking senior officer.*

A little less than a glass later, having unpacked his gear, Alyiakal makes his way to the officers' mess, which already holds a half score of junior officers, most of them older and clearly former rankers, and two overcaptains and two majers, one of them a Mirror Engineer. All of the four senior officers are at least ten years older than Alyiakal.

Alyiakal walks to where they stand beside the senior officers' table. "Good evening. I'm Alyiakal, and I just reported in today."

All four appear mildly surprised.

"I've been assigned to the Captain-Commander as his Tactical and Regional Information Officer," Alyiakal adds.

"Alyiakal . . ." muses the Mirror Lancer majer. "You wouldn't be the post commander at Pemedra, would you, ser?"

"I was until I got orders here."

"I'm Symmel," replies the majer quickly, as if he doesn't want to get into Alyiakal's past or possible reason for being in Cyad. "Shaarn is the Mirror Engineer, Tuuel the dark-haired overcaptain, and Fhamyr the other overcaptain."

"I'm pleased to meet you all. I hope I'm not assuming too much in thinking you all have duties at headquarters."

"I'm chief of staff for intelligence, under Commander Coeryn," declares Symmel, "and Shaarn is the same for Commander Zhaant." He then looks to Tuuel.

"Transportation and logistics under Commander Mhakyl." Tuuel grins and nods to Fhamyr.

"Training and personnel, reporting to Commander Staadt."

Symmel looks past Alyiakal. "Here comes Commander Coeryn."

Alyiakal turns. "Good evening, ser."

Coeryn's eyes go to Alyiakal's new insignia. "Congratulations, Subcommander."

"Thank you."

"Have you been assigned duties yet?"

"I'm the Captain-Commander's Tactical and Regional Information Officer."

"That certainly fits with your background." Coeryn gestures to the senior officers' table, then sits at the head.

Alyiakal takes the seat to Coeryn's right.

After everyone is served, Coeryn raises his wineglass and says, "To the subcommander."

Alyiakal lifts his glass slightly to acknowledge the toast, but does not drink, considering that would be in bad taste, and he suspects Coeryn would find some way to use it, sooner or later.

After everyone else has set down their wineglasses, Alyiakal wonders if he'll have to break the ice, but Fhamyr immediately asks, "Where do you call home, Subcommander?"

Alyiakal manages a soft laugh. "In one way, the Mirror Lancers are home. My father and grandfather were both lancer officers, and since my mother died when I was young, when I could I spent time at lancer posts. But for the past several years, my non-duty home has been in Vaeyal. It's a town some ten kays west of Geliendra on the Great Canal. In a way, I adopted the family of my best friend, who's an overcaptain at Northpoint."

Symmel nods. "Lancer officers tend to stick together."

"Especially junior senior officers," adds Fhamyr.

Alyiakal takes a sip of the red wine, far better than at any previous mess, if not as good as what Saelora served, and then a bite of the white fish in a lemon cream sauce.

"And Mirror Engineers," adds Shaarn, with an amused smile.

"I suspect that's only because there are so few commanders and subcommanders," suggests Symmel. "But there are doubtless other reasons." He offers an apparently guileless glance at Coeryn.

"There are always other reasons, Symmel," says Coeryn cheerfully. "Whether they're the right reasons is another question."

"Isn't that usually the case?" asks Alyiakal dryly. "Especially for those that seem the most logical?"

"You question logic, Alyiakal?" asks Coeryn.

"Not logic," replies Alyiakal. "Often the logic is faultless. What's usually not questioned enough are the supposed facts and precepts to which the logic is applied." The moment Alyiakal finishes speaking he can sense that in some ways his words have momentarily disconcerted Coeryn.

Even so, the commander laughs and adds, "Don't forget assumptions, especially those accepted as facts, as happened at Guarstyad." He looks to Alyiakal.

"There were several unquestioned assumptions there," agrees Alyiakal, "and I'm certain that you know far more than I do, but people do their best to forget their incorrect assumptions."

"That's one of the good aspects of engineering," says Shaarn. "You can't assume anything until it works in practice."

"Definitely an advantage," says Coeryn, "but people aren't machines."

"Especially the ladies," interjects Symmel, grinning broadly, "and I'm more than glad for that."

From there the conversation turns to lighter matters, for which Alyiakal is grateful, at least for the present.

After dinner, he returns to his spacious quarters and completes unpacking and arranging his gear before sitting at the table desk and starting his letter to Saelora.

More than a quint later, he finishes and then rereads what he has written.

My dearest Lady Merchanter—

I have arrived safely in Cyad, and you will be happy to know that I have been promoted to subcommander and assigned duties as the Captain-Commander's Tactical and Regional Information Officer. What those duties will entail will doubtless become clearer in the days ahead.

The Mirror Lancer headquarters building is a white granite marvel, five stories in height, with its own walled garden, and with quarters in a neighboring building . . .

Alyiakal skims over the next parts of the letter containing his initial impression of Cyad and a brief description of his journey but no details about any officers, but reads the closing carefully.

> *As I promised, once I'm more settled into my duties and I have a better grasp of Cyad, I'll write you a longer and more informative letter. I cannot tell you in a letter, nor should I, at least in any detail, how much I love you and how much I am grateful for your love, your insights, and your support over the years, and how I look forward to spending more years with you.*

Then he signs and seals it, so that he can dispatch it first thing in the morning.

LXXXII

Alyiakal wakes early on twoday, despite the gray mist that hangs over Cyad with the promise of rain. After washing and shaving he dons one of his new uniforms, then sets out to post his letter to Saelora, which he does with the quarters' duty squad leader before making his way to the officers' mess, where he finds, as Laartol has told him, that he's the senior officer present, which suits him.

At least until you know more about Coeryn.

After eating, he arranges to have his dirty uniforms washed, then makes his way to the tailor's shop, where the tailor is more than pleased with an order for four uniforms, particularly since two are the more expensive formalwear.

While Alyiakal has thought he might walk around the area surrounding headquarters, with the mist's change to a steady downpour he decides a local reconnaissance on foot can wait. Instead, he spends several quints exploring the quarters building and the adjoining stables, spending part of a quint talking to the head ostler and the captain in charge of the stables and the handful of carriages and coaches. He also discovers the armory at the stables' north end on a lower level.

Then Alyiakal returns to his quarters, where he gathers up his book of maps, removes any duplicate maps and rough sketches, and makes his way down to the main level. Then he covers the maps with an order shield and dashes through the rain to the headquarters building. While he has thought about using a shield for himself, dashing through the rain undampened will certainly raise questions he doesn't need.

He doesn't get too damp, partly because the high garden walls and the trees block some of the rain and partly because the distance from the quarters building to headquarters isn't far. He takes his time walking to the main staircase, sensing what he can about what goes on in the rooms flanking the corridor, but the general impression he receives is that the majority of activity is clerical.

But what else would you expect?

He smiles and starts up the staircase.

When he reaches the fifth level, he walks to Taysaan's desk.

"Ser?"

"The Captain-Commander requested my personal book of maps as early as convenient." Alyiakal hands over the book, then adds, "I used an older book of maps as a basis and updated where I could and added where there were no maps."

The senior squad leader's eyes widen as he takes the book. "He's meeting with Commander Staadt, ser, but I'll see that he gets it immediately after that."

"Thank you. Is there anything else I should know?"

"I already left a copy of the Captain-Commander's schedule on your desk. You'll get a copy every morning. It indicates what meetings you're to attend and when you're to accompany him when he leaves headquarters."

A polite way of saying that you need to check that schedule before asking. "I should have stopped by my study first, but I wanted to get the maps to the Captain-Commander straightaway. Thank you." Alyiakal nods politely, then turns and heads back down to his study.

When he unlocks his study door, he sees two sheets of paper on his desk. After lighting the lamp, he looks at them. One holds Laartol's schedule, which shows the morning senior staff briefing, but no other meetings until the second glass of the afternoon, when the schedule lists Commander Mhakyl with the notation "Transport Logistics."

"Subcommander Alyiakal" is also listed as participant for the meeting.

Alyiakal's schedule is blank, except for a notation, presumably from Taysaan.

> *Please let me know if you have meetings or appointments other than those required by the Captain-Commander.*

Since Alyiakal has no other immediate commitments, he sits down behind the desk and begins to think over how to structure his tactics and strategy report. A number of thoughts come to mind, and he takes out paper, inkwell, and pen, and begins to write them down.

A little more than a quint passes before there's a knock on the study door.

Alyiakal only senses a single person and says, "Yes?"

The door opens to reveal an older lancer ranker. "Ser, the Captain-Commander is ready to see you."

"Thank you. I'll be right there." Alyiakal carefully sets the pen on the small blotting pad and then stands. He doesn't lock the study door when he leaves, given that it's headquarters and there's nothing to steal.

When he reaches the fifth level, he asks Taysaan, "Is there a library here in headquarters?"

"Yes, ser. It's not large, but it's on the second level. You can take anything to your study, but nothing's to leave the building."

"Thank you."

"The Captain-Commander said you were to go in when you arrived."

Alyiakal still knocks on the door, slightly ajar, and says, "Subcommander Alyiakal, ser."

"Come on in."

When Alyiakal walks into Laartol's study, closing the door behind him, the Captain-Commander gestures to the desk and the holstered short fire-lance resting there. "You're to carry that at all times while on duty, even in senior staff meetings and even when meeting with the Majer-Commander."

"Not only to protect you both but to show your trust?"

"What else?" asks Laartol wryly, adding sardonically, "And who else?"

The last three words chill Alyiakal, but he says nothing as he picks up the holstered weapon, removes the firelance from the holster, and fastens the holster to his belt before re-holstering the weapon. While he can sense that it's fully powered, he asks, "Fully charged?"

"The armorer says so."

"Can I recharge it at the armory?"

Laartol nods, then gestures to the chair in front of the desk.

Alyiakal seats himself.

"I took a brief look through your maps," says Laartol. "You could almost have been a geographer's scrivener. From what I saw, your maps are better than most we have in headquarters." The Captain-Commander offers an amused smile. "Some would say maps don't make that much difference. How would you answer that?"

"If a post commander thinks they won't, then they won't."

Laartol chuckles, then goes on, "I received a report that you personally trained Mirror Lancer squads and companies in formations and maneuvers that are not usual."

Alyiakal has no doubt that report came from Baertal, if through Subcommander Zekkaat. "Yes, ser. I did so to enable lancers to quickly concentrate firelance bolts in ways that the barbarians and Cerlynese had never seen before. That way I didn't have to explain what I wanted in the middle of a skirmish or battle. It allowed for a more efficient use of the firelances and that meant more time between replenishments."

"I look forward to reading that section of your coming report on tactics and strategies, but as I already expressed, take your time and make it good. That's all I have for you right now. Be here just before the meeting with Commander Mhakyl."

"Yes, ser."

Because Laartol does not stand, Alyiakal asks, "By your leave, ser?"

"Of course."

Before Alyiakal closes the door on his way out, Laartol is already absorbed in one of the documents on his wide desk.

Alyiakal makes his way down the main staircase to the second floor, where he finds the library door halfway down the corridor on the right.

The older squad leader at the raised desk just inside the library door looks at Alyiakal's insignia and senior staff pin, then says, "You're new here, aren't you, ser? I'm Bhaarnyl, the head librarian."

"I'm pleased to meet you, Bhaarnyl. I'm Alyiakal, the Captain-Commander's new Tactics and Regional Information Officer, and previously post commander at Pemedra."

"Yes, ser. How can I help you?"

"One of my tasks is to write an updated tactics and strategy report, but I thought it might be wise to see what else has been written, either about Mirror Lancer tactics or about previous barbarian tactics."

"There's not too much on either, ser, besides the tactics manual written decades ago by one of the early captain-commanders. I *think* there's a very thin volume on tactics by someone from Suthya."

"I understand I can take them up to my study."

"It might take me a while to find them. I could bring them up, ser."

"That would be fine . . . if it's before second afternoon glass. I have meetings after that. My study's on the fourth level, the first door on the left. If you have trouble finding them, I'll come back later."

"I should be able to get them up there well before second glass, ser."

"Thank you." Alyiakal turns and heads for the staircase, knowing all too well the librarian wants to verify Alyiakal's credentials before loaning his precious volumes.

Less than a quint later, Alyiakal smiles at the knock on his study door. "Come in."

The librarian opens the door. "I have those two tactics books, ser, and another one I didn't recall."

Alyiakal stands and takes the three volumes. "Thank you, Bhaarnyl. I appreciate it."

"My pleasure, ser. I can see why the Captain-Commander wants you to do a report on tactics."

Most likely because you asked Taysaan, and he told you about me. "I wanted the books to make sure that anything I thought hadn't been tried had not, in fact, been tried. Incorrect assertions don't set well with superiors, especially at headquarters."

Bhaarnyl smiles. "Of course, ser."

"Thank you, again."

The librarian nods, then leaves, closing the door.

Headquarters is definitely an interesting place.

Alyiakal sets the three thin volumes on the desk, and picks up what looks like the oldest one and opens it to find it titled *Waging War.* Interestingly enough, he can find no quick reference to an author or anything resembling a date. The words, although clearly scrivened, are spelled so differently as to be almost unreadable, suggesting this is the Suthyan volume. The second, and thinnest, is entitled *Barbarian War Tactics,* written by Yuvallyr'alt, Subcommander, and dated 53 A.F. The third book is *Mirror Lancer Tactics,* and despite its title, Alyiakal is certain he's never seen it or even heard of it before. The name on the title page is Zaenth'alt, Captain-Commander, and the date is 43 A.F. At the bottom of the title page is another phrase—"Written at the behest of Kiedral, Emperor of Light."

Zaenth? Alyiakal knows that he's seen the name somewhere, but for the moment cannot remember where or in what context. Still, *Mirror Lancer Tactics* looks like the best place to start.

Alyiakal settles into his desk chair and begins to read.

When he sets it aside more than a glass later, he has not come across anything remotely different from what he was taught at Kynstaar, or by other officers, suggesting that Zaenth's manual was, and remains, the basis of current tactics, though Alyiakal has never seen the manual before. *But you've got more than a hundred pages to go.*

Alyiakal stands and slips the volumes into a desk drawer before he leaves and locks the door. Then he heads up to the Captain-Commander's study.

When he reaches Taysaan's desk, he asks, "Do I wait here for the commander or go in?"

"Go in. The Captain-Commander wants you there before Commander Mhakyl arrives."

Alyiakal knocks, then enters, and closes the door.

Laartol looks up from his desk but doesn't stand. "Take one of the conference-table chairs and place it even with the front of the desk and equidistant from my chair and the one in front of the desk, but where you can also watch the door."

Alyiakal does so but waits to seat himself.

"I thought it best that you meet Commander Mhakyl first, formally anyway, since you've already encountered Coeryn."

"Commander Mhakyl is in charge of logistics and transportation?"

"He is. He's very trustworthy."

Which implies that some commanders are not.

There's another knock on the door and a short but muscular commander enters, closing the door after himself.

Laartol stands and says, "Mhakyl, I'd like you to meet Subcommander Alyiakal. He's my new Tactical and Regional Information Officer, as well as my personal aide upon occasion."

Mhakyl glances at Alyiakal, eyes flicking down momentarily, most likely taking in the short firelance, then says, "About time, Laartol."

"He's also qualified in tactics—Guarstyad, Lhaarat, and Pemedra. The one disaster at Lhaarat was a year after he was posted to Pemedra. One of his tasks is to write a report on tactics and strategy."

Alyiakal says, "I'm pleased to meet you, Commander."

"I'm pleased to see you here, Subcommander. Some won't be, especially those who fancy themselves tacticians. They'll have a hard time disputing you, and I hope I'm there should that occur." Mhakyl offers an amused and slightly predatory smile. The smile fades as he says, "From what I've heard, you also have a decent understanding of logistics."

"Likely not as much as I should, but I think I understand its importance."

"Enough to badger headquarters for funds and to spend post golds, as well as a few of your own, I suspect, to build a road that should have been constructed years ago."

"It had to be done," replies Alyiakal, not totally surprised by what Mhakyl knows, but more that the commander would bring it up—until he senses Laartol's mild astonishment.

"You still surprise me, Mhakyl," says Laartol, as he gestures to the chairs and seats himself behind his desk.

"I can't let the subcommander be the only one to surprise you. Besides, Faaklyn and I go back a long way."

Faaklyn? Then Alyiakal recalls the Mirror Engineer who had given him the logistics tour at Ilypsya.

"You two are among the few whose surprises are welcome," replies Laartol. "Now, how are you coming on firewagons large enough to carry more supplies or lancers?"

"Not well, ser," says Mhakyl.

"Why is it that you always add the honorifics when you deliver bad news?" asks Laartol with a touch of humor in his voice.

"Because unpleasant news often requires respect." Mhakyl clears his throat and leans forward slightly. "Besides the intransigence I mentioned earlier, there's also a significant technical problem. Larger firewagons require heavier axles and wheels to bear the additional weight—"

"And heavier weight requires more chaos and larger chaos reservoirs," continues Laartol. "But if one larger firewagon replaces two or three . . ." He breaks off as he sees the commander shaking his head.

"It's not that, ser. I finally got a straight answer out of the Mirror Engineers. They can't build a larger mechanism that works well, not without excessive maintenance. Also, if they build it, the amount of chaos required to turn the wheels deforms the mechanisms quickly."

"Fireships are far bigger than firewagons," Laartol points out.

"They have three mechanisms for each ship, one for each screw," explains Mhakyl. "Putting two separate mechanisms in a firewagon would require so much additional space—not to mention the additional supporting mechanisms—that the firewagon would be too wide, and we'd go through wheels, axles . . ."

"In short, the existing firewagon is the most efficient possible, given what we know and can build?" concludes Laartol.

"Yes, ser."

"So the only feasible option is more firewagons, firewagons that the Mirror Engineers will not build?"

"They say they cannot build more because of the shortage of copper, because the chaos tower in Fyrad only produces so much chaos, and because the Magi'i limit the chaos we can have from their chaos towers here in Cyad there's not enough concentrated chaos to power additional firewagons."

"Given the limitations imposed by the Magi'i," adds Laartol, "and certain . . . projects ordered by the Emperor."

"Yes, ser."

Why do the Magi'i limit the amount of chaos available to the Mirror Lancers when the lancers protect the borders? Or does the rebuilding or refurbishing of the Palace of Light require that much chaos? Recalling Laartol's instructions, Alyiakal does not raise the question.

Laartol straightens in his chair. "Well, at least you have an answer, unlike your predecessor. What else?"

"With the death of Duke Taartyn and the Suthyan destruction of the remainder of the Duke's armsmen, the price of copper is up another tenth."

"That was to be expected," says Laartol, "once the Emperor, the Magi'i, and the Merchanters told the Majer-Commander that we were not to occupy Cerlyn." He looks to Alyiakal. "Your thoughts, Subcommander."

"I have no idea why that would occur, ser, save that the Merchanters must profit in some fashion by Cerlyn being independent of Cyador."

"Cautiously worded, but accurate. If . . . if Cerlyn became part of Cyador, import tariffs could not be levied . . ."

And the Imperial Tariff Enumerators would lose what they presently skim, at least if copper were carted south on the high road. Alyiakal nods and waits.

". . . and the price of copper and other goods could not be increased by passing through Suthyan traders and then Cyadoran traders," concludes Laartol.

And since the Suthyan traders wouldn't have copper as leverage, other outland traders would have a better chance of obtaining certain goods at lower prices . . . and bargaining for lower prices on other goods.

"All that is rather obvious," declared Mhakyl, "except to the Emperor, the First and Second Magus, and one other."

One other? The Majer-Commander? But why? Except Alyiakal knows the Merchanters have the power of golds behind them and the Magi'i have the power of chaos, and it appears that neither the Emperor nor the Majer-Commander can afford to anger either the Magi'i or the Merchanters.

"Is there anything else I should know?" asks Laartol.

"Mostly likely something has come up somewhere," replies Mhakyl. "It always does, but it hasn't come to my attention."

"Then I'll see you when it does," says Laartol.

"By your leave?" asks Mhakyl.

Laartol nods.

After Mhakyl leaves, Laartol gestures for Alyiakal to take the seat the commander has vacated. "I can see you understood most of what we discussed." He stands. "Just stay there. Don't get up, I'll be right back."

All Alyiakal can say to that is, "Yes, ser."

When Laartol returns within moments, Alyiakal does stand.

"The Majer-Commander is free for a while. It's time for you to meet him." Laartol motions for Alyiakal to join him.

The two walk past Taysaan's desk and toward the Majer-Commander's study. Laartol opens the door, and Alyiakal follows him into the study, closing it behind himself.

The study appears to be the same length as Laartol's, but is wider, with a conference table on one side of the chamber. Windowed doors open onto a roof terrace, through which Alyiakal can see the upper floors of the Palace of Light.

The officer sitting behind the desk has thinning jet-black hair, a long, oval face that hints at fleshiness, and broad but spare shoulders. His eyes are watery gray, and Alyiakal can sense what feels like indifference.

"Ser, I thought you'd like to meet the subcommander." Laartol pauses just slightly, then adds, "Alyiakal, Majer-Commander Mheryt."

Mheryt does not rise, nor does he motion for either officer to take a seat. He studies Alyiakal for a long moment, then says, "So this is the officer who's managed to make a number of senior officers look foolish. You don't look much different from any number of majers, even if the Captain-Commander has promoted you. Still, results speak louder than appearances."

Since Alyiakal hasn't been asked anything, he waits for Mheryt to speak again.

"Where do you lead from, Subcommander?"

"The front, ser."

"What would happen if something happened to you?"

"That's happened twice, ser. Once in dealing with the Kyphrans and once just after the company I led killed Duke Taartyn along with the forces in and around his palace. My officers finished the battles as planned and instructed.

In dealing with the Cerlynese over the years I split my forces, so a good part of the success was the result of the company officers."

"Why was it necessary to split them?"

"In order to surprise the Cerlynese before they could mass their companies, ser."

Mheryt frowns. "I suppose we can't argue with your successes over the years, Subcommander, but I will be interested to read this report, or manual, you're creating for Laartol."

"Yes, ser."

"It's good to meet you, Subcommander. I wish you well here at headquarters."

"Thank you, ser," replies Alyiakal.

Mheryt nods to Laartol, and the Captain-Commander half turns and motions for Alyiakal to precede him from the study.

On the way out, Alyiakal closes the door quietly but firmly.

"Back to my study," says Laartol.

Alyiakal opens Laartol's door more widely and lets the Captain-Commander enter first, then follows and shuts the door.

Laartol gestures to the chair before the desk as he takes his own seat. After a moment, he asks, "What do you think of the Majer-Commander? Honestly, now."

Honestly? Alyiakal manages not to wince. Finally, he says, "Based on that meeting, and from the little I know, he's perfect for the Emperor, the Magi'i, and the Merchanters."

Laartol's quiet laugh is bitter. "I wouldn't have put it that way, but I won't dispute your accuracy." He pauses. "You should know a few things. All promotions to commander must be approved by both the Captain-Commander and the Majer-Commander, and the Majer-Commander discusses those with the Emperor."

"Ser, might I ask, how often have you met with the Emperor?"

"Once, after I was appointed Captain-Commander, and only for a few moments. The second matter is that only the senior member of each branch of the Triad meets with the Emperor."

"Just the Emperor, the First Magus, the Majer-Commander, and the Merchanter Advisor?"

Laartol nods.

"What is the tie between the Majer-Commander and the others?"

"Only that he knows he'll be removed, or worse, if he directly opposes any of them."

Alyiakal hesitates, but knows he needs to ask the next question. "Why am I here, and what do you expect from me?"

The Captain-Commander offers a faintly amused smile. "To do your duty in the same fashion as you always have, to the same end."

Alyiakal manages, just barely, not to swallow. "Yes, ser."

ABOUT THE AUTHOR

L. E. Modesitt, Jr. (he/him) is the author of more than eighty books—primarily science fiction and fantasy, including the long-running, bestselling Saga of Recluce and Imager Portfolio, including *Fairhaven Rising* and *From the Forest*. He is also the author of the new series The Grand Illusion (*Isolate, Councilor, Contrarian,* and *Legalist*).

lemodesittjr.com